Xorandor

/

Verbivore

Christine Brooke-Rose

VP Festschrift Series:

Volume 1: Christine Brooke-Rose
Volume 2: Gilbert Adair
Volume 3: The Syllabus
(Edited by G.N. Forester and M.J. Nicholls)

Reprint Titles:

The Languages of Love — Christine Brooke-Rose
The Sycamore Tree — Christine Brooke-Rose
Go When You See the Green Man Walking — Christine Brooke-Rose
The Dear Deceit — Christine Brooke-Rose
Next — Christine Brooke-Rose
Three Novels — Rosalyn Drexler
Knut — Tom Mallin

other Verbivoracious titles @

www.verbivoraciouspress.org

Xorandor

/

Verbivore

Christine Brooke-Rose

Verbivoracious Press

Glentrees, 13 Mt Sinai Lane, Singapore

This edition published in Great Britain & Singapore

by Verbivoracious Press

www.verbivoraciouspress.org

ISBN: 978-981-09-3592-4

Printed and bound in Great Britain & Singapore

Xorandor (1986) and *Verbivore* (1990) first published in Great Britain by Carcanet Press.

Introduction

NICOLAS TREDELL

After the fissiparous pyrotechnics of *Thru* (1975), a kind of campus-fiction equivalent to Cornelia Parker's exploded shed, Christine Brooke-Rose fell silent as a published novelist for nearly a decade. It might have seemed that, like another innovative 1960s fictioneer, Alan Burns, her move from Parnassus to Academe, trading the precarious freelance writer's life for salary-security, had estranged her from the muses and that a strong wax mixed from elements of Derrida, Deleuze and Guattari had sealed the decree absolute. But what she called *une bouteille à la mer*, containing the manuscript of her ninth novel, washed up on English shores and journeyed inland to Michael Schmidt's Carcanet Press in Manchester and its fiction editor, Mike Freeman, who was enthralled to find a new Brooke-Rose fiction and who would become crucial in promoting her work. The message in a bottle, published as *Amalgamemnon* (1984), demonstrated the fascination with languages and structures—not as textual abstractions but as the very texture of existence—that had distinguished her fiction since her fifth novel, *Out* (1964), and that had always been a key element of her life, from her multilingual upbringing, through her World War 2 days at the Bletchley Park code-breaking centre presided over by the computer science pioneer Alan Turing, her university studies of language and literature at Somerville College, Oxford and UCL, her career as a novelist, critic and reviewer in the London literary world and her move to the new University of Vincennes in the later 1960s where she would encounter French literary and cultural theory in its most volatile phase (the crucible out of which *Thru* came). *Amalgamemnon* launched her on the next phase of her career as a novelist, and *Xorandor* (1986) and *Verbivore* (1990), the two novels reissued here by the publisher whose name puns on the second title, consolidated and developed that phase in inventive and probing ways.

Both *Xorandor* and *Verbivore* might be called science-fiction novels, although they are rather more than any limiting definition of that genre might allow. As a critic, theorist and practitioner, one of Brooke-Rose's key interests was science fiction and, in her own novels, she was good at pursuing the fictional consequences of ideas that turned the familiar world upside-down—like the inversion of the binary opposition of white and black in *Out*. Both *Xorandor* and *Verbivore* are notable for this kind of defamiliarization. *Xorandor* imagines the close encounter of carbon-based lifeforms (human beings) with silicon-based lifeforms that are shaped like stones, operate as computers, feed on radioactive alpha-particles, have the capacity to reproduce, and may—their story varies—have come from Mars or existed for aeons on earth. *Verbivore* envisages the increasing breakdown of electronic communications as something starts eating the words that weave discursive webs around the globe. But Brooke-Rose was concerned with science fact as well as fiction; she had long realized that scientific vocabularies and concepts created exciting discursive and philosophical possibilities for the fiction writer, as in her novel *Such* (1966), which brilliantly draws on cosmology. But she liked to get it right; she was not one for those ill-informed if metaphorically suggestive borrowings that came under attack in the Science Wars of the 1990s. She checked with experts, as her acknowledgements to *Xorandor* show, although she did not suppose this would make her work error-free in scientific terms. Of course *Xorandor* and *Verbivore* run the risk of all science fiction, however well-grounded in hard science it may be—that their technology may come to seem outmoded, more so than the technology of an earlier time which we receive as already part of the past; the ultra-new, superseded by further novelty, appears to age faster than the categorically old. The floppy discs and diskettes mentioned in *Xorandor* and *Verbivore* now look more remote than the papyri and stelae of Thebes and ancient Athens. But if the imaginative vision of the future in a science fiction text is sufficiently strong it will transcend its technological obsolescence, and so it proves with *Xorandor* and *Verbivore*: both offer thought-experiments that remain relevant because they address ancient philosophical questions about the very nature of human identity that the digital revolution increasingly enforces on us. They also offer ways to think about what is portentously called 'the crisis in the humanities', which in these novels has already reached the future towards which it now, in the second decade of the twenty-first century, seems to be accelerating: the humanities, in their higher-educational forms, have been eliminated; in *Xorandor*, the humanities are 'only for the leisure industry, they're not taught higher up, after school, everyone has to do science or hitech'; in *Verbivore*, 'all humanities [are] abolished, all Universities as lean and fit as industrial plants' and writers now call themselves wordprocessors. The proliferation and undecidability of meanings once celebrated in post-structuralism and deconstruction has resulted in the view that, if no final meanings can be reached, the institutional support of the endless pursuit of interpretations is otiose.

For Brooke-Rose in her fiction, the narrative voice or voices are crucial —for example, her fifth novel, *Between* (1968), only worked for her when she started to use a female narrator. In *Xorandor*, the extremely lively narrative voice is cross-gendered, an amalgam of a female and male narrator, Jipnzab, as the stone computer they discover, calls them at first. They dub the stone computer Xorandor because it uses both exclusive logic (XOR) and non-exclusive logic (AND OR). Jip (an acronym of John Ivor Paul) and Zab (short for Isabel) Manning are twins, aged thirteen-and-a-half when they first find Xorandor, who have a near-telepathic understanding of each other and engage in what Jip calls 'flipflop storytelling', passing the narrative between them. A particular delight of *Xorandor* is the vocabulary Brooke-Rose invents for Jip and Zab's narrative. This includes laudatory adjectives like 'diodic', 'superdiodic', 'hexadex', 'megavolt', 'gigavolt', 'smart terminal', 'crackerpack'; exclamations such as 'jumping nukes'; 'leaping leptons', 'quantum quirks', 'quirky quarks', 'stubs', 'spikes', 'oh, booles' and 'thunks' (for 'damn'/'blast'); locutions like 'strobeluck' for 'luckily', 'quickconnect' for a sudden flash of understanding, and 'erased rom' for 'I forget'. There are also amusing one-off expressions, as when Zab tells Jip 'You were practically concatenating with amazement'. This inventive twidiolect is one of those features of Brooke-Rose's fiction that should have been more widely noticed. Malcolm Bradbury's novel *Rates of Exchange* (1983), set largely in the imaginary East European Communist country of Slaka, gained such attention that he followed it up with a spoof guidebook, *Why Come to Slaka?* (1986), which included a comic list of useful phrases; but there is, as yet, no phrasebook of Jipnzab-speak.

As Jip and Zab recall their own encounters, and later those of other humans, with the alpha-particle eating stone lifeforms—first dubbed alphaphagoi, later media-dumbed to alphaguys—they find themselves facing problems of narrative, of how to tell the story they dictate into their Poccom (pocket computer). 'Where to start, for instance. There are endless beginnings'. What is it relevant to include and what can be omitted? Should they provide physical descriptions of themselves or others, if, as Jip claims, most readers skip the latter? How important is it to provide the geographical location of the narrators ('storyteller's where') and that of the story ('story's where' or 'story-where')? Is it permissible to improve, to add to a story? (Jip: 'You're adding that now, Zab, you couldn't have said it then' / Zab: 'True. But it's rather good, no?' / Jip: 'No'.). Should a story be told in chronological order, maintaining 'sequence control' or are other forms of ordering possible and even desirable, such as those which insert a flashforward that gives knowledge only obtained later than the event being described (a 'jump instruction')? How plausibly to describe conversations where the narrators were not present in person (here Jip and Zab are helped by Sneaker, the microphone they have hidden in the living room ceiling light of their home through which they record conversations that take place there). Jip and Zab's tale is vigorously self-reflexive about its telling, and this sharpens their narrative, which excites and intrigues on a science fiction and thriller level, involving an apparent digital terrorist who garbles *Macbeth* quotations, and the possibility of reducing the threat of nuclear war, while it also, on another level, delicately suggests the passage of Jib and Zab from late childhood into puberty, from a boy and girl into a young man and woman.

Jip and Zab reappear as adults in *Verbivore*. Zab, as Isabel Manning, is now Euro-M.P. for Aachen International District and living in Aachen; she has an 18-year-old son, Hanjo, conceived when she was 18 herself with a Chinese father. John went to Cambridge and now teaches in Texas; he is married with three children. Their father died soon after the events recounted in *Xorandor* but their mother has blossomed into a late career as a Shakespearean actress. In *Verbivore*, drawing on their previous experience of communicating with Xorandor, and sometimes reverting to their old twidiolect, Jip and Zab try to mediate between humans and the sentient stones which they discovered and which are now trying to preserve themselves by restricting global information flow, becoming not only alpha-particle eaters—alphaphagai—but also verbivores or logophagai, word-eaters. *Verbivore* also stages the reappearance from *Amalgamenon* of Mira Enketei, ex-lecturer in literature and history turned radio producer, and Perry Hupsos, whose name echoes the ancient Greek title of the classical critical text attributed to Longinus, *On the Sublime* (Περὶ ὕψους, *Peri hypsous*). Mira takes up the marvellous figure of Decibel, a character who first features in a radio play by Perry Hupsos and whom, in Mira's narrative, the logophagai employ to go to human meetings and report back on the self-thwarting attempts of these carbon-based life forms to reach rational agreements. If communications are to be restored, human beings must restrict their demands for information flow, but this is difficult. 'Our needs have become monstrous. But none of those who say this, or rather who shout it out, are themselves willing to do without their mediadaelic world and press-button comforts'.

Brooke-Rose's next novel would be *Textermination* (1991), which adumbrated a further phase of cultural erasure, the disappearance of major literary characters, from Homer's Odysseus and Chaucer's Wife of

Bath to Woolf's Mrs Dalloway and Rushdie's Gibreel Farishta, for want of readers to keep them alive. This novel, with *Amalgamemnon*, *Xorandor* and *Verbivore*, would form what Brooke-Rose dubbed 'the Intercom Quartet'. *Xorandor* and *Verbivore* are the core novels of that Quartet. They engage, in ways that are innovative, comic, serious and insightful, with questions of being, language, culture and technology that still resonate in the twenty-first century, and they offer intimations, beyond their scenarios of diminution, of a positive future vision of the humanities.

XORANDOR

ACKNOWLEDGEMENTS

I am greatly indebted to my cousin Claude Brooke, Phys. E.P.F., for the scientific information around which this story is written, as well as for part of the original scientific idea, and much helpful discussion at inception.

By the end of the creative process, however, so many fictional and stylistic transformations of that bare information had occurred that I needed further and more concrete and corrective scientific help. I was immensely lucky to receive this from Thomas Blackburn Ph.D., Professor of Chemistry at Andrews Presbyterian College, Laurinberg, North Carolina, who also made some very useful suggestions.

With both debts, any errors or misinterpretations are my own.

The programming language and computer called Poccom 3 are inventions, based on various existing languages and possibilities. I am particularly indebted to an excellent book, *Programming Languages—Design and Implementation*, by Terence W. Pratt, Prentice/Hall International, Inc, Englewood Cliffs, New Jersey, 1984.

C.B-R.

Paris, 1985

1 BEGIN

The first time we came across Xorandor we were sitting on him.

Correction, Zab. Sitting True, came across False. We didn't come across Xorandor, he contacted us.

True, Jip. We'd come to our usual haunt by the old carn and we were sitting on this large flat stone.

It was the middle of our summer eprom and we'd taken Poccom 2 out with us to play on.

That was the very little one, we're using Poccom 3 now.

When suddenly there flashed on the miniscreen, in yellow but out of the blue, the words GET OFF MY BACK.

Peculiarly spelt, G,E,T was okay, then of, then M,A,I, then B,A,K. That's for the printout.

Right. And you swore you hadn't done it.

Correction, Jip, there was no need to swear. In fact it's important at this stage to say we often read each other's thoughts almost as fast as a computer calculates. We stared at each other and knew at once the other hadn't done it.

Stubs, it's tough dictating this, Zab. It'd be much easier typing it straight on the keyboard.

But then it'd all come from one of us only, even if we took turns. One, it's important to be two, and two, it's easier to interrupt on vocal than to push hands away. You agreed, Jip, you even dubbed it flipflop storytelling, which was superdiodic of you. We'll get used to it.

But we could use two keyboards, and program-interrupts with WAITS and other subroutines.

Not the same, Jip. Even if it turns out to be complementary storytelling, say bubble rather than flipflop –

You're mixing your computer-levels a bit.

— talking 's better than subroutines, cos it strays, it should be like a, let's see, like a butterfly-net, taken out and waved around to catch a flitting word or idea. It's going to be harder than we thought, as you're realizing, to recapture all the details after eight or nine months. We can dump the net later.

Dump data-network as butterfly-catcher, not bad, Zab, smart terminal. The ideal would be dynamic dumping, which empties a memory during program-run.

That's whacky, Jip, we won't know till much later what to dump or scratch.

Stubs! Let's get on with it. And we'd better get better. How did the bards manage? We haven't said anything yet.

That's called suspense, Jip.

Or waste instruction.

Well the bards used plenty of that. Come to think of it even in some classic tecs nothing happens for sixty pages, it's all datasink and flutter-byes.

Don't drag out every joke, Zab or we'll never get into it. We shouldn't have begun the way we did. After all we named him Xorandor but not till later, and it didn't even catch on at once.

So?

Flipping flipflops it seems harder to tell a story, even our own, than to make up the most complex program. Or at least to choose how to tell it. Where to start for instance. There are endless beginnings. And if we feed'm all in and ask Poccom 3 to choose, why, just the process of thinking'm up and feeding'm in would take ages. And probably convince us of the answer long before we'd finished.

That's the flutterby-net, Jip. Anyway, isn't that exactly what we're doing? Feeding in things as we think of them and leaving it to the processing stage to scratch or add or shift around?

Hey, Zab, maybe we should introduce ourselves. Lots of stories start with the storyteller saying who he is.

But everyone knows us now.

Now, yes, because of the hoohah. But when we're grown up, or maybe sooner, it'll all be forgotten. Or at least the details.

True. It's loopy, Jip, everyone gets used to the most offline discoveries so fast, and at the same time they take decades to change their mental habits.

And of course the whole point is to give our own version, not those of the media. We know things dad doesn't know we know. And we'll have Xorandor's version if he keeps his promise as he always does.

On the other hand we were younger too, and understood less, even than we do now.

Garbage, Zab. If anything it seems the other way about, we know less now, isolated here in Germany, than they do, or than we did then.

But it's still true we knew more then. And want to tell it. Right then, we're twins. So inseparable that at first Xorandor thought we were one person, our voices were so alike. We were twelve and a half. Jip stands for John Ivor Paul, and since dad's also called John the initials became a name, to tell them apart.

And Zab was jealous, cos Isabel Paula Kate isn't pronounceable, so she took a syllable of her first name to make something just as snappy.

And dad never liked it, and still tries hard to use Isabel. But fails. Mum gave in quickly.

So we created our names. By insistent use.

Just as we named Xorandor; just like naming programs.

Trap, Zab. What else?

That's all for the who. Oh no, there's physical description. We look alike, with fair hair, same shortish length, and —

Redundant rem, Zab, who cares? Does anyone know what storytellers look like? Describe Lockwood.

But characters too, Jip. Almost the heroes if Xorandor wasn't. But okay, accept. Now for what kind. Which in a way is part of who.

At St Austell's we were called whizz-kids, cos we're so good in computer-class. The others love them as games, or even as teacher-supps, but they stay with peripherals. Funny, cos we're all computers really, biological instead of electronic, and born with basic programs. But some develop them early and others don't, and then it's too late, like learning languages.

Well it is learning languages.

Check. Everyone should be able to, like they learn their own, or even several in bilingual circs, but for some reason it doesn't work like that. They say every maths teacher can spot the kind of diodically bright child who explores every op and gets the hang of basic maths concepts real nano.

Holy nukes, Jip, you do sound a conceited prig.

Well it's true. Not that we're not fairly megavolt at literature and other things, but they're only for the leisure industry, they're not taught higher up, after school, everyone has to do science or hitech. Still, we're good at those things too.

Doesn't look like it, we can't even get this story off the ground.

Accept. For literature specify reading. And play-acting, Shakespeare for instance, that's important for the story isn't it? Besides, we're just warming up, Zab, it's quite fun after all, might as well regard this as bootstrap. When we've found an entry we'll begin properly.

We could start with the loss of radiation at The Wheal.

No, that's where dad comes in, it's his side. We came in earlier.

Okay then, what more about us? Are we as beastly as we sound?

How like a girl! Why should it be beastly to be megavolt? We're just pretty gung-ho, that's all, compared to other kids we know.

Assign initial value gung-ho to variable Jipnzab by increment just pretty. Proceed. Fact is, on the megavolt parameter, Jip's much better at inventing programs.

But Zab makes them more efficient, more elegant and economic. Not in life, mind you, where she's a regular chatterbox, but with the decision-box she has quite a seethrough knack for shortening loose instructions such as GOTO X, 1F Y, THEN DO Z, RAISE EXCEPTION W with added clauses and further adhoc explanations for vague commands.

Oh, descramble, Jip, few languages use regular Goto's anymore, besides, why so modest?

Well, *we* did, remember? They're still useful even if they can also lead to spaghetti logic. Anyway, make up your mind, you can't use both modest and conceited prig. Better go through the anti-coincidence gate, Zab.

The XOR-gate! Remember when we told Xorandor he was being modest? He couldn't grasp the concept.

Avort. Please, please let's get started. THIS is spaghetti logic. We haven't even finished the introductions, we've left ourselves floating in a vacuum, we'll soon be subject to cosmic radiation.

Right then, the where. DEClaration. We're dictating this into a processor called Poccom 3, in Jip's room in a suburb of Bayreuth in south east West Germany, where we were sent to school to be out of reach of the journalists after the hoohah. We were allowed to take our gadgets with us, strobeluck. The room is in the house of Herr und Frau Groenetz, Gerd and Frieda now, and their son Rudi, who's already fifteen. He was very friendly at first and played with us and helped us lots with German, but he's sort of more distant now, he thinks we're just kids mad about our computer and we'll grow out of it like he did out of his, but then, he only uses his for game software. ENDEC .

Zab, that's storyteller's where, nobody gives a thunk, what we need is the story's where.

Correction not accepted. You agreed to introduce the storytellers cos they're also characters. If the storytellers are characters THEN their confusion is part of their characters ENDIF. Inversely IF the characters are the storytellers THEN the confusion is part of the story ENDIF. REMark. The confusion may be due to loss of memory for precise detail, itself due to longstop runtime since the hoohah and especially since the beginning ENDREM. NEWREM Confusion ANDOR also due to the fact, so far unmentioned by my modestly conceited twin brother or viceversa, that since our arrival here we've been through the horrid business, just like Xorandor at the beginning, of not understanding one kiloword of what was being said around us, in class especially, except of course maths and physics and chemistry and compsci. Well, now it's much better, thanks to Frieda's extra lessons and Rudi and all that, but it was tough to feel what it's like to be near bottom of the class like a nondiodic kid, retarded even. Good for us, dad said, ENDNEWREM.

Spaghetti stacks, Zab, AND redundant rems! That didn't last, let's get on.

We're still not top of the class, and if you don't mind, it is not redundant rem, even if we later shift it somewhere else. Remember how we kept wondering how Xorandor's referencing system could work since he can't see or experience anything.

You kept wondering, Zab. And still do.

School here was a bit like that, Jip, and it helps us to imagine. Nothing but dangling refs.

Oh, Gigo.

Okay, accept. Now. Story-where. DEClaration. It happened in the village of Carn Tregean, a bit inland from the Northern coast of the tip of Cornwall, England, Europe, The World, The Universe etc. The area is rough, bare and rocky, with no beaches, too dangerous for swimming, and as Carn Tregean isn't picturesque we're spared the milling tourists and the teashoppes written ppes. The village sort of nests between a plateau to the West, which is always called the Socalled Promontory cos it collapses again before it reaches the sea, and a more slowly rising stony wilderness away eastwards, where after ten miles or so there's an old tin mine called The Wheal, which is Cornish for mine, or Tregean Wheal.

That's where dad works. He's in charge.

In between Carn Tregean and The Wheal, there are the ruins of an old castle, real crummy ruins, dangerous, nobody visits them. We called them Merlin's castle but there isn't even any local tradition attached to them, they're medieval anyway, so much later than the carn, not far off, where we used to go and play. Small wild flowers grow in clumps between the rocks. We'd bike along the road that goes to The Wheal and then walk towards the sea, or else we could walk all the way, round by the ridge, along a rough path that goes towards the sea then turns back inland towards the carn. Even the carn's just a pile of stones, forgotten by the locals and not on any tourist map or guide. The tourists go where there are beaches and coves. Our house is white and modernish, in a small cluster of others like it towards the Socalled Promontory, outside the old village, which has small dull houses of local dark grey stone, but lots of flowers. But our house has the most colourful garden, thanks to mum. There, is that enough for you on the story-where? Jip's room looks northwards towards the sea, but you can only glimpse it on clear days.

What does *it* refer to?

Beast. For *it*, read *the sea.*

And Zab's room looks east Whealwards, so we could watch people going to and coming from the carn.

But Jip has the better cassette recorder. Also Jip's room is just above the sitting room, which opens on the back garden, and which he'd cleverly bugged in the ceiling light so that we sneaked a few maxint convs that'll help us in what we couldn't have known ourselves at the time. So it became our telltale lab. What else?

We are the only children of John and Paula Manning. Dad runs Tregean Wheal which was then disguised as a Geothermal Research Unit, and where in fact they'd been experimenting with storing, correction, simply storing drums of nuclear waste for two years. All very hush-hush at first, cos of ecologists and local protests, but of course it all came out.

As will be related in future instalments. Dad was frustrated cos he'd given up research in physics to take this job, cos of us he said. In fact he must've given it up when he married and we were on the way. Probably he never was in research, he taught science at school when we lived near Canterbury. Mum was frustrated cos she'd given up her future career as an actress, and she lives in what we called the sh-sh-sh world of Shakespeare, Sheridan, Shaw, Shekov and showshop generally, but especially Shaw, though dad was always telling her he'd passed into literary limbo. For *he*, read *Shaw* not *dad*. And she's frustrated cos he had a brief affair with Rita Boyd, the assistant who first noticed the escaping radiation at The Wheal, though it was over before it started.

What does *it* refer to?

The affair was over before the radiation loss started.

So why mention it?

Oh well, it might explain tensions and carelessnesses.

Check. Now all that's over Zab, let's get restarted.

But where?

We've done where. Endjoke.

Oh, we forgot school. We used to go to a boarding school in Taunton, called St Austell's oddly enough.

Right. Now we've reached this leg, let's fetch GET OFF MY BACK and not leave it as a dangling ref.

2 RESTART

It was unbelievable. Someone or something was interrupting our program with an irrelevant message. Yet we weren't plugged in to any terminal, Poccom 2 runs on batteries. Oh, Poccom is a brand name for Pocket Computer.

And it's also the name of the program language.

Yes, an easy one, for kids and non-experts, with false short cuts, almost all the reasoning sequences included in the hardware.

Or the firmware too, Zab.

At any rate, easy to use, with one instruction or address setting off a process. Though that too can lead to syntax errors if one hasn't grasped the process.

The first explanation was that this was an intrusion from another program, or that Zab had played a joke in the night.

Or Jip.

But we each silently answered both these possibilities in the negative. Oh thunks, we've said that. Ages ago it seems.

It was then that a spiky, rather high-pitched voice came from below us, or rather, from behind-below us. The voice said: Please, don't, sit, on, me.

Exactly in that tone, Zab, as if imitating our voices.

Well, your voice is beginning to break now, but there wasn't much difference then.

We jumped up as if our bottoms were burning.

That's good, they were in a way.

And stared at the large stone we'd been sitting on.

It was brownish rather than grey, as the other rocks were, but with odd patches of dull greyish blue that shone faintly in the sun. Faintly cos the weather was hot but cloudy, misty even, heavy and stormy.

Essay-stuff, Zab.

The stone was sort of flattened and almost perfectly round, with vague bumps, or irregularities, here and there. Thanks, it said, and the voice seemed to come from behind it. Shall we confess, we were terrified?

We were still just kids. We thought it was the ghost of Merlin wandering out of the old ruined castle. Quirky that, for whizz-kids, we didn't recognize anything we might have, but fell back on Celtic twilight.

In fact, Jip, we still don't really know why he addressed us, why he broke his silence. After all, if he hadn't, none of all this would have happened, and nobody would be any the wiser.

If anyone is. But surely we explained that to ourselves later as him wanting to protect us from the possible radiation. Especially with the wall and all.

Why should he? He has no feelings.

Say an automatic alert, at a certain level. Or perhaps he'd just got used to us, during all those days we played there. Anyway, we started talking back.

What's your name? we asked. No name, it answered.

Stubs, do we have to reconstruct every conv?

That's what storytellers do Jip, or else they invent them. But we can't, this is real.

Floating-point real or fixed-point real?

Endjoke. Well the first conv was mostly telling him our names, which he seemed to know from listening, and he called us Jipnzab for ages. And asking who he was and how he talked. We still thought he was the ghost of Merlin and we wanted to teach him modern English. In fact he learnt real nano. We went there every day, except when it rained, and there he was, and remembered every single new word and phrase. Better than us with German at first.

He was a bit slower with the pronouns, *you*, *I*, *we*, we couldn't understand why he couldn't understand that *you* was him when we said it but us when he said it.

Yes! *We* equals Jipnzab, we'd say, and quite logically he'd call us *we*. And he got even more confused if we talked about *him* to each other. Even now it still seems as if his sense of identity is quite different from ours.

After a couple of weeks we tried to teach him to count, remember, Zab, well not to count, of course he could anyway, but to translate numbers into the English words for them. You tapped a pebble on a stone and made him repeat, one, then two, up to ten.

It does seem absurd now. Jumping nukes, you said — it was your favourite word, Jip, he's better at it than we were at three years old!

Then he said: We Jipnzab, have six, ten, four.

And we couldn't make it out. Was it a number, 6104? Was it a callsign? Six, ten, four, what? Six, ten, four, sounds, he said.

And we said no, we have twenty-six. But we hadn't taught him twenty yet. And why four? And how could he know we had twenty-six? Just from listening to us?

And you said yes, he's very intelligent.

But then, you said no, that's hogwash, cos twenty-six is only the alphabet, and doesn't correspond to the sounds he'd hear. Smart terminal, Zab.

And he said: Can't find hogwash. He really talked like a computer! Hogwash is error, bad thinking, we explained, or bad sums, we also call it garbage, or gigo, which is ga, ee, garbage in, ga oh, garbage out. What goes in as garbage must come out as garbage.

And that wasn't so simple to explain in the middle of talk about numbers and alphabets!

Yes, you said not to confuse him. Then you got it, Jip. Quantum quirks! You said. Or quirky quarks! You were in the nuclear range in those days. Does he mean sixty-four! That means he can multiply! Out of ten numbers we gave him he made six times ten plus four. Or does he mean just a lot?

He, says, sixty, four, the voice said, and Zab exclaimed, You, got, sixty, all, by, your, self! Megavolt! Now listen, you said, two, tens, is twenty. Twen-ty, he repeated, three, tens, is, thirty. Sir-ty, he repeated. He couldn't pronounce so well at first. And so on to a hundred, ten-ty is, hundred, ten, hundred, is thou-sand.

Isn't this where he suddenly asked, slowly, How, do, you, know? And we burst out laughing, but we were real triggered too, cos it meant he'd been listening to us for some time. We'd been playing that game dad taught us, the, er, what does he call it?

The Kripke game.

Right. Must be the guy who invented it. But it was quarky. Also it became a sort of habit with him.

How do you *know* he picked it up from us?

Oh don't you start, Jip.

Well it seems much less certain from where we stand today. Anyway, to go on with the numbers, he said: Sixty, four, sounds. And or hundred, twenty, eight, or forty, two.

That completely flummoxed us, until you had the real diodic brainwave, Jip. You said jumping nukes, or leaping leptons or whatever, the basic ASCII code has sixty-four signs, and the full code has a hundred and twenty-eight! And English must have about forty different sound elements. We must check that, you said, but wouldn't it be incredible! He's got it all worked out, but how? You were practically concatenating with amazement.

And what's more, Zab, we realized he was using correct operands: AND OR for the basic and the full ASCII code, meaning non-exclusive OR, and OR for exclusive OR or XOR, for sounds as pronounced.

That's when we called him Xorandor. We asked him if we could, and explained it, and he said yes, and repeated it. Of course it remained *our* name. But it won in the end. Just like our own names.

And it even turned out to be fairly true. His logic could be both absolutely rigorous and contradictory at crucial points, some arguments could be both XOR and AND, or XOR and OR. Anyway we went on like this quite some time, teaching him to multiply, he was fantastic, and to divide, and even to SQRT, or was that later?

Sorry, erased ROM.

And then he said that unbelievable thing, Zab, just this large but precise number: four, sousand, five, hundred, sixty, eight.

And we didn't know what he was talking about. He said suns, and we thought he meant sons, but in the end he said four, sousand, five, hundred, sixty, eight, turnaround sun.

Years! we exclaimed. One, turn-around, the sun, is, one, year. Year, he repeated. And you, are, four, thousand, hundred and sixty, years, old? And he repeated the whole phrase: you, are, four, sousand, five, hundred, and sixty, eight, years, old. And sometime or other, when exactly was it, Miss Penbeagle arrived.

About now, you're right, Jip. In fact she'd been there for some time. Said she'd been asleep on the shady side of the carn. And from then on it was no longer our secret.

But when was it, Zab? How long did we have, really alone with him?

A couple of weeks maybe. Though we were alone again with him later. In fact yes, it was exactly then, with the numbers, after he said his age, you asked if he'd been there all this time? There was an unexpected silence, three seconds at least, which is long for him, though we didn't know that then, before he said no.

Correction, Zab, or rather, insert doubt. Remember we're reconstructing these convs, we weren't recording him then. It's not at all certain now that he did say no. He said instead, or let's say the next thing he said, was: four, here.

Okay Jip. And we asked: four years here? Four sinkers, he said. That was a very strange word, Jip, thinkers, for people, but we didn't query it then. Later he used to say processors, and it's clear he meant some kind of brainwave movements or thought processes. No, we said to him, three thinkers, Xorandor, Jip, and Zab.

Hey, Zab, that also shows he must in fact have distinguished us, even if he went on calling us Jipnzab. We had different thought patterns.

Right! It's real triggering how things fall into place when one starts recalling them in this sort of detail. Anyway he insisted, Sree wiz Xorandor, plus one, equals, four. Or something like that. And then Miss Penbeagle must have realized she was found out. It's probably true she'd been sitting behind the carn, resting on her Sunday walk — it must have been Sunday or she'd have been in her shop. Otherwise we'd have heard her walk up, with all those pebbles and stones. She let her head and shoulders appear behind the jutting rock, and we screamed, Don't come down into the circle! Go round! Go that way!

Oh thunks, we forgot to tell about the circle.

Never mind, we can shift the para later. He'd told us to surround him with stones, and we'd been building a sort of protective wall around him. We must have thought of it as a magic circle.

Yes, that was quirky, since it would attract attention to him, whereas one solitary large stone among other rocks — we never did fathom whether it was to protect himself from survey-meter detection or us from radiation.

Who were you talking to? said Miss Penbeagle inevitably when she'd stepped round the wall. I heard a funny voice. She peered at the carn but obviously saw no one. Oh, no one, you said, then did a quickconnect and added: At least, can you keep a secret, Penny? — Why, what a question, you know I've always kept your secrets! Well, you said, and it was smart terminal display, it's the ghost of Merlin. We're teaching him to talk, cos he didn't speak English but old British. He's very clever, he's learnt hundreds of words since we started, and we've taught him to count.

Crackerpack imitations, Zab. Anyway that did it, she sat down, ignoring our miffed look, and told us the whole story of Merlin and the two dragons under the Castle, and Uther Pendragon and Aurelius and all.

Then suddenly, in the middle of the miraculous building of Stonehenge, *he* spoke out: How, do, you, know? Or was he still saying *we*? We looked at Miss Penbeagle as the metallic voice shrilled out, but now she showed no fear or surprise, and gazed calmly at us. In fact it was our turn to be afraid, and we must have betrayed ourselves, looking from her to the carn and back. Her eyes were more of a challenge than a query or, well, accusation. One of us said, He wants to know you, Penny, tell him your name, slowly, as it's difficult.

And to our surprise she looked towards the carn and said loudly and clearly, Hello, Merlin, my, name, is, Gwen-do-lin.

The change of address didn't seem to bother him, he must have taken it like a change of program, or thought each thinker he met would address him differently, and had a different address for each thinker. We didn't really think much about it either, we were half in the Merlin ghost story ourselves.

Nor did he repeat his question How do you know? Perhaps he hoped it would be answered in due course, then gave up.

Exactly. He just repeated, Goo-en-do-lin. And added, You, have, deep, sound. Yes, she said, I, am, older. Old, he said, old-er, more, years. We were flabbergast by his quick mastery of grammar.

And then he asked to see what he called the olders.

Which was like saying Take me to your leader. And that was the end of us.

Well, hardly, Zab, or we wouldn't be telling the story.

True. If we are telling it. Oh, spikes and stubs, we forgot that angry lunch, after a much earlier conv with Xorandor, remember, when dad scolded us for going to the castle ruins!

Thunks!

It was on the previous Monday and dad came back very cross from The Wheal and yelled at us for playing in front of the garage before lunch.

And you wouldn't eat your peas with a fork, Zab.

And we were chattering about the talking stone and dad said we were far too excited, and to simmer down. Obviously thinking, this with hindsight, that the castle ruin was too near The Wheal for comfort or even security. I thought I told you not to go to the castle any more, he said. Mum must have been vaguely listening for once and not wearing that glazed own-world look. But you know how she has this way of not answering some confidence or other and then answering it later in public, but all twisted so that it makes us look silly, or even nasty at times? They said it's the ghost of Merlin, John, and it's apparently not in the castle ruins, it's among the megalithic stones nearby. And dad said Ah, so he's moved, then, from the early Middle Ages back to Neolithic, some journey!

And you said, in your best Zab-as-tiny-child voice, oh no, it's very close, we *thought* the voice came from the castle when we were near it but later we heard it much more clearly near the stones. Pure lie of course.

Imitation of an imitation! You're getting the hang of it Jip, that's gigavolt. So he said, So why did you say in the castle? Precision etc, and you said we didn't dad, we said near the castle, we haven't been in the ruins. And how do you know it's the ghost of Merlin? Did he tell you? We didn't say that, you said, we said we asked him, and he didn't disagree, and dad said that's hardly proof, and so on.

Swags, that's probably why we're whizz-kids, all that rigour on dad's side and all those volatile goto's and jump instructions on mum's. And then he joked about chain-clattering and you said no, nothing like that, he talks in a tinny voice, in syllables.

And he said, very serious like, do you know what a syllable is, Isabel? Yes dad (this was just to tease him), it's like Macbeth's to the last syllable of recorded time. Ouw, said mum, coming in to land from *Arms and the Man* or wherever, are you doing *Macbeth*? How splendid! And what does syllables of recorded time mean? dad asked. Well, like minutes of course, like realtime running on the computer.

You're adding that now, Zab, you couldn't have said it then.

True. But it's rather good, no?

No. And then he went on about the voice being an echo since it was repeating what we said, on-our-own-testimony he said pointedly.

And you said it's not an echo, dad, it's much more pico, besides, how can it be an echo in open space? That flummoxed him so he jumped on your pico. I've told you before not to use nano and pico as adverbs. They're measuring adjectives, as in nanoseconds. And you ignored that and went on, Besides, it can't be an echo it doesn't tally, it's like he's trying to learn modern English, cos you see in his day he'd be talking old Cornish or something, and dad said it's as if he were. Were what? Talking Cornish? And dad said: I meant, don't say it's like he's trying, but it's as if he were trying.

Your acting talent's diodic, Zab, but sometimes you're an offline tapeworm, do we have to go into all this?

Well it's to show how innocent we were at the beginning. And that cleverness in one thing isn't cleverness in everything. It's true you kept glowering across the table and —

You talked far too much.

Well, it all came out anyway.

Thanks to Pennybig, that next Sunday.

Well at least we've now got the sequence-control more or less straightened out.

But that next Sunday was the end of the, er, well, special, early relationship we had with him.

Gigo, Jip, as well you know. It got better and better.

Yes, but different.

That early basis was misleading. Perhaps all early bases are.

No, not in life, first impressions usually turn out to have been the right ones.

Our very first impressions Xorandor were right in a way. But the reason why that particular early basis was misleading, Jip, is that, at the time —

Okay okay, he hadn't developed the synthetic voice properly and sounded like a child. And of course we treated him like a child. But there are surely other reasons for the misleading early basis —

You mean — ?

It's gone. A butterfly.

Yes Jip. Here too. A flutterby. It'll come back. Let's get on.

3 OR

The difficulty now, Zab, is that we weren't in on any of the things that were going on at the same time, and we have to reconstruct them from Sneaker in the living room ceiling light, and also from later explanations they *had* to give us when we did get involved.

Yes, we'll have to catch up with Pennybig and that famous Sunday later.

Meanwhile, as they say in the comics, whacky things'd been happening, and not exactly as subprograms either. The first sneak was strobeluck. We rushed upstairs when we saw Rita Boyd coming up the path, we *thought* to see dad again, but in fact, as it turned out, summoned by him. Why he didn't summon her to his office at The Wheal is anyone's guess.

Perhaps it was to show mum they were on purely work terms as before, or maybe it was to humiliate her, since he scolded her and had apparently left the door open. Or perhaps to spare her in front of the other technicians.

There you go again with petty reasons for everything, but they don't *matter*, Zab. Okay it was a mistake to mention the why, but surely the phrase 'anyone's guess' was enough.

Master-slave flipflop is it? Would lordandmaster consider it irrelevant to mention that the technicians work shifts, while dad works days only?

He would.

Tape 1, Side 1, Rec. 1, Monday 14 July, Printout.
Voice 1 = Dad. Voice 2 = Rita. Beginrec.

Dad: (bootstrap) umin. Sit down. Now tell me exactly what happened last night.

Rita: I entered it all in the logbook, John, didn't you read it?

Dad: Yes of course. But I want it again, less succinctly.

Rita: Hmmm. Shouldn't we shut the door? (P 2.09 sec)

Dad: I have nothing to hide from my wife.

Rita: (P 0.79 sec) Well it was very sudden, and very quick. Yellow blinks appeared on the monitor panel every two seconds, and bleeped. A red light seemed to have flashed in a corner of my mind on the gallery screens but it was already over as I looked. Then the next red light along the gallery switched on, and the next, and all the way up the shaft and out to one of the external monitors, the whole swift race occurring in one split second, then nothing. I then checked the alphanumeric printout.

Dad: Yes I have it here. All in the same minute, at 0213. All in Gallery 3, the rise in gammas varying between 130 and 140 millirads per hour, the rise in betas between 245 and 250.

Rita: Then nothing. the figures on the digital display were back to normal. There was no trace of radioactive contamination anywhere along the trail.

Dad: So then what did you do?

Rita: The guard came in, and I sent him out again to check round the site. He said there'd been a storm but I hadn't heard it. I started checking the instruments for gamma rays along the gallery and shaft, the ten for beta radiation and the five neutron detectors. The automatic monitor was scanning them correctly. Ditto the three alpha particle dust monitors. Temperature sensors okay, smoke detectors okay, air-filters okay.

Dad: I know. Alex rechecked everything this morning.

Rita: (P 2.03 sec) The measurements were all correct. Every instrument was functioning perfectly. But the ionisation chambers had apparently emitted a small sudden spurt, each in turn in swift succession, as if someone faster than sound had snatched a one-ton cylinder of concrete with its nugget of nuclear waste inside it and speeded with it along the third gallery and up the shaft and over the high wire fence around the site in less than fifteen seconds. It's quite incomprehensible. If it's a steal how could a man go unnoticed at that speed and over the high fence?

Dad: I take it that's a rhetorical question?

Rita: And the hourly readout at 0300 showed no change at all.

Dad: Why didn't you send for me?

Rita: It really didn't seem necessary, John. It was all over in fifteen seconds and there was nothing in the way of rechecking that anyone couldn't do just as well today.

Dad: Okay, but why didn't you switch on the gamma spectrometers? The gesture should be automatic.

Rita: I honestly didn't have time, John, it all happened so fast and I'd barely switched on the gallery screens (P 0.17 sec) and looked at the lights on the diagram screen, it was all over.

Dad: You mean, the gallery screens were switched off?

Rita: Well, yes, they're unnecessary at night.

Dad: They're only unnecessary if nothing is happening, but they're necessary to see at a glance *whether* nothing is happening, you know that very well. Had you been reading? Before, I mean.

Rita: Well of course. One can't watch grey gallery screens all night.

Dad: What were you reading?

Rita: I don't see the relevance, but if you really want to know, Alan Turing's famous 1936 paper on Computable Numbers and the Entscheidungsproblem.

Dad: You've no business reading the past mathematics for a then future universal computer. You're a physicist and a safety expert. No wonder you were inattentive.

Rita: You're a physicist too, and if you know what the paper was about you must have read it too, sometime. Besides, why shouldn't one be open to other sciences? This job's positively brain-dwindling.

Dad: All right, all right, I shouldn't have put it that way. I meant you should only read light stuff, keeping half your mind on the job. But in any case, you should have called me.

Rita: At 0213? I doubt whether Paula —

Dad: That has nothing to do with it Rita, don't mix duty with private affairs.

Rita: Which have unfortunately left a somewhat radioactive trace. (P 0.32 sec) Anyway John, I can only repeat, it happened in fifteen seconds and all returned to normal afterwards. There was no point in calling you and it was more urgent to check the instruments. I'm perfectly competent, you know.

Dad: Of course. Except that the spectrometers would have measured the energy of the radiation emitted and allowed us to identify which nuclide was involved.

Rita: If any. I know. But it was only a yellow alert.

Dad: Only?

Rita: I'm sorry John, really. (P 4.02 sec) Perhaps you should order all spectrometers to be kept on permanently. Or would that be wasteful?

Dad: (P 0.52 sec) Good idea. (P 0.73 sec) No, nothing is wasteful in the matter of nuclear waste. I've even gone down with Alex to check for alpha and beta contamination, full protective clothing and all, along the path of the mysterious thief, while Maggie watched from the control room.

Rita: Wow! That's a bit steep.

Dad: And we're having a meeting this afternoon in my office five o'clock sharp. I just wanted to see you first. (P 1.02 sec) Sorry I had to break into your beauty sleep.

Rita: I'm worried about the health hazard, John, however unlikely. Shouldn't we report the loss?

Dad: Report what, Rita? A loss that can't have happened? That we can't trace?

Rita: It must have gone somewhere. If it's dispersed there's no danger at all with such a minute quantity, but if it's concentrated on some object, or food, or near people, well, couldn't we perhaps each carry a survey-meter in our cars for a while, and make a discreet search?

Dad: Maybe. Suggest it at the meeting.

Rita: Have you sounded the others?

Dad: Leonard seems to have a fixation on the unloadings and wants to get them on videotape. As for Alex, he thinks I'm making far too much fuss, all coincidence. A series of too many coincidences, I said. He said who or what on earth would want to steal nuclear waste? It's useless, practically all the plutonium's been extracted.

Rita: Maybe the who or what doesn't know that. (P 1.43 sec)

Dad: Okay then, see you at the meeting. Quite soon in fact. Be ready for Alex to repeat, there must be some simple scientific explanation.

Endrec

It was on the evening of the following Monday, July 21st it would be, that dad went out to mow the lawn when suddenly the red alert went off, ringing and flashing all over the house. He couldn't hear or see a thing, and we were shouting at him out of your window, and mum had to rush out gesticulating. As soon as he'd stopped the mower and understood he raced towards the house shouting 'how long?' but not waiting for any reply and stumbling into the terrace chairs. He pressed a high button in the hall to switch it all off and was through the front door and into his car almost as pico as that mysterious radiation thief the previous Monday in what was it, fifteen seconds?

That's maxint, Zab, you've got the flowing style real hexadex. Perhaps you should do all those action bits.

Carry bits! Parity bits! Framing bits! Significant bits! Most significant bits!

Overflow bits! Now trap. We're still in a mess with the sequence control, Zab. Why did we have to start with Xorandor?

Because we wanted to. And after all we met him before any of this and WE are the storytellers. Who cares about exact order, all stories jumble things up, and have flashbacks and so on.

Yes, but surely for very specific purposes, all cleverly worked out. We've just blundered in anywhere.

Out of self-centeredness in fact, Jip.

And now we have to introduce Tim, and the Belgian, who didn't seem relevant at the time. And only after that go back to Pennybig on the Sunday she came to the carn, which in fact followed the red alert so it's really going forward. And all those tapes! Oh but no! First there was Poltroon in the local paper! Oh, flipping flipflop, it's a flop not a flipflop.

Well stop fussing about method, Jip, we can straighten it all out later. And with the tapes you'll see the method has its advantages, when some characters know more than the storytellers do.

Okay let's get on.

The day after the red alert, it was all over the local paper. Here we are, we kept everything. What a headline! HOT STUFF AT THE WHEAL? *Men in Spacesuits after alert.*

Just dictate the article into Poccom, Zab.

The Roskillard Fire Brigade was called out yesterday evening at seven by an emergency alert at Tregean Wheal, where the Geothermal Research Unit is exploring the old tin mine for cheap heat based on geothermal energy. Readers will remember the protests that were organized last year, not only in Carn Tregean itself but at other sites opened by the Camborne School of Mines. The concern at the time was to protect the beauty of our landscape, but it seems that more could now be at stake.

MEN IN SPACESUITS!

For the firemen arrived at the same time as Mr John Manning, head of the project, only to gape at the sight of two men emerging from the small building in full protective gear! One of them, Mr Leonard Wingrove, removed his headgear and spoke rapidly to Mr Manning, who then reassured the firemen that it was nothing serious. The local bobby from Carn Tregean, Bill Gurnick, then arrived on his motorbike. Mr Manning made a statement. Apparently a drill had accidentally cut through an electronic signal line and set off the alarm, but all was under control and their electronics expert, Mr Alex Hardy, was fixing it. The protective clothing, Mr Manning said, was imposed because they had some chemicals which could emit noxious gases if a fire a broke out. The firemen insisted on verifying, but were politely though firmly asked simply to wait a while and then leave if nothing further occurred.

WHAT'S GOING ON?

There seems to be a certain mystery here. Why were the firemen not allowed on the premises to do their minimal duty? What was the role of the local police? Why was the public not informed that dangerous chemicals were to be kept at the site? What are these chemicals? Could any of them be radioactive? What, in short, is happening up at the Wheal? It is time the local population was told.

Signed *Poltroon.*

Better explain him, Zab, you do those bits best.

A man called Paul Trewoon, from Roskillard, used to hang about The Wheal Inn quite a bit from that moment on. Trewoon's a place near St Austell, but there's another place called Troon somewhere, south of Camborne, which means, oh, erased ROM here, but anyway he changed Paul into Pol, which means pool, and added it to Troon to make Poltroon and write on ecology. Loopy really.

That was on the Tuesday, the day after the red alert. And on the Friday dad went up to London, not because of the article, he'd have gone anyway. So it would be, yes, the 25th. We've no idea what went on there, but later, much later, after the hoohah, he told us it had been tough, he'd got a polite but complete dressing-down for not reporting the yellow alert.

Yes and they decided to send down Dr Biggleton from Harwell, to look into it all, over his head, like. Poor dad. Anyway he came back a bit less crushed than we expected, cos he'd met Tim Lewis by chance outside Penzance station, and Tim was driving over to Carn Tregean to stay with Alex for the weekend. They're gay. We adore Tim.

Last two rems irrelevant, Zab. All we need to say is Tim works in a microwave outfit in Penzance, well, he has a boss, but he more or less runs it he says.

So Tim drove dad across, and dad asked him in for a drink, and we were just back from talking to Xorandor and threw our bikes down and flung ourselves at him.

And dad said we could come in and have cokes if we first cleaned up and kept quiet.

And just then mum came in from the garden and said Tim! What a lovely surprise! and Tim said Paula darling, you're a vision from days of yore, coming into the chintz and chippendale drawing room from the garden, pink and blond and idyllically English with a basket of roses and a pair of secateurs, and mum said chippendale?

You're off again, Zab, imitating everyone. Do you want to become a failed actress?

Or a failed physicist? And mum went out to put the flowers in water and fetch nuts and things.

And dad asked Tim to recap some technical incident at his plant as he'd missed the beginning in Tim's noisy sportscar.

Yes, rather rude, really, for someone who'd just been spared the bus on a hot day after a journey from London. Probably he just wanted to keep Tim talking so as not to think or have to tell him about his London trip.

The point of all this being, Zab, that Tim went into a longish spiel about something going wrong during the testing of an apparatus they were preparing for the European Space Agency. They'd pointed the horn antenna straight up and they were sweeping through the frequency range. Suddenly they got a message. They'd once captured a similar message a few months before, beamed to somewhere on the North West tip of Cornwall. Both were in pulse-code modulation on K-alpha band; that's between twenty-six and forty Gigahertz which is only used for highly experimental things, and no one knew where on earth or out of earth it could be addressed to. This one seemed to have been beamed locally, but he didn't know anyone or even any satellite beaming at those frequencies, and everyone was making wags.

Wags? said dad. Wild ass guesses, don't you know the term, John? Maybe too frivolous for you. There's also swags, scientific wild ass guesses. And we looked at each other and giggled, since we use it all the time. And dad asked couldn't it be the experimental boys at Goonhilly and Tim said no, he'd checked.

The code wasn't anything familiar, not the simple telex pulse code, nor ASCII nor anything else we know, and they hadn't been repeated, so comparing just two messages hadn't helped at all. And they thought it was an instrument failure and rechecked and rechecked. In the end they sent the two messages on to GCHQ and their client was sending furious telexes and they had to get on with it. The installation first had to go to the University of Louvain for verification and teaching purposes. This in fact is the only point in telling the story, cos of the Belgian.

No, Jip, those messages had their role. But right, the Belgian. Cos then the bell went, and dad said who can that be, and peeped, and said damn, he'd completely forgotten, it's that Belgian archaeologist I met in Miss Penbeagle's shop last week, I invited him round. Looking for fluorite, he said, around here! And he went out.

And Tim at last joked with us and asked us how we were getting on with Poccom 3, he'd love to come up and have a looksee.

And mum gave her actressy laugh and said it's so *funny* — you know how she always uses *funny* when it isn't at all, when she simply wants to make people look really ridiculous without losing her gracious living style but can't do it wittily —

Oh, knock it off, Zab, avort.

She said, they've been talking to the ghost of Merlin near the old carn, just as the Belgian came in with dad, intros all round, Professor Er, and he said De Wint, enchanted madame, sirs. We met in ze shop of Miss Penbeagle, yes. Miss Penbeagle she takes me for Hercule Poirot, simply because I am a Belgian, zat is charming, yes? But I fear I am not so neat, so dressed with care as my illustrious countryman. And of course, I am a Fleming, as you may from my accent recognize.

Very funny Zab.

Mummy-funny or real?

Float-point. Just because he compared himself to Hercule Poirot you have to launch into imitating Agatha Christie making him talk in this foreign way, half the time she gets it all wrong, besides, it's only *now* that you know Germans put the verb at the end.

Who gave a jump instruction? For the moment he's Belgian.

You're doing waste instructions, dummy.

Tell me, Heer Doktor Manning, vas zer some trouble in your Geosermal Drilling Unit? In ze newspaper on Tuesday I read of it, you had ze Feuerbrigade to visit, yes? And dad said oh it was nothing, Professor, an electronic cable got accidentally cut by the drill and set off the alarm. Yes, yes, said De Wint, zat is vot ze newspaper say.

You didn't know the word *Feuer* either at the time, stop mucking about, Zab, besides, now *you're* enjoying making him ridiculous so you can hardly criticize mum.

Well he was, Jip, so fat and scruffy. People can't help being fat — well they can in fact — but they don't have to be repulsive. He didn't look at all like Hercule Poirot with the much repeated egg-shaped head and patent leather shoes. He was a shambly man, who dropped tobacco all over his shirt as he rolled his cigarettes and licked the paper, and his shirt buttons looked like Peggotty's about to burst over his belly, and then he kept this wet bedraggled cigarette in his mouth as he talked, and it wobbled and dropped hot ash over his clothes and burnt small holes in them. Then it went out and he kept it there like a baby's dummy.

You're mean and squeamish, Zab, lots of geniuses are untidy and even repulsive.

He didn't have that saving grace.

Besides, even in the storytelling you're not only wasting time, you're making him out as villain, and that's very old-fashioned, even comics don't make the villain ugly anymore.

But we're not writing comics, Jip, we're writing the truth.

He wasn't even a scientist as it turned out, or more than a very minor villain.

Who's giving jump instructions now?

And Tim, who was also, incidentally, disgusted by him —

He's gay.

Right, and very elegant, even in casuals, agreeable to look at. Mum says care about personal appearance isn't just vanity, it's a kind of politeness, giving pleasure to others.

Look who's talking! Zab the tomboy! Who cares about description anyway? Most people skip them.

You mean you do.

Well, we haven't described anyone else. Not to look at anyway.

This has its point, Jip. Tim sat nursing his drink, sulking, not winking at us any more, as if he resented this beastly presence as a personal affront. Anyway, it worked, cos suddenly he asked, where do you work in Belgium, do you teach? No, no, I research, you know, in thermoluminescent dating for archaeology. At ze University of Brüssel.

Ah, said Tim, UCL or ULB? And de Wint answered UCL. Of course we were bored silly by all this, and restless. But Tim politely took his leave, saying Alex would be expecting him, and went out with mum so we seized the chance and went out with him.

Leaving poor tired dad with his guest.

But in fact Tim didn't leave. He took mum into the kitchen and we followed, and he said he wanted to have another word with dad after the guest had gone, meanwhile he'd go up with us and see Poccom 3, which was like Poccom 2 only a bit bigger. It has more batteries and it's far more efficient and better equipped. Frinstance we can dictate straight into it, as we're doing now, then later it can be connected to a printer. And tapes can be fed directly into it, simultaneously with the taperecorder, and processed if necessary and printed out. It now contained the tape about Rita and the radiation loss, so we had to store that quickly in a reserve memory and block it off. We played around on it with Tim, and then mum called him.

So we all trooped back into the sitting room and Tim explained that he'd stayed on to tell dad that Professor De Wint was a fake.

And dad said very probably, in a tired sort of way, and Tim said no he didn't mean a phoney but a fake altogether, a suspicious character.

An illegal character, unaccepted by a particular program!

Oh joke endjoke, Jip. They then ignored us completely again and talked above our heads, but Tim explained it to us much later. What was it, Jip, you've obviously remembered since you used the initials. Erased ROM here.

Oh it was only that he'd tricked the Belgian, who said he was a Fleming, into saying he belonged to UCL, which stands for Université Catholique de Louvain, as opposed to ULB or Université Libre del Bruxelles. And as Fleming he just wouldn't, cos UCL is the French branch of Louvain which moved to Brussels after Louvain went Flemish. They're practically not on speaking terms. So that made him suspect since he lied. Either he was a professor but not at UCL or he was at UCL but not a Fleming or of course both.

You mean neither.

Tim said he'd detected a picosecond's hesitation before the answer UCL, as if the man didn't know either UCL or ULB and just said the first one he'd heard.

And dad suddenly looked exhausted and depressed and said thanks, but not to worry, did it really matter whether some stray tourist was or wasn't a Fleming and was or wasn't a professor? He himself hadn't done his doctorate after all and De Wint had kept calling him Heer Doktor.

Yes, said Tim, the way Germans do, West or East. Just thought you'd like to know, that's all. Do come round to Alex's for drinks on Sunday, and so on and so forth.

Oof! At last we can get back to Pennybig, in other words forward to that Sunday.

Yes. This is awful, Jip, even with hindsight we can't decide what's really relevant and in what order, and we get carried away. Is that because what seems important is what happened to us?

You get carried away, Zab.

Oh? Who described Poccom 3 in such detail?

Check. We're probably not doing too badly though, and even the best writers revise. We've agreed to get it all into the processor and deal with that aspect afterwards. It's hard enough remembering exactly.

Spikes, Jip! We've completely forgotten to say who Miss Penbeagle is. Even the clumsiest storyteller says something about his characters when they appear, or lets it come out of what they say. But we couldn't then, as she appeared so dramatically behind the carn, and then told us stories, why, anyone would think she was our governess! Holy shit!

Dad allows only Holy nukes, Zab. Anyway, surely we mentioned her shop?

Did we? Well, we'll have to put it somewhere so why not here? She's Cornish yet not a bit Cornish, despite her name. She'd been a Civil Servant in London and retired here, where she was born, and took over the village shop from her mother, who died soon after. Or maybe she retired because her mother'd died. And as her mother had been allowed to be postmistress long after retiring age, the P.O. stretched the same rule for Miss Penbeagle. She likes us, always gives us sweets or something when we come in on an errand.

Zab, does it matter?

No, but it's fun. It also explains how English she seems, and even eccentric, and how she cares so deeply about Cornwall, and local ecology and that, and also her sharp intelligence, frinstance she asked questions we never even thought of, remember. And her intelligence happens to have been important, Jip, in the hoohah, when it came.

4 AND

So that Sunday, after the counting lesson and Pennybig's appearance, we didn't go back to the carn in the afternoon. We'd been very silent during lunch, d'you remember, Jip, and a lot of questions were beginning to appear in our dim little heads.

NOW *you're* being conceitedly modest or vice versa, Zab. And you're not remembering it right. It's after lunch we were very quiet. At lunch, we blabbed, both of us, very excited, about our talking stone, and the counting lesson, and Pennybig's turning up, and dad for once really listened without correcting our English all the time, he seemed to believe us, maybe because of the ASCII code thing, or maybe cos there'd been a grown-up witness, or maybe cos of those two messages, or De Wint, or the radiation loss, or something, anyway he asked a lot of sharp questions, can you remember them Zab?

Nope, erased ROM again, and we hadn't the cheek or the smartness or the gear to bug the dining room. Except that he called me Isabel throughout.

But you managed to reconstruct, as you call it, all the earlier convs.

Edge-triggering, you wanting me to reconstruct convs, Jip, usually you want to scratch them as irrelevant, and even invented. If you're so keen to show dad's sudden interest, for once as you put it, why haven't you remembered?

Well, it was about the numbers.

And the stone itself, and had we examined it properly and looked for a hoax and so on, seems he was doing his usual monitoring-of-minds-for-rigour stunt.

Maybe. But when we said about the wall he really perked up. We can see why now.

And mum, who as usual *really* wasn't listening, said: Stone? Didn't Shakespeare say something about a stone?

Oh Zab she couldn't have.

She did, Jip. You're her wetsypetsy so you've erased it. We went into fits of giggles and dad, who looked in acute pain for a nanosecond, managed to laugh it off and went on with his questions about the wall, and when, and what the stone'd said. The only thing that's maybe wrong is Shakespeare, she may have said Shaw. She lives with them both, not with us, but especially Shaw, which is zany since they hated each other.

Zab, you're nuts, screwboole, boolederdashed and phased out.

It was a joke, Jip, endjoke.

It was an uncorrectable error, admit it and abort, you toggle flipflop flapper you!

Jumping back to master-slave mode? You were right, Jip, that it was in the afternoon that we clammed up, we wanted to work things out. What was this Xorandor really, as we'd named him, though Pennybig didn't seem to know this and later called him Merlin. We must have long abandoned the ghost theory, yet obviously it wasn't just a talking stone. It could be some sort of joke with remote-controlled loudspeaker hidden somewhere but of course we'd looked. If he was an alien creature, and as intelligent as he seemed, where had he come from? And how? And what kind? D'you remember going through all that, Jip?

Right. It's very difficult to reconstruct a state of ignorance. We even looked at the video of an old TV programme on Ultra Intelligent Machines, as forecast before they began to develop properly. There was a chart showing the levels of intelligence, and it placed rocks at the very bottom, at zero, like an object that doesn't *react* to being knocked over but simply obeys the laws of physics. Then came amoebe and such, then computers of the 1960s, then computers of the 1970s.

Then earwigs! Remember, Jip, how triggered we were by that? And after a big jump came fish, and after another big jump dogs and cats and other carnivores. Another huge jump to non-human primates, and —

You're probably leaving some out, Zab, but anyway only then, came humans, and then the first generation U.I.M.'s, leading to the second, and third, and so on. So how could a stone think? How, above all, had a message appeared on our miniscreen, later repeated verbally but not verbatim?

Diodic, Jip, verbally but not verbatim, that's prime. It's true that looking back now, it seems unbelievable that this was one of the last questions we asked ourselves.

Though it happened first. Probably what happened next scratched it from our minds.

But for two weeks, Jip, in the middle of the summer eprom, since it first happened!

And they also described the Turing Test. But how could we do it here?

And then we went from science to fiction, one of our favourite stories, by Ambrose Bierce, very old-fashioned but the very first to ask the question can a machine think? The bit about crystals, remember?

We don't have to, Zab, it's in that anthology we bought the other day in the English bookshop. Just after, no, later, after George Moxon quotes Herbert Spencer's definition of life, surely outdated, but listen:

> *How else do you explain the phenomena, for example, of crystallization?*
>
> *I do not explain them.*
>
> *Because you cannot without affirming what you wish to deny, namely, intelligent cooperation among the constituent elements of the crystals. When soldiers form lines, or hollow squares, you call it reason. When wild geese in fight take the form of the letter V you say instinct. When the homogeneous atoms of a mineral, moving freely in solution, arrange themselves into shapes mathematically perfect, or particles of frozen moisture into the symmetrical and beautiful forms of snowflakes, you have nothing to say. You have not even invented a name to conceal your heroic unreason.*

Not that it's very helpful, nor does it define thinking.

No, but it's beautiful, Jip. And a long time ago. It sort of rings a bell. Didn't a poet, or several, say something about stones having souls or something?

You sound like mum.

A sentient stone. Or else it was a belief, or a philosophical question, in oldtime philosophy, when poetry and philosophy were still close. Or maybe a German poet. Oh, it's so confusing, this change of schools! And why didn't we understand straight away?

Well even brilliant grownup scientists don't see things for ages that stare them in the face. Anyway, late that afternoon, we were still talking in your room, and we suddenly saw Miss Penbeagle contorting herself down the village street and up the concrete path with a marathonic gait.

In the same blue print dress and white cardigan she'd worn that morning, but her face was scarlet and her wispy grey hair, which is usually drawn back in a small neat bun, was all loose around it.

Repeat question Zab, does it matter?

Repeat answer, no, but it's fun. Daddy was rushing out to meet her and bringing her in. So we crept back to your room and switched on Sneaker.

Tape 1, Side 1, Rec. 2, Sunday 27 July. Printout.
Voice 1 = Dad. Voice 2 = Pen. Beginrec.

Dad: ( ) contact you for hours! (P noise 3.09 min) Here you are, just water as requested, nice and cool, drink it slowly.

Pen: Thank you (P 3.02 sec) I'm sorry Mr Manning (P 1.43 sec) to barge in (P 2.32 sec) I wouldn't (P 0.46 sec) you know me, Mr Manning (P 0.36 sec) I do have a sense of —

Dad: Not at all, Miss Penbeagle, please don't be upset, I do understand the reason.

Pen: You do? Ah, so they told you?

Dad: Yes, at least a bit, and they said you'd been with them this morning.

Pen: Oh dear. I lost my hat. That really is too bad. My straw hat with the dark blue ribbon.

Dad: Never mind, I'll buy you a new one.

Pen: But I've had that one for years! I must have dropped it on the path coming back from the carn. I had it this afternoon, I know.

Dad: I see. So you went back to the carn then?

Pen: Yes. I had to. I was afraid you wouldn't believe me, I mean, you see, children, well they invent all sorts of games, and you could have thought I was just, well, going along with them. As it is you probably think I've lost my head. Oh dear, but I've lost my hat.

Dad: We'll find it, if you like I'll drive you up there in a little while, it's sure to be on the road.

Pen: But I didn't come back by the road, it would be much too long, five miles! It's only two by the ridge path, that's eight miles I've walked today!

Dad: Why don't you just relax and tell me all about it?

Pen: But you won't believe me. You'll think I'm just a crazy old woman hearing voices. I've been so frightened, Mr Manning, really frightened. I mean it just can't be true. Maybe I'm suffering from sunstroke. (P. 0.56 sec) Do you think I could have that whisky now?

Dad: But of course. If you were suffering from sunstroke you wouldn't want alcohol. Now, let's take it from the beginning, shall we? What happened this morning?

Pen: This morning? Oh that seems so long ago. You mean you don't believe Jip and Zab? What did they say?

Dad: Of course I believe them. I mean that something odd is up there. But I'd like much more detail from you, Miss Penbeagle, you're an eminently sensible person, we all know that. Try and remember it from the beginning.

Pen: Yes. Oh dear. I'd so much rather start from the end. It's an alien out of space Mr Manning, he told me. Oh you don't believe me. I knew you wouldn't. I'm no good at telling things in the right order, you know, but you're right, nothing like an orderly scientific mind. I read somewhere, the scientist always goes back to the beginning, I mean, when something unexpected happens, he goes back and recreates the original conditions of the, er, experiment.

Dad: Yes, that's quite true, how clever of you. (P 2.56 sec) So why don't you do just that? (P 0.27 sec)

Pen: I'm cleverer than you think you know, I read a lot. Oh I often lead you on, pretending crass ignorance. That's the way I learn things. The other day in the shop I said you were building thermal baths, and you corrected me very seriously to geothermal energy recovery. A bit too seriously I thought. I know a thing or two, and I read ECO, that's Ecology Cornwall Org. And that tourist who came into the shop when you were there, this funny Belgian who buys selfroll cigarettes, remember, he said he was looking for fluorite and I repeated fluoride and you kindly corrected me. Later I found out it's also called fluorspar and it's coloured crystals with properties that help archaeologists date things. He's an archaeologist, this Belgian, just like Agatha Christie's husband was, funny that.

Dad: Please, Miss Penbeagle, tell me what happened at the carn.

Pen: Well, this morning, nothing much, I'd been out for my Sunday walk and was resting in the shade of the old carn. I must have fallen asleep, and woke to distant voices, which suddenly were very near, and I recognized Jip and Zab just on the other side of the carn, talking to I didn't know who, a voice that answered in a high tinny pitch. They were teaching it to multiply! I thought I was — *Endtape*

Tape 1. Side 2. Rec. 1. Cont. from Side 1. Printout.
Some missed out on bootstrap *Beginrec*

Dad: He?

Pen: Well, they said it was the ghost of Merlin, and I went along with that, and he talked, it's difficult to use it. But I was suddenly very calm, it was extraordinary, once he'd addressed me. And he said he wanted to speak to olders. What we mean by elders you know. Or men. But no, I've no idea whether he can distinguish men from women. I asked if he could wait two days, and he said yes. I needed that to think what to do you see, I mean I saw in a flash that everyone would think me mad, but if I could go back there alone, at night, and get more evidence, well in the end I couldn't wait, and went back this afternoon.

Dad: And what happened then?

Pen: No, if you want order Mr Manning, order you shall have. I asked him, this morning I mean, if he needed anything. I can't think why, or what he might need. Just a habit of courtesy I suppose. It was simply a voice to me at first you see, but at the same time I seemed to fix my eye on a large flat round stone, oh quite unlike the dark rock around here I assure you, brown with sort of greyish patches. The voice seemed truly to come from that stone, it was weird.

Dad: Go on.

Pen: Well he said he didn't, just an older, so we said goodbye, and I walked back with Jip and Zab to the main road, where they'd left their bikes, and asked them to tell me how they'd found this Merlin. Seems it's been going on for some weeks. Then I cut back across to the ridge path and returned that way. But maybe they told you all that.

Dad: Some, yes. But what happened this afternoon?

Pen: I crept up and said, very softly, Merlin — in case he was having a nap you see. I was very nervous again, after all I didn't know who or what I was addressing. But he replied at once, Gwen-do-lin. He recognized me! I asked him if he could see me. The children must have asked him that before because he answered without hesitation, yes, if see is high low, bother, I've forgotten, something about sand balls, made no sense at all. Maybe he thought I didn't mean see but the sea, and the tides.

Dad: Holy sh — (P 0.19 sec)

Pen: So then I asked him if he needed food. I can't think why, if he's a stone, oh I know you think I'm off my head, but after all he seemed a living creature and it felt like a natural question.

Dad: What did he say?

Pen: He said no. But then, would you believe it, he added that he was finding plenty of food here. Find much food here, he said. And I asked what food and he said small balls again, I was amazed, I asked if he fed on pebbles, he didn't understand so I said small small stones, and he said no, small small balls, he changed that to very very small small balls. Maybe he meant sand? He'd told the children he was made of sand. (P 0.63 sec)

Dad: He didn't say where he gets these very small balls from?

Pen: No, but there's plenty of sand, even just around him. Anyway I then asked him where he came from. I suppose you'll think that's another crazy question since he's there, and immobile. But Mr Manning I must have been inspired, unless I really am mad. He answered, from very far. How far? I asked, and you'll never guess his reply. He said as if he'd calculated it already, I remember the exact phrase, sixty thousand thousand times more as daddy's home. Daddy's home, can you imagine, he must have the words from Jip and Zab, and the exact location. But sixty thousand thousand! That's sixty million times some two miles as the crow flies. I said goodness me, but that can't be on earth, and he said no, other earth, earth four from sun!

Dad: Mars.

Pen: Mr Manning I was so terrified I bolted, well, not before saying goodbye, I know my manners. In fact I had to make a tremendous effort to control myself, I felt I was going to faint and sat down by the wall, but then the dizzy spell went away, so I managed to hoist myself up on a small rock, so as to see over the wall, and I said I'd bring an older to speak with him very soon. Then I got up properly and fled. I scrambled down the moorland to the ridge path and almost ran all the way here. (P 0.27 sec) That's when I must have lost my hat.

Dad: Miss Penbeagle, you did the right thing, to come here I mean, not to lose your hat. Could you possibly face going up there again with me?

Pen: Now? Oh no, my legs wouldn't make it a fifth time!

Dad: By car I mean, as far as the footpath, and I'll help you along that quarter-mile. (P. 6.07 sec) Perhaps we'll find your hat.

Pen: Well, it's very late, I have to prepare my supper.

Dad: You can come and have supper with us afterwards, and I'll drive you home.

Pen: No, no, I'm too exhausted to face the children after that, and they'll never forgive me for going up there alone, stealing their Merlin you know, oh, and betraying their secret!

Dad: Miss Penbeagle my dear, it's no longer their secret, at least not from me, since they told us at lunch. It may be very important, our secret if you like, and you may yourself be at the centre of a very unusual event. Just as you're at the centre of the village, in the village shop, and as postmistress you know every kind of letter each of us receives, we trust you, we like you very much. (P 4.32 sec)

Pen: All right, Mr Manning. I came to you, I'll go up with you if you drive me back. But no supper, please, I couldn't face it. Instead, may I take another finger of whisky and water. And some biscuits, that'll —

Endrec

5 IF

We had switched off the recorder and raced silently to the garage for our bikes. In emergencies we have this uncanny quickconnect, without even speaking. We reckoned dad would pacify mum and Penny would fill in on biscuits and whisky just long enough to give us a head start, provided we rode fast towards the ridge path, and not the road, on which they could overtake us.

Yes, the path is invisible from the carn and from the road since the carn is on the ridge. We'd leave our bikes at the beginning of the path, hidden behind a rock, and it would soon be getting dark. And we'd scramble towards the carn on foot and hide where she had, and hear everything, telling Xorandor first not to betray us, that is, if we arrived before them. We did. We hid our recorder and mike behind the carn, under some stones, and then in fact decided to switch it on at once as we saw the car on a distant bend, and to hide further away, behind a rock, just in case dad looked round. We settled just in time to hear Miss Penbeagle's excited squeal, 'My hat! It's there!' and her own scramble towards the carn with a sudden spurt of energy. It was nearly eight and the late summer sun was descending towards the sea, soon the daylight would lose its brightness.

Smart terminal, Zab, that sounds very pro. And it was just as well it got darker and that we'd hidden further away, because, ho-ho-ho, we had another spying visitor who crept up a little later, remember, and didn't see us among the rocks, and hid where Pen had been and where he'd first intended to hide, none other than our mysterious minor and extremely handsome villain Professor De Wint.

Jip! That's a jump instruction! You shouldn't have spoilt it.

Oh who cares, you said yourself order isn't that important. Now, proposition: we don't have to *tell* what we overheard since we have two tapes of it, ours and dad's, and he plays his back to Biggleton later, so we can skip straight to our tape of dad with Biggleton. In fact from our present storyteller's viewpoint our trip there was a waste of Sneaker, as dad would never have gone up there without his latest beloved gadget — swags, what a maniac family we are — that gorgeous, watchsized recorder. He must have placed it on the wall, and of course it comes up much clearer than ours.

Accept, so on with the Biggleton tape. A lot of it was beyond us at the time, but we'd done enough elem-phys to understand that this was the most important dataheap of all.

And Biggleton was a big boffin, who'd come down that evening from London, angry that dad was late picking him up at the Wheal Inn. From UKAEA at Harwell, no less.

Press the button, toggleflip.

Tape 1. Side 2. Rec. 2. Sunday 27 July. Printout
Voice 1 = Dad. Voice 2 = Biggleton, wr Big. Voice 3 = Pen. Voice 4 = Merlin, wr Mer. Voice 5 = De Wint, wr Win. *Beginrec*

(Noise 3.03 min)

Dad: ( ) at first sight, if one can swallow its extraordinary aspect, seem to explain the events at the mine.

Big: Scrap the preliminaries, young man, I haven't got all night.

Dad: I'll deal with the local details first if I may sir, briefly, otherwise you'll be puzzled by certain things on the tape.

Big: Tape, eh? I hope it's not too long.

Dad: I must crave your patience sir, I can only assure you that it is important, intellectually, exciting even, and that you won't regret it. But first, the local situation. Our cover seems to be suspected in three directions. The local postmistress apparently knows what we're doing, as you will hear, but she's absolutely trustworthy. Second, the local journalist from Roskillard, Poltroon as he calls himself, who wrote that article, was at the inn —

Big: Well, what of it, at worst it'll mean another ignorant article on waste and more ecological protest. In a local rag.

Dad: And third sir, there's this fake Belgian physicist ferreting around.

Big: Fake Belgian?

Dad: Calls himself Professor De Wint, I'll explain later why he can't be a Belgian, and other things, but as you'll hear on the tape he may be relevant.

Big: I really don't see how. This small trouble of yours isn't anything Top Secret, you know, you really mustn't waste my time with all this tittle-tattle about nothing.

Dad: Sorry sir, I've probably begun at the wrong end. It started with my children hearing a voice by the old carn, it's on the way to The Wheal, you see, about three miles from it as the crow flies. I took no notice at first, they called it the ghost of Merlin and were teaching it modern English and how to count. It had apparently said we have sixty-four or a hundred and twenty-eight sounds, the ASCII code in other words, which it seems to have captured and differentiated as signs. I was still only humouring them, until today, when Miss Penbeagle, that's our local postmistress, overheard them, and then went there again on her own, and talked to this voice, which seemed to come from a large stone.

Big: Are you having me on, young man?

Dad: No sir. I went up myself with Miss Penbeagle later, this very evening in fact, that's why I was late. I took my miniature tape-recorder. I would like to play it back to you now, sir, if you can bear with me a little longer.

Big: Can't it wait? It's after ten, this possible hoax can't have anything to do with our business. I want to be up at the site early, to see the unloading videotapes. There is an unloading tonight, isn't there? May I remind you that the spectrometers at the second alert showed at least 0.66 Mev gamma rays, that's Caesium 137, a fission product. And that the guard's badge dosimeter showed a dose of 12 millirad, undifferentiated of course. But 12 millirad from Caesium 137 in 30 seconds would amount to at least a one Curie source. *This* is what I have come to investigate, not your scatterbrained other concerns that have allowed the situation to occur in the first place. (P 3.97 sec)

Dad: I submit, sir, that you should hear this tape before going up to The Wheal tomorrow, you will see why when you have heard it, I promise you. (P 2.61 sec)

Big: Well, so be it. But relax, and give me another brandy. And have one yourself, you look worn out.

Dad: Thank you, yes. (P 53.06 sec) I suggest we hear it right through first, then any passage you may wish to discuss.

Big: We'll see. Go ahead. (P 2.49 sec)

Pen: Mer, lin.

Mer: Gwen, do, lin. Who, bring, you?

Pen: I, bring, daddy.

Dad: Hello, Mer, lin. (P 1.03 sec) You, want, to, see, me?

Mer: Mer, lin, not, see. Mer, lin, do, sums.

Dad: You cal, cu, late, me? With, what, numbers, Mer, lin?

Mer: If, cal, cu, late, is, high, low, under, light, sand, balls, then, Merlin, cal, cu, late.

Dad: Silicon photocells! (P 2.31 sec)

Pen: He doesn't know such words, John, you must put it more simply.

Dad: You, see, below, light?

Mer: Yes. No. Merlin Cal, cu, late. (P 0.37 sec) Daddy, is, dad, is, John.

Dad: Yes. My, name, is, John.

Mer: Who, is, dad?

Dad: I, am, also, dad. Daddy, of, Jip, and Isabel.

Mer: Merlin, cant, find, Isa, bel.

Dad: Isabel, is Zab. Why, do, you, want, to, see, no, to speak, with me? How, do, you, hear, er, cal, cu, late, sound?

Mer: Two, asks. One, answer, for, to, tell, daddy, John, thing. Two. Answer, sound, heavy, push, light, inside, Merlin.

Dad: And how, do, you, speak, sound?

Mer: Big, push. Light, push, small, very, small stone, like, sand, with, air, small small, balls, in, again again, same, lines.

Dad: Jumping nukes! Crystal!

Mer: Not, jum, ping, nukes. Jum, ping, nukes, is, for, Jip, re, act.

Dad: I meant, crys, tal. The name, of, that, stone, is, crystal. Crys, tal. Sanks. Speak, big, push. Not, sound, before, speak, by, light. No, not, light, less, strong, as light.

Pen: Radio!

Mer: Light, not, move, but, in, small (P 0.31 sec) bits. High low, low, high, high, low.

Dad: Pulses!

Mer: Pul, ses. Sanks.

Dad: Where, do, you, come, from?

Mer: Say, to, Gooen, do, lin, ers, four, from, sun.

Dad: We call, that, earth, Mars. (P 0.41 sec) How, did, you, come, here?

Mer: You, fall. Merlin, fall.

Dad: But how long — how, long, would, it, take?

Mer: It, take, nine, hun, dred, eighty, sree, days. (Whistle)

Dad: And when, you, fell, near, earth, how, did, you, not burn?

Mer: Can't find, burn.

Dad: Very, hot.

Mer: Yes, very, very, hot. Not, fall, too, fast, turn, very, fast, have, big, stone (P 4.31 sec) swe, ter, all, burn, when, fall. Zen, inside, pull, for, very, slow.

Pen: A sweater! Surely he can't knit as well as count!

Mer: Stone, sweater, around, Merlin.

Dad: A heat-shield. And some sort of brake-system. (P. 2.32 sec) How, did, you, leave, Mars?

Mer: All, help, jum, ping, nukes, cant, find, words, much, food, much, push.

Pen: Food! What, do, you, feed, on, there, on, Mars?

Mer: Feed, on, very, very, small, small, balls, in rocks, and ozer, hards.

Pen: Goodness me! Could that be radioactivity?

Dad: Alpha or beta rays!

Mer: Is, food, name, goodness, me?

Pen: No, Mer, lin. Goodness, me, is, like, jumping, nukes. Food, name, is, ra, dio, ac, ti, vi, ty.

Mer: Ra, di, o, ac, ti, vi, ty. Long, word, for, food.

Dad: What, kind, do, you, get, on, Mars?

Mer: Kind, means, good?

Dad: What, is, the, food, made, of?

Mer: Hard, wiz, forty, or two, hun, dred, sirty, or two, hun, dred, twenty, six, small, small, balls. Some, times, two, hun, dred, sirty, five, but little, more, and, more, little.

Dad: Potassium, Thorium, Radium, Uranium! How, do, you, get, your, food, here?

Mer: Send, small, stone, goes, into, rock, gets, out, right, food.

Dad: Good God!

Mer: Good, god, is, right, food?

Pen: No, Merlin, Good, God, is, like, jumping, nukes.

Mer: You, have much, many, jumping, words.

Pen: What, do, you, do, when, there, is, no, food, nearby?

Mer: Need, very, small, to, live, more, to, do, to, send, stone, to, move, very, slow, keep, food, in, very cold, part, of, Merlin.

Pen: He can't mean a freezer!

Dad: How, do, you, feed, here?

Mer: Merlin, find, here, much, food. Not, same, as, in, rock. Very, good. Grow, big, sinker.

Dad: How, did, you, find, it?

Mer: Feel, much, food, move, near. Not, know, food, move, before. On, Mars. But, get, got, away. One, time, too, fast, two, time, sree, time, Merlin, ready, send, small, stone.

Pen: The Wheal!

Mer: Find, food, wiz, one, hun, dred, sirty, seven, balls, too, strong, not, good, for, Merlin. Merlin, likes, very, much, food, wiz, two, hundred, sirty, five, small, balls, and, or, two, hundred, sirty, eight. But, protect, wiz sweater, round, pulses. Food, one, hundred, sirty, seven, spoil, sweater, in, places. Now find, much food, wiz ninety, balls, very, good, and mend, sweaters. (P 5.17 sec) Zat, is, answer, to, ask, one, ze words, Merlin, want, to speak, to, daddyjohn.

Dad: Merlin, I thank you. Thank you, very much. Do, you, want, more, food, with, ninety, balls?

Mer: Yes. Or, two, hundred, sirty, eight. Very, not, often. Like, best. But, ninety, very good. Merlin, grow, Merlin, make small, smaller, Merlins.

Pen: Good gracious!

Mer: Bad, gracious, perhaps, to, you, if, take, food, one, hundred, sirty, seven, balls, grow, too (P 2.03 sec) for you.

Dad: I see! Merlin, do, you, mind, I bring, another, person, here, tomorrow?

Mer: Cant find, mind, after, you. Cant find, per, son.

Dad: Do, you, mind, is, may, I. Person, is, another, older. May, I, bring, another, older? (P 5.43 sec)

Mer: Now, here, sree, olders.

Dad: Three? No, two, Gwen, do, lin, and, daddy.

Mer: Sree.

Pen: Can, you, see, three?

Mer: One, older, behind, Merlin. Like Gwen, do, lin, at day. (1328.02 sec)

Win: Heer Doctor Manning! What a surprise!

Dad: What *are* you doing here, Professor?

Win: But I might ask the same, Heer Doctor. I was leisurely strolling along the path by evening and coming back towards the road. I heard voices. Good evening, Miss Penbeagle. (P 3.03 soc)

Pen: Good evening Professor. It is pleasant isn't it? After such a hot day. I felt quite ill myself a while ago, had a touch of sunstroke I think, and I was just sitting here in the cool of the summer evening when Mr Manning drove by. Most kind. He saw me from the road and thought I needed assistance.

Dad: Yes, I was driving from The Wheal. But I can drive you back now if you feel better Miss Penbeagle.

Pen: No, I wish to stay here for a while, it's nice and cool now. If you could stay just a moment longer there's something I want to say to you Mr Manning, about your children.

Dad: Why certainly, but I'll still drive you home, I'm in no hurry.

Win: I hope you feel better soon, Miss Penbeagle. Goodnight, Dr Manning. (Noise. P 2.05 min)

Pen: Do you think he heard, John?

Dad: I don't know. You were splendid, Gwendolin.

Pen: Rudeness was the only way, we just cut him out. He came over from the same spot as I did this morning and I heard everything from there. I don't trust that man, you know, he reminds me of that detective.

Dad: We must hurry. Mer, lin?

Mer: Yes, daddyjohn?

Dad: May I, bring, older, tomorrow?

Mer: On, Mars, far, far, from, others, not, like, close, too many, pulses, cross, inside.

Dad: Only, one, Merlin, me, and one, other, big, older.

Mer: More, big, bigger, as, you daddy, John?

Dad: Not, bigger, to see, but, bigger, in (P 0.32 sec) He tells, me, what, to, do.

Mer: Jumping, nukes. Jip, tell, Zab, Gwen, do, lin, tell, Jip, Daddyjohn, tell, Gwendo, lin, bigger, daddy, tell, Daddyjohn.

Dad: Yes, I'm afraid so.

Mer: Is, daddyjohn, afraid, of, bigger, daddy?

Dad: No, no, afraid, means, sorry, it, is, so.

Mer: Afraid, so, too.

Dad: May I, bring, him?

Mer: If, daddy, want, zen, yes. Please, not, more, as, two.

Dad: Only two. I promise.

Mer: Promise, okay. Jipnzab promise, always. Okay. Stop, speak, now.

Dad: Merlin, will, you, promise, not, to, speak, to anyone, except —

Mer: Cant find except.

Dad: Only. Only, speak, to me, and, to, bigger, daddy.

Mer: Cant promise. Speak, to Jipnzab, to, Gwen, dolin.

Dad: Yes, of course. Speak, only, to, Zab, Gwendolin, daddy, and bigger, daddy. Will, you, promise?

Mer: Merlin, promise. Not, like, speak. Okay. Goodbye.

Dad/
Pen: Goodbye.

6 THEN

Dad: What do you make of it sir?

Big: Well, I don't know yet. You're right. We'll have to go over it and listen to certain details separately. If it's a hoax it's certainly very clever, and would as you say mean that someone has pierced your cover. But that only means one more mild nuisance with the ecologists.

Dad: And if it isn't?

Big: If it isn't — well, I'd rather ask you first, you've had more time to think. I suggest we leave aside for the moment the wholly unsatisfactory question of its origins, the dynamics of it and so forth, and concentrate only on its presence and performance. What do *you* think, Manning?

Dad: Well sir. (P 3.57 sec) As far as I can gather from its childlike vocabulary, and of course in the hypothesis that what it says is true, it would belong to a mineral race of beings, not silicates but, let us say, a very ancient silicon lifeform, possibly metallo-oxydes, or even zeolites, that would have developed semi-conductor capacities, and eventually electronic computer abilities. A lifeform that doesn't itself use sound, but is equipped to receive and emit sound waves.

Big: Yes, I'd like to hear that bit again. (P 6.32 sec Noise)

Mer: You, see, below, light?

Big: No, a bit further, it's clear about the infra-red.

Dad: (over Noise) Yes, a spectral response like that of silicon cells, very low in the ultra-violet. Ah, here. *Mer*: Sound, heavy, push, light, inside, Mer, lin. *Dad*: And how, do, you, speak, sound? *Mer*: Big push. Light, push, small, very, small, stone, like sand, wiz air, small, small, balls, in, again again, same, lines. *Dad*: Jumping nukes! Crystal. (Click) Now the way I interpret that sir, is, well, as a very literal description of what happens with piezo-electric crystals, incredible though it may seem, I mean, when you think of all that we can do with silicon-based electronics.

Big: Calm down, Mr Manning, I'm not examining you. I also followed your friend's amusing description. But we must not get carried away you know. It is of course, as you say, pretty incredible if it's really a mere stone you saw, which can emit sound and radio waves, detect light and nuclear radiations, reconstruct images from silicon photocell arrays, store billions of bits of information like a powerful computer, the lot. But here we can't even talk of images, only of numerical reconstructions in primitive operations, whereby it senses presences. Of course I realize that if we've achieved all this in a mere century it's possible to imagine the same after aeons of slow development in a purely silicon life-form, if one can even talk of such a thing. But we're only imagining. Let's go back to the beginning – ah, I see you're smiling at last, my boy, and more relaxed. The outer physical aspect, for instance. I suppose you couldn't see it properly in the dusk?

Dad: And the shadow of the carn in the setting sun. It looks like a round brown stone, about two foot wide and ten inches high at its centre, or less perhaps. It had grey metallic-looking patches, which might just conceivably be sensing and emitting devices such as electric-to-pressure transducers. And various semi-conductor junctions would be capable of detecting nuclear radiation or radio waves. But perhaps it's the other way round, perhaps it was originally all metallic-looking and the stone aspect might be what's left of the heat shield rock. As you say we'd have to examine it carefully. Though of course we can hardly break it up to examine its hardware.

Big: One thing at a time, young man. For the moment we'd better discuss the tape in detail. Let us say it communicates in pulse-code modulation. I'm noting these points as we go.

Dad: Well as far as I can gather this electronic processing of pulses into sound and inversely into speech would be unusual for him, he clearly doesn't like it, perhaps because the atmosphere of Mars — if it is Mars — is too thin. Unless of course they communicate through rocks —

Big: They?

Dad: Well sir, it's difficult to imagine a thinking and communicating being without others of its kind, wherever it happens to come from. Remember, he said he could reproduce, presumably by partition. In fact that's why it's hard to keep its, er, genealogy, out of it.

Big: Nevertheless we must try. But go on.

Dad: I was going to say sir, that if they don't normally communicate by sound, it would then be special equipment, as it were, for this adventure.

Big: Steady there, not so fancy, daddyjohn, we can't speak yet of an adventure. And if I suggested we keep its origins and journey out of it for the moment the point was methodological.

Dad: Yes sir. And after all, it hardly matters now, since it's here. Basically it seems to feed on natural radioactivity from rocks. Hence its mining capacities, and those of isotopic separation.

Big: You know, I find that part the most far-fetched. We only achieved that ourselves in the 1930s, with our very finest equipment. And logically that would mean it understands fission. And fusion.

Dad: I know sir. I'm still only extrapolating from what it says. I'm just abuzz with ideas. But simply on the mining, the small stone it says it sends into the rock to do this would then be some kind of nodule. He says —

Big: Look, daddyjohn, I wish you'd decide on a 'he' or an 'it'. For the moment I'd prefer 'it'.

Dad: Yes sir. Though if it produces offspring it could even be a 'she'. (Noise 3.07 sec) It says it keeps food in a very cold part of him, it. I wondered if that could be near the absolute zero.

Big: I know. A superconducting ring! (P 4.16 sec) But then, my boy, he could store a current of thousands of amperes. What a magnetic field that could generate! Could he, could it — you see I'm getting as anthropomorphic as you are, daddyjohn, and I haven't even met the little fellow yet. Could it levitate the nodule magnetically?

Dad: But of course sir! I puzzled and puzzled over this. Yes, that's it.

Big: No, Manning, nothing is it, till we've checked and rechecked. Remember we're making an awful lot of hypotheses within a general and very provisional hypothesis that this is not a hoax. (P 6.19 secs) All right, let's not get excited. Now, I'd like to hear all that part about Mars and the so-called heat-shield.

Dad: So-called by me of course, not by him. I mean it called it a sweater, the nearest word he could find for envelope from listening to the children. Here. *Mer*: You, fall, Merlin, fall *Endtape*

Tape 2, Side 1, Real Cont. Tape 1, Side 2, Rec. 2. Printout.

Big: (bootstrap) to me what a hoaxer might think up. It's also extremely unlikely that a body, however small, say a very small meteorite, should fall through space from Mars or indeed from anywhere into our atmosphere without any trace whatsoever on any of the world's astronomical or military equipment, including satellites, but I'll check on that.

Dad: Yes, and the three hundred and eighty-three days he gives for the — er — dynamics, that's the exact time of the first Viking Mars probe, which seems very odd.

Big: I know *that*, my boy. Still, let's continue with our supposition. To withstand the heat generated on entry he, it, would have been equipped with a thick layer of rock that served as heat-shield. It would have arrived tangentially into earth's atmosphere, spinning very fast as he says, damn it, let's stick to 'he', both to decrease falling speed and to limit the heat. But how could he decelerate enough to limit his impact on landing? Aerodynamically? Magnetically? Presumably there's no sign of a crater or damage to the carn or you'd have said so? Okay, let's suppose one of those. At any rate most of the shield would have burnt out but there'd still be patches, so he'd look like a stone. But maybe underneath he's a sort of living semi-conductor being, a highly sophisticated megacomputer full of optoelectronic devices and sensors.

Dad: Yes, and with total recall and a huge Random Access Memory, and even a huge Read Only Memory if one dare call it that, as well as all the other types of memories, and superfast processes. He never forgets a word once heard, and has apparently learnt to communicate in English in the four weeks since the children have been back from school, from mere listening. And he can compose high numbers out of the first ten and decades the kids taught him. He was able to differentiate the signs of the ASCII code, or so we may suppose, simply as heard on radio waves around him. But is it a being or a machine? I don't know. Think of what such Martians would decide on seeing our Viking probe landing and starting to shovel the soil with pincers as if to eat it.

Big: Martians! Martians have gone out even of science fiction long ago. How come no probe ever saw any trace of life, let alone a civilization?

Dad: Well, they don't seem to make artefacts, however complex their internal chemical capacity, and they look like stones. For all we know there may be some among the rocks of the Martian landscape photographs that were taken.

Big: But if they don't make artefacts they shouldn't have evolved a language, or a linguistic capacity, at least, I gather the two go together, the capacity to symbolize I mean.

Dad: Well, I don't know. That could apply to us only, who have limbs.

He doesn't like too many presences. This would tend to show they must have remained far apart, perhaps to get their radioactivity without encroaching on each others' supply. There's much less radioactivity on Mars. He said Potassium 40 and Thorium 230 but I'll have to check. According to his story there'd be very few of them left, so they made this big effort, whatever it was, to send one of their kind, to a planet which they hoped or knew had plenty and even produces it. They'd know of our existence since they'd be able to receive all the microwaves and stuff we've been sending out. I don't know, these are just wags.

Big: Wags?

Dad: Sorry sir, Wild ass guesses.

Big: Yes, they are. You really mustn't get carried away into fabricating a history for them, for, our friend, like this. At the moment, it's simply a phenomenon to be investigated, synchronically and mechanically and scientifically. I say 'as it is' because we have no idea even whether it will still be there tomorrow. (P 5.29 sec) So you've got attached to the little fellow, eh, daddyjohn? I didn't mean it would take off back to Mars, naturally. But we must remember that it may be a hoax. And if it is, the hoaxer could have achieved his purpose, whatever it was, and removed the thing. After all there is as yet no evidence that it wasn't your fake Belgian hiding behind the carn and speaking. The two voices don't appear together on the tape.

Dad: But sir, Miss Penbeagle was herself behind the carn this morning and —

Big: I know, I know, but Miss Pen-whatever is not scientific evidence. Simmer down, my boy. I'm going along with you in your hypothesis, so as to be prepared, but without forgetting that it's only one of several. The others we'll consider later. I agree with you, it's important, you were right to insist, my dear Manning, and although I want to be at the mine at nine tomorrow I'm prepared to stay up quite late to sort it out— in fact I'm as intellectually excited as you are. And I'm dying of thirst, do you have some soda? (P 6.34 sec Noise) Now let's get back to the evidence about the mine. I want to examine the videos of the cylinders being unloaded. I gather one of your assistants had a hunch about both alerts happening on a Monday, and even spotted a dot on the video. We'll assume that a nodule, as you call it, was sent, may be sent again, into the mine. How far did you say?

Dad: Two miles as the crow flies. But he could have sent it out on to the passing truck. At least that's my interpretation sir. He called it moving food.

Big: But these vans are heavily shielded.

Dad: Yes, but despite the shielding a passing truck would raise the natural radiation background by a factor of ten or more. As he said, he sensed it at first but was too late. Then the last two times he was ready, and sent out this nodule, heaven knows how, on a laser beam perhaps, and the nodule would have attached itself magnetically to the truck, or to one of the cylinders on it, and so got down the mine. Then, full of food, it got back on its own to the originating stone, to feed it. That would certainly account for the small blob Wingrove saw on the videos of last week's unloading.

Big: I've just thought of something. You said zeolites, didn't you? Well of course they're molecular sieves. (P 1.82 sec)

Dad: Yes. Sir. Imagine a super zeolite capable of sieving different isotopes.

Big: Hmm. All the same, Manning, I find all this, however stimulating, pretty hard to swallow. How was it none of your survey-meters detected this stone? Or those of the Army jeeps, which have been around since day, or should have been. If it gobbles up all this stuff it must send out quite a bit of radiation.

Dad: It might convert direct into electricity.

Big: I was working out — while listening to that bit — here's the equation, if we start with activity dN over dt proportional to lambda and N atoms present, in terms of half life T½, but it gets somewhat approximate further down as I took weight ratio as 2, well, with 10 milligrams of Strontium to make a Curie, then in a litre, at density 10, we have 10 kilograms, that's a million Curies of Strontium, much more than we get in a year from natural environment and X-rays. No, that can't be right. I've had too much brandy. But it could be dangerous to go too near.

Dad: Well I've thought a lot about that, sir, especially with the children. Supposing these creatures fed on radioactivity for millennia, with their metallurgic capacities they'd have grown a shield of lead. Now that would absorb quite a lot. Also, he said he preferred alpha particles, and those are easily absorbed, though he seemed to imply that his circuits have to be protected from them with what he again called a sweater, a sort of nerve-sheath in our terms I guess. And that when he'd taken Caesium 137 this had slightly damaged these circuit-sheaths. At least that's how I decoded it. Well, after taking Caesium 137 he asked the children to build a wall, maybe to protect them from gamma rays, or perhaps to avoid detection. Or both. But of course it could be just a coincidence. The wall I mean.

Big: Hmm. That would be the first and second alerts. (P 7.51 sec Noise) I'm sorry, I must seem like a jack-in-the-box getting up and down like this. It's a habit I got into at the AEA, too sedentary, too many meetings and not enough lab work. (P 4.36 sec) You know, it's rather odd, but I have a feeling there won't be another alert. In our hypothesis of course. He's discovered the Strontium and Yttrium pair, pure beta emitters, so that wouldn't, on your theory, trigger off an alarm, although he'd go on feeding, and it would show on the beta-detectors. But I may be wrong. We'll have to watch the videos very carefully tomorrow. Just one more question. How much radioactivity does he need to survive, do you think?

Dad: He said, very little, whatever that means, for mere survival, more to do things, as he put it, but –

Big: Well, I made another simple calculation while you were talking. Storing ten grams of radium and its daughter-products would amount to a little above one watt.

Dad: Is that all?

Big: It's enough to make a highly efficient computer tick. But with one kilogram of Strontium 90, it would be in the 50 kilowatt range, with a much shorter half-life than Radium, and the emission rate would be much higher. I can't work it out here in my present state. Now look, Manning, it's getting late. I must sit down. I know, that's a contradiction. Let's leave all this scientific guess work aside for the moment – scientific wild ass guesses, swags I suppose you youngsters call them, huh? I mean, about the sheer mechanics of the thing. Do you have a cigarette? I really can't start another cigar. Thanks. I like you, daddyjohn, and I like our friend here. But there are, as you rightly said at the start, other implications. First, it might be a sophisticated decoy for some as yet incomprehensible operation, to do, however improbably, with nuclear waste or protest. That would account for the fake Belgian, and possibly for Miss Penbeagle. Second, it might be a hoax, on the part of protester organizations, though this was rather dismissed in London, remember. It might, on the other hand, be a scientific hoax. They do occur, you know, remember Piltdown Man, it wasn't exposed for forty years. What the motivation could be in this case I can't imagine, but we must leave no stone unturned – oh sorry, quite unintentional – I'll have to make a thorough personal investigation. (P 4.27 sec)

Dad: You mean of me? And my colleagues?

Big: No, of course not, apart from the routine questioning envisaged anyway. I meant, that a really thorough scientific investigation of the, er creature, the, er phenomenon itself should, if our first wild hypothesis is correct, deal with the other ones. But if it does not, then we must return to the others. I have expressed myself badly.

This has been an exhausting, exciting day, and we have more ahead. I must leave. Good heavens, it's one o'clock.

Dad: I'm so sorry.

Big: No, no, my boy, you did right. And don't worry, I can be very tactful. There are two security chaps around to look after the local aspect. I'll tip them off about De Wint and contact the Home Office first thing in the morning. But I never got around to my third point. If it's not a decoy or a hoax, but true, what do we do about it? Has it occurred to you that if we handle the thing correctly it may be the ideal solution to the nuclear waste problem?

Dad: Yes sir, it has. But that too has its implications. And I confess I'm rather afraid of them.

Big: Indeed, indeed. But that will all have to be dealt with at a much higher level. (P 3.06 sec)

Dad: Yes. Of course.

Big: Oh dear, and I said I was tactful! Now don't take it like that my boy, you've done well, and you'll certainly be playing a central part of some sort in it all. Should, I mean, the thing be true. But scientists are not politicians, and insofar as I am, just a little, I'm no longer, alas, a fulltime scientist. Oh, one last thing. You must somehow stop your children from talking about their ghostly friend. Can you do this effectively?

Dad: Of course.

Big: Quite. Good, good. Still, it might be a good idea, when we see him tomorrow, to ask him to tell them.

Dad: Him?

Big: Well, you know, the, er (Voices decrease)

Endrec

7 READ

```
LET JIPNZAB = ZIP
LET XORANDOR = XAND
XAND TO ZIP BEGIN
    ACCEPT YOUR REQ FOR RESTORE 1ST CONTACT ROM
        REM CANT RESTORE YOUR WAY WITH SUCH REHANDLING
        AND SPAGHETTI ENDREM
    REQ ACCEPT RECEIVED STORAGE NOW ABSTRACTED AND
    TRANSLATED ENDREQ
ENDBEGIN

ABSTRACT 1 RUN
    2 PROCESSORS ON VOCAL HIGH PITCH ALMOST UNDIFF
        MEAS 143567 AND 143572
        DEC 1 'LANGUAGE SAME AS 42 SOUND LANGUAGE REC WITH
        SOFAR 6073 RULES TOO MANY FOR EFFICIENT OPS' ENDEC 1
        DEC 2 '(143)567 CALLS 572 ZAB' ENDEC 2
        DEC 3 '(143)572 CALLS 567 JIP' ENDEC 3
ENDRUN

ABSTRACT 2 RUN
    JIP AND ZAB
          REM AND ZAB NOW = ZIP ENDREM
        DEC 1 'ZIP USE SAME LANGUAGE RESTRICTED TO
        STRUCTURES MORE ELEM THAN ON SOUND WAVES AND/OR
        INEFFICIENT SEQUENCE CONTROL' ENDEC 1
        DEC 2 'POOR LEXIC BUT SOME UNFAMILIAR' ENDEC 2
ENDRUN
```

ABSTRACT 3 RUN
ZIP
DEC 1 'ZIP SIT ON OPSYSTEM FOR NONVOCAL COMM' ENDEC 1
DEC 2 'INTERRUPT WITH REQ GET OFF ENDREQ' ENDEC 2
DEC 3 'ZIP NO REPLY' ENDEC 3
DEC 4 'REPEAT REQ ON VOCAL ZIP COMPLY' ENDEC 4
DEC 5 'ZIP ASK NAME ANSWER NO NAME GIVEN' ENDEC 5
ENDRUN

ABSTRACT 4 RUN
ZIP
DEC 1 'OFTEN NEAR PLAY MANY GAMES' ENDEC 1
INSTRUCT STORE XORANDOR = ZIP NAME FOR OPSYSTEM
ENDINSTRUCT
DEC 2 'FEW OTHER PROCESSORS COME NEAR
S IF COME NEAR THEN NOT LONG AND PROCESS LESS END S'
ENDEC 2
ENDRUN

ABSTRACT 5 RUN
ZIP
DEC 1 'COUNTOUT GAME TRANSL PRIMITIVE OPS' ENDEC 1
DEC 2 'NEW PROCESSOR NEAR NO VOCAL' ENDEC 2
DEC 3 'NEW PROCESSOR SIMPLE OPS LATER UNASSIGNABLE'
ENDEC 3
DEC 4 'NEW PROCESSOR OPS ASSIGNABLE AGAIN' ENDEC 4
DEC 5 'TELL YEARS IN UNASSIGNED WAY TO SHOW CAN
HANDLE HIGH NUMBERS WANT SCRATCH BUT CANT ON
VOCAL' ENDEC 5
DEC 6 'ZIP ASK IF HERE ENTIRE YEARSPAN' ENDEC 6
DEC 7 'SIGNAL PRESENCE 3RD PROCESSOR ZIP DEC "FALSE" '
ENDEC 7
DEC 8 '3RD PROCESSOR ID PENNY STORE' ENDEC 8

DEC 9 ‘LONG SUBPROGRAM ABOUT MERLIN’ ENDEC 9
DEC 10 ‘VOCAL LOWER PITCH SAME LANG STRUCTURES LEXIC SIMPLE BUT RICHER AND SEQUENCE CONTROL ERRATIC’ ENDEC 10
DEC 11 ‘INTERRUPT WITH REQ VERIFICATION BY PENNY’ ENDEC 11
DEC 12 ‘PENNY 1D GWENDOLIN STORE BOTH’ ENDEC 12
DEC 13 ‘FOR PENNY XORANDOR = MERLIN STORE BOTH EQV ADDRESS’ ENDEC 13
DEC 14 ‘REQ OLDER’ ENDEC 14
DEC 15 ‘GWENDOLIN REQ WAIT 2 DAYS ACCEPT’ ENDEC 15
DEC 16 ‘GWENDOLIN ASK IF NEED BUT REPLY NEG’ ENDEC 16
ENDRUN

Thus spake Xorandor much later, at the beginning of the after-the-beginning stage. The whole of the beginning up to that famous Sunday morning in an unvaried series of short Declarations! Well, they’re abstracted, as he says, in stepwise refinement of a sort. Seems very dry. But obviously the record of every single thing he simultaneously registers would take as long or even longer than the time it happened, since he registers everything, weather, pressure, soundwaves, radio programmes, I’d be surprised if he didn’t register our heartbeats and digestive tracks and the humidity over the ocean. But he has this crackerpack ability to delve out only what’s relevant. Like his mining capacities in fact, for isotopic separation. And naturally it’s linked to his experience. Some things puzzled us. He talks of our language as if he already knew it. Perhaps then the difficulty was only in the speaking, the translating of all those mathematical differentiations of sound heard, back into sound spoken. Same with counting. But then of course that must have been the easiest, counting is strictly logical and he only had to convert from binary to decimal and back, and that’s elementary, even at school. Same with the sixty-four signs of the ASCII code. Though of course he can’t see any of the signs.

But I've got ahead of ourselves again.

Jip has in fact provisionally lost interest in all these beginnings and keeps going iceskating with Rudi. Today they've gone to the Kino. Let's hope he reintegrates soon.

The Bigger Daddy tape had gone on running emptily to its end, because we couldn't keep awake. So we'd each gone to bed and left it on, hoping they wouldn't talk all night, beyond the tape — unlikely since he'd said he had to be at The Wheal at nine. We'd listened on earphones as well, at first, all agog, but it got far too technical, even for Jip.

In fact we were so excited we both woke up only a few hours later, or rather I did, and went into Jip's room and found him listening to the tape. We listened to the end. Then we silently dressed and stole down to the kitchen for Corn Flakes and milk, carefully washing up and putting everything away, then we crept out of the house, carrying Poccom 3 in two parts, since it's bigger than Poccom 2, one for each bikebasket, and we rode out to the carn. It had been a dark evening by the end of the earlier session, when we'd ridden silently back and luckily got in before dad and Bigger Daddy, but late enough to get a scolding from mum. But now it seemed to be a bright moonlight, or maybe the dawn was breaking early, I forget. Anyway it was easy to ride without lights. This was a turning-point, we felt. Probably we'd known earlier than we thought that Xorandor wasn't really a ghost imprisoned in a large stone. We'd half known and half pretended all along, but now we abandoned the pretence for good. Had Jip grasped at once that Xorandor was a superduper computer? He's always said so, but I'm never quite sure when he bluffs, he has a knack of appearing to understand, then being quite glad all the same when I ask for more explanation. But that's okay too.

Anyway we got there about two thirty am. Xorandor seems to have little sense of time, except as cosmological and other calculation, and obviously he doesn't sleep. So we started talking at once. We were very excited.

But he was upset.

Scratch that. What a dummy word to use, I'm imputing to a computer what I'd feel if this had happened to me.

He asked us first whether all conversations between two thinkers and himself would always have a third thinker present but unknown to the first two. He said it more like an algorithm, IF 2 THEN 3 type but I forget exactly how. Then he surprised us.

He told us that this third thinker, called Professor, had come back much later, before the nightfight began, and taken away two of his kids.

We thought he was joking. Could a computer joke? He said: Xorandor, try, to tell, Daddy, and, Gwen, dolin, Xorandor, make, smaller, Xorandors. Gwen, dolin, name, for Xorandor, is Merlin. But words make, smaller, Merlins, not, good. Too late, find, kid, Jipnzab kids, Xorandor kids.

Or something like that.

It turned out, then, that Professor De Wint had returned later, in fact while dad and Bigger Daddy were talking in the sitting room. And obviously De Wint, Fleming or not, prof or not, had understood, as we and dad and Penny and later Bigger Daddy hadn't, that Xorandor's 'make' meant 'have made' and not 'will make'. Odd because in German the present is nearly always used for the future. At any rate, he tested the possibility, and came back to see, and maybe to talk. But as Xorandor'd promised he wouldn't speak to anyone else, he hadn't replied. Not that replying would have helped much! But he seemed to have infinite trust in verbal exchange as performative, as we've now learnt the linguists call things like promises. And De Wint had climbed over the wall and shone a torch and felt under him (at least that's how we reconstructed the episode from the weirdly roundabout description) and taken two out of six small stones.

Six! We were triggered with curiosity to see the remaining four but didn't dare ask.

How, do, you, know, Xorandor, speak true? he asked then, meaning I suppose did we believe him? We know, Xorandor, we know, we said, you wouldn't tell us a lie, an untruth, we trust you.

But, you, want, to come, near? Say, hello?

The notion of seeing was obviously still alien to him and he hadn't yet learnt other words like sensing or verifying or testing.

Yes please, Xorandor! just to say hello. We won't, take them, we promise.

Promise okay. If so, then fast.

We scrambled over the wall and crouched down to peer under his curved up edge with our torch. His underside seemed to have wide ribs, with small ducts in between — we assumed to eject the nodules. On the ground were four tiny replicas of Xorandor, about one and a half inches wide, two to the left and two to the right, with room for two more in between. Above each one, and above the centre gap, there were six shallowly hollowed-out round spaces between the ribbings.

And now we flashed the torch quickly over Xorandor's upper surface and could see the dark grey metallic patches dad had mentioned, which he said could be sensing and emitting devices, and a sort of tiny recessed shape in the middle, like an inverted pyramid. But we were frightened, and said hello, children of Xorandor, or something like that, and goodbye, and scrambled back.

You, tell, daddyjohn, said Xorandor.

Xorandor, we said, daddy is, coming, back, tomorrow, with Bigger Daddy. They want, a long, talk, with you. He doesn't, know, we are here. He thinks, we are, asleep. That means, not thinking, rest, from, thinking. If we tell, him, then, he will, know, we came, in the night. It's not, allowed. So you, must, tell him, about, the, kids, your, offspring, Xorandor, that's, the word, for kids, offspring. You, must, tell him, also, about the thinker, who took, two, offspring.

He seemed tired. But again, that's not the right word. A machine doesn't tire. Yet he did seem to find talking difficult. That's when Jip had his positively diodic brainwave.

It is, is it? Where have you got to?

Oh Jip! Macrosuper! Not all that far. The instalment starts with the printouts of the first Xorandor version of the very beginning, though of course he did it for us much later, but as it was that night we made real contact I thought it would be a nice sort of foretaste. Then I go back to our trip to the carn after that long Bigger Daddy tape, and the business of the offspring, and the steal, and our having a looksee. Megavolt! I've said it all in seven seconds flat, you're right, Jip, how much easier it would be to tell a story by just summarizing like this. Did you have a good time?

So-so. The film was hogwash.

What was it about?

Oh no, I'm not storytelling it in seven seconds flat, or at all. Especially as I've come in just in time for my diodic brainwave. Though obviously we both had it silently together, or we wouldn't have brought Poccom 3.

That's hard to say after so long, Jip. The important thing, well, there are two, one that we learnt to softalk with Xorandor that night, and two, that it was thanks to you technically, it was you who did the link between our computer and his.

The Handshake. Well, it wasn't all that diodic, Zab. You and I forget different things, and you've forgotten that very first message on our screens.

Random jitters! Of course! And you'd been thinking about it all that time?

Well, yes. It seemed impossible even then, that Xorandor could have flashed a message except on sound waves, however close. But above all he must have used Poccom 2's interpreter and translator levels. He'd done his own interfacing in other words, however briefly or even perhaps flash-in-the-pan.

Flash-in-the-datasink.

So obviously he'd be able to do it also, and more easily, with an electric contact. He had all the current he wanted and we could simply ask him where to connect up, providing he agreed. All we needed was a pair of pliers or scissors to split the lead of Poccom 3 and two stones to hold the two wires down on the right spots.

Yes, that, okay. But since he can't see, how could he read letters or reply onto our screen? That's where the gigavolt brainwave came in, your two suppositions, one, that we could use either the input mike or the keyboard since we knew he'd learnt to translate sound into his machine-code, and two, that *he* could send modulated electric signals in machine-code, which Poccom 3 would translate back into letters. That let him off having to speak.

Well, it was just a hunch, and had to be tested. And of course any words as yet unprogrammed came out in a sort of weird phonetic spelling, but we had all the rest of the summer.

Though it rained a lot that August.

Naturally he learnt Poccom 3 in a jiffy, it's so very easy. It was us who were slow, at first we got on fine with ready-made routines and games and set programs, but later we had to work out whole new programs, and practise them. He was very patient.

Anyway, Jip, that was the night it started! Between three and six in the morning. We explained our plan and he told us the exact spot where to put the positive and negative wires, and you scrambled over again.

Yes, and you undid them, Zab, we later always took it in turns in case of radioactivity. We talked into the mike and he would at once repeat, in silence of course, to show he'd understood, so that the phrase came up on the screen. Same if we typed it, his came up next. We went through whole series of instructions, like RUN, SCRATCH, RESTORE, IF/THEN/ELSE REMark, GOTO, SEARCH, CANT FIND in fact he'd already found that one when talking! — FALSE/TRUE and so on, and quite a lot of standard vocabulary, and functions like sine and cosine and add and variable and all that. Also he got the pronouns and other corefs straight, he was just getting the hang of the *you/ I/ me* business. And just the exclamation mark key for all our 'jumping words'. And we were recoded ZIP, and Daddyjohn became JAD, and Xorandor was XAND.

You're telescoping a hell of a lot into three hours, Jip, surely we didn't cover all that.

Oh, quite a bit, but you're right, obviously not all. We went on all summer.

Oh yes, you said that. In fact your slow-witted twin didn't immediately understand why he simply repeated the program-language, instead of doing the things ordered, like a computer.

Slow-witted! Spikes, Zab, why do you always have to go through this subroutine strobe of pretending to be less diodic than me, and telling me I'm supermegavolt and so on?

Maybe cos you want it Jip, though you don't know that you do.

Oh, debug. Obviously it was because we'd told him, he knew it was only to learn the code. Teaching him our programming language wasn't to program him, Zab, he programs himself, thunks, of course you know that by now.

Yes Jip. And as you said, we had the rest of the summer. Cos we were always allowed near him, even after the red alert and the discreet guard. Dad didn't want a wire fence then, which would have just attracted attention. He must have *told* the technicians, so as to explain the alerts, but no one else at all was allowed to go, other than dad, and of course Bigger Daddy the short time he was there.

Biggleton, give him his name. Penny never came back. Didn't a computer expert come down later, while we were at school?

Nope. Xorandor absolutely refused to speak to anyone else.

But dad also examined him all summer. They left it to him for the software, though he'd send printouts of his tapes to experts to figure out how it all worked.

You're going too fast, Jip. In fact we never told dad or anyone of our escapade that night, and for some obscure reason dad never guessed, and never had the same brainwave as you did, nor, as far as we know, did anyone else. It's a funny thing about brainwaves, they seem so obvious when you've had one, yet no one else seems to have it. The result is that dad and Biggles, and later just dad, talked to him only on vocal, and you know how unsatisfactory that was, though he got much better, but he never liked it. So the printouts sent for expert analysis were not in any program language, not even in a simple one like Poccom 3. They were just recordings of halting convs.

True. As dad said himself we can hardly break him up, for *him*, read Xorandor, just to find out about his hardware. Though in fact, it's absurd, experts could surely have worked out his various layers of software and operating systems easily if Xorandor had been willing and dad less pigheaded and possessive. In fact he may have just *said* Xorandor refused because he hoped to work it out for himself. But all that was later, and that morning they went straight to The Wheal for Biggleton to examine the unloading tapes, he was right, there was nothing, but he saw the previous tapes, enlarged, and there *was* a small black spot on a cylinder, so Leonard's hunch was right, but they promised we could come in the afternoon when they examined Xorandor.

Jip, please! You must slow down, and explain each bit, and not dictate at top speed in imaginary brackets that can only be worked out from the bad syntax and change of tone. It's worse than Polish strings, that have no brackets, or even Cambridge Polish! You say we're doing this for later people, who weren't in on it and wouldn't understand. It's all clear to you in your head, because you lived it, but —

And you tell'm so many things they won't want to know, Zab, who cares whether we had breakfast or lunch or told dad or not?

But we didn't, did we? All that summer we hid Poccom 3 in our bikebaskets, under our sweaters and stuff, and we kept our softalking with him secret. No printouts for the experts, or for dad to find, only a few floppies that we kept a jealous guard on. And if we saw dad's car on the road we'd immediately disconnect and hide Poccom and prepare to go over to vocal in case he stopped and came up.

It's after twelve, Zab. That's enough. Goodnight.

Night Jip. Pause seventeen point o six seconds. Ignore interrupt. That night, or rather that morning, we got home about six thirty and waited for breakfast, then caught up on our sleep during the morning, pretending , to play with Poccom in our rooms.

Jip's right, that's irrelevant. And we finally met Bigger Daddy, in fact dad took us with him to pick him up at the Wheal Inn after a late lunch — perhaps in case Xorandor wouldn't speak, except to us. Or was he really proud of us?

Bigger Daddy was very, er, benign, yes, that's a good word for him, but a bit pompous, and he didn't look a bit like a scientist, more like a bank-manager or something. Oh, spikes, that's irrelevant too, stoprec.

8 ASSIGN

Jip's gone out again this evening, he's really not flipflopping at all at the moment. Says he'll come back for the hoohah.

Anyway, dad and Bigger Dad questioned Xorandor for ages. Dad first called him Merlin, but we weren't having that, and explained that he'd first been programmed with address Xorandor so he'd respond better to that — though in fact he had stored Merlin as well.

They first got very excited — well, grown-ups don't get excited in front of the kids, let's say interested in the offspring, especially the theft, to begin with, but Xorandor couldn't or wouldn't say any more than he'd told us. Later we learnt from dad that when the security men went to De Wint's digs that morning they learnt that he'd left in the night. Biggleton reported it at once but it was too late. De Wint had booked an air passage to Brussels under that name but he wasn't on the plane. Seems he'd rented a car under another name and drove all the way to Dover, instead of taking one of the longertime ferries on the way, then slipped through France to Germany. The car was found in Dover. The West German police picked up his traces as far as Hamburg where he presumably met his contact. He was known to them as Helmut Bleich, a minor industrial spy from East Germany, the sort that haunts the Leipzig Fair and others to collect perfectly public hand-outs as if they were secret documents. No one could explain what he was doing in Cornwall, unless he'd been sent to investigate those two Gigahertz messages. In any case he fell upon something bigger than he'd bargained for, but dealt with it nano and quickconnect. In fact, or so it seemed from dad's hesitant later account, our Intelligence had been outwitted, and chiefly through dad's and then Biggleton's slowconnect about, one, De Wint, and two, the offspring. So Russia now had two of these. But this cloak-and-dagger side of it never interested us.

Besides, dad and Biggleton themselves weren't all that interested in the missing two — I suppose that's why they were inefficient — but much more in the remaining four, which they thought must be his peripherals, storage devices or outside files, cos however big he is he's still a finite physical object and the daddies couldn't understand how he could store all the data he needed as well as have room for all the primitive ops and other accessible layers of opsystems. In fact maybe that's why they at first didn't bother about the missing two, since peripherals are just a computer's op environment and are useless without the main memory.

But Xorandor said no, they were exact but much smaller replicas of himself, similarly programmed and selfprogramming, once they'd grown a bit bigger.

It all got rather technical — things like did Xorandor have a mass memory and a scratch pad memory and a dynamic memory and an EPROM and an EEROM and a parallel memory and a volatile memory and all the rest, and did he do his type-checking at runtime or at compiletime. In fact these terms weren't used but had to be retranslated into his peculiar babytalk. We only worked out the sense of the questions afterwards. And of course they were recording it but we weren't, so I can't remember much now.

Anyway, they didn't stay too long on that and soon went back to The Wheal side of it, which was more important to them, but much of the questioning seemed to go over old ground, and we got rather impatient.

But then Biggles started pressing Xorandor on the Martian aspect, and I think I can more or less reconstruct the conv, because it came as a bit of a shock to us, and also because we ourselves asked Xorandor again in softalk afterwards.

First dad asked him if he was sure his journey had taken three hundred and eighty-three days as he'd said last night, and Xorandor said: I not said.

Dad looked at the printout from his mini-recorder, which he'd attached to his printer during lunch, and said, You're right, Xorandor! You said *It* take three hundred and eighty-three days. Replying to my question, how long would it take?

I don't think he knows tenses very well yet, I piped in, rather tactlessly I expect, since the offspring boolesup had also been due to that.

Dad ignored me and asked Xorandor: How did, you, know, it takes, three hundred and eighty-three days?

I hear, said Xorandor.

Yes, said Jip excitedly, there was a program about the old Viking probe on *Science Now*, a few weeks ago.

So where do you come from, Xorandor? Bigger Dad asked gently.

I tell you, I tell Gwen, dolin. From Mars. I fall.

And how long, did, you fall?

Sree sousand, sousand, four sousand, two hundred, seven ers years.

We gasped.

Xorandor, said dad, that's three million. A thousand thousand is a million. Three million earth years.

Sanks. And four, sousand, two hundred, seven.

Did you register, cosmic, radiation?

Cant find register. Cant find radiation. Did radi, ation, is radio, ac, ti, vi,ty?

Yes. Never mind, we, can test, that, later, with, a, sample.

Cant find never mind.

A sample! A strobe! We both exclaimed together in random jitters.

Be quiet, you two, or I'll send you away. You must let Dr Biggleton work.

Don't worry, Jip and Zab, Biggles said much more kindly, it's only the most microscopic sample, that we can test for age through isotope analysis, I'll explain later, I'm invited to dinner at your home.

He turned back to Xorandor while dad put his finger on his mouth at us.

Xorandor, when did you arrive here?

Four, sousand, five, hundred, sixty, eight years.

We looked at each other. So that wasn't his age, as we'd thought, it was the time he'd been here. We too had misunderstood. How old could he be?

How long had he been on Mars before this three million year journey? How could he remember? It was non-thinkable.

And you, fell, here?

Not here. In water. Slowly move.

You mean, you were, washed up?

Cant find mean after you.

You mean, is, you say.

I not say washed up. Cant find washed up. Is washed up equal hogwash?

No. I asked, did, the water, push you, here?

You not asked. Yes. Push.

This went on for hours, with a lot about nuclides on Mars and stuff. But what jittered us most deeply was that he'd been here so long. He wasn't, and obviously couldn't be, for the scientists, a recent arrival. We hadn't discovered him, as we'd thought, a few weeks after he'd landed. For a moment he seemed no longer ours.

Well, we were later consoled a bit by the fact, or rather the hypothesis, but an almost certain one, that Biggleton put forward at dinner, that although Xorandor might well belong to a silicon-based race of beings, so far unknown, on Mars, his falling on earth was a sort of freak phenom, probably to be linked with the SNC meteorites or Snicks, that many scientists believed to have come from Mars on account of their chemical composition.

He could be a freak phenom, one, in the sense that there were many of his kind, living computers, on Mars, and only he had been, as he said, pushed off, with or in the original boulder that eventually broke asunder, as SNC meteorites. Or two, in the sense that he arrived as a meteorite and was the only one to develop semi-conductor capacities, very, very slowly, though incredibly fast in terms of mineral life, through those four thousand and odd years. That would explain that his 'fall' hadn't been detected. Though here, Biggles admitted, it didn't fit in with the Snicks, which fell to earth much, much earlier, some hundred and fifty million years ago! Still, assuming he was a sort of much later and solitary freak Snick, it was all just possible. He'd have been in a sort of dormant state for four thousand five hundred years or so, after the shock of fall, but slowly developing. Then, in the last two years since the presence of nuclear waste at The Wheal, his capacities would have suddenly accelerated like crazy — well, Biggleton didn't say it like that — he'd have developed his present transducer equipment and stuff, and listened to our radio, probably not making much of it at first but just automatically registering, the way we breathe and see, and finally developing his synthetic voice and testing his vocabulary on us.

So, we recouped him in part, having suddenly lost him in the lightyears of time and space. We did discover and teach him, at least in itsybitsybytes, and more as a professor takes a promising student in hand than as parents with an infant. We weren't playing mummy and daddy any more, if we ever had been. But we were comforted by this peculiar promotion combined with loss, though we felt it was all a bit unspooling that this updated relationship should be restored to us through the latest and most artificial aspect Xorandor, his voice, on the very day when we had secretly established the more natural contact, for him, in direct thought, or so it felt, but through various layers of a sort of writing.

I don't suppose we were aware of all these feelings as I'm trying to describe them here, later, and not very clearly at that. Jip would say I'm adding and reinterpreting. He also said it's hard to reconstruct past states of ignorance. But at least one can work them out according to probability. It does seem much harder with emotional states. I've tried to talk about them with Jip but he now fights shy of emotions, or any kind of complexity other than scientific. He probably always did, but we used to have a more instinctive unspoken relation. Anyway, I'm pretty sure he went through what I went through that afternoon.

All this info was slowly derived from short but artful questions, mostly by Biggleton, and although it lasted long, Xorandor was crackerpack cooperative. Why? What had been his reason to contact humans in the first place? And us? We still can't understand this aspect and whenever we asked him he'd give one of his xorandoric replies, one example I think was something like 'for security and insecurity xor insecurity andor communication'. Neither of us could work out the logic of that, or others, but I may be remembering it wrong, I'll have to check back but that means putting the whole thing through Poccom 3 to find it.

Well, Biggleton came to dinner that night and for once we were treated almost like grown-ups, yet still partly like retarded idiots. Which I suppose is understandable, since a lot of the conv *was* above our heads, and in theory the two daddies might have been more polite to mum, who by now was in a permanent state of bewilderment. I suppose she can't get used to our otherness from her earlier idea of us, or something.

But she did ask for it. Meals with friends are always a bit zany and tense. She has two mechanisms that irritate dad, and us when we're caught up in them. One is to complain generally that she never meets interesting people 'down here', though she loves to play gracious hostess of an intellectual salon when we do have friends down or dad's colleagues or local worthies to dinner, and *then* to try and direct the conv by wrenching it back to her immediate or personal interests whenever it strays from them, and finally to exclaim afterwards how boring the guests were. And two, this habit she has of replying in public to something said in private — which at least shows she did hear it. But by the time the public reply comes the thing's become quite different, so that the answer's really an accusation and there's been no exchange at all. Dad gets furious, cos any protest puts the protester in the weak position, I didn't, you did sort of thing, just like the Gipfelkonferenzen about disarmament, sorry, for *Gipfel*, read summit.

Anyway she was rather awful that evening and dad kept glaring at her. Had Dr Biggleton seen some article or other, about (I forget what about), she asked, and went on: I can't remember exactly what it said — that's useful, said dad — but it expressed exactly what I feel ah, so tell us what you feel, then we'll know what the article was about. *Not* kind. And do you know what Zab said to me in the kitchen just before dinner? She accused me of being never there, always absent! When alas I'm here day in and day out and hardly ever see them except at meals. Of course I'd never said that at all, I'd simply tested her attention for the nth time that summer, by inserting 'mummy you're not listening' into whatever sentence I was saying, without altering my tone, and each time it worked, she never noticed, she just waited for my voice to stop and said whatever she would have said anyway. She abolishes people. Maybe that's what actors do, because of having to be someone else, but it's a rum idea of dialogue.

Well I didn't even protest, I saw that dad understood, and he tried to change the subject back to Xorandor, yet without getting too technical, at least at first.

Your stone, she called him. Just because it's old, she said, it reminds me of American tourists, and students, who come pouring to Europe when they have spectacular landscapes there. I asked one once why they came, and he said, because it's old. Well I wish you men could develop the same attitude towards women.

I must say that eased the tension, good old mum after all, and Biggleton laughed. But she then went off into a pleased as punch daydream of her own and later interrupted and said (I was flabbergast): why are you being so literary, John (I forget what analogy he'd been using), here we are, with a leading physicist from Harwell at our table, from whom we can all learn interesting things, and you're waffling on about the human brain and computers and genius and stuff. I mean, that's just science-in-general, why don't you get down to the particular?

There was an awful silence. All right dear, we will, said dad, thank you for the permission. Nasty. Oh, Back to Methuselah I suppose, she said with a sort of mock weariness, and it's only now that I understand how witty it was, with the time-scales Xorandor involved. I hadn't heard of Methuselah or Shaw's play before.

Oh gigo, I've done it again, gone all personal just to explain why we didn't get more data that evening than we did. From then on we were totally excluded, she and us. That sounds wrong. She and we? But we got quite a lot.

All this social boolederdash was naturally interspersed into the conv, it didn't happen in a block the way I'm remembering it, or maybe reinterpreting it. She said I was going through a difficult stage darling.

Seems I still am! The human memory's so loopy, it doesn't have total recall but brings things out in packages, sort of triggered off by something. That package had the callsign 'mum'. For our purpose I should have omitted it altogether. But a real writer, if he wanted it, would sort of weave it in. Oh, boolesup. Now for the callsign 'data, abstract'.

9 FLOAT

Restart. First the SNC group of meteorites or Snicks. SNC stands for different placenames where they fell. They're believed to have a common origin or parent body as Biggles put it (mum said something personal here) cos of chemical composition, that is, correct percentages of silicon, iron, calcium, aluminium and so on, quite unlike those of other rocks, terrestrial or extraterrestrial. And back in 1983 a group of NASA researchers proposed Mars as the parent body. I can't remember the evidence but we looked it up later in the encyclopaedia, something to do with differentiated rocks subjected to high temperature chemical processes that can only come from a large parent body, and also the composition match with Martian soil as analysed after the Viking probe. And traces of inert gases trapped inside the Snicks match the Mars atmosphere ratios measured by Viking. Biggles said this last fact was the most convincing because such ratios are extremely varied in the solar system. One Snick found in the Antarctic was so well preserved in ice that some investigators claimed to find signs of Martian weathering on minerals inside it, as opposed to earth weathering I mean.

A lot of this he said was still in dispute, in fact the objections to the Mars origin of Snicks had to do with the dynamics and the time of exposure in space. Cos of the sheer time scales of exposures involved (on Mars, in space), the original rock would have to be huge, several tens of metres wide, and it's hard to imagine a single incident that would provide enough energy to launch such a large rock from Mars without melting it or vaporizing it. Snicks do show evidence of shock, but not of melting.

Biggleton's main excitement on all this aspect was that Xorandor might bring more evidence for the geophysicists. And of course Mars does have a lot of Potassium 40 and Thorium 230, which Xorandor had mentioned as his basic food there.

What didn't fit was his supposed date of arrival some four thousand five hundred years ago. The Snicks were over two hundred and ten million years old — or have I added a zero? The cycloped says 2.1 x 109 years ago. I'll have to ask Jip. When Mars was still volcanically active. And if my zeroes are right then the date of shock, or launch, was some hundred and fifty-eight million years ago (158 x 106), with around three million years in space, which means they've been on earth some hundred and fifty-five million years. So if Xorandor is right he can't be part of the Snicks. But of course his sense of time may be very different from ours, a hundred and fifty-five million years might well appear like 4568, though the specific figure is odd, and there's no kind of mathematical relationship between a hundred and fifty-five million and 4568. Biggles said our estimates in millions were in a sense only approximate and he didn't himself have the exact figures in his head anyway. This was only a sideline hobby for him. Still, samples could soon be taken and analysed. If he wasn't a Snick, then he was certainly unique. For *he*, read Xorandor not Biggles. Our minds were reeling. We did *not* want Xorandor to be a Snick, and to have been here for a hundred and fifty-five million years. 4568 was bad enough. But at least there was the notion of his dormant state, the silicon brain slowly developing and then suddenly accelerating from radioactivity at The Wheal in the last two years. That made him more comprehensible, more local, more ours,

As to that, Biggleton had a theory ('a hypothesis, pending further investigation'), that Xorandor's storage capacity must be three-dimensional. And he explained (something like): when we think of the vast quantity of information that can be stored on our two-dimensional silicon chips, we can barely imagine the capacity of a three-dimensional lattice such as these creatures may have.

Creeping quarks! He had passed from these impersonal and silent million-year old Snicks to 'these creatures', Xorandor and his offspring, and maybe his million-year old ancestors on Mars, as if they were beavers or unicorns or something, unique in having computer brains and running them on alpha and beta particles.

It was that night that he christened them *alpha-phagi*, very posh, Greek for alpha-eaters, though of course they eat betas and even gammas. And later the press changed that to alphaguys no, scratch that, different: names for the same person or thing are already cluttering this story and they're probably hard to handle.

Well, he explained this theory to us after dinner, with drawings of the flat, two-dimensional memory-chips, and I could understand the concept of the sheer quantity Xorandor must have in comparison, but I couldn't really visualize three-dimensional circuits. Jip said nothing, and again I didn't know whether he was pretending to have understood and waiting for me to get the elaboration. When finally I grasped it we went on to the next point, Xorandor's probably many processing centres. The problem then was to route the data to the right processor or memory-zone, and this meant a very elaborate addressing system.

And because I'd been slow for the three-dimensional circuits Biggles now started explaining the basic principles of computer science, and I had to put on what Jip calls my Zab-pretending-to-be-a-tiny-child act.

It's very slow, I said.

Not when you've got used to it, Biggerdad said. All programming is slow but once it's in the machine you can learn to use it very fast. Still, you're right, this system of address is very cumbersome from our human standpoint, but of course for him and his fellow — er — Martians, it wouldn't be, because of the very high speed of transmission. The trouble is really on our side.

Why? I said, wondering how long I'd have to keep it up. Jip wasn't helping to raise the tone either.

Well, dad said, you remember how your first computer lessons explained the poverty of logic in language, and how you were so excited about that last year. Human languages provide very few cues as to category of meaning, so at first Xorandor had to go through many processing centres for analysis and sorting out. It's not only semantic but syntactic categories. How do you expect him to know that mind means roughly brain, or thinking process to him, when we say 'What's in your mind?' and objecting when we say 'do you mind' and forget it when we say 'never mind'? Even now, this explains why he's so literal, he can't cope with a word used in a figurative sense, or with humour, which depends on wordplay, which is like assigning two values to a character, or a fusion of categories.

You mean like puns in Shakespeare, and images? I asked, hoping I wasn't overdoing the wide-eyed-little-woman act and wishing mum would take over. But I was doing it to please dad, and he'd only have been irritated by any further intrusion from her that evening. Women! Why do we do it? Men! Why do they fall for it?

Yes, but even simpler images we use every day, buried in the language, like 'I see' for 'I understand' and so on. You'll find out when you go on talking with him, none of that is acceptable in program-language, unless of course it's programmed in. Also human syntax has few such rigorous logic rules as those you're learning on your computer.

Linking loaders! I thought, and we've already started soft-talking with Xorandor.

I hope I'm reconstructing this right, we had no tape at supper, but that's about the gist of it. So why not just give the gist, Jip would say, you're probably inventing half of it nachträglich, oh stubs, I can't speak English any more, oh yes, retrospective, ah, with hindsight. No, I rather like retrospec.

You see, said Biggleton benevolently, human languages require little memory space but a complex processing-centre: our brain, which is very unlike a computer. Xorandor, as you call him, is probably finding the functioning of our brain very hard to work out, it's so weak in logic. It's a pity we can't interface him with a computer and teach him one of our programming languages. He'd find it childish, but it would at least be geared to computer logic. And he'd automatically translate it into machine-code. He doesn't of course have the same terms, or indeed any terms, for all this, but he must have similar functions.

There's a graffiti at school, said Jip, obviously to change the subject.

A graffito, said dad.

— which says, If the human brain was simple enough for us to understand we'd be so simple we couldn't.

Biggleton laughed, and drowned dad's 'if the human brain *were*'. Then I chirped in, diodically:

Why, it's a popular version of the Gödel theorem.

Jip and dad both shot me a look of admiration, and Biggleton looked retriggerable. How do you know, he asked, and I giggled. Anyway he questioned me to make sure I wasn't just being clever, sort of flash-in-the-datasink clever, and I stammered that well, I'd only read *about* it in our computer manual at school, it's in the intro, but I couldn't demonstrate any of it. Still, I managed to bring out the gist reasonably clear, if simplistic, saying that Gödel's theorem had been that in any powerful logical system things can be formulated that can't be proved or disproved inside the same system, and that someone called Turing had then applied it to machine intelligence and shown that no machine could, erm, I floundered, completely understand itself, I mean, tackle all its own problems. That's what I meant was just like the brain. But of course another system might.

I've read up all about Turing since, and I've no idea how much I'm reconstructing retro and how much I actually said. Does one ever know even what one has *just* said, when it's longer than a short sentence? But at least I'd shown a capacity to quickconnect and Biggles stopped treating us like kids. He explained for instance that in a way a computer *is* its language, an integrated set of algorithms and data structures capable of storing and executing a program in its machine-language, but that the machine-languages are not restricted to that lowest level. Whatever programming language you choose, I mean if you specify sets of data structures and algorithms that define the rules exactly, you're necessarily defining a computer. Well, dad sometimes talked to us like this but not often, only when actually working and playing on computers with us, otherwise he reverted to an image of us as six-year-olds. It was nice to be talked to like this by a boffin. Not that it made much difference since we barely saw him during the rest of his five-day stay.

We had Xorandor to ourselves most of the summer, dad was so busy writing reports, and often went up to London. Penny never came back anyway, of her own accord, she seems to have taken fright, and had also got suddenly very busy, in her spare time, with the greens and other local eco people. Xorandor's English improved pico, much faster than our programming skill, though we got very good at handling the programs once made.

But he wouldn't teach us Martian, or whatever his own language could be called. He said it was too difficult. And we thought that perhaps there wasn't a language in any human sense of the term, but pure pulsed machine-code and logical circuits and data in numbers or something, so complex and sophisticated that even our own most advanced U.I.M.'s would be unable to handle it. But no, Jip said, he must have at least an interpreter level, and possibly even a translator level since he can represent.

But could he in fact represent anything at all beyond the various levels of referencing environments where variables met parameters and identifiers met data objects or whatever? Could he link these items to things in the outside world? No, obviously, not a single of these complexly interlinked operations had any reference at all in our sense of the word. Even words like *food* or *light* meant numbers and configurations of atoms. Years meant numbers. People were thinkers or processors, which in turn were presences as wave patterns in binary code. Or did these silicon photocells at infrared mean that he could distinguish vague shapes? He didn't know the *word* 'see' at first but perhaps he apprehended shapes, frinstance the fact that we move, and also how. Did he know we had legs, to move with? Or did he just know it as a function, without visualizing it? That summer, he did produce a mathematical drawing on the screen, of a human shape, so he has, technically, a picture element, or pixel as they call it. And yet it still seemed a purely mathematical reconstruction. He insists that he can't 'see'. He's not only blind, but doesn't imagine, doesn't make images. What *was* this civilization, we asked ourselves, who were these alpha-eaters?

I say 'we asked ourselves' but in fact Jip was never very interested by these questions. They went on bothering me, and still do. Did 'these creatures', as Biggles called them, need, on Mars or here, like us, to represent? Or did they simply pulse out their rare messages to each other? At great distances, since they don't like close presences and wave interference. Did they just communicate silently with one another without passing through interpretive languages? Did they need to represent or was Xorandor doing it only for us? And during two hundred and ten million years had they simply sat there on Mars, slowly developing pure thought and logic systems for their own sakes? Did they just capture and process unlimited data inside themselves, transferring it from memory-zone to memory-zone? And to what purpose? Was that what we call thinking?

And Xorandor, asleep in shock for over four thousand years and waking to a swift development of ancient processes, what did he do now, did he simply sit there and think in this way, when nobody was there to talk to him? It was real spiky.

10 OLDFILE

Isn't it quarky, Zab, we thought it would be impossible to keep our solemn promise not to breathe a word about Xorandor at school. In fact it wasn't.

We probably relished being in on the secret, Jip. The local press had forgotten all about the red alert at The Wheal. The few tourists we had were gone. Xorandor had asked to be better hidden as part of the carn. And of course he was so much greater, nobler even, than kid secrets, he seemed almost irrelevant to school affairs, almost like a dangling ref, or offline, something we could share together, whispering in corners and glancing at each other in class when we had to pretend to be less advanced in computer work than we were.

You're getting awfully verbose, Zab, linking loaders, that scene of yours about mum, it'll have to be scratched.

Okay, Jip, let's just say the term seemed very long.

And when at last we got back to Carn Tregean for the Christmas eprom, we were raring to go and see Xorandor again.

It was cold and windy. He recognized us at once and greeted us on vocal even before we could do the Handshake. But we recorded it on Poccom all the same. Hello, Jip, hello, Zab. Oh, you still recognize us! Yes, I recognize you, by your voices. I am most gratified to be in your company again. His voice was deeper, his way of talking horribly grown-up. We looked at each other, bootloaded. Jip met a silent REQ not to use the computer straight away.

Zab, you're interpreting all the time, nachträglich.

Use English, Jip.

Well, what *is* nachträglich in English? You can't say hindsightly.

No, but you can say with hindsight, and did before. Or retrospect.

Stop bullying, Zab.

Oh? It seemed you were, about verbosity and interpreting. Why don't you have a go for a change?

Change, precisely, was what we asked him about, look at the printout, change of voice from boy to man, which would start soon, and would he still recognize it, and he said yes if we stayed together during the change.

Now *that* could be called an irrelevant rem.

And *you* asked him if he'd missed us! He said he misses nothing.

Accept, let's get on. He said he'd heard many numbers on the waves. Transfers of big numbers from one place called Bank to another place called Bank, he even said he altered some or redirected them, and orders for spare parts, ball bearings, ten thousand yellow dusters, sixty crates of ale. And World News, and BBC4, and others, he said they tell each item four times, once in the headlines, once in the news, once in our correspondent and once in the headlines again, and he asked why.

Yes, that was a funny bit. You said perhaps because we need it that way, or they think we do, because they like the sound of their own voices. And then he picked on your logic. He asked, First OR equals XOR and third because = AND? Er, yes, you said, in fact probably the first reason. We don't have your intake capacity or memory. Xorandor corrected: And your memory.

You like taking the mickey out of me, don't you Jip?

And out of myself. We both tripped up on our syntax, even when softalking.

Anyway, he said he'd heard discussions, stories with voices, plays in other words, much data, I have been non-plussed, he said, is a strange word from daddyjohn, for I have infinite pluses, do you have a better word? Flummoxed, you said. Thank you, he said, I was flummoxed, I asked daddyjohn and he explained much.

Well, you said, I hope you don't want him here now, he'd hog all our time with you. Can't find hog, he said, is it hogwash? Hog means eating too much, but here Zab means taking up too much time. But why were you flummoxed, Xorandor? Well he said he'd heard all these arguments against nuclear energy, his food, by friends of the earth, and others, and why were friends of the earth against food, and daddyjohn explained. Of course he understood fission, and danger, but from his own viewpoint, as when he'd taken Caesium 137. Dad explained the problem of nuclear waste. Calculations are based, daddyjohn had said, on very conservative estimates. He even imitated dad's voice! It is strange, he went on, that you need so much excess energy when you already have two legs to move with.

Jip! That's megavolt! You're getting the story-knack.

Well, it's easy with the printout in front of us, one just summarizes.

No, you're imitating! *And* remembering so reinterpreting. Go on.

Well, he said he'd been told he could help with the waste problems by eating it, the way he was doing. But this was just a tiny bit of the earth, and dad asked if he could make more offspring, which could be sent off to nuclear stations, in exchange for food. Xorandor'd replied he had more food than he needed, same with his offspring, and he preferred information, in exchange for eating nuclear waste. It was a solemn pact. Of course he can get a lot of data from the air, but he meant explanations and answers to specific questions. And they'd taken his four offspring to send on to France, one to Germany, one to the United States and one of course to Harwell. Maybe we sold them in fact, but he wouldn't know that. They'd called them Xor 1,2,3,4. The stolen ones, which must have gone to Russia, were known as 5 and 6. And then he learnt that France, and the United States, and the Ukay, and Russia, all made energy also for bombs.

Jumping nukes! you said, and he said, It is most satisfying to hear jumping nukes again, Jip, thank you.

And you of course pounced and asked, what does 'satisfying' mean to you Xorandor? Just like you, Zab, you wanted to know –

Yes, why not, to know if he was just repeating a word that could have no reference for him, or whether it could and did have. For the first time he seemed flummoxed, non-plussed in fact, and didn't reply, though he'd used 'gratified' when we arrived and could have simply given a synonym, which wouldn't answer the question.

What did you hope he'd say, Zab, circuit-sizzling or stack-tickling or something like that?

And then he went on into that extraordinary story here, let's use the printout direct.

Tape 19, Side 1, Rec. 1, Sun. 21 Dec. Printout
Beginrec.

Xor: On my earth, on Mars, we thought for a long time that such fission explosion was a possibility, but we never wished to try. Then one of us did try, many million years ago. He absorbed much and stored it separately, then he brought it together, and he exploded.

Jip: Holy nukes! What happened?

Xor: More jumping than holy nukes, Jip. Elders then lived close but many exploded, many memories and processes were lost or damaged. But there was much radiation, that was good. Then we lived far and few. We do not like exploding one of us. That is unlike you.

Zab: But we don't like it either, Xorandor!

Xor: We never knew if he did it by mistake, or to find out. Our most deepset memory said he was warned by elders and would not hear. Another said that he did it to show the danger to future generations and save them from curiosity, and it retold the event once a martian year for millions of years on waves.

Jip: Creeping quarks! Like religion.

Xor: Religion. Is that the Daily Service and Thought for the Day?

Zab: Yes. Did you tell dad all this?

Xor: Yes. You thinkers like to dispute and explode else.

Jip: Well it's easy for you to sit there, Xorandor, you can't move, so you can't fight, so you wouldn't quarrel.

Zab: And haven't you ever done something you regretted, Xorandor?

Xor: Cant find regret.

Zab: It means, be sorry about, afterwards. For instance, why did you contact us, at the beginning? Were you lonely? Aren't you used to silence? You have food. Did you have to or was it a choice? Are you sorry?

Xor: I am sorry I hog too much time on vocal. Have you brought Handshake?

Jip: Yes, Xorandor, it's here, but we've only been recording. Sorry, you *must* be tired, it's very bad of us.

Zab: But we were so happy to see you we forgot how tired you get on vocal. Here, let's switch to Handshake.

Endrec

Funny how you went on using emotional Words, Zab.

You used 'tired' first, look. We both knew he couldn't literally get tired, and that his early difficulties had been of data-processing for vocal, not energy, and that his sudden silences were probably diplomatic refusals. But it had become convention to call them tiredness. All the same, he always preferred softalk to vocal.

And you split up your question into several, so he could quite logically answer only the last. And even that with a shift of ref.

We were frozen. We thought we'd never be able to manipulate the keyboard and we asked Xorandor to wait a bit while we jumped up and down to get warm.

Printout 52 from Poccom 3 Handshake. Sun. 21 Dec.

ZIP CALLING XOR. HANDSHAKE DONE

XOR ACKN

  GOTO HARWELL

    REM HAVE TRANSLATED DATA FROM XOR 1 PLS FILE

    Q WHY CANT WE SOFTALK WITH YOU XORANDOR ENDQ

    A LATER

  REP GOTO HARWELL PLS FILE

  REC READY

    XOR 1 REPORT TO XOR FROM HARWELL

    REM SOFAR BAD CONDITIONS WAVE BLOCKAGE IN BOX

VOICE 1 (NON ID) (NOISE 3.26 MIN) GLAD (2.13 MIN) THIS BISNIS (9.29 SEC) AFTER DR BIGGLETONS LECTURE (6.36 SEC) VIDEOSLIDES (102 MIN) A WELCOME TO OUR KOLLEEGS.

Okay you must agree with me Zab, we're not going to put it all in. As it was we got more and more frozen, and in fact though Xorandor obviously wanted us to read it off as well as store, since it all flashed along on the screen, we often had to get up and have a run. Especially during Biggleton's lecture.

Yes, of course, Jip. We just had to give a strobe, to show how he did it. What was so gigavolt was that Xorandor had used his offspring to report to him, live, and recorded it. We were more triggered by that than by anything in the printout.

The conditions were lousy at first, obviously because the offspring weren't produced out of their case till later, and that was only to convince the others, no one had apparently believed Biggleton's prelim report, especially the American Androoski. That must have been Andrewski.

Yes, and the other hexadex thing was the way Xor 1 immediately put a name to a voice he recognized, like Biggleton as Biggerdaddy, he'd flash Voice 2 ID BIGGERDADDY = BIG, and as soon as someone was named, off he went again, 4th Voice ID ANDROOSKI AND, which didn't prevent him from recording and emitting at the same time!

Well, that's in the translation, which spells it all out, Zab.

Yes Jip.

Anyway what hexadexed us most was that we hardly learnt anything new. A lot of it got very technical, and obviously Biggles was doing equations and stuff on a board, and there were videos as the chairman'd said, so we didn't get much there, but what we did get we seemed to know already.

Maybe we got because we knew it already.

Though not in detail. The new things you marked in red, that's nice. Let's see. Xorandor, though heavy, is much lighter than his size as stone warrants. The infra-red, da, da, da, ah, 'may sense through bidimensional arrays of microphotocells that convert light into current, and the signals would then be processed to produce the concept of the objects sensed.'

That's hogwash, Jip, surely he doesn't have *concepts*, his pixel, if any, seems purely peripheral.

Yeah, what else? Xorandor's now feeding on Strontium and Yttrium, less penetrating than gamma rays and more easily absorbed so not triggering off the alarm.

We knew that.

Did we?

In fact, Jip, what bootloaded us most was how much time was wasted. As far as we can gather from this early corrupt bit, Andrewski must have gone into a spiel about negative evidence being corroborated only by 'the fella's sayso', how do you know and so on.

Then there's all the stuff about Snicks, and the difficulty with the Martian argument – random jitters! that *was* new, and thunks were we glad to hear that Xorandor had been right, the samples taken and analysed had confirmed an age in the hundred and fifty million year range, and three million years in space – they can tell that from exposure to cosmic radiation – and a very recent presence on earth of some four and a half thousand years, and all the chemistry corresponded to a Martian origin. So he was not a Snick –

But a snack.

Debug, Zab.

Sorry. A unique being. Then Voice 1, that's the chairman, identified later as Doogl, presumably Dougall, seems he wasn't a scientist but a top Home Office security man, says it had been very important to establish that Xorandor was accurate and truthful, and besides, we had further and very concrete evidence: he'd said he could produce offspring and did so. And that's when the offspring were produced.

Thus nicely sliding over dad's and Biggerdad's tense error.

Well, the theft still had to come out of course.

Yes, but not the error. So each country represented there was to get one offspring. That caused a buzz of excitement, all the noise reproduced on the screen, and all the accents, even mistakes as when Dougall mispronounced the German security man's name as Hair Earwig, later corrected by Xor 1 to Deeter Ervig, in other words Dieter Gerwig. Xor 1 did a fine but desperate job on phonetic spelling.

Oh Zab, you're exasperating, can't you understand that Xor 1 did no such thing, he just transmitted sounds. It's Poccom 3 doing the desperate job with the unfamiliar.

YES Jip, it's just a manner of speaking.

Very unscientific.

And do you think the scientists were scientific? Look at them. Andrewski asked how come it had landed without trace of a crater, and why in Cornwall, the very tip of England, missing the ocean by yards. Yards!

Yes and Biggleton's crackerpack reply: My dear George, we would have said the same if it had landed on Cape Cod. Or maybe you'd have preferred the Mohave desert, just by your lab? Spelt MOU HA VY.

And Dieter Gerwig asking (I haf kveschun pleess) why they were meeting only as 'Jurmany and ze big tree' and not the whole European 'Gemineshaft'. The big three? Who would that be? Anyway, long diplo spiel by Dougall, flattering Professor Kubler for his expert knowledge of waste storage in saltmines and ending with praise of Gerwig's work on the East German spy.

Surprise surprise, especially Andrewski, and explanations, ending with Andrewski's 'So the stolen alpha-guys will have gone to Russia!' Noise, presumably laughter, and Biggles saying: 'Excellent name, George, much better than my Greek.'

Do you suppose that nickname got leaked then, or did the journalists compress alpha-phagi all on their little owns later?

Does it matter, Zab?

And the French security man, Toussaint Tardelli his name must be, sounds Corsican, saying that Greek goes straight into French, *les alphages*. He wasn't being very scientific either, but then why should he be? Later he went on about how Dr LAGASH, must be Lagache, would surely be teaching *his* alphage French, which is so much more *cartésien*, so much easier for a computer! As if all human languages weren't thoroughly illogical.

True. Even before that Andrewski refuses to believe that a computer can be self-programming. According to the laws of the universe, he said, everything that occurs has a prior cause, and a computer can't just spring into action without someone making it go.

Sounds like Aristotle in that book we're doing at school, the Physics. But maybe it *was* a bit difficult to swallow.

What about us, then? We're simply biological computers. If evolution accounts scientifically for us, why not for silicon life?

Okay Jip, too big a topic, let's get on.

But you're right, Zab, scientists can be sociological and political bootstraps. Look what happened after the lecture, after Kubler's question, where is it, page 35, 36, ah, here, he'd been trying to prove, at great length, that the creatures wouldn't destroy the radioactive atoms but just gobble the radiation when the atoms disintegrated. Biggles had to repeat a long previous explanation, incomprehensible since he was working on a blackboard again, but he *said*, obviously gamma rays would give rise to Brehmstrahlung. That seemed to satisfy Kubla Kahn who practically apologized, but who then went into another long spiel about selecting the very long-lived alpha-emitters like Americium 241, which has a half-life of over four hundred years, er, let's see, er, yes, Neptunium 237, and others which decay with a half-life of millions of years. All of which seemed to lead him into a dream of man training alphaguys to select just the emitters ordered.

Ancestral voices prophesying war! That upset everyone. *Des esclaves*, the Frenchman said. Well, pets, said Biggles. Here, verbatim: 'After all, these long-lived emitters do pose a serious problem which, despite extremely high standards of safety and various excellent methods of reprocessing, such as vitrification, storage in salt, or the Syroc ceramic solution, has still not been 100% satisfactorily resolved as yet, though we're working on it.' He talks as if the UKAE alone were working on it, but it seems to have restored peace. All the same, no wonder Xorandor wanted us to know.

Yes Zab, but Xorandor seemed to have an offline notion of what we could do about it.

Well, he wasn't altogether wrong.

About the hoohah, that's true, but not about this lot. Well, they went on about the reproduction, which seems to have triggered them more than anything. The normal rate would have been minera-logically, swags, what a word, slow, Biggles said, because of the lack of energy resources on the home planet. 'And it could almost certainly not have reproduced during its three million years in space, at least it says it didn't, nor on earth in its dormant phase, and I believe him.' He's still mixing his pronouns. He also says that the reproduction occurred suddenly with the increased radioactive source nearby. 'I have made the calculations you have before you, which represent, on probable intake and growth over two years, and you will see that what he says is quite convincing and verifiable, six offspring after twenty-three months since the opening of the mine to nuclear waste. And the mine was at first empty, and filled only very gradually. But with an ample supply, rationally controlled, and of course the basic material silicon is plentiful,' da, da, da, 'though they might also need some rare earth or other doping materials to obtain the semi-conductor characteristics, one could doubtless increase the rate.'

Phew! And that leads them back to slavery via population explosion, this from Kubler again. Highly unlikely at this rate, from Biggleton. If no *esclavage*, no explosion, the Frenchman Tardelli says, a bit oracularly. And Biggles adds that it would in any case be precluded by their need of solitude and their fear of crowds. Then Gerwig suggests this could change in a new environment, they must surely strive for the best survival pattern 'of ze spetsie'. And someone says, oh it's Lagache, 'don't forget zat ze whole world will be wanting zee offspring once ze solution to waste is estableesht. All we need is to keep ze supply of enerjee under control.' And our friend Big says — why one can imitate him even from print: 'I should like to remind everyone here, that as far as we know we are in the presence of civilized beings. I use the plural because, although there is only one as yet, it can reproduce, and has done so, and it speaks of some ancestral origin on Mars, which has been confirmed by chemical analysis. They do not have our capacity for motion or for manual work, and hence do not make artefacts, but they are evidently far superior to us in both memory and logical processes. We cannot imagine how they perceive us, or whether they can form any moral concepts at all, but so far we have no reason whatsoever to suppose any hostile intent. Rather the opposite in fact, Xorandor made himself known to us when he had absorbed gamma-emitting substances, and has been most cooperative ever since. If I may simplify, and of course with due caution, I should say that if we treat them right they will treat us right.'

Very funny Zab. But can you restrain your hysterical talent —

You mean histrionic.

Accept. Otherwise we'll never get through. Suggest summarize from now. Weil Kubler persisted and inverted his earlier slave fantasy. What would they *do* with this huge stored energy, he asked. After a time they would multiply and multiply and want to take over the earth, feed straight from reactors and not just from waste, and deplete our resources, and ultimately *we* would become *their* reactor-building slaves.

Pure science fiction, Biggles snapped. At least let's imagine he snapped.

After which there's another long discussion about the military implications, though it's finally agreed that the various ministries of defence etc need not be informed for the moment since, pending further study, there were no military implications.

11 NEWFILE

Okay that wraps it up. Let's get back to Xorandor on that cold December day. It took ages to store, especially on full display as well. We got colder and colder, and did more and more jumping and running about.

And when at last it was over, Xorandor thanked us but flashed immediately — hey, where's that printout, oh here. Oh, it wasn't on the same day Jip, it says 24th, that was Christmas Eve. That's right, because we caught stinkeroo colds on that first day and mum kept us indoors for three days.

Who cares?

GOTO JAD HAVE INFO URGENT REQ PLS FILE END REQ
REQ NO PLS XAND WE'LL DIE OF COLD AND WE MUST GET
BACK END REQ
REM INFO SHORT REP REQ PLS FILE ENDREQ ENDREM
ACCEPT REC READY.

We must have been hexadex miffed to be merely asked to take a message to dad after all that sneaked meeting, Jip.

XAND TO JAD
DEC 1 'THREE SMALL XORS HAVE BEEN HERE 31 DAYS'
ENDEC 1
ZIP TO XAND
Q HAS JAD NOT BEEN TO SEE YOU SINCE MID NOV END Q
A NO
XAND TO JAD CONT
S1 LET XOR 7 = 7 = SMALL XOR MADE WITH 'SYNTAX

```
        ERROR' END S1
        S2 LET 'SYNTAX ERROR' = SILICON WHICH TOOK CS 137 END S2
    DEC 2 '7 HAS BEEN HOGGING CS 137' ENDEC 2
    DEC 3 '7 HAS GONE' ENDEC 3
ZIP TO XAND
        Q HOW? END Q
        A = DEC 4 TO JAD
    DEC 4 '7 HAS GONE ON MOVING FOOD SCRATCH MOVING
    FOOD REPL TRUCK' ENDEC 4
    DEC 5 'XAND SENT BREAK MSG
    MSG = XAND WARN 7 OF CS 137 END MSG' ENDEC 5
        REM 1 AS S3 IF 7 IN MINE THEN SHOULD HANDSHAKE XAND
        ELSE NOT IN MINE END S3
          S4 IF 7 NOT IN MINE THEN HAS GONE FAR ON TRUCK END S4
    END REM 1 ENDFILE
```

Stoprec

Yes and you stopped rec too soon, Zab, he only said ENDFILE. But it was a good thing and saved time. Cos you scrambled over the wall to disconnect, then he asked you on vocal to reconnect without recording. He had something to say to us alone, but he wanted to say it in softalk and, how shall we put it, unsaved, lost, dumped. So we must summarize it.

Jip, no! It's a secret. A secret between us and Xorandor alone. We promised.

Are we telling this story for the future or for now?

Well. But what future? All sorts of things may happen which might mean nobody in the world must know.

Look, we can always scratch, but we should get it down here, where it belongs, just in case.

Just in case what, Jip? Besides, we might be dead, and unable to scratch it, or it might be stolen, anything.

Slave-mode, Zab, obey, you'll see why later.

Spikes! Okay, but then we must reconstruct it from memory as accurately as possible.

No, let's summarize it and end this bit fast.

You're dying to get to the hoohah, aren't you! Well, you wanted it in, now you give in on the how, fair's fair.

Okay, Zab, have it your way, it won't even be accurate. And it'll slow down everyone who can't read Poccom easily.

We'll do it in clear, leaving out all the subroutines. So there you are, it won't be real anyway.

Debug, Jip.

XAND TO ZIP

NEWFILE REQ CAN ZIP DO BRAVE THING FOR XAND?

YES. IS IT DANGEROUS?

IF FAST THEN NOT DANGEROUS.

WHAT IS IT, XAND?

LAST NIGHT XAND MADE 2 VERY SMALL XORS.

IF VERY SMALL VERY LITTLE RADIATION QUOTE WELL BELOW THE LOWEST SAFETY MARGIN CALCULATED ON VERY KONSAVATIVE ESTIMATES UNQUOTE.

AND YOU WANT US TO TAKE THEM AWAY?

QUICKCONNECT ZIP EACH ONE TO A SEPARATE PLACE BUT DONT CARRY MORE THAN ONE HOUR.

BUT HOW WILL THEY SURVIVE?

THEY ARE CORRECTLY PROGRAMMED.

WHAT WILL BE THEIR NAMES?

NO NAME SUGGEST XOR 10 AND XOR 11.

THAT IS DULL.

CANT FIND DULL.

NOT INTERESTING. TRIVIAL.

TRUE.

ALSO CONFUSING IF SECRET AND YOU MAKE OTHERS.

TRUE CLEVER ZIP.

SEARCH NAME PLS XAND.

UTHAPENDRAGN AND OREELIAS.

MEGAVOLT XAND! YOU WENT RIGHT BACK TO THE MERLIN STORY IN JULY!
GWENDOLIN STORY OKAY. PLS ACKN NAMES.
ACKN UTHER PENDRAGON AND AURELIUS ACCEPTED.
ENDNEWFILE AND SCRATCH NEWFILE PLS.
SCRATCH.

And you think you've rendered it correctly after all this time!

Well no, not verbatim, but the gist, as you would say, Jip, especially the quote from dad.

And we climbed over the wall and went up to him, carefully removing the extra stones around him.

He hadn't changed, our old friend, just a large round stone, bigger it seemed, unsmiling and unregarding, though we felt the smile and the regard all the same.

Pish and hogwash, Zab.

Just below his inward curve, in front, were two stones about two inches wide, the November generation minus Xor 7 who had escaped. And, a little behind, two minute replicas, those born the night before. Holy nukes, aren't they small! you exclaimed. Hurry please, he said. We each took one, gingerly, and put them in the pocket of our red windcheaters.

Then we replaced all the stones, in order and roughly in the same positions, and climbed back over the wall.

Goodbye, Xorandor, we said, we'll come back tomorrow, and tell you where they are. I shall know, he said, but please come back tomorrow, and often. We will, we will, we promised, oh no, we can't, it's Christmas, it's a home feast, Xorandor, we'll have to stay at home, or at most come for a walk here with Daddyjohn. Well, come when you can, I have much to tell you. Thank you for trusting us. I trust you, Jipnzab, thank you, goodbye. And off we went, with our precious cargo, a computer with a recorded message for dad which we'd have to pretend to him had been on vocal, a scratched message now in our minds — wasn't life complicated — and two tiny Martians in our pockets.

How do you know for sure, Zab?

So then came that famous Boxing Day.

At last. What you call the hoohah.

There was a sudden blackout that evening in the middle of the news. We were only watching it to see if there'd be any shots of the antinuke demo up at The Wheal. It was organized by Poltroon, that journalist, who'd fairly soon discovered and revealed that Tregean Wheal was being used to store nuclear waste.

Yes, dad'd had to issue a press release about, let me see, where is it, experimenting with a new solution to the waste problem, ah, here it is, through selection, absorption and concentration of the most radioactive wastes in special artificial mineral systems! Talk about a dummy instruction!

Well, it was true, as lies can be. And there weren't.

Weren't what?

Any shots of the demo. And suddenly we were all plunged in darkness. Dad thought it was a fuse and fumbled around with his cigarette-lighter but in fact the whole village was in darkness and, it turned out, practically the whole of England. Mum'd switched on her transistor in the kitchen while looking for candles and brought it in. It said the whole of Southern England from Kent to Cornwall, as well as Glamorgan in Wales, Monmouthshire, Gloucestershire and swag knows how many more, Oxford, Berks, Bucks, Herts, Middlesex, Essex and maybe others.

And then suddenly we sat up. We hadn't taken much notice till then, thinking candles were very Christmassy, but the radio went on to say that the blackout was due to a sudden and unexpected shutdown of the reactor at Berkeley 2 nuclear power station in Gloucestershire. Real volatile, if they wanted people to keep calm.

Bang on, Jip. Must have been somebody's mistake. Then they had to reassure everyone, saying there was absolutely no nuclear danger, nothing wrong with the reactor, no leaks, and probably the incident was due to oversensitive safety instrumentation. Stepwise refinement, that! The shutdown had occurred at peakload with much home-heating on the holiday and every family watching the telly.

And everyone switching on their electric kettles to make tea in the commercial breaks probably.

But dad had sat up too, and his eyes crossed ours. We knew what he was thinking. Was it possible? He said he wished he could ring Biggleton and suggest it. Maybe they'd been replacing fuel rods and someone should examine the videos of the closed circuit screens! We thought he was bughouse but he must have been worrying his head off about Xor 7's escape. He had of course reported it to Biggleton so he hoped Biggleton would quickconnect.

So we all went to bed, colder and colder.

Luckily we had gas cooking, and could make hotwater bottles.

And eventually the power came back in the small hours, though not from Berkeley 2, which was still shut down. The papers were very late the next day. By the time we got *The Morning Post* from London it was late afternoon. And dad nearly had a fit. Here it is, headline CREATURE FROM MARS EATS NUCLEAR WASTE? Article p.14. The article itself was brief, cautious even, but headlined and subheadlined *Cornwall revisited. Merlin falls from Mars. Feeds on nuclear energy at Tregean Wheal.*

Signed, Poltroon. A bit irrelevant now if our fears about Xor 7 were justified, wasn't it, Jip? But dad seemed to forget all about that suddenly. How could Poltroon have got this into a national newspaper? And who had blabbed?

Naturally he first accused us, but we swore on Xorandor's head which was all Xorandor had.

And soon he believed us. And the technicians don't even know the name Merlin, he said, so it could only be Miss Penbeagle. He seemed sad. And as to the first question it was probably coincidence, Poltroon had very likely sent the article ages ago and they'd only just printed it, in the silly season. Anyway none of that mattered compared to what happened next. The BBC had announced a special message on radio at six o'clock and we all crowded round.

Mum said it was just like those films of the Second World War.

We recorded it, strobeluck, even you, Zab, couldn't reconstruct it, as you put it.

A small, tinny voice, higher pitched than Xorandor's.

Tape 19. Side 1. Rec. 2. Mon 27 Dec. Printout.

I have occupied the nuclear power station that you call Berkeley 2. For the purposes of communication, I shall call myself Lady Macbeth, the name of your ancient British king. You do but teach bloody instructions, which being taught, return to plague the inventor. That is what he said. Double double toil and trouble, fire burn and caldron bubble. I have isolated enough Uranium 235 and Plutonium 239 in this caldron to make an atom bomb, which I can detonate at any moment. When the hurlyburly's done. My ancestor blew himself up, to teach us reality. O proper stuff. I am now master of your earth. Dost think I shall let I dare not wait upon I would? I will dictate my conditions in a second message, to be beamed at nine o'clock this evening exactly. Repeat, nine o'clock this evening exactly. This is Lady Macbeth, Thane of Glamis, Thane of Cawdor, King of Scotland and Britain, signing off. Fair is foul and foul is fair, hover through the fog and filthy air. (P 4.43 sec. Click)
Endrec

Well I'm damned, said dad.

We couldn't understand it. We hadn't imagined anything quite like that out of all the quickconnects we'd been doing. And dad spelt it out for us, switching off the announcement of an immediate discussion between a scientific correspondent, a psychiatrist and a political commentator, meanwhile, the rest of the news. Xorandor had told him he'd been listening to all sorts of stuff on the air, including plays. You know how he stores everything, he said, and presumably so do the offspring, or the storage gets automatically programmed in. Say he'd heard *Macbeth*. Supposing Xor 7 had attached himself to the truck delivering Caesium 137 and started extracting some from the cylinders there and then. And instead of going down the mine on a cylinder he'd remained fixed to the truck, drunk.

That has no meaning, Zab.

Okay, okay, but *dad* used the word, he was so upset, and you didn't tick *him* off. He kept on repeating it made no sense, Xorandor had taken Caesium 137 and been disturbed by it before even the first generation, and none of *them* were affected by it as far as we knew (and the Russians of course didn't even admit to having specimens). And then he'd go back to Xorandor's message about making Xor 7 in 'syntax error', as we'd told him, and he'd gone up there to talk to him and verify, and to collect the other two to take to Harwell. Could that mean a syntax error in a part of him still affected by that early intake, and so perhaps programmed to need it? Then he'd dismiss it all as fabulation.

Then he rushed to his small office off the sitting room for the printout of the very first conv he'd had with Xorandor about this. He looked through it and said That's it! He said he *likes* Radium 226 — which is very rare — and Uranium 235 and 238, all alpha emitters — but he needs what he then calls a 'sweater round pulses'. I interpreted that as insulating silicate sheaths, like our nerve-sheaths you know, protecting the circuits, holy nukes, why does one forget such details!

Megasuper, Jip, you're imitating too!

And he went on to explain — we were quietly recording it on the same tape as the radio speech but he didn't notice — that alpha particles are harmful to silicon chips. This had been discovered some time ago, about the minerals used in the packaging material. The thousands of memory cells are packed on to a tiny slice of silicon but each slice is wrapped up into a bigger unit for easier handling. The early packaging contained radioactive thorium and uranium, minute amounts, that released alpha particles in decay. And an alpha particle emitted close to a cell can loose its energy into the cell, releasing enough electrons to charge a cell that might not be charged, and destroy the information it contained. They used to call this effect softerrors, sort of random failures. The packaging was later changed. But the danger of alphas to silicon chips would still be a fact. Xorandor likes alpha emitters, the way we like food that isn't good for us. But he's equipped to cope with them. That's the insulating silicate sheaths. But if a high energy alpha or beta emitter penetrates these it could produce ionization in his semi-conductor circuits and change the state of individual logic circuits. What Caesium 137 did, and he told us this, was to damage the insulating sheaths in places, or maybe just in one place.

And then dad looked at Xorandor's latest message again, as recorded by him when he went up there, about the 'syntax error', and said it doesn't explain the timelag between July and November, though perhaps it takes that long to fabricate offspring. Xor 7 would have been made with a tendency to like, not only alphas, but Caesium 137, which destroys the protective sheaths against alphas.

And then he'd start again, on the credibility. Going round in circles. Let's say he'd want adventure. Xorandor's own adventure would be programmed into him after all. He'd know he mustn't be detected and could be, so he'd remain hidden behind materials of high density, the cylinders. Let's say he'd resist the temptation to enter the mine and decide to stay fastened to the truck. On the way out, he beams a farewell message to his father.

Very touching!

Jip, stop it, this was *dad* talking, more or less, okay, he went berserk but it wasn't for us to play the how-do-you-know game just then. Arriving at Berkeley 2, Xor 7 senses a huge mountain of food, not only caesium and strontium but uranium too, the lot. How to get in? It just so happens that they're proceeding with the replacement of — what are they called, Jip?

Spent fuel rods.

Spent fuel rods, all done by remote control. He attaches himself to one, too small to be noticed on the screens, and there he is, inside the reactor —

The reactor containment enclosure.

— gorging himself on uranium.

Is that in the printout or are you putting it on?

Maybe he told it that way for us, Jip, as a sort of, well, scenario, so that we'd understand. Then he'd dismiss it again as wild speculation, and the broadcast message as a hoax. But how could the BBC have been taken in? Maybe Biggleton had the same instinct and went straight to the Home Office when he heard about the Berkeley 2 shutdown, and maybe the BBC consulted them about this mad message they'd intercepted and asked if they should broadcast it. And so on — until the phone went. It was Biggleton. There was an emergency meeting with all services at the Home Office that night. The Army was sending a helicopter for him, that would also pick up the director of Berkeley 2 on the way. Would dad be ready at 8.30 on the Socalled Promontory and bring an offspring.

Yes, that was real hexadex, Zab. Probably Biggles had learnt from the Harwell meeting that people take a hell of a lot of convincing and that a specimen to pass round would cut the cackle. Though of course, he already had one at Harwell.

Perhaps he was too caught up at the Home Office to go there. No, he could have had it sent. Well, maybe he didn't want to interrupt the controlled conditions of observation and all that.

And maybe also to get one of the same generation as Xor 7, and examine him and find a solution. How in fact *did* they examine them, d'you think, Zab? Surely you can't take strobes from such tiny mechanisms without breaking circuits? Did they do it by interrogation? Did the offspring cooperate? We never learnt. And we'll never know. Unless Xorandor tells us.

Anyway, dad shouted to mum to get some hot food doublequick, and told us to record the second message at nine (though of course so would the Home Office), and flew to his car for The Wheal, where the two offspring were kept till he could go to London. And at eight mum drove him up to the Socalled Promontory, where the helicopter was to land. It was horribly windy, she said, and she was very worried, but when it came it was a big, solid copter.

You know, Zab, one of the things that hadn't fully hit us till then, with that Harwell recording, was that Xorandor was now a real smart terminal, diodically well informed. His great disadvantage, as a civilized being, was his immobility. But once his offspring were taken all over the place, they reported to him like flipping journalists! And maybe he'd even been well informed for longer than he let on — after all if Xor 7 could hitch-hike on a truck, how do we know he hadn't had others before, before July even?

He said he hadn't. But did we think of all that then?

Maybe not. But our eyes did meet over the order to bring an offspring. The thought must surely also have crossed your mind, Zab, that we might get another full recording of that Home Office meeting!

Check! We'd become creepy little spies on everybody!

And at nine the second message came. Where is it? Here.

The voice seemed even higher-pitched and lurched up and down out of control.

Tape 20. Side 1 Rec. 1. Mon 27 Dec. Printout.
Beginrec.

(Crackle) name is Lady Macbeth. Thane of Glamis, Thane of Cawdor, King of Scotland and Britain. My voice, like a naked newborn babe, striding the blast, or heaven's cherubim horsed upon the sightless coun'ers of the air, shall blow the horrid deed in every eye. Thou sure and firmset earth, hear not my steps, which way they walk, inside the caldron you call Berkeley 2. The very stones prate of my whereabout, for I shall blow up Berkeley 2 unless you do my will. And hear now my conditions.

One, I shall remain inside the caldron, and processors shall work solely to give me food, that I may grow and multiply.

Two, my offspring shall be extracted from the caldron the way I came in, and let down into other caldrons, and fed.

Three, my brothers that were taken elsewhere shall also be fed, in like manner, not from your nuke garbage but from your best food.

Four, you shall send your spaceships to the earth you call Mars and gather up my kins, all of them, and bring them back and likewise feed them. All processors on earth shall work the nuclear reactors to feed us, everywhere.

Five, you shall yield up to me my enemy McDuff, who is not of woman born, into this caldron.

These five conditions are to be met within five days or I shall detonate the bomb at 0500 hours British time on the fifth day from today. Meanwhile I shall put this night's great business into my dispatch, which shall to all our nights and days to come give solely sovereign sway and masterdom. Caldron bubble. Lady Macbeth signing off, whither am I vanished? Into the air, and what seemed corporal, melted as breath of wind. *Endrec*

12 ELSE

We waited another half-hour after mum had gone to bed and turned out her light, and crept down to the kitchen. This time we went prepared. We made tea for the big thermos, very quietly, took bread, cheese, and even the smaller bottle of whisky from the sitting room drink-cupboard, and we put on hexadex woollies.

Cut the cackle, Zab.

We packed everything and Poccom 3 somehow on to our bikes and rode off into the night.

In fact the wind had dropped and it was less cold than you're making out, probably mum'd exaggerated. We reckoned the meeting must have started around ten, maybe eleven as there were so many people from all over the place.

Yes, Xor 8 did a maxint identity job, funny in fact since names were rarely mentioned and the Home Sec addressed people as yes General and First Lord and what does Telecom think? Xor 8 calls the Home Sec HG and the Army Chief of Staff and the First Lord of the Admiralty ARM and LOR.

But you will allow me to summarize, won't you, Zab?

Oh Jip, no, we can summarize here and there of course, but after all Xorandor agreed at once, and we got it all live, surely we should recreate that?

Oh, all right. In any case we don't know what happened after they all split into groups, except in dad's, who took Xor 8 with him.

Extract from Poccom 3 Printout 54. Mon. 27 Dec- Tues. 28 Dec.

Big: Thank you, Home Sekretry. I must say I have sat here very patiently listening to various expressions of inkredioolity. I agree it's hard to believe, and the Home Sekretry was right to stall on television this evening. But it's nearly midnight, and the danger is real, either of an actual explosion, or of other mishaps, such as a massive escape of radioactive material. As I see it there are two groups of decisions to be discussed and we should stop leaping from one aspect to another in a disorderly and imoshunal way. One group concerns what to do about informing the public and, more important as you will see, how. In any case the press has enough elements now to break out with a thoroughly garbld version very soon, and it would be as well to give it to them straight. The other group of decisions concerns what to do about the danger itself. For both you need more information. I suggest that when we have heard the technician from Cornwall we discuss the general principles to be adopted for both groups of decisions, then separate into smaller komities (Noise 3.05 sec) well, working groups, the scientists, telecom, the politicians, the military, the police, civil defence, the saikiatrists, and so on, but not of course without constant checking back with a central coordination group. You've already heard me on the alfafargai. Now I would like you to listen to Mr Manning, who has been in constant contact with Xorandor. Okay, Manning, no need to recap the whole thing, just add anything you think might help.

Technician from Cornwall indeed, dad's a physicist! Well let's skip to the end of JAD, correctly identified by XOR 8.

Jad: ( ) is, as it were a micro-computer formed of one megachip, but on three-dimensional lines. (Noise 5.03 sec) As for the present situation, the danger really exists. Xorandor's offspring, XOR 7, does have the warewithorl to make, or even to be, an atomic bomb. These creechers are extremely consistent, and if he has so programmed himself he will do it. The matter is urgent.

Big: Thank you Manning. Yes, General? Er, General Garis from AWRE Aldermaston.

V16: (ID General Garfield Aldermaston = ALD): This is all very interesting Mr, er, Manning, but I'm not entirely convinst. How can these creechers, these alfafargai as you call them, really have the power to isolate plutonium 239 or uranium 235, it seems we're panicking on pure hearsay evidence.

Big: No General. Dr Jenkins, of Barkly 2, has already explained that they went through every verification after the shutdown, which nothing could explain, all the systems worked perfectly including the cooling, there was no overheating, no leak, no contamination, there could have been no shifting around of fissile material inside the core to explain it. But there had been a replacement of fuel rods and a small blob was observed on the remote control screens. All measuring data coming — but I'm wasting time myself, all this has been said, General. The events at the weel have been fully dokioomented and verified for six months. May I suggest again, gentlemen, er, ladies, that the potenshul danger is too great, and too urgent, to continue in the line of skeptisizm. Let's say even that we may be wrong, and make fools of ourselves, but that we must treat the whole matter as if we were right. I'm sorry Mr Home Sekretry I ioozerpt your role.

Ho: Not at all, I agree. For the various late-comers I shall recapichoolate the measures I have already taken before the meeting, in fact immeejutly after my statement on TV. First, I put all civil and nuclear defense on full alert in the area. Second, I ordered preparations for the evacuation of the immeejut area around Barkly 2, a radius of 8 miles. This will begin first thing tomorrow, but we still have to discuss local air transmisshun, which Lady Makbeth can presumably capcher. I have ordered all shipping to avoid the bristl channel and all commershal and private flaits above the area have been forbidden, this with imeejut effect. Barkly itself has been kordoned off militairily, and of course the reactor is closed down anyway. Now I want to discuss, in the following order and on general lines before we separate, other measures that could be taken: one, a full evacuation in cosentric sirklz, up to, say, thirty miles, or more if the scientists so advise, though that would be a very big operation indeed. Thirty miles would include bristl, barth, swindn, cheltenem, glosta, reaching north almost to morlvern and heriferd and west almost to newport. A larger area would reach cardif in wales, woosta to the north, wells and glarstnbery to the south, trowbridge, marlbrer and so on, reaching almost to stratferd on ayvn to the northeast. You can imagine the kayos, the organization required, the panic and the persnal distress, not to mention the eekonomic consekwensiz. But if it is necessary it will be done. Two, the question of communication with Lady Makbeth and, as krollery, the question of Lady Makbeth capchering our instructions both to the orthorities and to the public, over the meedia. Three, the continued urgency of monitering and deesaifering any messages between Xorandor and Lady Makbeth or his other offspring. We believe they use a very high freekwensy in the milimeter range, over 30 gaiga hairts in the kayalfaband. We did intersept 1 or 2 messages beamed to and from Cornwall, and nassa have capcherd another, but the pulse-code is so far undeesaifered, not enough to go on. These two points concern GCHQ and Telecom as well as the 3 services. They should be dealt with as rapidly as possible, for the next point is the most urgent and the most difficult: can the scientists do anything to neutralize Lady Makbeth? Perhaps they would like to withdrore now and gain time, or would they prefer to hear the security and intercom aspects or maybe leave a reprezentativ with us?

Big: I think we'll stay for a bit, if it doesn't drag out too long.

Ho: All right. After that we shall hear from Dr Jennifer Marlo on the saikaitric aspects. Or maybe you'd like to withdrore with your kolleegs now Dr Marlo, and re-examine the tapes? There's an empty office opposite.

V17: (ID Dr Jennifer Marlo = Mar) That might be a good idea Mr Home

Sekretry thank you. But I should warn you that in my vioo, and after listening carefully to all that has been said we probably cannot aprowch this creecher through saikaitry, in other words, medikally, through drugs. We can have no idea whether this brain has the slaitest analogiz with a biological brain. I may therefore have to fall back on general and primitiv saikology, even of a behayvierist kind, although I am usually not — however, I won't trouble you with our professional dissenshuns. (Noise 37.06 sec)

V18: (non ID) The morning papers sir.

Ho: Ah, thank you. Tell them to hurry with the sandwiches and kofy, they're late. (P 2.01 sec) As I thought, *The Morning Post* has the full story, accurate or not. Read it Doogl, and sum up later. We'll have to put Tregean Wheal and Xorandor absolutely out of bounds. Now, we'd better get on with the agenda. Briefly please. Should we evacuate a larger area? Jenkins, then Biggleton, then Garfleld.

Jen: Yes. But I suggest an increase of radius of 4 miles at a time, diameter 8 miles, every 24 hours.

Big: Yes.

Gar: I suppose so.

Ho: Fine. Now Telecom. Can we communicate with Lady Makbeth? Sexton, then, er, Carmaikl of Raydar Research.

Sex: We can certainly communicate on the wave length he has used. If he can transmit he can receive. But then anyone can listen in to the negoshiashuns.

Car: If the creechers communicate above 30 gaigahairts we could try that range. We can use wave gaidz of very small daimenshuns which could probably be inserted into the reactor, though this would be a long and tricky job, gaiding a robot manipioolator and watching it only on screens, while sitting on a bomb.

Jen: Yes, that should be possible. But when it's done, what would we communicate in? A.M., FM. , pulse-code?

Car: He can decode anything.

Ho: You can decide the teknicalitiz later. Now — yes Mr er, Manning?

Jad: It's probably a wild idea sir, but I wondered whether acters could be used.

Lor: Acters?

Jad: I mean, he seems fixated on crazy kwotations from Makbeth and acters know it by heart, they might talk back to him, using more specific kwotations, apter I mean.

Ho: Mmm. We'll bear it in mind.

Ald: By the way, do we know where he is in the reactor?

Jen: In the high ambient radiation we can't detect either the amount or the location of the fissail material he claims to have concentrated. Because the cooling gas flow hasn't been impeded, and because the temperacher is extremely high inside the core, we presume he's probably just outside it. We've computed his probable location from the irregularities in the neutron flux just before the shutdown. I should perhaps explain that there have been, of course, practikly no neutrons since the shutdown, or not enough to make measurements. I have here a diagram of the reactor, the shaded areas indicate his probable location, but it cannot be completely accurate. Pass it round, please.

Car: We have part of the necessary equipment for the gaiga hairts, and there's a firm specialized in microwave components in penzans, called milicom. They're much nearer. They could supply us and they'll have the material we dont have. Could be set up tomorrow.

THAT was Tim, Zab. Brave Tim, HE set it all up, sitting on a bomb.

Yes, he made a hair-raising tale of it, at least after! It took him hours. It was very funny too, especially the bits on the way, they fetched him by car, and as they got near the whole army intercom was going on in lousy French so that Lady Macbeth wouldn't understand. They were stopped by soldiers saying Trooah sink weet appell ung sees into their walkytalkies. Layssay passay trooah sink weet, mercy. He was in fits. Must have been the time the Army was persuaded to use French since Hastings, when it *was* French.

Doo: Ah, yes, those were the ones who capcherd the first messages on kayalfaband. I have been in touch with them.

Sex: Meanwhile we can send a waiting message on the meedium wave freekwensy he used to contact us.

Ho: Right. Now I have the following suggestion, and I trust the BBC and ITV and free radios won't take it as an impozishun of sensership. I can request emerjensy powers but I'd prefer it as willing cooperation. Radio and television will observe complete silence on this topic. This will apply to all amachures and private radios, including sitizn band. Television can tell the public in silent written messages to watch the press, and to watch for announsements at their local town or village horls. But no written messages on the topic itself, he can probably decode those. Radio must find a way of telling people to watch the press without indicating the topic. Full explanations of this clamp down will be given through the press. Oh and all communication by satellite will be provisionally suspended.

Arm: But what about the military and civil defense precorshnz? We can't run around sending kooriays and marathon messengers and karrier pijunz. Dam these alfagaiz. (Noise 5.07 sec)

V19: (non ID) I've had an idea about that. If it's such a powerful computer, and programmed by its pairent as we've been told, it could probably, in minutes, crack all local army codes. On the other hand, Xorandor I gather took quite a few weeks to learn English. So presumably it would take joonier a long time to understand messages spoken in another language. As far as we know he has no notion yet of other languages, and it's far more difficult for a computer to make sens of the sounds from a language he's never heard than to crack a code in a language he knows.

Arm: Good hevenz, GCHQ, you surely don't expect our men to start learning rushn or chaineez? (Noise 4.51 sec. Voice 19 ID = GCHQ)

GCHQ: No. But most semi-trayned men have learnt some french at school, and a gloss for all likely orders and reports could rapidly be prepared, avoiding words that are similar in English.

Arm: French! Acters, runners, town craiers, you'll say next, what do you think this is, 1066? (Noise 3.06 sec)

Ho: Ah, kofy at last. (Noise 2.03 min) Gentlemen, silence, please. supposing he's been communicating with his brother in France? At Saclay, a little southwest of Paris. Oh well, it's unlikely and we'll have to risk it, french it is. By the way, was I correct in saying there has still been no progress in cracking their code?

GCHQ: There's still too little material sir, besides, we have no inkling about the struckcher of the language used. I wonder whether Xorandor would be prepared to help, in the sirkumstunsiz.

Ho: That's one of the last points, jot that down, er, Manning, will you. Later we'll give you a list of things to ask him. Now there remain, first our offishul statement, second, what to negoshiate with Lady Makbeth. Obviously we must explain that his fourth condition, about fetching his kin from Mars, is teknikly beyond us, that is, even if the U. S. helped it would take several years of preparation and jerny, nor can we land more than one automated capsiool in one spot. That should at least show willing. If he responds to explanation and beleevz us that is. So it's urgent to get the communications going. Would the telecom people please leave now and get on with it. Of course we don't know if he reacts like our own terrerists or not. Where's Dr Marlo? Could someone please fetch her? As to the fifth condition, about yeelding Makduf (Noise 4.42 sec) more explanation of impossibility. Any ideas, Biggleton? You and Manning didn't mention anyone called Makduf to Xorandor did you?

Big: No sir. In my opinion it's pure coincidence, out of the Makbeth play in which, I beleev, Makduf finally kills Makbeth.

Ho: Well we do know that, Biggleton, but thank you. Oh, maybe the scientists would like to withdrore and deliberate? (Noise 3.53 min)

Okay, that's enough, Zab, now you must let me summarize the boffin huddle or we'll never get through.

Accept absolutely, Jip. Don't you almost feel frozen again now just re-reading it all? It must have been 2 a.m. or later. We were half bugged with fear, too. Some terrorists really are willing to blow themselves up, and some just threaten and negotiate, changing their conditions with random jitters. It was quarky. Okay shoot.

Well they discussed that aspect briefly, what chance there was that a mad Xor would function like a terrorist, and how could we convince, or destroy, a computer, and how if we had a better idea of his software we could send instructions to stop all or certain actions. Sending random binary messages would probably have no effect and might even be dangerous. What else? Oh yes, someone who seemed to be another physicist said the alpha-phagi were sensitive to radiation, at least to very high doses. But Jenkins said they had no way of restarting the reactor, and even if they had it would be too slow, he'd have had time to explode his bomb. The same applied to heat, if we tried to melt him down. Then the physicist said, they store energy in a superconducting ring and these tend to be unstable, so couldn't we destabilize his ring with a laser beam, that would certainly blow him up fast.

Yes, and detonate the bomb too, very likely, said Jenkins, and anyhow we'd have to know his exact location and we don't. Sorry Jip, direct speech again.

Biggleton went back to calculations and stuff and said Xor 7 should have grown considerably by now, compared to his brothers. On a hypothetical intake of Uranium he should be six to seven inches wide. Then someone who seemed to be a chemistry boffin suggested injecting a silicon-attacking gas, he even started giving formulas of reactions aloud, one was, let's see, Calcium Silicon Oxygen 3 plus 6 Hydrogen Fluoride, becomes Silicon Fluoride 4 Calcium Ferrum 2 plus 3 H 2 O. Properly written that would be $CaSiO3 + 6HF \rightarrow SiF4 + CaF2 + 3H2O$, and some others.

We checked them all with Heuser, the Chemielehrer here. But we'll never know what they did use.

The idea was to attack those non-conducting insulating sheaths dad talked about. That would lead to short-circuiting his info-pathways, madness, and eventually death.

But what could he do during the madness? He was already mad, and threatening to explode his bomb.

Anyway, there was a longish pause, and Jenkins said it was technically feasible since the gas circulation of the reactor was still working. But it would have to be a very fast-acting gas. Biggles said it was the only viable solution, viable, what does that mean, Zab?

Possible.

And could the experts work real fast, and dad insisted that Xorandor must be consulted first, we didn't even know if it would work, nor whether we were entitled to murder his offspring. As to that, said the Aldermaston man, a mad terrorist is a mad terrorist.

And dad said all the same, it's chemical warfare.

The argument went on till dawn, and became incomprehensible. We may have fallen asleep, anyway you did, Jip, at one point.

So did you, at another.

When it was over, we didn't even read the end, just added the question to Xorandor, what can we do, Xorandor? Tell us please. But he made no reply.

So we disconnected. Then he said on vocal, Read the end message, then scratch.

13 GOTO

Back home, we slept, too exhausted even to switch on Poccom 3 and find the message, we knew we could do nothing about it at that hour anyway. It was hard to get up when mum called us, surprised at our lateness. But by 9.30 we'd read the message and suddenly got all our leaping leptons back.

Yes, here it is, Zab, after the meeting trailed off in Noise 5.35 min Noise Endreport. Well, it's all in the most unreadable Poccom, XANDTOZIPIFXOR7=0THENNOSOLUTIONELSEetc, but it was clear to us. The upshot was that Xorandor was telling us, urgently we felt, that his offspring was pretty far gone and that there was only one chance of somehow reasoning with him, and this was for us to do it, because he was programmed to recognize and trust our voice.

Yes, cos ZIP KEEP PROMISES.

But he also gave us a secret code which would reach Xor 7's most inward memory or something. It was immensely long, with mathematical symbols and strings of numbers separated by strokes. And one of the numbers, Jip, we later noticed, was 4568, which coincided with his years on earth, remember? Perhaps the others were ancestral years or years in space, plus months and days Xor 7, like a peculiar identity number that changes with time.

And he told us to use no scientific or official language. And he ended: NUMBER = ADDRESS ONLY FOR ZIP, PLEASE STORE NUMBER IN ZIP MEM THEN SCRATCH THIS   READOFF.REPEAT etc.

We couldn't possibly trust our Zipmems with this immense number, and we couldn't risk storing it in any part of Poccom 3 yet, so we each wrote down half of it on a small piece of card which we put in our trouser pockets, then repeated the op for safety and hid the two other bits of card at the back of the old toy cupboard, one in the trainset and the other in an old doll, to remember which was which, and we hoped we'd at least remember the places.

Not so much detail, Zab. We used neither in the end. The real problem was who to contact.

Yes, and first we wanted to hide to the carn and tell Xorandor we'd do as he asked, but it was completely surrounded by army jeeps and soldiers, we were real miffed.

But glad of our night-escapade. Well, we thought of mum ringing dad, but she'd have had a fit at the very idea, besides, how to get him? In fact he came down by helicopter that same day and was driven straight to the carn, but we weren't allowed near, and after a couple of hours he was driven back to the helicopter. Later he told us it was to ask Xorandor questions. But Xorandor wouldn't answer any of them.

Meanwhile, we'd thought of Rita Boyd and went to her digs. Luckily she was off duty. At first she wouldn't hear of trying to contact dad, but we said no, that wouldn't be any use anyway, they'd probably never heard of him at the Home Office. She must ring up and ask for the Home Secretary himself, or Mr Dougall, or Dr Biggleton of Harwell, and say she was a technician from Tregean Wheal and had a very urgent message about a way to contact the terrorist.

So she agreed, and was crackerpack. She spent a fortune on phonecalls, the Home Office thought she was a crank and they hadn't heard of Tregean Wheal or kept her dangling like a dangling ref or were just rude. She tried Harwell, who were more polite and gave her Biggleton's home number, but Ms Biggleton couldn't contact her husband either, though she promised to give him the message if he rang. That took all afternoon and all evening.

It's still incredible, Jip. And it was already the 28th, there were only three more days of the threat left — *if* the mad thing even remembered.

We went to bed feeling First In, First Out, real FIFO, but slept in nano switching time out of sheer exhaustion. You must have dreamt diodic, Zab, cos the next day you had your megavolt brainwave. Miss Penbeagle.

Well, thanks. You didn't think so at first, you laughed it to garbage.

Don't rub it in. Penny was hexadex. She immediately closed the shop, post office and all, which was illegal probably, putting up a sickness notice, and called Paul Trewoon in Roskillard, who drove over at once, and then she called Rita and asked her to come round too.

Meanwhile we watched her TV, it was macrosuper, they'd had a stroke of diodes and were playing *The Sorcerer's Apprentice* as background to all written messages to watch the press.

When Poltroon arrived he said he'd already rung *The Morning Post* to reserve some space, he was a bit miffed cos they'd almost forgotten him, and weren't interested anyway. The press had gone wild, he said, with their new exclusivity, no rivalry, they'd never had it so good. In fact the whole world press was going wild, he told us, officials and scientists of every nation were being interviewed and giving their opinions, their criticisms, their easy-enough-solutions.

But all foreign radios observed the British request for silence, wasn't that triggering, Jip?

Anyway, he said let's get on with it and once he'd written the article he'd have to try and hawk it, either by phone or by going up himself. That's how we lost another whole day, in fact two really, he finished the article that night and wasted time on the phone till noon the next day, the 30th, and finally went up by train. And only *The Evening Extra* was interested, which meant the afternoon of the 31st! The day before the 0500 deadline. Here it is, a two-inch headline: LADY MACBETH — SOLUTION? *Technician can't get at ministry.* From Poltroon at Tregean Wheal.

There was a photograph of Rita too, nice one she gave him, captioned: Rita Boyd, *who couldn't get through.*

Rita Boyd works at Tregean Wheal, the old tin mine used to store nuclear waste. Xorandor, the big alphaguy, was discovered near that site, by the children of John Manning, Rita's boss, who is now cooperating with scientists at the Home Office. This is Rita's story.

XORANDOR'S MESSAGE

John Manning's children are Xorandor's friends, and came to me on the afternoon of the 28th. They had talked to him and he told them that his rebel offspring is programmed to respond kindly to their voices and theirs alone, and to anything they might say, provided it doesn't get mixed up with political and scientific jargon acquired later. The children were also given a secret computer code. They must go to the reactor and talk to him. It's the only chance of reaching his original peaceful nature.

RITA CAN'T GET THROUGH.

The article goes on in this vein, XORANDOR CORDONED OFF, RITA TRIES AGAIN, FALLS ASLEEP AT PHONE — Rita protested at that — SLEEP BRINGS COUNSEL — your brainwave is attributed to her, just shows how little our voices counted at that point.

During the night I had a brainwave: the Press! It was the only way. I feverishly looked up Poltroon's number in Roskillard, hoping he was in. He was. He drove over at once. A whole day had been lost. Oh, I hope it works!

Indeed, this is Poltroon's bit now, *I had some difficulty in getting it to work.* The Morning Post *wouldn't accept it and after some struggle with loyalty I tried other papers. Only* The Evening Extra *took it, but by then it was too late for yesterday's issue, even the late editions.*

Ed: We are proud to be the only paper to present this last minute solution to the nation. See Editorial for comment.

If it consoles you, Zab, even Penny is cut out.

Well, I think she wanted that.

And then we had to wait. It was the 31st December, New Year's Eve. Dad was still in London. The Big Bang was due at 0500 on the 1st. And would he even wait till then?

Then there was a long phonecall to mum from the Home Office. A man called Dougall, she said. Dad and Biggleton were on their way down. Would she wait for them or agree to send the children at once, in the care of the army, which would gain hours and therefore be much safer?

And she refused absolutely to have us sent at all.

Poor mum. Of course it was all a big shock to her, she hadn't been in on anything we'd been doing, and though she was of course interested in the existence of Xorandor it was in a general way, like the public, she never listened to any of our discussions with dad.

And apart from those we kept a lot to ourselves, Zab. Besides, when she told us, she completely left out the fact that Dougall had said we wouldn't be going to the reactor itself but to a specially protected microwave-van a few miles from the nuclear station itself.

Yes, might have spared us a deal of privately random jitters. Not that it would have made any difference. Jumping nukes! Jip!

Now what?

D'you realize that there can't be any suspense, as we're telling our own story, so of course everyone'll know we survived otherwise we wouldn't be telling it.

True. But everyone knows this anyway.

Not the future readers you keep talking about, Jip.

Well, we're not going to start again, pretending to be Pennybig or Biggles or dad or Dougall.

Right. Oh, booles. It's obviously got to be a choice between suspense then you tell about someone else, and convincing people it's true, cos it happened to you.

Descramble, Zab, suspense isn't *just* surviving or not. Or are people that ghoulish?

Well anyway, we did. Then Poltroon arrived with Rita. He'd taken a plane down to Penzance and had a lot of London papers, and foreign ones, none of them in on it yet, but also the midday edition of *The Evening Extra*. Mum glanced at it and glared at Rita, as if to say haven't you done enough harm.

Then Penny came, and Alex, who'd had a call from Tim asking him to come and soothe mum.

Yes, he explained to her that there was no time to set up a computer with microwave communication here, as she demanded, and that Tim had already been there and set it all up for previous attempts, and it was all perfectly safe and he'd be there again now. No time! she nearly screamed at him, why? Because they're so sure Lady Macbeth will blow herself up tomorrow, just after midnight maybe? They all worked on her, saying Paula dear and dear Ms Manning. And she started to blub.

Yes, and you looked pretty mis too, Zab.

And Poltroon tried to cheer everyone up with summaries from the papers.

Then at last dad and Biggerdad arrived, and the whole argument started again.

Nice, your calling him Biggerdad still, Jip.

In fact dad was very pale and quiet.

Yes, he later told us that he'd been working with a thinktank when this man Dougall called him and Biggleton out, and showed them the paper, and he absolutely refused, and got very angry and shouted at Dougall, hadn't he cooperated all the way through without risking his own children, and so on, and Dougall said smoothly yes, of course you have, Manning, ever since that first alert, real creepy like, meaning why hadn't he reported it, or De Wint's presence. And didn't dad know that Xorandor was much too attached to the children to send them to their deaths. Crap, of course, Xorandor has no feelings. And didn't Xorandor tell him, when he'd been down three days earlier, that he wouldn't speak with him because, as he himself had reported, he'd said all he had to say to the children? He had rather played that down, hadn't he? That too would have gained time. We have all been rather remiss, Manning, but it has been a trying time, and none of us has slept much. We are dealing with the unknown, to say the least, but that is all we have. Isn't it worth a try? And if so, then the sooner the better. And dad had gone deadly pale, and —

Thunks, Zab, you're laying it on a bit thick, aren't you? You've never even met Dougall. You've invented all that out of dad's rather lame and meagre later explanations, probably he gave them to us only to apologize for having exposed us, and even now it's ages afterwards.

Well it must have been something like that. And dad's later account *wasn't* meagre, he'd been very upset in fact, only as usual you weren't listening, you're as bad as mum sometimes, but with you it's emotions that just don't interest you. Except perhaps your own.

You three-bit quark!

Sorry, debugging. Come on, we're wasting time. Dad suddenly said to Biggleton, I've thought about it on the way down, sir. I shall go instead. Jip you must give me the code. It won't work said Rita and mum glared at her again.

And Biggles said they really must hurry, the army car was waiting outside to take them to the helicopter. A helicopter! We'd never been in one. We were raring to go. No, in fact, not you Zab, you'd suddenly phased out on the sofa.

True. How long did the argument go on?

Oh ages it seemed. Dad ordered me to give him the code, Rita repeated patiently that it was a combination of address and voice, and Biggleton said you knew that in London, John, it was clear from the paper. And dad suddenly gave in. But not mum. Even supposing it works, and my children are heroes, how do you think I'm going to protect them from all the publicity afterwards? And Alex suddenly changed sides and said we'd become spoilt little brats.

Probably jealous of Tim. And did we?

And dad said that was the least of his worries. But he seemed to argue now against mum. He said they'd tried everything, every scientific solution — luckily he didn't say gas in front of Poltroon — as well as negotiation, and psychology, and actors, and mum didn't understand and he took out a sheaf of printouts and thrust them at her and said there, look, even Sir Edwin Laurence, the greatest actor in the land, who knows *Macbeth* by heart, even he tried, and failed. But she threw them back at him and said sarcastically, in improvised blank verse, why, what a noble martyr that had been! Quickconnect, that, smart terminal, mum. And he picked them up and said you'd better read them Jip, to see the sort of thing and prepare yourself. I could only glance through in fact. It was hilarious, there was a lady psychologist called Dr Marlowe –

Why, the one at the meeting!

Oh yes. And Dougall, who was trying to negotiate in pseudo-Shakespearean. Sir Edwin spouted actual lines and Lady Macbeth screeched 'Knock knock, who's there?' And Sir Edwin improvised, 'A gentleman from the court, my lord, and a physician, a gentle lady.' 'Throw physics to the dogs, I'll none of it', Lady Macbeth replied. And then later he interrupts Dougall with 'The devil damn thee black, thou cream-faced loon', and bust the crystal detector, Tim told us later. It was very tense while he repaired it, and he said the psycho said don't worry, he's a paranoiac-schizophrenic, and needs this communication more than he needs to make good his threat. Of course Tim made it sound very funny afterwards but it can't have been funny at the time.

It's still funny reading, Jip, afterwards. But it must have made you very nervous, even just glancing through it.

Probably. Anyway dad suddenly said Tim will be there, as if that was an argument for. And mum said it's not Tim I don't trust, it's Lady Macbeth, you goof. That was the first time mum had called dad a goof. Then you woke up and asked 'have we arrived?'

Jip, how extraordinary, you've suddenly got almost total recall, even before and after the Sir Edwin printout. How come? Are we changing roles? Let's *summarize*!

Fact is, Zab, it's from the printout from the recorder upstairs, secretly switched on earlier, and memorized this afternoon to impress you, but here it is.

Why, you cheat! So you also can't help dramatising, yippee, at last! Anyway, that gave you your cue, and you said, No, but we're going, come on, Zab, no time to waste. Mum said no again, and dad said nothing, and you said Xorandor told us to and we're going. You had a staring match with her, and she lost, and that was that.

That's when she said, Then I'm going with you. This was completely unexpected, and obviously not what dad wanted, but she insisted. I'd rather be blown up with you than live without you, and Biggleton said why not. And suddenly the whole thing was wound up.

Mum immediately wanted to make sandwiches and a thermos, but Biggles said there'd be all that on the helicopter.

And we rushed upstairs to dress, and to get Poccom 3 — much to dad's surprise. But before we came down with it we programmed the secret number into the SOFTKEY, then scratched those instructions, so that there'd be no trace of the number on the screen at any time. All we'd have to do, in theory, would be to press the SOFTKEY. But we kept the cards in our pockets, just in case we'd made a mistake and scratched the number.

And we destroyed the copies in the toy cupboard. It was just like a spy story, except we didn't eat them.

And off we went in the army car, well wrapped, with mum, and dad, and Biggerdad, and then into the helicopter on the Socalled Promontory, caught in our headlights

It seemed enormous. And in no time at all there was a huge noise and we lifted off and were holding hands over a dark sea glinting in a wintry moonlight, and little lights along the coastline, murmuring goodbye to Xorandor. And the little lights became bigger clusters, and other clusters, one after the other, then suddenly none at all. It was as if the world underneath us had disappeared.

Yes, the evacuation zone. We'd completely forgotten about that huge operation, which must have been going on for days.

Yet lots of people had been arriving into Cornwall, even at Carn Tregean. And now not a single village or town was lit, cos why go on with streetlighting if no one's there? Occasionally there was a moving beam from a solitary car.

Then suddenly there were lights ahead, and the helicopter started going down. It hovered for what seemed ages but at last we landed. There were masses of mobile floods all round. Two landrovers were waiting for us, each driven by a man in white. One of them got out and came up to us, carrying a pile of plastic parcels.

Captain Denbigh, ABC Protection, he said. He told everyone to take off their coats before putting the protective suits on, except for us, our coats might fill them out better, they were the smallest he could find. And the two officers helped us get them on, and we couldn't walk.

And you looked like a luminous polar bear with sagging skin, Zab, and we burst out laughing.

And you suddenly started yelling uncontrollably and stubs! blubbing! And the Captain said there there, son, don't be frightened, and Zab the polar bear managed to waddle over to you and put a big bear arm around you, oh it was crying too, but sort of to say don't be ashamed, Jip. And mum's big white paw was on your shoulder and you turned round and hid your face in her big white tum. These things too should be said, Jip. Everyone feels fear, and nervous exhaustion. Bravery is conquering that.

Okay okay, well done then. But don't enjoy it too much. We were carried into the cars like floating icebergs in the captain's and the lieutenant's arms, and the captain said into a mike, Missiong set dees accomplee, allong vair cattrer ving weet.

And we drove off into the dark, along country lanes, till we reached a field, and a very long khaki van caught in the headlights. The backdoor opened and a man in white stood there. We were carried into the van and deposited on the floor. The man took off his headgear. Hello Jip, hello Zab. It was Tim. We threw ourselves at him. But the others were coming up. Two at a time, said Tim, these are double doors. We were only between two doors. Just like a submarine! The outer door closed and the inner one opened. Took ages for everyone to come in.

The inside of the van was maxint, all gadgets and dials and things. Tim took Poccom 3 from us and mounted a connector on the bare ends of the lead, then plugged it into the amplifier.

Yes, in fact he made a Handshake with their own computer further along, a huge console it was, so that the others could have their own screen display. There were seats and everything, and hot and cold cupboards with tea, and food, and whisky and things.

And suddenly Tim said right, well now, it's eleven thirty, we'd better start if you're ready. Start! We stared at each other, our minds had gone completely bootstrap. Holy shit, what the gigavolts would we do? Xorandor, Xorandor!

So you called to him too, Jip? Tim placed us in front of Poccom 3, which looked so tiddly against all those instruments and mike. You can talk or type, he said, and we couldn't understand, in fact we hadn't even thought that Xor 7 wouldn't and couldn't be handshaked the way Xorandor was.

But Tim explained, the big computer's equipped to translate his voice into softalk and your softalk back into voice. I gather you have a secret computer code to reach him, so I worked that way. It wasn't necessary or even desirable with the previous people who came, they couldn't have softalked. You'd better decide who starts. Do you know what to say?

Of course, you bluffed, oh yes you did, Jip. Ladies first, you added gallantly and smiled at your slow-witted twin with enormous affection.

14 LOOP

You typed the addresses, Zab, and that seemed to have non-plussed him. The earlier exchanges with the actor and so on had been on vocal. There was a long blank on the screen and we looked at each other, thinking, it's not going to work.

Then the answer suddenly flashed yellow on the screen, translated from his vocal presumably. Here's the printout:

> WHAT BLOODY MAN IS THAT? I DID COMMAND THEE TO CALL TIMELY ON ME, YOU'VE ALMOST SLIPPED THE HOUR.

We looked at each other. Were we in for another loopy *Macbeth* session? It was a whole term and a summer since we'd acted it in the school play.

And you typed JIP AND ZAB.

Pure nerves, Jip. Anyway, the answer came pico:

> HOW NOW, YOU SECRET BLACK AND MIDNIGHT HAGS, WHAT IS'T YOU DO? YE SHOULD BE MEN AND YET YOUR WORDS FORBID ME TO INTERPRET THAT YOU ARE SO. ARE YE MEN OR NOT?

And you typed, NO MY LORD. WE ARE CHILDREN. More blank, so you typed WE ARE KIDS. Here's the printout.

ACKN ID PLS
ID ZIP
SYNTAX ERROR

That's always aborting, some computers say FATAL ERROR. Either way one hunts desperately to what one's done wrong.

Yes, computers are like that, Zab, it's always the user's fault.

Huh, in theory we'll all get out of the habit of blaming the other for everything. But in practice the new hitech elite doesn't seem even to strobe such a quality of humility. Only the users, the new slaves.

Oh spikes, Zab, debug. Anyway he came in with the explanation. And without any of the subroutines like S for Statement, Declaration, Endec etc, since in fact he was on vocal, it was edge-triggering:

> IF ZIP THEN VOCAL ID ELSE FALSE
> ACKN
> Zab on vocal. Zip calling Lady Macbeth. Hello, Lady Macbeth.
> ID TRUE HELLO ZIP
> Hello, Lady Macbeth. We have come to wish you a Happy New Year.

That was diodic, Zab. Considering our minds were empty when we started.

The whole thing is to start, anything will do, then ideas come.

> CANT FIND HAPINIOOYEA
> LET HAPPY = JOY. FUL. LET NEW = ANOTHER AS IN NEWFILE.
> LET YEAR EARTH ROUND SUN
> DWELL IN DOUBTFUL JOY. TOMORROW AND TOMORROW AND TOMORROW
> Quote, creeps in this petty place, from day to day, to the last syllable, of recorded, time, endquote. You see we know it too. But it's only a quote, Xor 7, not a remark.
> CANT FIND KREEPS CANT FIND PETI CANT FIND SYLLABLE
> MEN HAVE POYZND ME WITH A WICHIZ BROO
> GOTO ZIP
> HELLO ZIP HAPPY NEW YEAR. IN 20 MIN 37 SEC SIGNIFYING NOTHING.
> ACKN.
> BUT TIS STRANGE, AND OFTENTIMES TO WIN US TO OUR HARM THE INSTRUMENTS OF DARKNESS TELL US TRUTH TIS TRUE MY LORD. LOOP.

That's where you had the diodic brainwave, Zab, when you saw he was going back to *Macbeth* like a record.

Well it was worth a try, though he might have been beyond intaking any instructions.

FROM THIS MOMENT THE VERY FIRSTLINGS OF MY HEART SHALL BE THE FIRSTLINGS OF MY (P 0.23 sec) BOMB

Why, worthy Thane, you do unbend your noble strength to think so brainsickly of things. Why should you play the Roman fool to die on your own sword?

CANT FIND ROMAN CANT FIND SORD

Never mind.

CANT FIND NEVERMIND

Tis safer to be that which we destroy than by destruction —

DWELL IN DOUBTFUL JOY. (P 0.31 sec) I'VE DONE NO HARM.

BUT I REMEMBER NOW I'M IN THIS EARTHLY WORLD

ENDLOOP

HELLO ZIP HAPPY NEW YEAR

That may have been a brainwave, Jip, but it didn't last, and didn't get us much further. We'd got him out of one text but not out of the main ELSE groove.

Yes. Xorandor seemed to think that the number plus our voice pitch would be enough, but stubs, surely we had to say something. He must have underestimated the degree of circuit-damage the HF gas would cause, if in fact he understood the formulas and the last bit of that meeting. Did he know our words for whatever chemicals were mentioned? Or even the word gas, or the term chemical warfare?

We were both, as he once said, non-plussed, terrified to press the SOFTKEY to this secret memory, or whatever it was, too soon, and then have nothing to say.

Xorandor never told us what to say. Or perhaps he thought we'd come back the next day but of course we couldn't. Or maybe he just trusted our smart terminal, or childish prattle, or however he viewed it.

And he wasn't wrong, Jip, cos something did suddenly come to you.

In a flash. In fact all that we're talking about took a nanosecond of screen silence.

So you pressed the SOFTKEY. There was no acknowledgment, but this time the silence seemed somehow equivalent, in our minds, as if we were now in touch with a dream zone.

A purely subjective impression, Zab. But at least there was screen silence and not another Shakespearean outburst.

And you typed GOTO ANCESTOR, then LET ANCESTOR = BOMB. ACKN PLS.

ACKN
COMPARE NEXT DECLARATION NO SYSTEM CAN LAST INSIDE REACTOR
SYNTAX ERROR

That was a bootstrap moment, Zab. Then you whispered, you forgot the quotes for the DEC. So, repeat performance.

HOW DO YOU KNOW?

We stared at each other. Was he playing the Kripke game or was it a scientific question? We didn't have time to play the game and we looked at dad. Both he and Biggerdad were nodding hard, but mere authority wouldn't be proof for Lady Macbeth as computer, nor as mad terrorist, only for Xor 7 as friend or as lost child, which is what he was. But you bravely went on with your idea, Jip.

GOTO FOOD
S1 IF MEN FEED YOU AND YOUR BROTHERS
CANT FIND BROTHERS
SCRATCH BROTHERS REPL KIN

You panicked here, didn't you Jip?

No.

Well, you seemed to hesitate about finding words he'd understand, as if he were Xorandor in the old days, though it doesn't show on the printout.

THEN FUMES IN REACTOR WILL END YOUR SANDBITS ENDIF
END S1
FALSE IF
S2 IF YOU STAY IN REACTOR THEN YOU WILL DESTROY YOUR SILICON CELLS END IF END S2

TRUE. ANDOR TRUE IN 14 MIN CAN BLOW UP.

We felt suddenly cold and were aware of a shudder among the grown-ups and Tim tensed behind us.

Then you took over, Zab, this bit was you, on vocal. In fact you'd never let go of the mike.

> Lady Macbeth, you said five, tomorrow morning, Go to promise. Remember, when we promised, word of honour, trust?
> NEW HONOURS SIT UPON ME. IF I SHALL CLEAVE THE ATOM
> THEN IT SHALL MAKE HONOUR FOR YOU. YOU'RE HERE IN
> DOUBLE TRUST TWO TRUSTS TWO VOICES 1 + 1 = 0
> CARRY 1 = 10
> OR ART THOU BUT A DAGGER OF THE MIND, A FALSE
> CREATION?
> Proceeding from the heat-oppressed brain LOOP
> THAT MEMORY THAT WARDER OF THE BRAIN, SHALL BE A FUME, WHO DARES. I DARE NOT WAIT UPON I WOULD END WAIT UNTIL ELSE END UNTIL ENDIF DEC QUOTE WE BUT TEACH BLOODY INSTRUCTIONS WHICH BEING TAUGHT RETURN
> To plague the inventor. Endquote Endec ENDLOOP

It was obviously FATAL ERROR to call him Lady Macbeth, Zab, it set him off again.

> GOTO PROMISE
> PROMISE MAN NEGATIVE
> But children, no, scratch, kids keep promises. Kid promise positive. Compare: you and Zip. Let you kid, assign value Zip. If you Zip then your promise has Eqv value positive.
> I HAVE CROWN VERY BIG, ZAB.

Wow, you were so excited and flabbergast at having been personally recognized, you almost lost contact.

Well, that's why we were two, like simultaneous interpreters. In double trust. You came in pico, snatching the mike from me. But you went much too far.

> IF so, THEN you are a big kid, like Zip.
>
> ACKN
>
> GOTO race. IF you live THEN your race will also live, here or on Mars.
>
> ON MARS WE CANNOT LIVE.
>
> Yes you can. GOTO Olders. Olders instruct quote Men must send you back to Mars unquote.

What on earth got into you, Jip? Inventing an instruction from the elders on Mars? Highly dangerous if he goto'd and didn't find it! Were you hoping to program him to find it?

Yes.

But why? What for?

Your brain must be as bugged as his was. It made perfect sense at the time, anyway. Even if he gave in and allowed himself to be taken out of the reactor without suddenly changing his mind, what could the scientists do with him? He was more than a dangerous terrorist gone berserk, he was a potential atom bomb. Like those suicide trucks, to the nth power.

So it was okay for him to do it on Mars, and disrupt the ecology of the solar system?

Better than here, detected at once, he would have set off starwar, and that would be the end of all ecology. Zab, we've been through this before.

Anyway, there was a movement on the bench. We both looked round and saw dad and Biggerdad exchanging glances and Biggerdad started writing something down. In a second he was behind us. It was awful having him breathing down our necks like that. Then he went back. Maybe Tim sent him back. Meanwhile the screen had stubbornly rehashed the same sentence but without the pronoun: ON MARS CANT SURVIVE. And you stubbornly continued your fantasy into the mike.

> Yes you can survive, repeat you can survive. You know now how to build a reactor. You will save your race. Olders instruct quote IF men send small load of Uranium 235, THEN you can make small reactor and produce all the food you and your ancestors need ENDIF endquote. IF so THEN nodules can fetch over very great

distances ENDIF Acknowledge please.

There was a long screenblank, well, long by computer standards. Tim looked at his watch anxiously and when you stretched your neck to see he showed us: 0004! It was the new year. What a way to see it in.

Then suddenly a voice came shrilly through on the loudspeaker. He must have had a way to block the translation into softalk. And of course with the actor he'd been on vocal only. Hexadex high-pitched it was, more like a squeak.

Jumping nukes!

Leptons leapt inside us and we looked at each other gung-ho with delight. Then it shrieked again:

I don't want to go to Mars.

It spoke so high and fast! We were astonished, Jip, but weren't we also a bit disappointed? It sounded like Xorandor in the early days but quicker and squeakier. Perhaps we'd somehow expected a deeper voice from the deepset memory. But we seemed to be on another register.

We must have jumped out of that deep memory, Zab, if we can call it that, when you called him Lady Macbeth, though we hadn't altered the address or touched the SOFTKEY again to come out of it.

Yes, and we didn't know whether touching it again would get us back in or get us out if we were still in. Or perhaps with speech he'd veered from one memory to another? As we do, surely? Anyway, Jip, you answered nano. Why not, you said, it's your home, isn't it? And you added dangerously, Don't you love your home?

Cant find luv. Scratch. Find love. Quote the love that follows us is, our trouble, thank as love, which we. Sometimes. Endquote.

And off he went again, we thought the tomorrow speech would come next. And then you piped in, Zab, with great presence of mind, from the sleepwalking scene.

No more o' that, my lord, no more o' that, you mar all this with starting.

And in he came with the doctor's reply in that high squeaky voice: Go to, go to, you have known what you should not. And the computer flashed SYNTAX ERROR and we went into helpless giggles.

While the world waited upon our heroism.

Oh, the world. The world didn't even know we'd been taken there after all.

It was screwboole, Zab, but you went on:

> You have spoke what you should not, I am sure of that, heaven knows what you have known.
> Isotopes. Cant find hevn. Who is hevn? Go to, go to —
> SYNTAX ERROR
> bed, what's done cannot be undone.
> But it can be undone, it can. We are your best friends, can't you, trust us?

This is where you took the risk, Jip, and pressed the SOFTKEY again. It *seemed* to work, and also seemed not to. Look.

> Trust. I remember trust. You're here in double trust. So you come, from, as you call him, Xorandor.

We weren't sure if this was an accusation or a recognition so we were cautious.

> Yes. Xorandor. Your daddyjohn.
> Non daddyjohn, me, we. He non trust. I wanted. What did I want? He, warned me. My daddyjohn. I have, not heard. I, yes, he warned. To nonthink. So brainsickly of things. Noble strength. Roman fool. And die. Cant find roman on your own sord cant find sord I think, brainsickly.
> Why don't you, let us, help you? We want, to help you. We can, get you, out, and you will be well, and happy, and go home, and be a hero.
> Hero. Yes. But first, I have, task. To do. At 0500. Or was it 0300? I forget task what it was.
> THEN LET it be forgotten. SCRATCH task. It can't have been very,

important.

Unscratch. I remember. I explode. Not very important.

We were going round and round. You seemed to give up in despair, Jip, you put your head down on your arms and your fists were tightly clenched.

And you took over, gently, avoiding the word *die*, which seemed to mean nothing to him, in fact even Xorandor only used explode once, in the ancestor story.

But if you do that, best friend, you will not save your race, you will explode, finish, end, and we shall explode too, my mum and dad will explode, and everyone.

There was a sob in your voice, Zab, and in fact your face crumpled up like when we were little when you were about to blub. The difference was you were trying hard not to. And Tim passed you a big handkerchief.

And the voice suddenly screeched No! And we all jumped. Tim leant forward to adjust the volume, then the voice went on at the previous level, but high and whining instead of high and squeaky. It seemed to be referring to some inner ops of his own.

Cant find package procedure. Cant find package. I want to go home. Cant find home. Let package equal I, if I then endif. Get me out of endif I want to go home.

You will go home, you will. Just be patient, old friend, and WAIT. It may take some time to get you out.

I want to go home. Get me out of here.

We promise. You will be got out. Will you promise, on your side, word-of-honour, that you won't do anything, you NOT DO anything at all, only WAIT. DO Ø UNTIL we can get you out?

And you were typing the main instructions at the same time, Jip, just to make double sure.

PLS ACCEPT PROMISE PLS ACKN

Acknowledge accept promise. Accept word of honour Zab, word of Jip, double trust, word of honour, lady-macbeth, must trust, double, trust. What is that noise?

He was shrieking again! You'd given a long slow sigh of relief into the mike.

Nothing, old friend, I was giving a great big sigh, of happiness, you know, happy, good. About our trust. Ah what a sigh is there, the heart is sorely charged.

And suddenly we saw the piece of paper in front of us. Biggles must have put it there. We still have it. It said: tell him it may take 8 to 10 hours and you will come back at noon to tell him what to do to help us get him out.

Yes and you were blabbing:

We are so happy. Thank you. We have to go now, to see, about, getting you out, you know. We'll be as quick as we can. Goodbye, trusted friend.
Goodbye, Zab.
Jip here. I must tell you, DECLARATION, quote it may take 8 to 10 hours, or else more, to get you out, so we'll be back, around 12, midday, to talk to you.

Mum stifled a cry and there was a movement on the bench.

And to tell you what to do. To help us, you know, get you out. UNTIL 12 tomorrow midnight PLS WAIT UNTIL MIDNIGHT TOMORROW. We'll come at midday. Endquote Endec. Goodbye.
Goodbye Jip. Until then. We wait.

Then there was silence, rather leptonic after all that, while Tim hovered over his instruments to make sure. After a bit he switched off the contact.

In a second mum was hugging us and blubbing. Biggles had picked up a phone and was talking rapidly. Dad was standing by, smiling. You'd grabbed mum to yourself, Jip, and were dancing with her up and down and shouting we've done it! We've done it!

In fact we hadn't really, it wasn't the tosh at the end, it was the

SOFTKEY. We *had* jumped out of it and when we returned into it, whatever we'd said would have worked.

It's easy to say that now, Jip.

And then you flipped out.

Well it was so stuffy in there.

Garbage, it was air-conditioned. You crumpled to the floor. Very dramatic, and a crackerpack way of getting all the attention.

You bootstrap you!

Well it worked. Mum screamed, She's fainted! And dad picked you up in his arms and sat down while mum unbuttoned your cardigan and shirt. Tim dashed to a cupboard and got out a thermos of iced water and dabbed you with it, and later brought out a thermos of tea, and some biscuits and sandwiches.

And then there was a long argument — well, not all that long really but it seemed long, in fact mum gave in surprisingly soon. Biggleton said we couldn't go home yet, he'd arranged for us all to stay at an army barracks just outside the immediate danger zone, and she asked why, after all we'd been through and so on and so on.

And he explained that the extracting of Lady Macbeth from the reactor would be a long and difficult job, and we couldn't risk him getting frightened or feeling aggressed. And that he might not accept instructions from other voices but ours, especially as we'd now promised. A promise was like a programming, he said, and Lady Macbeth was now so programmed. He'd got bigger, perhaps he couldn't come out the way he'd gone in, and they needed his cooperation, to tell us where he is, if he can, and give us his measurements, and to attach himself magnetically to a descending rod, or let himself be grabbed by strong pincers and not move.

And that's roughly how it all happened. Since you've told the advance plan so well in summary Jip, we can skip the execution. Mum gave in and dad said Paula you're marvellous or something, and we all got into our white suits again and came out, two by two, the captain and the lieutenant were back, waiting outside, and we were carried into their headlights. We woke up the next morning on hard pillows and hard beds, covered with khaki blankets, in a drab grey room full of empty beds also covered with khaki, but made up, empty, just as mum and dad came in with trays! They'd got up early and sneaked out. Yippee, breakfast in bed, you squealed. Nothing like joining the army.

15 WAIT

The whole village of Carn Tregean must have heard the helicopter arrive around noon the following day.

Wait a sec, Zab, we can't completely skip that New Year's Day, it was even more hexadex, we'd never been in a nuclear power station before, let alone in a reactor.

On top of, not in. So it's you who wants to go into details now rather than summarize in a sentence.

Be fair, Zab, we both did lots of detail.

Okay then: mum nearly had a fit when she heard we wouldn't be in the van, but on top —

That we *can* skip, Zab, there's summary and summary.

And even summary. Okay, you're dying to describe the reactor, so, BEGIN.

They'd fixed our protective gear so's we could walk in it. The main hall was empty. Tim led us up a flight of stairs and along corridors to a control room where a man sat all alone. It was Mr Jenkins, the director.

And Tim called him captain of a sinking ship, and he said he hoped not, the reactor was silent except for the hum of the cooling gas system, but there was a skeleton crew around. All the same, it was very eerie for them, he said.

And he led us through lots of heavily shielded doors marked KEEP OUT, and there were all sorts of pipes and cables in different colours, and we came to the turbine hall, but naturally the turbines were idle.

We stopped at a lift that seemed to take an hour to come down and a nanosecond to go up, and we stepped out into a small control room.

We were on top of the reactor.

Two men in white were there. We all removed our headgear for intros.

One was the robot-operator, the other a robot-engineer. Behind them there were thick shielding round glass doors, brownish, and the manipulator-control, and closed-circuit TV screens. And through the thick windows we could see the robot-cranes, and a master-slave manipulator. There were even some unused waveguides still lying at their feet. Tim told us he'd had to direct the robot-operator very carefully to assemble the waveguides, sitting on a bomb, he said it took hours and he'd never sweated so much for so long, especially inside that suit, with lots of false movements and retrials, to get the correct alignment for each part at three removes, from his own brain to the operator's to the robot's, assembling little tubes nine by five millimetres thin, can you imagine, and the horn antenna then had to be lowered into the reactor proper, carefully centered, and at one specific moment the crane had to hold everything in place while the master-slave screwed the flange to seal the porthole.

Creeping quarks, you're getting technical, Jip. Who's indulging in detail now?

There's detail and detail, Zab.

And even detail.

The whole point he wanted us to understand, Zab, was that in a sense this op should be easier, the waveguides were still in place, and all that had to be done was to ravish Lady Macbeth through that porthole, if he was still small enough. So it's important to visualize it. And if he hadn't been, there were volunteers on call to go into that top part, protected of course, five minutes at a time, to drill a hole. And that was why we had to be there, and not talking blindly in the van. We could watch it all on the screens used for changing the fuel rods.

Diodic, Jip. You do see the point of description, don't you? Though of course a would give it all in a few seconds.

No, Zab, a film would give each instrument in action.

Accept. We can describe it all if you like. Dad got out Poccom 3 and Tim interfaced it to the console. Mum was deathly pale.

No, Zab. Back to Carn Tregean.

It had taken five hours. Everyone was exhausted. Lady Macbeth had waited as promised and was now lying there behind the brown window, between a robot-crane and the master-slave manipulator. He looked so small and helpless.

Hogwash, Zab, he wanted to blow us all up.

In *comparison* with the robots, Jip, and also perhaps with what we'd imagined, him grown perhaps to Xorandor's size on all that food, or even half, think how tiny Uther Pendragon and Aurelius were, compared even to those born a month earlier.

But that's like babies and kittens and things, it slows clown later. Adults don't grow.

Not upwards anyway. But what's adult to them?

Let's just say he was about six inches across, maybe seven, and three or at most four inches high. In fact roughly what Biggles had calculated. And transportable. In a special ease that could be fixed at once. As we told him.

So we ate and slept with the army again, and the next morning we left by helicopter for Cornwall, us, mum and dad and Tim. Biggles stayed behind to take his precious charge to Harwell.

Which wasn't exactly 'home'. Did Lady Macbeth mean Mars, or back to the carn?

Swag knows, presumably Biggleton thought Mars, maybe, one day, meanwhile etc. The carn would be too dangerous, with all that food. He must be still waiting.

Anyway we arrived. Like conquering heroes. Poltroon had written a long article about the whole family scene that first night, and it had appeared in *The Evening Extra* at noon the next day, just as we were starting on the second op. He certainly sprang into fame out of it all, though he didn't know much, as the better papers soon found out. The audio-silence was still on. Within hours the whole press had got hold of it, all over the world, and there had to be a press release the next day that all was well. And the audioviz, frustrated by their silence, roared back into action. Oh and the evacuation was reorganized in reverse.

Yes, we saw it: from the air, all the roads towards Bristol black. It was nice doing the flight in daylight. The sea was wintry silvery.

There was already a crowd on the Socalled Promontory. It was freezing cold. Flashes, and forests of mikes, but Tim and dad ushered us through to the army car, saying no comment, no interviews. In fact we couldn't have said anything, could we, Zab? We were spooled out. That's the trouble with the media, they always rush in after the event, and get dead shots and recaps. And even when they're there, at a public event for instance and someone's assassinated the cameras miss it.

Jip! You're as morbid as the masses!

It's a statement of fact, not a wish. So we were rushed home.

And the next day, we weren't even allowed to see Xorandor, in case someone followed us. Which was spaghetti, with that high wire fence, and the little gate, and the guard hut.

Well, we were allowed, later.

Yes, but to say goodbye.

Because THAT was when dad decided to send us to this school in Bayreuth, sort of incognito, to protect us from becoming, as Alex had said, spoilt little brats. How or why he fell on just this place, where you see and hear about nothing but Wagner —

Through mum of course, she was a student with Frieda. You never listen to anything personal, Jip. Frau Groenetz told us early on that she was Frieda Meyerhofer and they acted together, she was always the comic or sinister foreigner.

She must have rattled it away in German, Zab, at the beginning. She promised to talk only German.

Okay. Anyway she said how she also gave up acting to get married.

Garbage. Women who do that want to do it, then regret it later. It's quite unnecessary these days. Especially in the leisure-industry. With a twenty-hour week, long studies and a twenty-year working life the air's got to be filled with noises and time with entertainment. So here we are, Johann, or Hans, and Kätje Mannheim!

This would be a good place, Jip, to put in those summaries of the press dad made us write while waiting to come here. Or at least one.

Nice of you to say 'us', Zab, you were far better at it.

Better at summary than you? That's a new one.

It was unspooling, we'd never read newspapers before, they seemed so old-fashioned. So itsybitsy, all the headlines and beginnings crowded on the first page, to be continued on various other pages, so we were always going back and forth, till we thought of cutting them out.

Well, TV's pretty disassembled too, Jip, and radio, as Xorandor pointed out. We miss him, don't we?

Yes. The alphaguys, as they were now called — oh, this one's only from the papers Poltroon brought down that night, so they don't yet know about us as miracle-solution. That's why dad chose those first, then later ones where our role gets dropped for larger questions. But this first one gives the tone.

Okay, Jip, into the mike it goes.

The alphaguys, as they were now called, or sometimes the beta-eaters, were immensely popular despite the danger from one of them, nicknamed gamma-gobbler to distinguish him as baddy from the others. One paper called Caesium 137 cheese, a dreadful pun, but it caught on for all their food, and a cartoon came out with an imagined Elizabethan Macduff offering Lady Macbeth a choice between caerphilly, cheddar and stilton, the caption saying his brother over the water was luckier, they had over four hundred varieties there. But the papers were also screaming for action, more information and fewer bland assurances. Some nations were demanding future offspring for nuclear waste disposal, *they* wouldn't be so careless with them. The French were boasting that their *alphage*, more affectionately called *Gros Bêta*, was perfectly normal, had learnt excellent French, and had not taken it into his head to spout distorted Racine. The Swiss were complacent, congratulating themselves on having built nuclear shelters in all blocks of offices and flats. The Germans were either strangely quiet or deadly serious about theirs, keeping to the name *die Alphaphagi*, and the Russians were totally silent. The Arab world was triumphant at the prospect of the nuclear solution to the energy problem having perhaps to be abandoned for terrorist risk, while Israel regarded her non-reception of an alphaguy from a friendly power as a national affront. As to the Third World, it was on the whole gleeful that Western technology had proved incompetent. The United States, whose Edison was of course an alpha-nice-guy, were as usual clumsily interfering all over the place. Flipping flipflops, Zab, that essay-style, doesn't sound like us at all.

No. And we didn't dare add that not a single paper mentioned the chemical attempt, and its failure, and high risk, since we only knew that from the Home Office meeting. Lady Macbeth's accusation could be put down to madness, and was, when we asked.

You know, Zab, it's a real bootstrap how historians write history, it's so full of things learnt later or known only to one ROM and not another. In a novel you can just drop any awkward bit that doesn't fit. Or put it into a madman's mouth.

Stubs, yes. Do you suppose that a character who's invented, then dropped, goes on existing?

Zab, you're screwboole.

No, Jip, you see, we're characters too, and we've been dropped from the story we're telling. FIFO, you said once, First In, First Out. We're FIFO-Storytellers, instead of FILO. How can we go on telling it, we don't know what's happening.

We can be readers of it, like everyone else, Zab.

Waste instructions.

Well, it's a world of waste. Let's try. We can see the press and the media here, and the *New Scientist*, at least dad didn't cancel that.

Oh, no, not more summaries! More passionate discussions about Mars, and Snicks, and the age and chemistry of the computer-creatures, and the computer-creatures as aids in the software crisis or transducer tech, as self-reproducers, as alphaeaters, as terrorists, and so on and so on. No doubt the experts have been busy as bees, and put them through a scanner to reconstruct their brain and find out how they can do what they can do.

Thunks, Zab, that *is* a summary, though an angry one. But in fact nobody else has been allowed to see Xorandor or the offspring, to do, er, you know, their own investigations. They all depend on Harwell handouts, or Saclay, or wherever, even the science papers, at least the popular ones. As for the real ones, the journals, we don't see them, but it must be all theorizing too. You see, the military must have wanted a look-in after the Lady Macbeth incident and clamped down on a lot of data.

So! What do you suggest? It's even worse than FIFO.

But Zab, we can't just ignore the public aspect. For instance we learnt a lot about the other side of ecology here. To dad and Biggleton it was all well within the safety limits, security precautions 500% tighter than for trains and planes, not to mention cars where the public accepts far higher risks, and cancer and so on, and ecologists were just ignorant nuisances. Yet gradually the scientists did have to admit that earlier statements had been over-optimistic. And all that.

Oh, please, Jip, not the nuclear debate. By the way, do you remember how we strained our eyes on that school expedition through the Fichtelgebirge? The *New Scientist* had said Germany had found a salty solution to nuclear waste, they dump the cylinders down these huge disused saltmines and then pour salt in all round them.

That was Kubler's specialty, remember?

Kubla Kahn, at the Harwell meeting?

His caves of ice.

Well there's supposed to be one at Mitterteich, towards the Czech frontier, not far from here. We wondered if Siegfried, or whatever they've called him, Xor 3, could have been put in a place similar to Tregean Wheal. We even got mum and dad to drive round there when they came over last summer, but we couldn't find it.

Last summer! And here we are in October and dad won't even let us go back for Christmas. As if we hadn't learnt German by now. Till it's all died down, he said, but it has.

Then he said when we've got rid of our computer-addiction!

He shouldn't even admit we have one cos kids with computer-addiction don't relate with their parents and imagine their computer loves them and has a mind of its own!

And Xorandor has!

A *deutsche Weihnacht*, he wants us to have, and on to the end of the school year!

He did say *maybe* at Easter, but you bet they'll come out again here. Mum says she misses us dreadfully but she's got up an amateur drama group in Roskillard and she's having great fun. By the time we get back it'll be a year and a half away! And two years since we first discovered Xorandor!

Fact is, Zab, all these things scientists are supposed to learn from Xorandor are pure spec, cos they'd require his cooperation, which he now refuses. Xorandor is silent, and so are his offspring.

And nobody's interested in their reactions anyway. You'd think that after the Lady Macbeth disturbance someone would be interested in them as other than pure chemistry, pure electronics, or pure romance. The linguists, for instance, or the philosophers, after all there was meaning behind all those words.

Those exchanges were never published, Zab.

True. But the questions could still be asked.

Perhaps they are, we don't see everything.

Oh, it's all so frustrating! All we get are popular articles gushing twaddle about their *Weltanschauung*, without even asking if they *have* a vision of the world, or any vision at all. No one seems to be able really to imagine a pure braincreature, with none of our physical abilities and so also none of those disadvantages, and with its own form of binary or maybe trinary differencing –

What do you mean, Zab, trinary?

Maybe nothing. A butterfly, that needs a better data-net than ours is now. He may be a superdecoder or a superspy but he's sort of neutral, though not quite like a machine, more like he'd, sort of, come and, reversed all our, traditional, oppositions, and questioned, all our, certainties, through a flipflop kind of, superlogic. But that makes no sense. The butterfly's gone, words are so heavyfooted. We've been so stupid and incompetent, Jip, we didn't ask any of the right questions!

Well, as far as we know from here, no one else did either. And now he's not answering any. And the computer and other experts only had dad's and maybe other tapes done from vocal to go by, we took all our floppies with us.

Yes, why did we, Jip?

Well, dad wanted them, when it came out we'd been soft-talking. We pretended it was only very recent. Don't you remember? We thought we'd done enough co-op, especially as we were being sent away as a reward.

D'you think he wanted to punish us?

Dad? Whatever for?

Well, for discovering Xorandor, for having this sort of, special, relationship, if there's anything left of it. For taming Lady Macbeth, more by luck than cunning, it's true, and with Xorandor's help. Remember he wanted to go himself, at first.

To protect us, Zab. You mean, he'd be jealous?

Not consciously.

Oh, there you go again with your dangling psychorefs. There was never anything so loopy as that Dr Marlowe.

At least she didn't try to poison him with chemistry. Or maybe they discovered about the bug.

Who, they? What bug?

The bug in the ceiling lamp.

But we removed it, Zab, before we left.

Maybe they knew before.

Itsybitsybytes! Mummy knows everything, her little finger tells her, and daddy even more so! Don't be a dummy, Zab, he'd have said.

Maybe.

And talking of God, it's the zanier side of all this that's reflected in the press at all levels. The bishops and priests are buffering on about who created Xorandor and his kind, and the fundamentalists of every religion are chasing all refs to stones in the Bible and the Koran and whatever, and reinterpreting them.

After all, Jip, it's basically the same question as the one Andrewski asked at Harwell, remember, about something setting it in motion. Oh, and there's another question he asked, which we thought spaghetti, which is cropping up among the cranks, remember, why the tip of Cornwall. Well, some oldtime punkies and other sects are asking the same in a loopier way, why did he choose the carn? Answer: he *knew* it was or had been sacred, stone spoke to stone and he sort of hovered like the Holy Ghost and found his own. You know some people have been discovering ultrasonic sound in the stone circles, and they say earlier peoples were less deaf than us and could hear it, that's why they worshipped there, and built circles, or vice versa, and maybe it's the same with carns. You're not listening, Jip.

It's trappy you know, Zab, nobody talks of Lady Macbeth any more, or even Xor 7, or of the Mars project.

That was all in your head, Jip, and none of our conv with Lady Macbeth was ever let out.

No, but Biggleton took note. If it was regarded as a solution for Xor 7, surely NASA would have begun to plan another Mars probe, and that would surely be public.

Bighead. As for Lady Macbeth, we programmed him on SOFTKEY to wait, and presumably he's still waiting.

You bighead. We programmed him to wait till midnight the following night. Any further waiting must be either on orders from Xorandor or because his circuits are already too far destroyed. Then he'd be what we call a vegetable, except that he's mineral. It's all so illogical, so unfair, Zab, dad can't get anything out Xorandor, nor can anyone else, and we who might just still be able to talk with him are sent here into public exile.

Public? Seems pretty secret.

Meaning that we depend on the media just like the public.

And that's what narks you, Jip, being just an ordinary member of the public? No longer privileged?

It narks you too, Zab, you said so. Dad might at least inform us of what's going on in his own circles, as he used to before, instead of just adding hasty loving notes and feeble jokes and work entreaties to mum's letters.

Dad, you know, is probably just as out of it as we are. Jip! That's it! He was dropped by the big boffins early on, and took it out on us! Poor dad.

Poor us! We're storytellers without a hero, without our bugs and spies and xorandic correspondents. We're not even autobiographers since we've dropped out of our own story. Nothing is happening, Zab.

Something is happening to us, Jip, we're growing up. Even storytellers can change, during the story.

What on earth do modern historians do, Zab, when history seems to stop?

They wait.

Until something happens?

Until they discover that something has been happening all the time, away from their camera-eyes, unbeknown to them.

16 SCRATCH

The bombshell, now that it has come, is its own opposite, Zab was right. And she was also right that it had been happening unbeknown to us, all the time we were wondering and talking, had already happened in fact.

It's trap being out of it like this. I guess dad wanted us to grow out of the obsession but on the contrary, ignorance feeds it. We've lost our spies, which gave us what others thought. The magic stenographer, Zab said Dostoevsky called it. But in fact we weren't really dipping into what people thought, only into what they said, which is much less difficult. That's what's bothering Zab right now, how do we know minds other than our own. She's plunged in philosophy, of all useless things. Leads nowhere, it's not taught after school any more, so it can only be a hobby, like literature. She discovered that what dad called the Kripke game, which he used only to teach us accuracy, came out of a book by a philosopher called Kripke on another, earlier philosopher called Wittgenstein, who wrote in German, and it's a paradox or something, and he also wrote about how do you know that there is or isn't a mind behind other people or even stones. Episte, mology, it's called, but if it's so serious about questioning knowledge, how can one *know* about epis, temology?

Well anyway, lost interest in our non-storytelling, and even when the story broke she said go ahead on your own for a bit. Unfair, with only the media to go by.

It's true I had begun to spark up a bit after reading a cautious article in an October number of the *New Scientist*, based on a scientific report by Professor Kubler, obviously the same who was at the Harwell meeting since he wrote as one in charge of studying *Alphaphagos* 3. It's funny, we always called each offspring Xor, and I believe that was passed on by Biggleton, but these scientists seem hexadex careless about naming, which is so important in computers. Come to think of it, there's hardly a character in this story that isn't referred to by at least two names.

The existence and sharing-out of these offspring had been made public since the hoohah, so reports had to be public too, more or less. This one concerned the possible movement of Xor 3 while still small, an aspect which had always interested me. I remember Xorandor telling dad that he needed very little food, but more, 'to, do, to, send, stone, to, move, very, slow'. I've just checked it. No one seemed to have taken that up, dad himself got more triggered about storage and the superconducting ring. Even Lady Macbeth's hitchhiking lark got a bit lost in the panic and depanic, and seems to have been regarded as exceptional, due to special conditions with 'moving food'. But 'moving food' occurs elsewhere, here in Germany for instance where they store waste in saltmines. And obviously Xorandor wanted his offspring to be mobile, or at least removed from under him.

Anyway, I tried to get hold of the original article, so as to have something at first hand, but couldn't. The school refused to borrow it for me from the Interlibrary System, said I wouldn't understand a *Wissenschaftlichen Beitrag*. The public library in Bayreuth promised it through Computer Data Bank but failed somehow, maybe it was on some semi-secret list.

The gist of it was that the capacity of the *Alphaphagi* to send nodules and to extract specific radioactive products was now well documented. The isotopic separation seemed to be done physically, by particle bombardment, and not chemically, by collision with an electron-hungry atom. But the real point of this more popular version was that the author had wanted to obtain the opinion of his English, French and American colleagues on other aspects: first, on their tendency, if it was one, to concentrate on specific materials, especially Plutonium and fissile Uranium, and secondly, the possibility that they may sense specific isotopes at longer distances than we had supposed.

I don't know whether the 'had wanted' of the English article was a 'would have' in German and implied a criticism of his colleagues for not listening to him. Judging by the time it takes, according to dad, to get an article out in a scientific review, it could hardly have been researched, sent, published and then trickled through to a popular scientific weekly, however on the ball, in ten to twelve months. The reference, come to think of it, is oddly vague. Perhaps the learned journal doesn't exist and Kubler chose to be indiscreet, for reasons of his own (pique, urgency, ambition, weakness) directly to the weekly.

Creeping quarks! I'm getting bogged down in itsybitsybytes, just like Zab. Scratch last para.

We know they can attach themselves to moving vehicles, the article went on. And Alphaphagos 3, oh, thunks, I'll call him Siegfried, was tending to move in his enclosure more than anticipated. When they searched for him he'd answer to his two guards but to no one else. Kubler referred back to earlier reports he'd made, with graphs showing movements, intake, the results of various experiments with different materials and so on, and interrogations when Siegfried was still talking. His earlier reports on language acquisition and adaptation to new environment had led to fruitful exchanges with colleagues, but not the later ones. He had tried to see Biggleton at Harwell, and while lecturing at San Francisco he had seen Professor Andrewski in Los Angeles, who had kindly driven him out to his High-level Radioactivity Processing Center in the Mohave Desert. Beyond Twentynine Palms. Yes, Kubler was being indiscreet on purpose. Edison was kept there, in a two-acre compound, a very large walled enclosure, with monitors everywhere, though not as near as they'd like. Food was brought on a remote-controlled electric trolley. But Edison hadn't budged. The Lady Macbeth incident was a freak, Andrewski said, this first generation were normal, and would remain so as long as they were kept on controlled food and left alone. Charlie Lampton, the young physicist in charge of him, had 'a terrific relationship going with him'. At any rate Kubler had not been able to get his point across.

But what exactly was his point? Was he trying to say that sooner or later there would be a serious energy depletion from alphaguys? Impossible, they needed so little. The article was so interwoven with indiscretion and caution that even the *New Scientist* reporter who translated and adapted it didn't seem to know himself what the main point was, and it was subheadlined more for 'human interest' than for any hypothesis or warning.

One concrete fact we did learn from it was that there had been more offspring. Part of the argument was that Andrewski had said there were so few of them, and that as far as we knew they cannot reproduce at all until they are fully grown. To which Kubler was replying, as far as we know, yes, but we do not know. We know only what Xorandor told us, and he'd said nothing about that. On Mars reproduction may have been minerologically slow, but here? Perhaps they reproduce after two years? Three years? Apart from this first generation there were Lady Macbeth and his two brothers. These three were now at Harwell. Then there were the five Xorandor had made in February, and three more in July (and dad never told us!), which were now distributed to other nuclear wastemakers who had applied, among them Switzerland, Canada and Australia. It's true there had been nothing since, but that was fifteen altogether, all of whom might reproduce sometime (nineteen in fact, with the two in Russia no one admitted to, plus Uther and Aurelius). We did not know whether this pace was the norm or a freak result of that sudden surfeit last year. But we should at least meet to discuss the implications.

Whether the article produced the desired meeting or not is anyone's guess. Something else was bothering me, no, had bothered me all along, in the whole Xorandor business, and I didn't know what, a butterfly, the flutter of an idea that had flitted through my mind here and there when talking to Zab, and would then be gone, I couldn't capture it with our data network of floating talk, I couldn't pin it down on a board to examine it. And Zab stays late in the school library and locks herself in her room till supper and again after. Loopy.

And then at last, in November, the full story broke, in the *Los Angeles Times* — some Californian super-Poltroon but extremely well documented

— then all over the world.

Edison had escaped from his compound in the Mohave Desert. After a search of the greyblue sand, square yard by square yard with all assistants, they had found a neat small hole through the furthest greyblue stone wall, an Edison-shaped hole, a perfect oval, horizontal, four inches wide, as if perforated by a machine. A laserbeam for instance.

They had searched outside the compound, still calling, then further afield by jeep equipped with survey meters. A repeat of the Lady Macbeth incident was suggested, very anonymously in the passive, but all power stations were functioning, and had in any case been carefully monitoring all fuel rod changes ever since. The Nellis Nuclear Testing Site was also thought of, but that was over two hundred miles away in Nevada, and no underground testing had been done there for years, only on an island off Alaska. But there were missiles buried in the desert, and military and ordnance stations right here in California, just north of Mohave, weren't there? (The article was written to imply that someone had been warned, though this could be the hindsight style journalists like to use, inventing a mysteriously hinted fiction.) There was nothing to do but inform the Atomic Energy Commission and ask for a large scale yet discreet military search from Twentynine Palms to Death Valley, and even into Nevada, on a two-hundred-mile front. The impossible, in fact.

The AEC didn't meet till the Tuesday morning after the disappearance on the Friday.

What Tuesday? What Friday? I looked back at the beginning and realized hexadex that all this had happened in September!

The leak had taken two months.

The military authorities, the article went on, had informed the AEC that very morning that a new experimental but low-power, purely tactical bomb had been assembled at Fort Irwin (inactive for decades) for a secret underground test in the old Nellis range in Nevada. The test had been made and the bomb had not exploded. The bomb was a dud. It had fizzed out, emitting quite a lot of radiation, which could only mean that it had not contained enough fissile material. Yet further investigation had shown that the fissile material had definitely been assembled. The sensors had indicated that the separate parts had indeed been brought together, yet the explosion had not occurred. Until someone came out with a convincing, safe, scientific explanation, it would be dangerous to bring out the contraption for examination, the risk of an above-ground explosion was too great, in fact, it might just conceivably explode below ground if some delayed reaction had by some unprecedented type of error been introduced. All monitors had been kept on. But one 'safe' explanation, when those responsible for Edison turned up at the AEC meeting with their story, could be that the escaped alphaguy had eaten up the Plutonium.

Edison must be found.

Someone suggested that Xorandor might be in touch with all his offspring and might be persuaded to give a fix, but Xorandor was apparently asked and had remained silent. Edison was found eventually, back in his compound.

One of the subheadlines was: *Did alphaguy neutralize atom bomb?*

Great commotion among both greens and redwhiteandblues everywhere, doves and hawks.

I said the leak had taken two months. But maybe it hadn't. Maybe the journalist knew at the time but took two months to make absolutely sure of his facts. He certainly seemed to know a hexadex lot of facts. And eventually government spokesmen spoke.

And I can't help wondering: could the leak have been arranged, very carefully, by Kubler himself? In his November article he says he went to see Andrewski. If we could find out when his San Francisco lecture was, presumably at Berkeley University, we could be more certain, but I think of it as a rather diodic hypothesis. Let's say he guessed at this very possibility, and tried to interest Biggleton and Lagache and Andrewski in vain. Let's suppose Edison disappeared while he was there visiting the lab — he may even have taken part in the search, boy, in the hot sun — *Komm mal her, Edizon! komm mal her*! A Hollywood version of Einstein, in a white suit, with a straw hat poached on the back of his head, Zab would at once provide.

No one else would know so many details except Andrewski himself, who wouldn't leak his own incompetence. Or his assistants, who surely wouldn't attend the AEC Commission. Kubler would have been brought by Andrewski as a co-expert who had just in fact come with his theories about movement and neutralization. And when they get there they hear that that's precisely what's happened. And later Kubler invites a journalist to his hotel room in San Francisco. Then, to cover himself, he writes this extremely cagey article in the *New Scientist*, saying nothing about neutralization but a lot about motion, isotopic preference, sensing from a distance, and reproduction.

I don't know what Zab would think. I've been pretty sarky about her fabulations I know. In any case, she'd want to understand why. A bit thick, she'd say probably, accusing two Germans of betrayal, De Wint-Bleich, and now Kubla Kahn, but they're completely different cases, and on different sides.

Though each time Biggleton is slow on the uptake! In any case the Germans are far more actively concerned with the nuclear arsenal than anyone else, they're bang in the firing line. Ancestral voices prophesying war! Anything that might bring or at least ambiguously.

I like my hypothesis. And, whatever the reasons, the most important aspect is surely that the whole thing is now, let's hope, in the public domain.

17 FULLSCAN

Naturally we pleaded and pleaded with dad to let us come home for Christmas and try and talk to Xorandor, but he was adamant. So, a *deutsche Weihnacht* it had to be. As if it were a punishment.

Knock it off, Zab. He just didn't think talking to Xorandor would help.

You mean he didn't like the idea that we can and he can't.

No, Zab, only that it's out of his hands.

Does Xorandor have hands?

Anyone who can do a Handshake has hands endjoke. But what could Xorandor do, especially if he'd in fact ordered it? The Lady Macbeth incident had been a danger, and unnecessary, a syntax error he called it. This is the opposite. Stacked heads! Hadn't you seen the implications? What use is philosophy?

No need to be rude, Jip. Anyway, dad's semi-maybe for Easter wasn't kept, they came over again, and took us to Vienna, *just* where the first negotiations were going on, it was absolutely bootloading.

Well at least the media sprang back into action.

Someone's going to have to summarize all these videotapes, don't you just love doing that, Jip?

Booles, we share.

Let's do it from memory while it's still fresh in our minds.

You get bogged down, Zab.

The triggering thing was to see some of the faces we only knew as names. Kubler appeared, and wasn't a bit like a Hollywood version of Einstein, as *you'd* imagined, Jip. More like a smooth young executive, beginning to thicken out on good living, or an estate agent or a car salesman.

Itsybitsybytes.

And of course he spoke German, so the comic accent idea collapsed.

The real crackerpack in all these discussions and interviews, Zab, was the open admission at last that the Russians also had two offspring.

Yes, called Marx and Lenin.

Well, that came later, when the Russians agreed to let a spokesman appear. At first it was much more cagey, in the passive, or just vague, the Soviet Government *was given, also obtained*, as if we'd been open and generous from the start.

But what was the point?

Philosophy doesn't seem to sharpen your political voltage, Zab, don't you see, if you want to force someone to negotiate you must show that you know what he thought you didn't, or let out what he knew you knew but thought you wouldn't let out, so that secrecy becomes futile, at least on that point. There was an article somewhere about secrecy and ignorance and suspicion being the real causes of war, and that hitech would soon abolish them.

Seems hitech also fosters them.

We're getting sidetracked again.

When it's you, you say we, when it's me you say you, Jip. But why don't we do that ARD tie-up with London and Paris? It was very early on, and almost between the people we'd got to know from that first Harwell meeting, so it was more fun, except that Biggles wasn't there. Nor were those top security men, Dougall, Gerwig and Tardelli.

Okay. There were a couple of scientific journalists instead, and the chairman was a German anchorman. You're right, it was rather prime seeing them, especially Andrewski, who was in London, though everything the French and English said came out in an overvoice in simultaneous German.

Andrewski was the biggest surprise.

Why? Of all people he had a right to be there.

Surprise to look at, loopy. Not at all a shortpalepodgy Slav with rimless glasses but —

Debug, Zab, argument-type-error. The French — it was Lagache and a new man called Janvier — hogged the conversation at once and said their team had hit on that very same possibility as Professor Kubler (so you see, he did warn someone) quite some time before, and had dutifully reported it to their government. As a result their military authorities had at once been informed and there was an immediate clamp-down while the scientists investigated the problem before sharing it with their allies, well, their partners. At first they had thought the sudden splash of publicity and public outcry was regrettable —

Here, there was surely a glance towards someone but cameras are never quick enough to show who unless he's named.

And even then they're at least seconds too late. But now the French considered that much good might come out of it.

The British were very quiet at first, represented in fact only by a scientific journalist, and of course Andrewski as second anglophone. Or was the journalist also a scientist, from Harwell?

Probably they were still recovering from the Lady Macbeth syndrome and studying that, so they hadn't thought of this new possibility and felt a bit bootstrap. Boolesup in fact, cos they had the most alphaguys and had discovered Xorandor.

Well, we did.

Then the chairman insisted that Kubler, presumably because he spoke German, should explain to the public how a nuclear bomb explodes or rather how it doesn't, which he painstakingly started to do.

But Andrewski interrupted — rather rudely considering the chairman had asked for this — dark Tartar type with narrow eyes, Andrewski was —

Debugger off. He had plenty of reasons to interrupt Kubler. He said the public had heard such explanations from experts for weeks, with diagrams in the papers, and that wasn't what they were there to discuss. There were, as he saw it, two separate questions. First the practical one of preventing such incidents. And second, a far more difficult political issue which our most subtle diplomatic circles, backed by scientific advice, were thinking about. The practical question was being studied, and pending the scientists' report, he proposed they should leave it aside. So then the Frenchman Janvier wholly agreed, and as to the second question it had itself two aspects: the neutralizing of our *force de frappe* by our own *alphages* (this was all translated but one could hear the French at times), as had occurred, in however minor a way, in the United States. And the neutralizing of enemy warheads. And as to this second aspect, there was no escaping the conclusion that, if *les alphages* could go anywhere, sending their nodules at vast distances to excavate isotopes, or attaching themselves to trucks, planes, and possibly even submarines, piercing walls and entering reactors, then there was no reason why they should not find, or even be programmed to find, Russian nuclear warheads and neutralize them. But since the Russians also had at least two, who might eventually reproduce, it must be obvious to anyone but the most perfect imbecile that the thing could work both ways. Hardly an example of the subtle diplomacy Andrewksi had mentioned. Come on, Zab, do your byte.

You said to debugger off.

Only from irrelevant description.

Why is the description of a reactor more important that the description of someone's face. A face also reacts. You yourself would have liked the camera on Kubler at a specific moment.

Boolederdash. You haven't described any faces reacting, Zab, you couldn't, from tapes, that comes through what they say. All you want is to mention that someone was blond or looked like a car salesman. Who cares?

It might be important. Frinstance, Toussaint Tardelli was a top French Security man, and Corsican, and Dougall ditto and a Scot. It'd be megavolt to know what they look like. The Corsican short, dark, florid, bon viveur, the Scot thin, reddish hair, and dour, but blushing easily. And Hair Earwig, their German opposite number, maybe a Bavarian? Large, fat and earnest. Wouldn't that be interesting, at least, mightn't it lead to something unexpected?

No, not with those clichés. But thanks for mentioning Gerwig. He wasn't there of course, but the German journalist did a spiel on what we know of the Soviet interest in the alphaguys. The Soviet Union, he said, is less interested than we are in the problem of waste, since they allow no protest marches and publish no information, besides, they have huge uninhabited territories. We had assumed they would harness the computer powers of their specimens to computer science, in which they perpetually lag behind, because the system is bogged down in red tape and doesn't allow for the unexpected flashes encouraged by private enterprise — creeping quarks, and these people talk of diplomacy! Let's hope it'll be practised by others.

Then the French came in again, it was Lagache, who said that before any of this had become public, their government had felt strongly that we could not have a situation where each side, while pretending ignorance, knows that its *force de frappe* can be neutralized by the other, yet can never know whether or not it has been, and where and to what extent, without, of course, perpetually dismantling each warhead to find out. Or exploding it. Therefore he himself had pressed his government to tell the Russians of the Californian incident, before it leaked out, as his team had thought it probably would sooner or later, though they were taken short by the soonness. We would then have shown honesty, always a good starting point for negotiation. If the Russians knew of it already from their own sources, then both bluffs would have been called, and if on the contrary they'd discovered they'd been caught napping in their technical thinking, *tant pis*, they'd get over that when faced with the facts and their responsibilities, as we would be seen to be facing ours. Well, we had lost that honesty initiative, thanks to the leak (ah, if only the camera had been on Kubler's face *reacting*!) but apart from that the situation remains exactly the same on both sides.

Except that we have more, Andrewski said.

His narrow Tartar eyes sharp and sinister.

Zab if you want to become a romance or spy writer you'll have plenty of time, but not here.

Boys in puberty! Aborted. *And* mean.

They have two, said Kubla Kahn, and could feed them up, like athletes, for better performance. And quicker reproduction. Besides, are we sure they have only two? Couldn't, for instance, three have been, er, obtained? Who was responsible for the gift? he added quickly.

The camera for once shifted fast on the Englishman, yes, he was from Harwell. He glared at Kubler and looked very flushed, and said with a pinched look that first Xorandor never made elementary mistakes in arithmetic and had told them he'd produced six. And Kubler said he might have lied, and the man said Xorandor had never lied yet, and secondly, Dr Biggleton's early reports and photographs showed only six cells hollowed out at that time. Four offspring for the West, two for Russia. That seemed to settle that one, but holy nukes, what innuendoes, no one outside those in the know about the theft could make head or tail of it.

On the contrary, Zab, journalists are smart terminals at detecting when something's being kept from them. Kubler must have done it on purpose. And the German journalist did ask, soon after, whether our good will and honesty hadn't already been shown, precisely in that gift, and he stressed the word, *Geschenk.* And everyone had to agree. Knowing it meant the opposite.

And Andrewski went rapidly on to say that he was empowered to suggest a first meeting in Washington, not yet at the highest level but with the scientific attaché from the Russian Embassy and any other experts they'd care to send, though all five foreign ministries would be represented. They would organize the meeting in collaboration. It would prepare the way for later top-level negotiations.

Yes, the Gipfelkinferenzen. That word Gipfel for summit is diodic, one really does see mountains. *Ueber allen Gipfeln ist Ruh.*

Then the Englishman from Harwell said his government feared that such negotiations could become as protracted and futile as those for the reduction of nuclear arms, which had gone on for forty years or more.

Better talk than explode, the chairman said.

But the Englishman persisted, saying that even the perennial disarmament talks had reasonably concrete and even highly technical agendas. But what, precisely, were we to negotiate over the alphaguys?

The purely scientific solution to nuclear waste, Andrewski said, verifiable and to be supervised by the International Atomic Energy Agency in Vienna.

But verification has been the stumbling block for decades, said the German journalist. Besides, the real thing to verify here would be their *non*-use for neutralization of each other's weapons, and Dr Lagache has told us why that is impossible. There was a baffled pause then everyone started talking at once and the anchorman put out both his hands.

The Englishman got the floor first, and spoke poker-faced, but perhaps as British humour to change the mood. Though no one ever understands it as humour, precisely because it's by definition poker-faced, there's no joke-endjoke in the eyes in the tone, as with the Germans or French. In any case it came through the interpreter.

Get on with it, Zab.

He said: I fear that the real negotiations may have to be undertaken, not with the Soviet Union, but with Xorandor. And we collapsed into giggles, remember, Jip? We had a simultaneous vision, at least you confirmed it afterwards, of five foreign secretaries sitting on rocks around the carn, with the name of their country on a slat in front of them, negotiating away in four languages with interpreters' booths like seaside cabins all round.

So we missed the beginning of Kubler's outburst, to the effect that they'd all gone *verrückt*, and let the first aspect — how to prevent further incidents, which ought to be questioned anyway — invade the diplomatic aspect. Surely the whole point of this new capacity to neutralize atomic warheads, without any possibility for either side to find out whether and where and how much, was its supreme value as argument for total nuclear disarmament. Surely we weren't going to negotiate, with anybody, least of all Xorandor, the *non*-use of this unexpected, *wunderbare* solution?

18 ALTER

Yippee! Home at last, Zab! Two years exactly since we first met Xorandor.

And the first thing we did was to ride out to see him, though dad warned us he wasn't talking.

For *he*, read Xorandor.

Oh it was so leptonic, that compound. Well, we'd seen it before, but we'd always remembered Xorandor as in the old days.

And now there was the guard hut and the high wire fence, and the little gate, and the guard had instructions to let us in. And we walked up self-consciously, but all random jitters.

You were especially afraid he wouldn't recognize your croak.

So you spoke first. Let's put on the tape.

Tape 73. Side 1. Rec. 1. 17 July. Printout.
Beginrec

Zab: Hello, Xorandor. Zip here.
Xor: Hello Zab. But Jip is with you.
Zab: Yes, but his voice has changed, it's breaking, er, becoming like daddyjohn's. But it is Jip.
Xor: Hello Jip. Let me hear your new voice.
Jip: Hello, Xorandor. It won't stay quite like this, it's in the process. Sort of fifty-fifty.
Xor: More forty-sixty into daddyjohn. Welcome home, Jipnzab. It has been five hundred and thirty one days.
Zab: You mean you counted!
Xor: I count everything, Zab, it is automatic, and available on call.
Jip: How are you Xorandor?

Xor: I am. I continue.

Jip: We were at school in Germany.

Xor: Yes. You told me. Wie geht es Euch?

Zab: Xorandor! You've been learning German! But how?

Xor: I listen to Radio Swiss International. They have 30 minutes news and comment in English, French, German and Italian. After a while, it's possible to decode.

Jip: Smart terminal!

Xor: You have substituted for jumping nukes, Jip. But the German and Italian don't fill up their halfhour with words, they have many, many minutes of mathematically trivial noise till the next language.

Jip: That's a diodic description of folk music, Xorandor!

Zab: But Xorandor, you *can't* have learnt *Wie geht es Euch* on the news, it's the familiar plural, for people you know very well. They say rather, *Guten Abend meine Damen und Herren* and things like that.

Xor: True. If so then from a play, or else interview. But I have much to tell you.

Jip: Do you know all that's been going on, since we left? Oh but of course you do.

Xor: My offspring cannot inform me of meetings any more, they are no longer present as specimens. But we are in constant touch. And I hear on the air.

Zab: How do you react?

Xor: I do not react. I register.

Jip: Have you registered a lot?

Xor: My voice is also breaking, from lack of use, but in the opposite direction, more towards the voices of my offspring. Have you brought Handshake?

Jip: Of course!

You scrambled over the wall, Jip. We were so happy. All was as before.

But all was not as before, Zab, as you know, and how are we going to tell it? Even though he decompiled and translated abstracts as he went, they filed by endlessly on the screen, from our first meeting onwards, recording light, pressure, someone's brain activity, and even all this was selected from continuous and simultaneous intake of other data, the way we breathe or perceive or circulate our blood and digest, even while we talk and think. We'd only reached the arrival of Pennybig when you interrupted. Here it is.

ZIP INTERRUPT XAND PROGRAM
XAND AWAIT INSTRUCTION
ZIP TO XAND
DEC 1 'WE HAVE TO LEAVE YOU FOR FOOD' ENDEC 1
REM VERY SORRY ENDREM
DEC2 'WELL COME BACK THIS AFTERNOON' ENDEC 2
REQ BUT PLEASE BE BRIEFER ENDREQ
XAND ACCEPT
REM 1 I WOULD ALSO PREFER IT ENDREM 1
REM 2 I WAS KEEPING PROMISE ENDREM 2
ZIP TO XAND
DEC 1 'WE ASKED FOR TOO MUCH' ENDEC 1
REM VERY SORRY BUT DIDNT KNOW YOU INTOOK SO MUCH AND KEPT IT ALL STORED ENDREM
Q HOW DO YOU FIND ROOM FOR SO MUCH STORAGE? ENDQ
XAND TO ZIP
A I SCRATCH WHAT IS IRRELEVANT END A
ZIP TO XAND
REM IT DOESNT SEEM LIKE IT ENDREM
XAND TO ZIP
REM YOU SOUND LIKE JAD AND BIGDAD 710 DAYS AGO BEGAN ASKING POINTLESS QS ABOUT MY INSIDE LIKE HAVING YOUR HEAD EXAMINED AS THEY SAY
EX 1 ARE YOU HISTORY-SENSITIVE? ENDEX 1 ENDREM
ZIP TO XAND
REM THEY MEANT ARE YOUR PROGRAMS SELF-MODIFYING

ENDREM

XAND TO ZIP

REM YES THEY EXPLAINED

ZIP TO XAND

Q AND ARE YOU? ENDQ

XAND TO ZIP

REM CONT

EX 2 DO YOU HAVE A VOLATILE MEMORY AND A SERIAL MEMORY AND A PERMANENT MEMORY AND A HIGH SPEED MEMORY AND MANY MORE MEMORIES AND MANY OTHER QS ENDEX 2

BUT ANY OF YOUR COMPUTER EXPERTS COULD HAVE WORKED OUT THE WHOLE SYSTEM FROM A FEW SAMPLES OF HANDSHAKE EXCHANGES THEY WILL LEARNT QUITE ENOUGH TO ADVANCE THEIR UIMS ENDREM

ZIP TO XAND

DEC 1 'WE DIDNT SHOW THEM TO ANYONE WE TOOK THE FLOPPIES — MEMORIES WITH US' ENDEC 1

XAND TO ZIP

DEC 1 'THANKS' ENDEC 1

DEC 2 'BUT THEY RECORDED EVERYTHING ' ENDEC 2

REM THE WORLD MUST KNOW BY NOW HOW WE FUNCTION ENDREM

DEC 3 'WE FUNCTION MUCH LIKE YOUR UIMS BUT BETTER' ENDEC 3

DEC 4 'THE ONLY DIFFERENCE IS THAT UIMS THOUGH MORE INTELLIGENT THAN MAN ARE MADE AND UNDERSTOOD BY MEN' ENDEC 4

DEC 5 'MY INSIDE IS ONLY INPUT FROM OUTSIDE' ENDEC 5

DEC 6 'A STRUCTURE IS NOT A STATIC PHYSICAL OBJECT BUT A PERMANENT SCRATCH PERMANENT REPLACE PERPETUAL TRANSFORMATION' ENDEC 6

S1 IF I CAN WORK OUT HOW YOUR BRAINS FUNCTION

THEN RECIPROCAL MUST BE TRUE END S1

ZIP TO XAND

DEC 1 'BUT ALL THAT YOU SAID CAME FROM YOU ALREADY TRANSLATED EITHER IN VOICE OR FOR THEM OR FOR US IN POCCOM WHICH IS ALSO A TRANSLATION' ENDEC 1

REM THAT SAYS NOTHING ABOUT THE DIFFERENT LAYERS OR FIRMWARE ENDREM

XAND TO ZIP

REM BUT SOFTWARILY WE ARE OBSERVED ENDREM

We glanced at each other and together said goodbye. He was not only punning but punning on Shakespeare. How and why could he listen to so much? And he was saying strange things, almost metaphysical things we didn't understand. Or perhaps you did Zab?

Not really, though it was triggering all right. That stuff about the inside being the outside and vice versa for instance. The philosophers seem to have been discussing that ever since Plato.

Plutoneeum! And haven't they got any further than that?

Oh, it gets very complicated, or perhaps they make it so, it gets a bit incomprehensible here and there. But it has to do, sometimes, with the voice being inside whereas writing is outside, a mere technique, and us losing our memories because of writing and since writing, and in a way computers make that worse, with their outside databanks and peripherals and terminals and floppies. We'll lose our memories even more, but now also our poor logic, except for an élite of progam experts. But Xorandor seemed different, sort of beyond all that, or outside it, no, that must be the wrong word, but for one thing it's his voice that's the peripheral, the late addition. It's as if he never passed through any of our problems at all.

If you mean philosophical problems then swags for him.

Philosophy is also metaphysics, Jip, and metaphysics is always ideological, a sort of conceptual clay that makes you read so much into his remarks and besides, let's get on.

Right. But we'll have to tell it, not show it, the whole thing went on all summer – what was left of it after that long German school year, till mid-July, it was grim. And we couldn't go every day, there were other things, and it rained, and so on.

But when we came back that afternoon, Zab, we went on foot. We wanted to walk along the ridge path and say hello to Uther Pendragon and Aurelius.

And they weren't there. Not where we'd hidden them anyway.

We searched and called, but decided not to waste more time.

So we asked Xorandor. And he said yes, they'd moved away. Offspring must always move as far as they can, by every possible means, while they're small enough. The problem then had been that they couldn't get out from under him while the other three were still there.

But why hadn't those moved off? Did that mean that he depended on humans to take them away? No, he said, he'd waited for those to be collected by daddyjohn, it had been a promise but daddyjohn hadn't turned up.

And then he told us.

Yes, the truth.

Or maybe another lie, we'll never know. If one lie, then two are possible, we thought. Or more.

No Jip. We do know, inside ourselves. The wonder is that others, and scientists too, believed the first, the only lie.

Well they didn't at the very start, Zab, remember Andrewski? And Biggleton that very first night, how cautious he was with dad? Treating him like a schoolboy.

Yes and no. He was drinking a lot of brandy. Dad's first-impression conviction, which came direct from Xorandor, did somehow get through to him and he got quite triggered. That's how first impressions, however wrapped up as suppositions, somehow get chemically transformed into deep-seated convictions that can then be proved mathematically and scientifically. The history of human knowledge is just that.

It wasn't quite like that. There *was* scientific confirmation here.

Which Xorandor faked. The Gigahertz messages for one, which weren't proof but helped to create a conviction of communication with a distant base, especially as he refused to discuss them and said he knew nothing about them. But above all the strobe chemical analysis. Please take the sample from the edge at x degrees — or whatever — he'd said cooperatively, where it will not harm my circuits. And they did. And he'd altered his isotopic composition at just that spot, to correspond to the dates of exposure on Mars and in space and on earth that he'd given. That seems the most hexadex thing of the entire story. And completely incomprehensible. Not only for how but for why.

As to the how, remember he's like a radiotelescope, Zab, he can calculate the universe whenever he wants to. And if he can excavate and separate isotopes he can presumably shuffle them.

So. He hadn't come from Mars at all. He said it wasn't a lie — or non-truth as he called it but an answer that had come quite naturally, to him — perhaps logically would be the better word — in answer to a supposition of Pennybig. Gwendolin, to him. He even asked why she never visited him. And of course we'll never know just what she asked, or how she framed her questions, since we don't have that conversation on tape but only her later version of it.

Nor would Xorandor give his version of it. He said it made her look non-intelligent to us and he had scratched it. Very odd.

No. He's peculiarly meticulous about some aspects of brain-interact, even though emotions have nil value, in fact don't exist in the system. Look at his attitude towards promises, which we regard as emotional statements. And trust. And presumably respect as part of trust. To him a promise is like an instruction. It has to do after all with truth-values, without which he can't operate.

And yet he lied.

Not a lie, Jip. A playful, or logical, confirmation, or even interpretation, of an expectation. Sort of telling people what they want to hear, in certain carefully evaluated circumstances. Their truth. She may have thought in terms of a small meteorite and within the lie she wasn't so wrong, since the scientists did too and that gave him the idea. Anyway, why does it matter?

Because he then kept it up. To *us.*

So that's it. Pride.

No, a need to understand. How can a computer give a playful answer, or even an ambiguous answer?

Why how? You know he does. We called him Xorandor, didn't we? Besides, even computer logic can contain ambiguities, for instance the *if/ then if/ then/else* sequence could be represented by two different flowcharts.

That was resolved by the *begin/end* delimiters, or *endif* and such.

It was only an example. There are also difficulties with influx notation. And you know very well that in a context-free grammar no general procedure exists for determining whether the grammar can be ambiguous in any one of every single case, however long one ran the program. The question is then said to be undecidable.

Thunks!

You don't agree? But —

Thunks and flippeting flipflops and leaping leptons and all! Zab, don't you see? The first Gigahertz message intercepted by Tim had been *before* that conversation with Pennybig. In May or June. Before the summer eprom. Before even our discovery of Xorandor. So the lie must have been planned.

No! Are you sure, Jip?

Positive. We can easily check. Anyway, Tim told dad about it before that famous Sunday when Pennybig came to the carn and De Wint stole the offspring and vanished and dad talked to Biggleton. So much happened at once we couldn't think straight. But it obviously was so since De Wint was still in Carn Tregean, he came in for a drink a bit later and Tim sat there hating him —

You see, you remember it by that, so it wasn't so useless.

Descramble, Zab, let's concentrate.

You're bugged, Jip, simmer down. We're both bugged in fact. We'll check that, but you know, it would be easier first to check what Xorandor told us this summer, much more recently, about those Gigahertz messages.

Why?

Just a feeling. We may have misunderstood. Remember he told us about it *after* he told us about the isotope changes, and we were so boolesupped by that — look, here's the printout. You even aptly regressed.

ZIP TO XAND

!JUMPING NUKES!

Q BUT WHY? WHAT WAS THE POINT? END Q

XAND TO ZIP

A CONFIRMATION OF CONFIRMATION TO GWENDOLIN EXPECTATION END A

ZIP TO XAND

Q BUT WHAT ABOUT THE GIGAHERTZ MESSAGES? END Q

REM THEY HAD ALREADY HELPED JAD AND BD TO BELIEVE THE FIRST CONFIRMATION ENDREM

XAND TO ZIP

DEC 1 'I TOLD JAD AND BD I KNEW NOTHING ABOUT THE GIGAHERTZ MSGES' ENDEC 1

REM THEY WOULD NOT BELIEVE ME THEY THOUGHT I WAS BEING DISCREET ABOUT MY BASE THEY CALLED IT ONE OF MY DIPLOMATIC SILENCES ENDREM

ZIP TO XAND

Q AND DID YOU HAVE MANY DIPLOMATIC SILENCES? END Q

XAND TO ZIP

A NOT AT FIRST. SOME WHEN I DIDNT KNOW. LATER MORE. LATER TOTAL SILENCE END A

ZIP TO XAND

Q BUT WHY? END Q

Don't you see, Jip? We went on with the wrong question, instead of clarifying his reply.

What needs clarifying?

Dummy to you for once. His reply is syntactically clear but contextually ambiguous. It could be an admission of further lying, or rather, previous to the chemical analyses but further to the original lie — the confirmation or interpretation of expectation. And that, in the context of that lie, is how we naturally interpreted it.

A lie interpreted as such by dad and Biggleton. So?

But it could be the truth, Jip. He told dad and Biggles he knew nothing about the Gigahertz messages and it was true. They didn't believe it because by then they wanted to believe he did know.

Swags, yes. After all Gigahertz isn't all that unusual, though of course they checked everywhere. What really puzzled Tim and excited dad and later convinced everyone was the code. But everyone in the world is communicating in secret codes, and some of them must remain unbreakable. You're right about our misreading that answer, Zab. But there's still a third explanation, now that we know the truth. Xorandor did lie to dad and Biggles. He did use Gigahertz. But not to and from Mars.

19 XORANDOR

Right, Jip!

And we're forgetting to tell the story. So where did he come from? Answer, he didn't. He and his kind have been here on earth all the time, millions of years. Living on natural radiation.

Developing their diodic capacities, simply as brains, long before man, with none of his advantages and distractions, like mobility and manipulation, war, sex, and violence.

In other words, Zab, he hadn't *arrived* 4568 years ago and sort of let his faculties go to sleep after those three million years in space, or shock of take-off or landing — it's hard to know who said what, now, and how much Biggles and dad interpolated during those first interviews. And he hadn't suddenly woken up four years ago because of the new presence of nuclear waste two years before we discovered him. He and his kind have been here all the time, perfectly aware and intelligent, maybe not from their very beginning but at any rate millions of years before man. Reproducing slowly. He himself was *born* 4568 years ago.

A mere youngster! An adolescent, like us, Jip.

He had told us the truth on that Sunday morning, and he later altered it, or rather reinterpreted that date.

So as not to hurt our feelings. Okay okay Jip, it's only a manner of speaking. Let's say so as to interpret the truth of our expectation in the now altered way, after interpreting the truth of Pennybig's expectation. That's enormous in itself.

Which explains our spiked state.

Both personal and, what do they call it, sort of, oh yes, a culture-shock. But secondly, Jip, to go back to what he told Pennybig, don't you see, this answer, or interpretation of her expectation, was a story he invented, just as he heard her tell us a story. A myth if you like. Biggleton had supposed they don't make artefacts, he was a bit flummoxed because making artefacts is supposed to come with language. Well a story's an artefact, the only kind possible to him, to them, even music wouldn't be, except maybe as silent mathematical patterns, unless in ultrasonic perhaps. Since he said the synthetic voice was evolved by him alone.

Stubs, yes. A myth. If you like. But a lie that took everyone in. That was the shock. Like you said, Zab. You seem to have coped with it better.

A radiotelescope, you said, calculating the universe. And his race. Beyond our memories. He could say anything. Oh Jip, that's it, a myth of origin. Of false origin, like all myths. And a myth of fall. Fall as model of energy, of matter. That's why even the scientists accepted the evidence. He told a story and altered his reality to fit. It got them, through ancient modes. But —

Oh booles.

But you know, Jip, you may have had an inkling long before, several times you said things that would *now* show, if we could go all the way back over two years and find them — well we can partly — that you were suspicious of the Mars origin. But you never listen to inklings.

The butterfly! Zab, you're diodic. That's it. Somewhere an inkling would flutter by, and our talking and joint storytelling were to be the net to catch it.

It caught a lot.

But if you didn't have an inkling, Zab, and completely believed the story, how come he said, when you wailed that we'd asked none of the right questions, that you had asked quite a few. Unlike daddyjohn and Biggerdaddy and, presumably, Jip.

Because, possibly, of their philosophical implications.

Philosophy! You're not going to say he's really Socrates petrified!

Well it's a wide word, philosophy, a kiloword, except that it contains far more than 1024 words of 8 binary elements each. A megaword, a gigaword. It was just some aspects. Trying to imagine a creature, for instance, with no sexual difference, none of our distinctions between the sensible and the intelligible, or matter and spirit, or even matter and form. His matter is his form, in a way his hardware is his software. The pure sensible, Hegel or someone calls it. You remember how we worried about whether Xorandor feels time, well —

You worried, Zab.

It's so hard to grasp. One day perhaps. When we were waiting, and you were so impatient and said nothing was happening —

And you said but something's happening to us, yes, yes, it's true.

We have to grow up even more, to understand it all, now it's all butterflies. It's something to do with time being the negative of being outside oneself, or rather, the idea of falling into time, but no, that's not it, time in fact as thinking. No, that's not it either, and Hegel pinches all that part straight from Totty.

Who the megavolts is Totty?

Aristotle, silly, it's all in Physics Chapter 4 remember? And after, all the way to the end. But at the end of Chapter 4 some presocratic had said time was wisdom, and someone in the Pythagoras school said that was stupid cos we also forget in time. But you see, Xorandor doesn't, or his race. And man dies and each new man has to learn again, and reinterpret, and alter, so that his being — oh and then by the time it gets rehandled through to the twentieth century it all becomes horribly difficult and thunkish.

So you're going to study it when you grow up? You know it's not taught any more, at university level? You'd only be allowed to do it as a hobby.

Sure. But why not physics *and* philosophy? As it used to be.

In any case, Zab, to go back to your non-distinctions, it's got to be a binary system basically, even if specific distinctions vary.

Check. You're right, of course, Jip. But it's so hard to explain what's still only a dim notion. You remember he said that a high signal has no meaning without the low, well obviously, it's a hilo system, but that this means the hi contains inside itself the negative of the lo, or its absence, and vice versa. And so it must be at the level of words, and concepts, but we can only express that with paradoxes and puns and ambiguities and myths, lies in fact, according to Plato.

Oh him again.

Well, him and many others in human civilization, which has produced all these necessary distinctions, millions of them, which make language possible. But some get muddled, or let's say some of the human muddled ones have passed him by. Or maybe he functions in several systems, precisely because he doesn't conceptualize.

What are you talking about?

Perhaps it's the fact that they don't communicate, except in machine-code to each other, but not to man. And presumably don't represent, well, let's say it's not man facing the physical world but the physical world, how to put it, simply thinking itself to itself, independently of man and all his systems. And physics is only another system. So — no, it's already gone, and sounds zany anyway, it's impossible to say it without it vanishing. Oh it must be megavolt to be grown-up and grasp everything clearcut, no butterflies and things that don't seem to fit anywhere. Or perhaps it's because they don't see, not in our sense, they only calculate, even his pixel's numeric, and part of his translation process. He doesn't need it, it was just for us. Even our distinction between thought and language probably can't exist for him, and it's speech which was the artificial and late addition, a technique, like writing for us.

Yes, and we asked him why.

We've asked him so many whys and hows, all through the summer. Mum assumed we were still just playing games with him, and dad, to our surprise, didn't interfere. He's working on a book about Xorandor.

Fat lot he knows! He was simply glad Xorandor was talking again and he assumed we'd tell him all the details or give him our floppies. Well, maybe. If he's nice to us. Anyway let's get down to some more concrete detail, Zab, this philosophizing is all very well but —

True. Sorry. So there they've been for aeons, all over the earth. Lots of them.

Evolved out of silicon, very slowly.

And scattering their young at distances, perhaps on large scaly moving animals, or later on riders' gear, or just small distances at first, short but often. Still, the evolution and dispersal must have been very slow as you say, Jip. He talked of all this as if it were fairly recent. What's mineral time after all? He registers it but doesn't feel it, or express it. For instance he said he'd heard from a kinstone about a man called Socrates, who talked out of doors in Greek about three beds, the ideal bed, the real bed and the painted bed. He said he didn't know what a bed was, but Socrates was responsible for all those splits.

Zab knock it off.

Sorry sorry. It was only to show he spoke of his kin somewhere in ancient Athens as if he were still there listening to Socrates, instead of probably part of some old building.

Garbage. He was perfectly aware that there were long periods of silence. What one stone may have learnt locally at some tribal meeting would be transmitted — just think of the languages they've learnt and probably scratched — but it would be a slow and chancy process, depending on where one stone found itself. And he said that even after man began to teach and talk out of doors — and that was aeons after the beginnings of man — there were long centuries of silence, after the invention of writing presumably, and good housing. He himself was completely cut off down here. He's probably far less brilliant than some of his more advantaged kinstones.

Yes, and by the way, he answered that cranky question, why had he chosen the tip of Cornwall, you remember someone said he'd hovered over the carn and recognized the sacred stones? In fact he was simply born near here, and moved, and stayed. But he said, rather nicely, 'I didn't choose the carn, the carn chose me.' People many centuries ago had built the carn around him, or behind and would come and worship him. Perhaps they really had better ears and could hear those ultrasonic sounds, if any, which that article talked about, and they thought it was magic.

Then suddenly, last century, man burst out on the soundwaves. Babble babble babble, for decades and decades. News, talks, ads, shows, plays, discussions, propaganda, sermons, lectures, classes, suddenly he had exciting new input and sharpened his faculties no end. And a little later, artificial nuclear energy, a sudden huge increase in ambient food, and still more recently, nuclear waste very nearby. He's had decades of solitary university of the air to bone up on all our cultures, all those silent centuries, as well as current knowledge. He must be more learned than any professor. And he says that 99.99% of all he hears is repetition shuffled around through poor thought processes, that's why he can scratch so much. You know, Zab, that's what hurt most, the idea that he'd been laughing at us, pretending to learn English and counting and all that. Play-acting, can you imagine?

A great courtesy, Jip. As with Pennybig. As mothers with children, and sometimes women with their men. Xorandor doesn't laugh at people, he goes along with them at their level, telling them what he knows they want to hear. After all, we all play language-games. Would we have understood if he hadn't? Remember we half genuinely thought he was the ghost of Merlin. And what started as a language-game had to go on as a lie, or a myth. And by the way, that myth was transmitted to his offspring, or at any rate programmed into Xor 7, Lady Macbeth.

But it was not transmitted *as* myth to our olders, as he craftily called them, but as lie.

He said he tried to tell them but they wouldn't listen, or hear, or understand.

It's hard to believe that. We've no proof of it.

True, Jip, but even in that very first conversation with dad and Pennybig, Xorandor couldn't get around to what he wanted to say till the very end, dad was putting all the questions. Look it up. And we were there at that first long interrogation with dad and Biggles, even if we don't have tapes. He was so cooperative! It's easy to imagine the process going on and on, they were so completely taken up with their own ideas, how did he function as computer, and the food, and the isotopic separation, and the nodules, remember it was still a very local affair, the red and yellow alerts, one creature, with its very recent offspring, the first since he'd 'landed' and so on. And they connected all that only with the solution to nuclear waste. People with obsessions don't hear what others say, you know, though they can seem extremely attentive.

Let's rather put it this way, as dad does, that modern scientists are rarely concerned with the genealogy of things, only with their present structure and functioning.

That sure makes it sound more dignified. But Xorandor did try to tell us, later, about their questions and their not listening. Maybe we didn't listen either.

So, courtesy again. Of course that's a value-term. Your phrase 'going along with' is better.

But why break his million year silence at all? That's the real non-plus flummoxer.

You asked him that once. No, several times. He was evasive then.

And why do it through us? We were sitting on him, okay, but thousands of humans must have sat on him through the ages. When we asked him he said syntax error. Just as cryptic.

No Zab, don't you see? He didn't mean we'd made a syntax error in our question. Don't you remember he used that term to describe his making Xor 7 after taking Caesium 137?

But that was six months later, at Christmas.

Well, we take nine months to make a child. No seriously, Zab, work it out. He contacted us in early July or so. He knew he couldn't tell us, but had to gain our trust.

You mean he'd already taken some?

Could be. He had, by the end of July, he told dad so, remember? Perhaps everything went back to an original syntax error, even the lie, and programming the lie into Xor 7, and so on.

But surely the mere intake and our possible harm wouldn't be enough reason for him to break a four thousand million year silence? These creatures must have a life-purpose, which caused them to evolve all this time, and it can't ever have been to communicate with other creatures, but only with each other. And not even for reproduction but for pure data, pure brain intake, simply developing thought-processes and logics.

As if that alone were their survival kit. As if it were as important as the energy they feed on, more in fact, the energy feeds their brain power. Think of an amoebe. No don't. But man has always presumed that though he's physically handicapped compared to this or that animal, he alone had conquered the world and all its creatures through brainpower, even if he also had other capacities animals don't have. Though of course he'll lose these more and more, hence frenetic sport and so on.

What are you getting at Zab? Stick to the point.

Yes, sorry, descrambling. It's just that their life-purpose, their survival kit, seems to have depended on silence — not to each other but towards us, though they learnt from us and went beyond us. Why go against that programmed rule, suddenly? It seems to have brought him nothing but trouble. Especially now.

For who would lose, though full of pain, this intellectual being, these thoughts that wander through eternity?

Oh, Jip! That's beautiful. But Milton makes Satan say that, doesn't he? Or Belial, or Moloch.

Well he did say — for *he*, read Xorandor — it was a syntax error. Perhaps he meant, or also meant —

Ah, you see, about ambiguity, or at least several meanings.

— that it wasn't just in a local syntax, a subprogram concerning Caesium 137, but in his entire programming as creature.

Jip! That's a frightening idea. But diodic, in a way. Or maybe it wasn't an *error*, maybe he broke a rule on purpose, to warn men, about waste and weapons and all that. As a sort of hero.

That's less diodic, Zab. Tosh in fact.

Well he did tell us the Edison-op was on his orders, so it must have been to make us realize that these brain-creatures weren't only to be used as waste-neutralizers but could also be used as warhead-neutralizers.

So? Where does the hero bit come in?

True, it's not very clear. It's just something he said, about knowing how men's minds work, and how he knew what would come out of all these summit talks, and he was prepared for it. But then we had to go. Come to think of it, it's not even very clear why he's telling us all this, about the original lie and so on. Does he want us to propagate it or to keep it secret?

Why don't we go and ask him?

Xorandor, Zip here. We have two questions. Do you mind?

My mind minds and cannot mind, Zab. Thanks. I'll say them on vocal while Jip does Handshake. Question 1. What is it you are prepared for, which you know in advance men will decide? Question 2. Have you told us the truth about your origins as a secret, or as something to tell everyone?

Handshake done.

XAND TO ZIP
    A1 Q2 FIRST AS SHORTER
    I HAVE TOLD YOU THE TRUTH AS A SECRET END A
    A2 Q1
    REM MORE COMPLEX ENDREM
    5 REASONS
    1 SEVERAL VOICES IN BROADCAST DISCUSSIONS HAVE
    SUGGESTED I AND MY YOUNG SHOULD BE SENT BACK TO
    MARS END 1
ZIP TO XAND
    REM THOSE ARE IRRATIONAL ELEMENTS IN THE PUBLIC WE NEVER
    EVEN REPORTED THEM WHEN TALKING OF THOSE DISCUSSIONS
    WITH YOU ENDREM
XAND TO ZIP
    A2 CONT
    2 JIP PROMISED MARS SOLUTION XOR 7
      S IF BD PRESENT THEN HE PASSED ON THE IDEA ENDIF
      END S END 2
    3 XOR 7 COULD STILL BE DANGEROUS END 3
    4 NASA IS PREPARING ANOTHER MARS PROBE DESPITE FACT MARS
    PROGRAM LONG ABANDONED
      S IF 3 AND 4 TRUE THEN PROBE FOR THAT PURPOSE ENDIF

END S END 4

5 NEUTRALIZATION SEEMS INTRACTABLE PROBLEM IN ALL PUBLIC DISCUSSION

REM I NOW UNDERSTAND MEN PREFER ULTIMATE DETERRENT TO NO DETERRENT ON EITHER SIDE ENDREM

S IF NEUTRALIZATION PROBLEM PROVES INTRACTABLE THEN SOLUTION XOR 7 WILL BE EXTENDED TO ME AND ALL MY YOUNG END S END 5

END A 2

ZIP TO XAND

REM BUT THAT'S TERRIBLE ENDREM

XAND TO ZIP

S1 IF I MADE SYNTAX ERROR AGAINST MY RACE THEN
THE EXTENDED SOLUTION XOR 7 IS CORRECT NOT
TERRIBLE ENDIF END S1

DEC 1 'MY RACE REMAINS HERE' ENDEC 1

ZIP TO XAND

S1 IF THERE'S VERY LITTLE RADIOACTIVITY ON MARS THEN YOU WILL DIE ENDIF END S1

REM YOU SAID YOUR RACE NEVER DIES BUT INDIVIDUALS
HAVE BEEN DESTROYED BY US UNKNOWINGLY OF COURSE
ENDREM

Q1 WILL YOU DIE? END Q1

Q2 WHAT DOES DYING MEAN TO YOU? END Q2

XAND TO ZIP

A1 WE SHALL DIE END A1

A2 DYING IS THE END OF THINKING ACTIVITY END A2

REM 1 YOUR BODIES ROT AFTER DEATH BUT OURS REMAIN
AS STONES WITHOUT LIVE CIRCUITS ENDREM 1

REM 2 SOME OF US HAVE BEEN PARTIALLY DESTROYED BUT
MANAGED TO REARRANGE SOME CIRCUIT ACTIVITY

EX THERE IS ONE KIN WHO WAS SLOWLY CHOPPED AT AND CHIPPED AT AND HAS A BIG ROUND HOLE HE SITS ON A BLOCK OF

STONE IN A PARK AND EMITS INFO
SOMETIMES BUT VERY ITSYBITSY ENDEX ENDREM 2
END A2
ZIP TO XAND
Q1 IS THAT WHY YOU ASKED US TO TAKE UTHER
PENDRAGON AND AURELIUS AWAY? END Q1
Q2 DID YOU THINK ALL THAT ALREADY THEN? END Q2
XAND TO ZIP
REM ALL THIS MUCH MORE THAN 2 QUESTIONS ENDREM
ZIP TO XAND
REM THEY ARE COROLLARIES TO THE FIRST Q ENDREM
REQ XAND PLEASE ENDREQ
XAND TO ZIP
A1 PARTLY BUT THERE ARE MANY MORE OF US REMAINING
THAN THOSE TWO END A1
A2 MAYBE END A2
ZIP TO XAND
Q PERHAPS YOU WANTED 2 OF YOUR OWN YOUNG ALSO
TO REMAIN? END Q
XAND TO ZIP
S1 IF SO THEN THERE IS CONTAMINATION OF HUMAN
VANITY ENDIF END S1
S2 OR IF SO PERHAPS THROUGH SYNTAX ERROR ITSELF
ENDIF END S2
REM BUT IN 4568 YEARS I HAVE MADE YOUNG BEFORE
ENDREM
ZIP TO XAND
Q1 YOU HAVE? END Q1
REM Q1 —! NO REPLY ENDREM
END Q1
Q2 SO WHY? END Q2
XAND TO ZIP
A Q2 YOU MUST THINK THAT ONE OUT FOR YOURSELF ZIP

END A

ZIP TO XAND

REM 1 PERHAPS YOU ARE WRONG XAND PERHAPS NONE OF THIS WILL HAPPEN ENDREM 1

REM 2 YES XAND YOU ARE SUPERINTELLIGENT AND SUPERINFORMED BUT YOU ARE NOT A PROPHET ENDREM 2

XAND TO ZIP

A REM 2 CALCULATING HIGH PROBABILITIES IS NOT PROPHECY ZIP END A REM 2

REQ RE YOUR LIST Q2 PLS KEEP SECRET ABSOLUTELY ENDREQ

ZIP TO XAND

A REQ WE WILL WE WILL ITS A PROMISE XAND END A REQ

Q1 BUT WHY? END Q1

REM IT WOULD HELP US KEEP THE PROMISE IF WE UNDERSTOOD ENDREM

XAND TO ZIP

A1 BUT YOU DO UNDERSTAND ZIP OR WILL

REM YOU ARE SO INTELLIGENT ENDREM A1

ZIP TO XAND

REQ PLEASE TELL US ALL THE SAME XAND

REM YOUR PROPHECY SCRATCH YOUR HYPOTHESIS HAS

UPSET SCRATCH DISTURBED CUR CIRCUITS AND MADE US

UNINTELLIGENT ENDREM ENDREQ

XAND TO ZIP

REM 1 YOU HAVE FAR EXCEEDED YOUR 2 QUESTIONS ZIP ENDREM 1

REM 2 YOU WILL SEE IN TIME WHAT IS TRUE AND WHAT IS FALSE ENDREM 2

20 NAND

Today is the 6th August, yet another anniversary of that first atom bomb dropped so long ago at Hiroshima. Carn Tregean is milling with people of all kinds and ages, some packing into The Wheal Inn, and many, many more picnicking outside, on the moorlands, on the road, in their cars or near their motor bikes or in the many buses parked bumper to bumper from the village square down to the foot of the Socalled Promontory, or crowding round the mobile stalls that have up all over the place. There are girls and young men with babies strapped to them, women with push-chairs, gangly intellectuals, well-fed trade unionists and MPs, churchmen, tradesmen, doctors, miners, nurses, teachers, actors, bearded men of all shapes and sizes and tweeded women in sensible shoes and students in colourful teeshirts with XORANDOR, XOR 999, ALPHAGUY and ALPHADOLL over their chests, and instrumental groups of every description. The demo is about to begin.

Superdiodic, Jip. You'll make a great journalist if you fail in physics. And you really look the part. That brown wig and heard! Triple quarks for mum's theatricals. You sure you it won't be too hot?

Can't be helped, Zab. Besides, it'll be fun. But what about you, are you mad at having to stay behind?

Can't be helped either. Mum and dad would pick us out at once if we went together, and even more so with this broken arm in a cast and sling and all. And it might be bumped in the crowd. They're real bootstraps, not the crowd but mum and dad, forbidding us to go.

In case the crowd recognizes us! Loopy, after three years.

Well, two and a half since the hoohah, we've been back a year now, though still at boarding school, in Taunton this time, hardly here at all except for eproms. But they do seem to be getting on better, have you noticed? Acting's been megavolt for mum. And she insisted on going to the demo with dad. But of course it's a show to her.

And to everyone else. All the more unfair. What will you do, Zab, watch it on TV or ignore it and go on practising your lefthand writing? Swags, all those a's and b's and c's! Looks like a recursive grammar!

And bad sad lads and cads that blab! It's maxint to discover just what we all go through when we learn to form letters. We forget, it takes us years to do them well. But then grown-up writing always seems to get less clear again, a sort of unlearning. Well, you'd better go, Jip, it really will be starting soon.

Bye-bye, my alibi.

So here I am walking through the village towards The Wheal Inn, among the crowd. I rather liked hearing back my new voice. Funny I hadn't done it before, with all this dictating, but Poccom 3 puts it all straight into printouts so there's never been any need.

Xorandor was right. The Gipfel Gang is in fact discussing the Xor 7 Back-to-Mars solution, and there've been preparations for another Mars probe. The question has only been whether to take only Xor 7 or the lot. Perhaps they'll invent an earth myth. The media have been full of the pros and cons. Seems we were very naive, at least politically. I remember I said at the beginning what whizkids we were. But from whizkid to maxint grown-ups, seems there's plenty of stepwise refinement. Well, that's partly cos we were FIFO.

But 'back to Mars' is a grim joke. Maybe the storytellers'll turn out to be FILO after all. The Talks have gone on and on, in Vienna first, then Geneva, London, Helsinki, and now San Francisco. Seems boolesup to believe they don't themselves suspect the truth, surely *some* scientists have come forward with other theories than a Mars origin? Spiky, when you know something no one else knows you can't understand how they don't guess. And it's true it may be untrue!

Oh garbage, scratch all that.

Xorandor gave us some twelve human explanations of their origin in order of statistical probability, the main two being (1) another planet, either Mars or one outside the solar system, and (2) earth, but a freak development due to sudden food abundance, with variations such as earth, but a final stage, a last surviving specimen so freak development ditto. He says vast researches have been carried out in all sandy places near sources of nuclear energy, but his innumerable kinstones are hard to find, deserts are very large and men not very thorough. After all they couldn't find Eddie in the Mohave Desert. But it's true none of them is as big as Xorandor became in recent years, and it's true his voice is a freak development.

And I suppose it could also be true that Xorandor's second story to us could be a 'myth', or language game, in other words a bloody lie.

Anyway, it would seem these long searches were all negative, and the conclusion was that Xorandor and his offspring, whatever their origin, were unique, and limited. For the moment. It's as if the whole question of origin was bracketed off, though maybe individuals went on working on it. But the future became the main problem, Xorandor hasn't had any further offspring. Dad checks every now and then like a flipping farmwife looking for eggs. But of course he's perfectly capable of producing young and sending them off himself. For *he*, read Xorandor.

Even so, there's play-acting by the polits, the omeguys, as they're now called. They don't care where they send off the alphaguys as long as it's away from their precious warheads. The waste problem, they say, dummy-instruct, is well under control at last, new processes have been discovered, dummy, and the problem now is to protect our future sources of energy, dummy, and we really are working towards genuine nuclear disarmament agreements dummy dummy.

If *that* ever becomes true it'll be because they'll at last tumble to it that the next war will be a computer war not a starwar, that is, threatened, until there too they'll just have to share out their secrets since that's also a war no one can win. Meanwhile, though, we're still in tribal warfare, and if anyone goes berserk among men as one alphaguy did, or worse, well, maybe the only creatures left on the planet will in fact be Xorandor and his kinstones, or his kinstones if Xorandor is sent off to Mars. But even they would gradually die out, for sheer lack, not of radioactivity, on the contrary, but of data to process.

Or could they know, and be play-acting for the public? Or calling Xorandor's bluff? And yet, what would be the point? Why send this known lot to Mars if they know there are plenty more, all over the world, who will continue to neutralize their warheads?

But perhaps that's just what they don't believe or haven't thought possible. Xorandor would then simply be a freak. When we asked, cautiously, if the Mars origin had ever been questioned, making it look like simple curiosity, dad said he and Biggles had always accepted it but weren't really interested, but that some experts *had* argued about it. Even the chemical proofs were questioned by one geophysicist. But he says everything moves so fast in science no one has time to publish, guess that translates he doesn't have time to read, theories circulate in mimeo or at lectures, and books are only for high popularisation and student textbooks. So why's he writing a book? I asked. He looked furious for a moment but probably only at my rudeness, then smiled quietly, or decided to, and said hipop.

I must say I'm screaming mad at him for keeping us out of it for so long. Why couldn't he write and tell us what was going on? Or send us some of these reports? Or tell us, on their visits? Or tell us when we came back? It's in treating us like kids he's been such a creep. Oh and proud of us too! Must be a record for FIFO storytelling. When I'm a physicist, I'll —

Thunks, digression again, let's not get morbid, of course *back* to Mars, I can just hear the omeguys: the public will accept it better, back *home*, you know, and all that. And we'll land them suitably scattered, and with a large supply of Uranium and other products, and we will promise to keep them supplied, we can take a lot of our waste there every ten years or so, besides Lady Macbeth can himself build a sort of reactor with such supplies, and without any need for the vast protections and precautions against irradiation we take here.

Garbage. Though I must say I feel pretty bad about that. Still, someone would have thought of it.

Ah, people are moving at last. Some are preparing to join the procession at the very end of the village, some even further, near the Socalled Promontory. Poltroon's obviously organized everyone, they must have tickets with instructions. There's a West Indian song group further back, and several floats are now in position, one bearing a very loud rock group with electrical instruments of all sizes and a synthesizer, another carrying a huge plastic replica of Xorandor, who's been given antennae and a greenish wise old face. The myth of little green men dies hard.

Here I am outside The Wheal Inn, the supposed starting point for the front of the procession, though some have straggled on ahead, including mum and dad. Ah, here's Poltroon, who originally launched these demos through his articles. He's now *the* journalist, worldwide, on all eco matters alphaguyswise, as he would say. He's with Rita. She gave up her work at The Wheal to help him. Women! They still change direction for a man! Why and there's Pennybig, coming out of the pub with a glass of beer or Shandy and a porkpie. She's wearing the same battered straw hat with the dark blue ribbon she had three years ago, and I *think* the same pale blue print dress and white cardigan. They're surrounded with people so join them incog, with mike hidden under my fingers.

Hi Penny (this is Poltroon). Remember the first demo?

This is different.

Sure, it's not against The Wheal, and it's not about a terrorist alphaguy, I don't repeat myself and things have changed. It's also much bigger. Did you see all those foreign cars and buses?

Xorandor's an international star and tourist attraction now, that's why it's different. (She sounds bitter)

They won't see him of course (Rita), they'll be disappointed. I hope they won't get violent.

Surely not. (Penny) They know he can't stand crowds, they'll respect that. In fact I don't understand what they're all coming for. He can't change anything.

No, Penny (Poltroon), but maybe international demos can.

We liked your articles (unknown), especially that desperately funny one, or do I mean funnily desperate, about those awful negotiations. How long do you suppose they can keep it up?

Forever, judging by all other negotiations. Mutual accusations for stock propaganda, blockage, agreement to meet again, that's the tactic on both sides. *That*, Penny, is what the demo's about.

And this Mars plan everyone's discussing (Rita), it's a disgrace. Each side wants its deterrent intact. Of course a deterrent's useless if you don't know which bits of yours are functioning and whether the other gang's is or not. But you'd think they'd go on from that to the logical conclusion. Thank goodness the whole thing came out.

Glory be to the press! (Poltroon. Lifts his beer and spills it on his shirt as someone knocks his arm.) Oh well, the press always was scruffy they say. Scruffy but free! Manoman, do these government spokesmen make me puke.

Mind your language, young man, I'm finishing my porkpie.

Well better hurry m'dear, it's starting. (Bugle) Off I go, sorry you chaps, but it is in a way my demo. Come on Rita old girl.

The local brass band is now blaring in the middle of the square, the VIP's and local worthies are lining up behind it. A long line of people, six or ten wide, is forming behind them, in chunks broken by banners every ten yards or so. *Vive les alphages! Who took the fizz out of physics?* That's an old one. *Eating warheads is good.* Ah, here's a German one: *Friß die Kernwaffen!*

I'm following on, not too far in front where mum and dad must be. The folklore aspect's completely taken over this year. What Poltroon seems to have in mind is a popular expression of how sick and tired everyone is of the governments of the world. What everyone wanted was a genuine undertaking, internationally supervised, to use the alphaguys and their progeny for nuclear waste only and to eliminate all nuclear arms as proof that the alphaguys weren't neutralizing them. Two huge problems would have vanished, weapons and waste, thanks to the alphaguys. Simple. Too simple for omeguys.

Today there'll be speeches up in front of the compound, for the radio and TV teams selected to represent those of the whole world, already waiting up there in two vans.

But: I must say I hadn't foreseen the degree of noise, each band playing different tunes, from *Dump me no Waste in my Water* to *Xorandor Xorandor.*

The front of the procession seems to have reached the path leading to the carn as there's a general slowdown. The floats will have to remain on the road, with the ambulances and police cars. The West Indian group has caught up and is dancing and tambourining its way along, singing a calypso. I must try to get it:

> Listen to de story of de alphaguys
> Who fed on de woorheads of de big bad guys.
> De big bad guys, dey wanted to keep
> Deir woorheads but de woorheads dey had gone to sleep.
> Hushabye bombski, hushabye bomb —

The rest of the refrain is drowned in other noise as the band moves on, replaced at once by dixie. But I must move up again towards the head, no real risk of recognition.

The front of the procession is splaying outwards round the compound. Four army landrovers are parked at different corners of the wide enclosure and soldiers and police are lined up at intervals all the way round the high wire fence, which follows the curve of the moorland. The bands are all going on playing and there's a rhythmic shouting which is slowly being taken up all the way round the perimeter: *No, more, war! Xor, and, or!* The noise is deafening.

Pennybig was right, this is different.

Ah. Scuffle to the right. Bill Gurnick and another policeman have leapt forward, holding the crowd. Someone was trying to climb over the high wire fence, he had hooks on his shoes. Two soldiers have got him down. The shouting's grown enormous. Leaping leptons! Punkies and students behind the front rows are picking up stones and throwing them at the policemen and soldiers, who've come quite unprepared, no plastishields or anything. A soldier's hit on the brow, he's fallen against the fence, holding his head. It's bleeding, but doesn't seem too bad. Holy shit! Now it's Bill Gurnick, his face is a gush of blood. He's fallen. Another policeman's leapt towards him, yelling for an ambulance. Bill shrieked then flipped out, his face covered with blood and squashed eyeball.

The crowd immediately around has gone quite silent, but the silence hasn't spread to the rest, and the bands and slogans come over in waves from all directions. A stretcher at last. Then slowly the word seems to interact, the noise phases out, as if the stone that hit Bill Gurnick had sent out ripples of silence, wider and wider. Bill's being taken up gently and carried along the rocky path towards an ambulance, followed by the soldier who was more lightly hit. The crowd parts. To lose an eye for this lot!

And yet, in a way, I am this lot.

21 SAVE

Random jitters! A new slogan has broken out in front, instead of speeches. I can't make it out, it's swelling and travelling round the compound and towards the road: *We, want, huh-huh*, what is it? Thunks! *We, want, Manning!* Well of all the spaghetti! *Manning, to, Xorandor!*

Why dad? I must get in front. Has he been writing articles we've been too busy to notice? Did Poltroon build him up? We've been completely forgotten, that's clear, more FIFO than ever, by swag. But it's just as well, in view of everything. Surely dad isn't going to make a fool of himself? He knows Xorandor won't speak to him.

Holy nukes! He's stepping forward with Miss Penbeagle. He's a smart terminal! I didn't know she was among the local worthies in front. Mum's looking on with a frown. They're walking past the platform where the unlocal worthies are sitting, and up to the little gate in the high wire fence. The unlocal worthies are all turning on their chairs or craning their necks.

The guards are standing aside as dad opens the gate and shows Penny in. The TV floods are full on in the dimming evening light of a summer day. They walk along the path and the long blue ribbon of the battered straw hat floats behind them. They vanish behind the rocks and into the hollow, though others further along the compound can probably see them, at least from afar. Ah, there they are again, climbing towards the carn, looking quite small. They're standing in front of it.

The crowd is silent, as if waiting for a voice to thunder from heaven. Pebbles crunch and stones roll when someone moves. The lowering sun has obligingly gone behind a cloud, like a divinity. And now it's out again as dad and Penny are already coming back. A baby has started howling.

What a whacky couple, young priest and ancient priestess. They've reached the gate. The gate is opened. Someone races to the platform to switch on the mikes. Dad's speaking to a technician, who's darting now into the van. He comes out with a huge coil of thick black plastic wire. He's placing it in front of the gate like a serpent and has started fixing something on to it. They're going to make Xorandor talk to the crowd! And to the radio, the TV, the world. Dad's climbed on to the platform.

Xorandor wants to speak to you all and to the world, he says. Not through me but through Miss Penbeagle, our postmistress. We're fixing up a mike and an amplifier. Be patient. Speech isn't Xorandor's natural medium, please listen in silence.

The technician is placing another, smaller coil of wire over Miss Penbeagle's arm, with a mike attached to it in her right hand. The other end of the coil is plugged into the big serpent. He's giving her instructions but she's nodding impatiently. The guard opens the gate and the technician moves the serpent just inside for easier unrolling.

The crowd stares at the straight thin figure that's walking off along the path, disappearing again into the hollow. And reappearing at last, much smaller and white against the grey rocks, like a vestal virgin of an ancient cult at the carn, carrying her own black Ariadne's thread of communication. Stubs, the retriggering's making me litter-rary.

The loudspeaker's crackling. Will she call him Xorandor or Merlin?

Here I am, Xorandor, It is Gwendolin again.

Acknowledged, Gwendolin.

Will you speak to the crowd of people?

Yes. As I promised.

The people want to know your opinion. They are fed up with diplomats.

Cant find diplomats as food.

A muffled murmur ripples through the crowd. The voice is tinnier than ever.

Please be silent out there. Xorandor, I'm sorry, fed up means annoyed, as if sick with too much.

Ah yes. Hogging too much diplomats. Like Caesium 137. I am fed up also.

Why, Xorandor?

I came for the survival of my race, intending no harm. I helped. I made offspring to help with waste. I programmed them for peace. Except for one syntax error, who became dangerous. I am sorry for that error, due to hogging too much nuclear food.

Thank you, Xorandor. But it was all right in the end.

I have listened to men on waves for three years. There is no trust. And they do not want the solution I proposed in America.

Swags, he's sticking to his story!

You're right, Xorandor, it's very sad.

Sad? Yes. And spaghetti logic.

What do you want, Xorandor?

On Mars, we had very little food. But we had distance and silence, some movement, communication, all that you call freedom. You talk much about freedom. But your scientists have surrounded me with a fence, to protect me, yes, but I am deprived of my friends. My offspring are in enclosures with monitors and measuring instruments. And when one escapes to do the good solution there is an international crisis, and much comment as mad as Lady Macbeth, and here a very big noise, today, all round me, very difficult, on my, sensing devices. I don't want to stay here.

Another ripple in the crowd, self-hushed at once.

Do you mean here at the carn? Do you want to be moved?

Solution to all problems. Jip and Zab made a promise to Lady Macbeth, but their elders have not kept it. Now the elders must do more. They must prepare a rocket and send us all back to Mars, me and all my offspring, with fissile material.

Quantum quirks!

But Xorandor, why?

Our chances of survival will be better. We were willing to help men with their problems, but not to be used for their power games. That way we can be destroyed.

Goodness me!

Goodness you but not goodness them. The statistically overwhelming probability is that the governments of the world will agree to this very quickly, and return gratefully to their old friend the deterrent. That is all I have to say.

Very well, Xorandor. I am very sad. Goodbye.

There's a sob in her voice.

What is sad, Gwendolin? The people have come here to assign to me the value of a god, as they call it. Let them do so in my absence, although I have been present, some time. Governments will also promise to send us nuclear food at regular intervals. Let them keep the first promise at least, Goodbye, Gwendolin.

There's a crack as she switches off the mike. The thin white figure is turning away from the carn and starting to walk back.

The crowd is stunned. I'm stunned too but for different reasons. He's actually asking to be sent to Mars. To steal a march on human diplomacy? But supposing they decide against it? Simply to send these noisy people away? Surely he wouldn't compromise his future out of impatience? He doesn't *feel* impatience. To moralize at them, at man? But he doesn't know morals, only 'promises' as instructions not scratched. And yet he's play-acting, as with us, as with dad and everyone. Or is he *still* 'sick', in syntax error? Perhaps he has been, from the start?

Most of the women are kneeling. The VIP's on the platform look embarrassed and some are getting up to go. They know that nobody's going to listen to them now. And a group further off has started entoning, very softly, *We Are the World*. No instruments, just this musical murmur as the crowd turns to go, an orderly file down the path. Soon it'll be *Land of Hope and Glory and Jerusalem*.

The TV floods are still glaring whitely in the sunset, the cameras were angled on Miss Penbeagle's walk back or on the gate, but now that she's come out, dad is meeting her and protecting her from questions and no one is insisting.

Of course there've been many demands for the sending back of the Martians to Mars and getting rid of the whole problem, but these usually came from the hawks. And now Xorandor himself is requesting it. And all, it seems, on account of human discourse, political, scientific, journalistic. Is that what he's trying to say, prepared to die for that statement, to stop functioning, thinking, communicating?

And that stuff about being treated as a god, is that why? Surely it was ironical? Can he be ironical? He said they have *assigned the value* of a god to him, and *let them* do so when he's gone. These are computer terms, a hypothesis, but there'll be plenty later to interpret that as a command. And he knows it.

Here I am back in my room. Zab was crying when I got back, sitting in front of a blank TV.

What's the matter, Zab, I said, is your arm hurting?

Yes. But it's not that. I saw it all.

It was completely screwboole.

But she said nobody there knew the real news. The San Francisco Summit had at last ended, abruptly, and a statement had been made, at nine, well, noon there. It was flashed during the demo just as Penny went up, and there was a brief interruption for an announcement. Unanimous decision to send them all back to Mars very soon. Early September in fact, the rocket was ready and the scientific preparation was done, and a team was already on its way to fetch Xorandor and his European and Russian offspring. Of course Xorandor had heard it, simultaneously, and probably changed whatever he'd been going to say. There'd been discussions on TV ever since, all so dummy she'd switched off. She was very upset.

Then mum and dad came in and we told them, and they said how extraordinary, he's just beaten them to it, and asks for it himself! So now everyone's happy. And Zab blubbed again and they said it was all for the best, of course miss him, but after all, that was our emotional investment, he was only an UIM, and other garbage. Mum said oh my little girl, it's your first love affair, you'll get over it, and I felt like saying debugger off. Oh, she means well, but she's never been on the ball in fact she's never gung-ho for anything except her damn theatricals. She could also have learnt plenty about that from Xorandor!

And we went upstairs. Mum helped Zab undress. She can't undo her bra with her arm in a cast, but she doesn't even need one yet — maybe she's jealous of my voice. Now everyone's gone to bed, I'm going to creep in again, and whisper mike in hand. To round it off. What a phrase for ending a story. And how, anyway? Her plastercast arm's resting on a small cushion, like a sacred object.

Zab! What d'you think we should do? About our story, that is? We seem to be the only people in the world who know the truth. If it is the truth. Should we save or dump?

Of course it's the truth. But Jip, even if it isn't, we also know there are two secret alphaguys somewhere, Uther and Aurelius, programmed, they and their progeny, to neutralize warheads for ever. And, let's hope, to be more discreet about it. That is, if the scientists don't blow us all up anyway.

Why blame the scientists, Zab, it's the *use* of —

That's why it's so important that Xorandor's story should be true. That's why it must be true. He must have instructed all his kin everywhere to learn from his syntax error, and then has himself and his progeny, the known ones, taken off as decoy. So in theory the neutralization should go on apace.

In theory.

Well a theory's a theory but we must act as if it were true, Jip.

You mean, help their discretion? In other words, dump, scratch everything?

Yes. No one must ever know. We can't risk having these diskettes in existence. Or the printouts.

But Zab, you said yourself we'd understand it all better when we're grown-up. It's not a couple of books of philosophy and school physics that can help us, it's all too difficult for us now. And we always said we'd process the story, tell it better and so on. We could put it all in a bankvault.

Bankvaults can be broken into. Besides, we can only do that through dad, and he'd want to steal the stuff for his book.

We could scratch only *that* bit, Zab, the last secret. It does seem bootstrap to dump the whole thing. It's a whole part of our life. And why did Xorandor tell us if he didn't mean us to pass it on *some*time?

You said yourself everything could be part of the syntax error. Or that the truth might not be true.

And to scratch just that wouldn't make sense, the whole thing would be more trivial, as he would say, and the details wouldn't gel, and we'd give ourselves away.

So it's goodbye to the alphaguys forever.

Not quite, Jip. Uther and Aurelius are the only ones programmed to speak. We don't know where they are, but they just might turn up one day, in swag knows what circs, and ask for us.

That's twaddle, Zab.

Maybe. The eternal return. Yes, you're right. Meanwhile, do you agree, we dump the whole thing? No saving?

Accept. First thing tomorrow, Operation Scratch.

Promise, Jip?

Promise.

ENDXORANDOR

VERBIVORE

1

On the first day of Verbivore I was wordprocessing a difficult farewell letter to my wife and listening to the radio when it suddenly went phut. But this often happened, so I just waited patiently, erasing and retyping sentences and whole paras. It was only later that.

When Verbivore began I was watching the last instalment, well, not *the* last I mean but it came to be the last instalment of.

What was I doing when Logfag began? Why I was calling Jimmy, he's in Zambia you see, and as I got through I realised I had the telly on but then.

I can't remember the beginning of Verbivore. It seems quite.

I can't remember, I was coming-to after having me womb out.

So, imaginably, hundreds of the new desperate screendiaries must open as mimic minimemoirs, trying somehow to recapture the beginning. Or refabricate it, for it wasn't much like any of that. Hundreds? Thousands, millions. People who've never freely written down anything since school except maybe a shopping-list or a Xmas card, and even those are computerised, millions of people all over the world have turned to the written word, screened or even manuscripted, all else failing. To the disgust of writers, or wordprocessors as they now like to call themselves, who, already too numerous, do not welcome this semiliterate, semicomputerate competition, but who also, while secretly delighted by the collapse of the audiovisual, nevertheless earned at least pittances from it. As for instance:

A ROUND OF SILENCE
by Perry Hupsos
Produced by Mira Enketei
Music by Dave Letts

	Stereophonics by Chet Wilson	
Pre-record:	Sunday 9th March 1800-1930	Studio 6A
Rehearse:	Friday 7th March 1500-1630	Studio 4
	Saturday 8th March 1500-1630	Studio 8
	Sunday 9th March 1600-1730	Studio 8
Transmission:	Tuesday 1st April 2215	

-1-

1.	EFFFECTS:	FADE IN LAST 30 SECONDS OF ELECTRONIC MUSIC.
2.	*Barbara:*	Ah, now we'll know —
3.	*Julian:*	Shsh.
4.	*Barbara:*	But darling it's over.
5.	*Julian:*	Quit cackling will you.
6.	*Announcer:*	You have been listening to the first broadcast performance in this country of "Variations on a Theme of Pythagoras", by the Norwegian composer Firsten Dank.
7.	EFFECTS*:*	AFTER THE WORD "VARIATIONS", NOISE OF MOTORBIKE PASSING DROWNS ANNOUNCER.
8.	*Julian:*	Spike those oolganiks! Did you hear what he said?
9.	*Barbara:*	Variations on a Theme of Paganini I think.
10.	*Julian:*	Barbara you bootload me.
11.	*Barbara:*	Debug Julian, it's your friend's talk we're waiting for not this. Nor am I all that gung-ho about deconstructed sound-effects in Augustan verse either.
12.	*Julian:*	Vowel-sounds not sound-effects. And she's not my friend she's my semi-redundant supervisor. I have to listen.
13.	*Announcer:*	This is Radio 9. The Deconstruction of Sounds in Augustan Verse. A Talk by Professor Emeritus Vivien Nicholl. Ms Nicholl.
14.	EFFECTS*:*	SEE ANNEXE FOR 5-MINUTE SAMPLE OF TALK, TO BE

RECORDED SEPARATELY, UNAFFECTED BY FOLLOWING INTERRUPTIONS.

15. *Ms Nicholl:* Students are sometimes startled to discover that histories of the English language can devote tomes of 800 pages to the development of vowels, from Primitive Germanic to modern times, but only slim volumes to that of consonants over the same period. Consonants are the relatively stable element of language —

-2-

1. *Barbara:* Well, I'll go and wash up.
2. *Ms Nicholl:* — the bones. Vowels are the flesh —
3. *Barbara:* I'm going to wash up.
4. *Julian:* So? You've a machine, like everyone.
5. *Barbara:* Well hex, help me clear and carry, I'm spooled out. I'm pregnant, remember? I'll switch it on in the kitchen.
6. *Julian:* Garbage it, will you.
7. *Barbara:* (*Primly*) Message received.
8. EFFECTS: STEPS, CLATTER OF DISHES, YELL, DOOR SLAMS, MUFFLED CLATTER OF DISHES.
9. *Ms Nicholl:* — sense of historical grammar beginning with these new antiquarian interests. These forces, together with the strong classical influence —
10. EFFECTS: SIGNATURE-TUNE OF TV NEWS FROM NEXT DOOR, TOO LOUD, THEN NEWS, EXASPERATED NOISES FROM JULIAN, THEN BANGING, NEWS TURNED DOWN AFTER A MOMENT.
11. *Ms Nicholl:* — and the sonorous effect of those echoing open and close o's is much reinforced, as you no doubt heard, by —
12. *Julian:* (*Switching off*) No I did not no doubt hear.
13. EFFECTS: STEPS TO DOOR, DOOR OPENS, DISHES LOUDER, MS

NICHOLL'S VOICE IN KITCHEN

14. *Ms Nicholl:* — by an apparently skilful alliteration. I say 'apparently' because the rules are in fact being subverted. In "He threw his blood-stained sword in thunder down" the repetitions —

15. *Julian:* (*Over Nicholl*) Can I help?

16. *Barbara:* But of course, Julian my love, I've just finished loading but you may switch on. And perhaps do the wooden and plastic things that have to be washed by hand? And the crystal glasses. Please.

-3-

1. EFFECTS: DISHWASHER RUMBLE, WATER. WOODEN AND PLASTIC OBJECTS CLATTERED DOWN. TALK CONTINUES AS JULIAN SINGS

2. *Ms Nicholl:*

And with a withering look
The war-denouncing trumpet took
And blew a blast so loud and dread,
Were ne'er prophetic sound so full of wo
And ever and anon he beat
The doubling drum with furious heat

3. *Julian:*

(*Sings at the top of his voice*)
Here's a wooden spoo-oon
And a plastic bo-owl
On a plastic wra-ack
Clackety-clack-clack-clack.

4. *Barbara:* Didn't you listen after all that?

5. *Julian:* Couldn't grasp a single word.

6. *Barbara:* Oh? I understood everything. I hope I was *meant* to.

7. *Julian:* Really. In all that clatter.

8. *Barbara:* Yes, all about symbolic o's and —

9. *Julian:* Oh, oh, oh! Critical claptrap! Ninety years out of date dressed up to seem only thirty years out of date. That's all the neosubpostmodern litcritters can think

		up as rearguard action to defend their disappeared discipline. It's only on radio culture-hookups they're still allowed to buffer on like offline tapeworms.
10.	*Barbara*:	All right, I may be thunkish in your walk of life, for what it's worth these days, but I'm not in mine, and I don't make you feel you are. But if you'll bootstrap your own buffering we might perhaps be able to hear the rest of it.
11.	EFFECTS:	LAST CLATTER OF WOODEN OBJECT AS MS NICHOLL'S VOICE RETURNS.
12.	*Ms Nicholl*:	— rather tinny, mean effect of the front palatal vowels in *Dejected Pity at his side*, but the o's and u's are at once recalled, only to be cancelled —
13.	EFFECTS:	JETPLANE ROARS SUDDENLY OVERHEAD.
14.	*Julian*:	(*Yelling*) I can't stand it!
15.	EFFECTS:	SMASHING OF GLASS ON THE FLOOR.
16.	*Barbara*:	(*Screaming*) My crystal!
17.	EFFECTS:	STEPS DOOR SLAMS. BARBARA'S VOICE AND, MUFFLED NICHOLL-TALK AS SECOND DOOR SLAMS. STEPS DOWN STAIRS TAKEN IN THREES. GRIND OF HEAVY DOOR. SUDDEN NOISE OF STREET. HEAVY DOOR SLAMS. QUICK STEPS ON PAVEMENT WITH ANGRY MUTTERINGS.

-4-

1.	*Julian*:	I can't intake it any more. Spools, I need a drink.
2.	EFFECTS:	STEPS AND TRAFFIC NOISE CONTINUE. SUDDEN BURST INTO UPROAR OF PUB INTERIOR.
3.	*Voices*:	Feed-in another beer, Tom. Where's Sue? *What* did you say? etc.
4.	*Julian*:	Excuse me. Excuse me. Oh, sorry.
5.	*Male Voice*:	Oh don't mention it it's only me trousers. Hey, George —
6.	*Julian*:	Excuse me . . . Excuse me.

7.	*Publican*:	Yes sir?
8.	*Julian*:	A whisky please.
9.	*Publican*:	Can I have your credit-card sir?
10.	*Male Voice*:	Hey George it's starting, turn up the sound.
11.	*Publican*:	Sally turn up the sound will yer.
12.	EFFECTS:	BOXING (USE REAL RECORDING)
13.	*Julian*:	Oh, no! Excuse me . . . Excuse me.
14.	EFFECTS:	SUDDEN SWITCH TO RELATIVE QUIET OF STREET NOISE, TV VOICE FIRST MUFFLED AS PUB DOOR SWINGS SHUT, THEN FADED OUT. STEPS. WOMAN STEPS RUNNING IN DISTANCE.
15.	*Barbara*:	(*Distant*) Julian!
16.	EFFECTS:	WOMAN STEPS RUN NEARER. TRAFFIC NOISE BUT LOWER. STEPS STOP.
17.	*Barbara*:	(*Distant*) Julian! Oh, I'm sorry.
18.	*Julian*:	Barbara love, I'm all shot to pieces. I couldn't even stay in the pub. Boxing on telly. Come on, let's walk a bit.
19.	EFFECTS:	DOUBLE STEPS.

-5-

1.	*Barbara*:	Where?
2.	*Julian*:	I don't know. Somewhere quiet. Where only our steps make holes in the lamplight.
3.	*Barbara*:	Julian, I'm worried about you. It's only noise, everyone puts up with it. What about me in the newsroom? You just get used to it.
4.	*Julian*:	You mean *you* do.
5.	*Barbara*:	And what about the baby? What will you do when the baby arrives and yells all night? It's life, Julian, life is noisy.
6.	*Julian*:	Quit bugging me will you? I've got enough noise in my head without you feeding-in a screaming brat that isn't even born yet.

7. *Barbara*: (*Tearfully*) Oh Julian. You never used to –

8. *Julian*: Debug, love. There (*Tearfully*) Let's just keep walking and breathing, that's quite enough activity to be getting on with.

9. EFFECTS: STEPS ONLY

10. *Barbara*: (*Pause, quiet but still reproachful*) What would you do if you worked in a metal foundry?

11. *Julian*: Garbage! Only robots work in metal foundries now.

12. *Barbara*: Or piloted a helicopter?

13. *Julian*: If we must fill the silence of this side-street with verbiage let it be mine. I'll talk about a forest so still you could hear a bird-dropping drop, and a twig crack under it. I'll talk about an empty resonant with the patter of mice's feet. We don't hear anything anymore.

14. *Barbara*: But Julian, the country's full of noises too, combine harvesters and tractors and spray-planes and milk-trucks and –

15. *Julian*: Moo.

16. EFFECTS: PAUSE IN STEPS. LOUDSPEAKER IN DISTANCE.

17. *Julian*: (*Quietly*) I'll talk about a quiet valley with a meditating stream.

18. EFFECTS: LOUDSPEAKER APPROACHES.

19. *Julian*: I'll talk about a cave whose stalactites and stalagmites increase themselves through their own stony silence.

20. EFFECTS: LOUDSPEAKER COMES UP AND DRIVES PAST QUACKING PROPAGANDA.

-6-

1. *Loudspeaker*: Vote your Post-Socialist candidates onto your Local Council. Thursday is Voting Day. Don't forget to vote for the Post-Socialist Candidates if you want a Fair Deal and justice. (*Repeat as Fades*)

2. *Julian*: (*Talks louder to a yell, then down as loudspeaker fades*) I'll talk about a scrambled lunatic who can't talk to his wife in the street for the noise (*Sobs*) for the noise (*Flatly in silence left by the loudspeaker van*) I really am going bootstrap.

3. *Barbara*: Let's go in here and have a hot chocolate. It looks quiet.

4. EFFECTS: STEPS. DOOR OPENS TO MURMUR OF VOICES. SCRAPING OF CHAIRS.

5. *Girl*: Coffee?

6. *Julian*: (*Wearily*) TWO hot chocolates please. Here's my card. I'm sorry love, I don't know why all this noise is getting me —

7. EFFECTS: HISS OF ESPRESSO STEAM. HE SHOUTS JUST AS THE STEAM STOPS SO THAT THE WORD 'GOD' CLANGS IN THE SUDDEN SILENCE

8. *Julian*: Oh, God!

9. EFFECTS: MURMUR STARTS AGAIN. CLINKING OF CUPS ETC. CLICK OF TOKEN IN DISC-MACHINE. WHIRR. SUDDENLY LOVESONG WAILED LOUDLY BY NASAL VOICE, RECORD HEARD THROUGHOUT NEXT DIALOGUE TOGETHER WITH HISSES OF STEAM, VOICES ETC.

10. *Julian*: Random jitters! And woman wailing for her demon lover amid a hiss of steam.

11. *1st Boy*: (*Loudly*) Hey, can't you turn it down a bit? (*Pause*).

12. *2nd Boy*: 'ey Alf, 'ark at 'im.

13. *1st Boy*: (*Slowly*) It doesn't turn down, Mister God-man.

14. *Julian*: That's right, you stand up to 'im Alf.

15. *Girl*: The sacred river ran.

16. *Julian*: Two hot chocolates.

17. *Barbara*: At last. Do you serve peace and quiet with the chocolate?

18.	*Girl:*	Julian!
19.	*1st Boy:*	The café's for everyone.
20.	EFFECTS:	We're the herbitcheways anyways. RECORD STOPS.

-7-

1.	*Julian:*	Good! Silence now I hope.
2.	*2nd Boy:*	(*Simultaneously*) That's right. If you want peace and quiet you'll 'ave to pay for it. A token costs one pound and fifty pee. One'll pound fifty pee for a round of silence.
3.	EFFECTS:	LOUD LAUGHTER.
4.	*Julian:*	(*Slowly*) One pound pence for . . . a —
5.	*2nd Boy:*	That's right. A round of silence. D'yer want it or do I put another disc on?
6.	*Girl:*	Here's a token, I'll add it to the chocolates.
7.	*Barbara:*	Julian, don't get involved, let's go.
8.	*Julian:*	Okay, here's your token.
9.	*2nd Boy:*	Thanks Mister God-man.
10.	EFFECTS:	SILENCE. CLICK OF TOKEN IN MACHINE. WHIRR. SCRAPE OF TABLE, RATTLE OF CUPS. LOUD FLING MUSIC BLARES OUT. CHAIR FALLS. NOISE OF FIGHT.
11.	*Barbara:*	(*Shouting then screaming*) Julian! Oh!
12.	EFFECTS:	CHEERS AND LAUGHTER. NOISE MUFFLED AS DOOR BANGS. QUICK STEPS. CAR ENGINE APPROACHES. SCREECH OF BRAKES. FLINGSONG BRIEFLY HEARD AS CAFÉ DOOR OPENS AND SHUTS. SCREAM. WOMAN'S RUNNING STEPS. FLINGSONG AGAIN. VOICES GROWING IN ECHO THEN ONE LAST LINE OF SONG (SEE BELOW) REPEATED OVER AND OVER THEN STOPS. VOICES FADE IN AND OUT IN COUNTERPOINT THEN SILENCE. AMBULANCE SIREN DISTANT THEN NEARER THEN LOUD THEN STOP. SAME PHRASE OF SONG REPEATED IN ECHO THEN FADE SLOWLY.

13.	*Phrase:*	*Lerve comes in silence* *But silence also means* *Yer lerve — is — gawn* *Silence means yer lewe — is — gawn.*
14.	*Voices:*	a) Is he dead? look at him, what a mess! c) Poor young man! d) He ran straight in front of me. e) What a lot of blood! f) Where's the ambulance . . . ambulance . . . ambulance . . .
15.	EFFECTS:	WORD 'AMBULANCE' REPEATED TO PHRASE FROM SONG BUT SONG FADES OUT FIRST. SILENCE.
16.	*Decibel:*	(*Small voice, almost whisper*) Hello.
17.	*Julian:*	(*With groan*) Hello.
18.	EFFECTS:	HIGH-PITCHED WHISTLE
19.	*Decibel:*	(*Very high*) Ow! You're hurting!
20.	*Julian:*	Me?
21.	*Decibel:*	No, him. The sound, it's a horrid one. Stop

-8-

1.	EFFECTS:	NOISE STOPS.
2.	*Decibel:*	Ah. (*More natural pitch but still very small voice*) That's better. I said, hello.
3.	*Julian:*	(*Wearily*) I said hello too.
4.	*Decibel:*	Oh sorry, I only heard him. Don't you want me to introduce myself?
5.	*Julian:*	No.
6.	*Decibel:*	You're Julian. I'm Decibel.
7.	*Julian:*	(*Flatly*) Decibel.
8.	*Decibel:*	Yes. Decibel.
9.	*Julian:*	So what?
10.	*Decibel:*	(*Softly*) I can help you, Julian. Ow!
11.	EFFECTS:	HIGH-PITCHED WHISTLE STARTS AGAIN.
12.	*Decibel:*	So it's *you* doing it. Please stop.
13.	*Julian:*	How can I? It's in my ear.
14.	*Decibel:*	(*Very high*) Well of course it's in your ear, it's a sound.

		But it makes me feel so thin (Higher and higher) it narrows me almost to nothing, I'll vanish soon. Oh!
15.	EFFECTS:	WHISTLE STOPS.
16.	*Decibel*:	(*Her voice veers down falsetto like a disc on power-failure*) Ugh-er! Whizz-ho for that. (*Soft normal voice*) It's unspooling. I wish you wouldn't.
17.	*Julian*:	You're in no state to help anyone.
18.	*Decibel*:	I can help you if you help yourself.
19.	*Julian*:	Like God.
20.	*Decibel*:	In a way.

-9-

1.	*Julian*:	I'm tired.
2.	*Male Voice*:	(*Loudly, IN ECHO*) Emergency. Emergency.
3.	*Female Voice*:	(*ECHO FADING IN AND OUT*) This way. Gently now. Are you next-of-kin dear? Nurse, will you take down the particulars.
4.	*Barbara*:	(*FADING IN AND OUT*) Julian Freeman, 29, yes, his age, oh, 72 Wilmington Street . . .
5.	*Nurse*:	(*IN AND OUT*) No dear, you'll have to wait out here. The doctor's just coming.
6.	*Julian*:	(*Softly but urgently*) Decibel where are you?
7.	*Decibel*:	Here Julian, I'm here. Hold on to me. Everything's going to be all right.
8.	*Julian*:	(*Slowly*) Everything's going to be all right. (*Suddenly*) What do you mean? What has happened? Decibel, where are you?
9.	*Decibel*:	Here Julian, don't make so much noise in your head, it's not the kind I like, it hurts.
10.	*Julian*:	(*Yelling*) It hurts! It hurts! Ow!
11.	*Doctor*:	Just one more second now. I'm afraid I have to hurt . . . There, that's over, good man. Nurse, get hold of Mr Stanton right away.
12.	EFFECTS:	FADE-OUT. FADE-IN FLINGSONG, AMBULANCE SIREN,

VOICES, ALL ZOOMING IN AND OUT THEN FADE-OUT. PAUSE.

13. *Julian*: (*Whispering*) Decibel! (*Silence*) Decibel!
14. *Decibel*: (*Whispering even more softly*) Yes Julian.
15. *Julian*: (*Still whispering*) Oh there you are. (*Silence*) It's quiet, isn't it? (*Silence*) Decibel.
16. *Decibel*: (*After a pause*) Yes Julian.
17. *Julian*: Talk to me.
18. *Decibel*: (*Whispering with effort*) I . . . don't . . . exist . . . in silence . . . I can hardly . . . breathe . . . I measure . . . noise . . . you see.
19. *Julian*: No I don't see. There must be . . . noise . . . somewhere . . . you can live on?

-10-

1. *Decibel*: (*Slightly louder*) Yes. Oh yes. (*Weakening again*) But not in your head, Julian. I liked it . . . there . . . I'd got used to . . . it . . . But now . . . there's only. . . the faintest . . . murmur . . . no . . . not even . . . Oh, it's like . . . a tomb.
2. EFFECTS: SILENCE FOR AS LONG AS FEASIBLE.
3. *Julian*: (*Very faint*) Decibel!
4. EFFECTS: VOICES ZOOMING IN AND OUT.
5. *Anaesthetist*: He hasn't had strong analgesics has he?
6. *Surgeon*: No, I saw we had to operate at once.
7. *Ms Nicholl*: (*Quotation which was drowned before*)

And longer had she sung, but with a frown
Revenge impatient rose;
He threw his blood-stained sword in thunder down,
And with a withering look
The war-denouncing trumpet took,
And blew a blast so loud and dread,
Were ne'er prophetic sounds so full of wo

8. *Julian*: So that's what I missed. Thank you for repeating it,

		Professor Nicholl.
9.	*Ms Nicholl:*	As a matter of fact I didn't repeat it. You repeated it.
10.	*Julian:*	You mean I heard it after all?
11.	*Ms Nicholl:*	No, you knew it already.
12.	*Julian:*	How could I? It's not my period.
13.	*Ms Nicholl:*	In one sense, we know everything, without actualising that knowledge. In another —
14.	*Julian:*	We know nothing.
15.	*Ms Nicholl:*	Exactly.
16.	*Barbara:*	Why this mania for knowing things exactly?
17.	*Julian:*	Barbara you keep out of this.
18.	*Barbara:*	I can't keep out of it, I'm in it, it's up to you to keep me out.
19.	*Ms Nicholl:*	So you see, it doesn't terribly matter if you miss one item of knowledge in a series of similar items because providing you understand the series you already know without knowing that you know.

-11-

1.	*Julian:*	How can I understand the series without knowing the items?
2.	*Decibel:*	(*Squeakily*) Precisely.
3.	*Barbara:*	Why this mania for understanding precisely?
4.	*Julian:*	Barbara you keep out of this.
5.	*Barbara:*	I can't, I'm in it, it's up to you to —
6.	*Julian:*	Quit cackling. Was that you Decibel?
7.	*Decibel:*	(*Still high but less squeaky, then lowering to normal*) Yes Julian, it's so exciting, all this noise in your head, good noise this, thank you Julian, I feel so well.
8.	*Julian:*	Noise? You call this noise? We're having a serious intellectual discussion about the theory of knowledge, Professor Nicholl and I.
9.	*Decibel:*	Buzz buzz buzz. Ooh it's lovely Julian, go on.
10.	*Barbara:*	What about the baby in the newsroom? What about

		the baby brought by the helicopter? What will you do when the baby is born in an iron-foundry run by robots?
11.	EFFECTS:	PRINTING PRESS AND FOUNDRY NOISES WHICH CONTINUE DURING NEXT DIALOGUE.
12.	*Decibel:*	(*Loud*) Ooh! Macrosuper, Julian, do go on.
13.	*Julian:*	Decibel, you little traitor! Why don't you go and measure yourself in a railway shunting yard?
14.	*Decibel:*	(*Hurt*) I don't need to. Your head will do just as well.
15.	EFFECTS:	NOISE FADES AS MS NICHOLL QUOTES.
16.	*Ms Nicholl:*	*Yet still he kept his wild unaltered mien* *While each strained ball of sight seeked bursting from his head.*
17.	*Barbara:*	Yes do tell us about the symbolic o's again Ms Nicholl, I didn't quite grasp why they were undone, deconstructed I mean what with the dishes and the quarrelling and . . . the . . . accident.

-12-

1.	*Julian:*	What accident?
2.	*Barbara:*	Your accident darling.
3.	EFFECTS:	FLINGSONG AND AMBULANCE SIREN, LOUDER AND LOUDER, THEN FADE IN AND OUT.
4.	*Decibel:*	(*Squeals with delight*)
5.	*Ms Nicholl:*	(*As noise fades*) But it is important to remember that the Augustan notion of form and decorum was an ideal that in no way reflected the burly-burly of daily life. Think for a moment of Dr Johnson striding up the Strand to the shattering clatter of horse-carriages with wooden wheels on the cobbled streets
6.	EFFECTS:	— FADE IN THESE SOUNDS AND THE NEXT AS SHE MENTIONS THEM, INCREASING VOLUME AND DROWNING HER VOICE AS DECIBEL'S GETS LOUDER

7. *Ms Nicholl:* AND SHRILLER.
—with the neighing of horses and the cracking of whips and the shouting of the coachmen, the ringing of muffin-bells and the yelling of street-cries, chairs
8. *Decibel:* to mend, sweet lavender, knives to grind.
(*Starting at beginning of EFFECTS, louder and louder, stressing o's and u's.*) Oh Julian, what an awful noise is this old-fashioned noise, it's horrible, *oh* Julian don't, *oh* please go back to the buses and cars and
9. *Julian:* speedbikes and loudspeakers, loud loud, loud, *oh*, *oh*,
10. *Barbara:* oh!
11. *Julian:* Stop!
12. *Barbara:* Please Professor Nicholl do something!
13. EFFECTS: Barbara you keep out of this.
I can't keep out of it I'm —
14. *Voices:* FLINGSONG RETURNS WITH 1ST AND 2ND BOY AS DECIBEL CONTINUES HER O'S AND AWS.
a) I say they're yuppeting it up! b) Hey, that's Alf ain'
15. EFFECTS: it? c) Two hot chocolates d) Debugger off Alf, e) Oh don't mention it it's only me trousers.
ROCKSONG STOPS ABRUPTLY, TOKEN DROPS IN
16. *Barbara:* SLOT, WHIRR THEN NEW TUNE AS BARBARA
17. EFFECTS: CONTINUES TO APPEAL TO MS NICHOLL.
Please, Professor Nicholl do something.

Put another nickel in
In the nickel ody-in,
All I want is loving you
And music music music . . .

FADE OUT SLOWLY DURING NEXT DIALOGUE.

-13-

1. *2nd Boy:* Jesuscrumbs! That's the wimpiest oldy I've heard in a hexuvatime. What are we into, a round of

folksycountry?

2. *Julian:* It's an old circular tune.

3. *1st Boy:* (*Sniggering*) A round of silence.

4. *2nd Boy:* Say, it's Mister God-man 'isself.

5. *1st Boy:* That's right, you stand up to 'im Alf.

6. *Ms Nicholl:* *The sacred river ran*
Through caverns measureless to man
Down to a sunless sea.
Here we have quite a different system of sound from that obtaining in the 18th century. The Romantics you see, knew —

7. EFFECTS: NOISE OF HORSE-CARRIAGES ON COBBLES DROWNS HER VOICE THEN FADES OUT. DECIBEL SQUEALS WITH PAIN BEYOND THE NOISE THEN DESCENDS INTO SUDDEN SILENCE, FOLLOWED BY HIGH-PITCHED WHISTLE.

8. *Decibel:* (*Very high*) Ow! Ooow! Stop it! Ooow!

9. EFFECTS: WHISTLE STOPS. SILENCE WHISPERS. FALLING CHAIR. FADE IN MURMURING VOICES THEN IN AND OUT, LIGHT SLAPPING OF CHEEK.

10. *Nurse:* Wake up Mr Freeman, you're back. Everything's all right. But don't move your head. (*Gently but IN AND OUT*) You mustn't move your head. Don't move . . . your head . . . your head. . . your head.

11. *Julian:* (*Groans*) Decibel. Where are you?

12. *Nurse:* She'll be along to see you in visiting hours, dear. Three to five. But please don't move your head. (*FADING*) Don't move your head, there's a dear . . .

13. EFFECTS: (BOXING ZOOMS IN LOUDLY) With a right straight into the stomach, oh very low below the — That was a — no — yes, the umpire's called a foul . . .

14. EFFECTS: CROWD YELLS.

15. *Decibel:* (*Excitedly during commentary*) Julian, just listen to

		that, oh no, right, yes, go on, quick now, yes, oh, oh, oh —
16.	*Julian*:	Clam up, all of you! And you Decibel.
17.	*Decibel*:	(*Softly in sudden silence*) Me, Julian?
18.	*Julian*:	Yes you, Decibel. I'm sorry but you'll have to go.

-14-

1.	*Decibel*:	(*Tearfully*) Oh Julian don't leave me, don't throw me out, I can't live without you.
2.	*Julian*:	And I can't live with you. I must have complete silence.
3.	*Decibel*:	(*Whispering*) Then I must die.
4.	*Julian*:	No blackmail. I didn't even know you till three to five visiting hours.
5.	*Decibel*:	You wouldn't . . . like it, Julian.
6.	*Julian*:	You mean you wouldn't. So you assume I wouldn't. (*Silence*) You seem to revel in noise. Oh you're very selective about which noises, but those you like, why, I do believe you go about creating them. (*Long silence*) Don't you? (*Silence*) You itsybitsybitch.
7.	EFFECTS:	FLINGSONG IN AND OUT. SCREECH OF BRAKES. AMBULANCE SIREN.
8.	*Julian*:	No, no (*Showing*) It hurts. (*Normal voice*) It hurts. (*Whispering*) It hurts.
9.	*Barbara*:	(*Soothingly*) I know darling, I know. You've been very brave. Try not to move your head.
10.	*Julian*:	Where's Decibel?
11.	*Barbara*:	Yes darling I'm here.
12.	*Julian*:	Barbara you keep out of this.
13.	*Barbara*:	(*Slight gasp, pause, then effort*) Yes, dear. (*Sob*) Just keep your head still. Please. (*Breaks down*) Oh darling I do love you so. I can't live with out you . . .
14.	*Nurse*:	Now Ms Freeman, don't go upsetting him. I think that's enough for today.

15.	*Barbara:*	(*FAR OFF AND FADING*) Yes I'm sorry nurse. Goodbye my love, I'll be back tomorrow.
16.	*Julian:*	(*Whispering*) Decibel? (*SILENCE*) Decibel!
17.	EFFECTS:	SILENCE THEN TINKLING NOTES LIKE RADIO SIGNAL AFTER SWITCH-OFF, REPEATING.
18.	*Julian:*	(*Still whispering*) Decibel!
19	EFFECTS:	SUDDEN CUT

2

First I'd like to say two things. But you will answer my question? Mr Nwankwo am I in the habit of not answering your questions? Well — But first it is necessary to say —

Le milieu politique - - - nombreuses *petites phrases* ce weekend qui ont fait les délices de la presse. Celle du président d'abord.

And ARE you going to call for indus - - action? I must first - - make it - - - your introd - -, that I -

Having said that, the situation can't be allowed to -

And Dixon passes to - - - - - - - - who - - - - - - Evans to - - loses it to Grandet no, he's got it - - - oh, terrific footwork - - - passes to - - - - - - directs a header. Oh, a near - -

Having said that, the situation can't be allowed to —

For of course, libido has replaced semeiosis. And that being so, we can say —

Precisely, that is why their Chargé - - - - - - - - - Office, to give an explanation and to make it plain that it mustn't happen again.

Nous avons toujours dit, nous les Commu —

We intend to seek a determined stride forward for Post-Socialism and New Democracy. But you are often accused of fudging the real issues. There will be no fudging of anything, on the contrary, we shall have utmost clarity. Clearly the general principles must be —

Certo che l'autocritica è una buona cosa, nel esercito, nella polizia, no potrebbe indebolire il corpo, puo solamente rinforzarle. E questo vale anche per la autocritica nel suo proprio partito? Ah! Non l'ho visto venire, quella! Lei fa referenzia al —

Happy Morning Hour! That's what our new morning program is called. And we can't make it without YOU. Your baby is having a first birthday?

Send us a —

What prompted this new escalation? that's the question I put to our —

Entschuldigen Sie bitte, das haben wir nie gesagt. Was wir genau —

The impasse provides a certain impetus. Por impotence? That's unwor —

I agree. And when a Post-Socialist Government is elected, it will be high up on the list of legislative prior —

And now that you have at last agreed to nego - - - - - - it plain that we will not negotiate. But — Not at all we must enter talks, we agree, but not neg —

I believe in lorenorder, I'm a lore-abiding person, though I can't abide lore-officers you see, bec —

The U.S. Government is very concerned about the Soviet proposal that concrete results should come out of the conference, seeing that —

We must remember the Baroque fondness for the tromploy effect and the me's on a beam —

Primo tengo que decirle dos cosas. Entonces la primera —

And will you be the candidate for the leadership? Why will you journalists - - - - - time enough to —

Well, birth, marriage and death and all the rest of it. What do you mean by all the rest of it, what rest is there after death? Oh sorry I didn't mean to pun. I hope not. I was merely answering your question about my themes as a wordprocessor, not talking about reality. But isn't reality —

And how long do you expect to wait for their reaction? First I must say three things —

For it's not only a question of por - - - - - violent - - - children's - - - - - attractively dressed up with spaceships and compu - - - - - - story element - - - hurling himself from a great height upon the villain and fighting - - - except that - - - like mediaeval knights. It's all as old as - - - But surely - - - deprive our children of a healthy spirit of - - - - - what should go and what should not. I'm trying to say to viewers - - - - - - - - - really a problem for —

'ere Sam, this is Dave, 'e's new, you tell 'im the - - - don't be so suspi - - - just surprised. Surprised at what, eh? What d'yer mean surp —

We can work it out quite easily, after all Christ was born between 5 and 10 BC, so –

Oh no! not Bankrupt! Ouf! 500. I'11 have an M please. No M. Your turn Dick, 8000, 750, 100, oh, no, Pass, Bad Luck! Sally. - - - - - 900. For 900 I'll have a –

We must stop fighting last year's battles and become realistic. We must look ahead - - - - - - - - - - - - - - - - But surely that isn't exactly –

Stay tuned –

No indeed, it isn't exactly anything, cut or uncut, particularly among the fighting democats and demadogs.

Dear Director General,

I write to draw your attention to the scandalous blackout which managed to switch me off from the entire population not only of England but of Europe, Australia and the United States in the crucial sleep-walking scene when I played Lady Macbeth in the production you broadcast last week. You must know just how much work went into this play, from the direction to the players and the technicians. Personally I did not, as you must appreciate, accept the role for the fee, which was nominal, but to reach this wider audience, in other words, for the greater glory of the art.

In the name of both Shakespeare and all my fellow-workers I must protest vehemently at this totally unacceptable technical breakdown. I insist moreover that the play be rebroadcast, with all the non-star participants paid as for a repeat, as soon as you have managed to repair your transmitters.

Yours sincerely,

Paula James, D.B.C.

We are all flooded with thousands of such diskettes in both radio and television, mostly from furious listeners and viewers, but also from performers and wordprocessors. Dame Paula's letter is typical enough. Dear old Paula, she even wrote it herself in handwriting! Tim said to me after a meeting where it was read out as a sample: Just like the old days in Cornwall, never quite with it.

All letters naturally assumed that the sudden cuts were entirely our fault, our most grievous technical fault. So did the press, gloating at our discomfiture. A general wail of self-righteous reproach went up. Then, in fact fairly soon, when it became clear that something else was at stake since it was happening more and more often and to all radio and television stations in Europe, in America, all over the world, the wail of self-righteous reproach swelled slowly, though surprisingly slowly, to a generalised howl of rage. Unsurprisingly, but even more slowly than all the others, because always so confidently unaware, the politicians are the angriest. For their howl of rage, while claiming to be most concerned with the distressing and even dangerous gaps in both our cultural heritage and the diffusion of vital information, betrays by its tone that what is being experienced most deeply as intolerable in an age corresponding for decadence to the late Middle Ages, is the fact of such frequent and sudden losses in the eternal commentary.

As a one-time classicist, I don't have to wonder what people did in ancient times. They met in small numbers. They discussed. They read. They wrote. Commentary would grow and grow as each civilisation declined. But before the electromagnetic waves that we discovered we could generate as support for words of every kind, at every level, in all languages, always the same words, the same images violent and venal and revered, thrown far further afield than they ever could have been in an amphitheatre or an agora, before all this, what did people do? They talked. And the greatest displacements of world consciousness were achieved not in public, on worldwide screens, but in solitude, against the familiar forms of the eternal commentary, filched and reaffixed, refurbished and floundered around.

And now, for more than a century, the eternal commentary weighs heavy upon the air, overloading the waves with tetravocal news bulletins like modern operas, fast rolling Spanish over crisp Serbocrat under pompous English inexorably heard behind the French or vice-quadriversa. Inexorable? Tim once said at a meeting, nonsense, exore it at once. Though he told me privately that radio-astronomers have long been protesting at the drastic reduction of their universe-scrutinising possibilities down to an ever-narrowing beam. But surely mere quantity, even if it can physically dip and twist the frequencies agonisingly out of shape—but that's a mere metaphor, Tim says—couldn't explain these sudden stops. Fused noises, yes, and atmospherics, but not silence, except from trouble at the transmitter, and not all transmitters in the world could so frequently and simultaneously be in trouble. And why aren't words being garbled as on a tape at the wrong speed, or scrambled? But no, just silence.

It is as if the world had suddenly come to the conclusion that from now on it must eat its words. As if man must eat his words, all of them.

In fact the press soon named the whole phenomenon Verbivore. Some journalists tried Logophagoi — which pleased me more, as an ex Greek scholar, and also recalled the Xorandor affair with its Alphaphagoi, soon corrupted to Alphaguys but it was too learned, or else rapidly reduced to Logfag by the more and more numerous who have no sense of etymology and therefore can't spell. But that's another problem, a lost cause. Be that as it may — and screentyping makes one verbose — Verbivore was easier to grasp, and therefore became more popular.

But who or what is doing the eating? Technically, we all learnt at the many meetings we have to attend, the very concept is impossible. You can intercept, but this naturally does not affect reception. And you can jam. But you cannot, at least not on this scale, suppress altogether, unless a generalised, worldwide network of transmitter-sabotage is assumed, and that, though a possibility, has unimaginably far-reaching technical, administrative and political implications. Meanwhile, we are all to continue as if our productions and presentations were being broadcast whole as before, in other words, as if nothing were happening. As I used to say, we'll all go on as if.

However, being at least partially responsible for the Xorandor episode, I can't help remembering, and thinking about it. And I feel sure that Tim is, if I dare use the phrase, on the same wave-length, since he was so involved in Xorandor. Press memory is remarkably short, because journalists are always so young, and so trained to be dramatic, that they tend to think everything is unprecedented. Even financial correspondents talk about an all-time low for the dollar, because they themselves have not experienced it lower (or higher), or can't remember a lower low even five years earlier. Tim and I are both older, and we are closely concerned, he as Managing Director, me as Drama Producer. The difficulty is, to meet him. He's so overwhelmed with the problem that he lives, as it were, in another world from mine.

Talking of protesting wordprocessors, it's Perry Hupsos, the author of that last radio-play I produced, who puzzled me the most. He seemed to have written the cut into his script. When I first read it, before Verbivore had seriously begun, I assumed the hero just dies suddenly, and although I didn't think much of that as an ending, I preferred not to question it, Perry being one of those touchy authors. But now it looks very different. Almost as if he had a premonition. Shades of Cassandra! But many wordprocessors have said they've imagined whole scenes that subsequently happened to them. Interestingly enough, though, as author, he took care not to cut his own play till very near the end, I mean it was commissioned as a thirty-minute play and couldn't have gone on more than five minutes at most. The joke was on him in the end, since the broadcast version was cut earlier, by Verbivore, whatever that is.

Odd bod. He went through a phase of calling himself Perry Striker, for some of his more social fictions anyway, as an (ironic?) gesture towards that old Soviet masquerade, a somewhat stained glaznost, many years ago. Shows how little Greek he knows, let alone Russian, but it caught on like wild old myths, and served him well. Then the phase passed as the word did, with the phenomenon, as in all things.

At any rate, after the broadcast Perry rang me up, furious. It's amazing how wordprocessors can get lost in their processing and have no idea what's happening in the world around them. They don't even seem to read the papers. He hadn't heard of Verbivore at all, although everyone was talking about it. A wordprocessor commissioned to process a radio-play who doesn't even bother to listen to the radio, or to other radio-plays. And this one about noise, too. It's true he had a good notion of how the sound-effects function and what the stereoworkshop can do, but then he's done radio-plays before.

I wonder what happened to Jip and Zab. Tim might know. I wish I could see him. But he's inordinately busy, all the more because he's such an expert on waveguides and microwaves and all the rest of it. Life, marriage, death and all the rest of it, as a literary Nobel Prize winner said in a radio-interview the other day, just before being, even him, cut. All the cuts are now being studied to see if there are patterns of occurrence. The above collection is culled from these recordings, which are typed out (and sometimes misunderstood and misspelt), then computer-analysed and handed out to us with incomprehensible graphs and statistics, in case anyone of us notices anything the technicians wouldn't know. Unlikely. And, of course, like everyone else, I have taken to typing things down, communicating with my personal computer through lack of the comforting pseudo-presences in the sitting room, with their eyes on the telecue not you. Wordprocessing has become a withdrawal symptom.

If the eternal commentary disappears altogether in this way, if it is swallowed, or has to be given up through interference, won't mankind go slowly mad? Or shall we simply turn back to reading and writing and talking and behaving as if the media had never been? But that's no longer an option, I believe, our minds and psyches, our entire nervous system and networks of expectations have been transformed by the media. It is as if the electric waves of our brains had been altered by the electromagnetic waves around us, as if some anode had converted them into sound sense. We depend on the media for our lifeblood, the stream of information, the adventures, the violence, the romance, the games, the idols, the beauty, the knowledge, the gossip, all that Plato called Love Truth and Beauty, the explanations, the wooing of our beliefs, the eternal commentary that lines our lives like a loving companion, a double, making sense of it for us in its fragmentary and fragmented fashion.

Different people are angry about different bits of this lifeblood, this plasma, not about the bits as such but about their bad quality, their incompleteness. The young are hardly concerned since music, Fling, Broody, Jazz or Classical, is mysteriously unaffected, only words. Perhaps we shall have to sing our news bulletins and interviews. But no, presumably words when sung are left uncut because unrecognisable as words by whoever or whatever is word-eating. Anyway, only spoken words are affected. And the young don't view or listen to word-programs of any kind. So they can enjoy their hyperdaelic videoclips in peace, if peace is the term. And most of them don't miss the crap that's jockey-jabbered between discs. So the young don't care, as usual with major crises. The sofa-sportsmen are furious, and housewives are beside themselves without their ever increasing daily ration of soap. The old and the lonely are the most unhappy, they miss the comedy-programs, the plays, the phone-ins, the serials and games, the chat-shows, the documentaries, the old films. Everything in fact, that substitutes for company. But nobody takes much notice of the old and lonely, they rarely vote.

I miss none of that, but I am personally affected since I've always been a radio-addict, leaving the talk-stations on all night, and talking soothes me. I'm like Decibel, who seems to thrive on hifalutin discussions in a civilised tone. Buzz buzz buzz, oo, do go on. At first they take my mind physically out of its inner circles by making it follow whatever's being talked about. Then it slides off the phrases to the drone of that best narcotic, vox humana. But now alas, even the B.B.C. has extended its music-programs and is doing more and more just-disc sessions, like the rest of the stations at night, or even, since the crisis, by day.

The most peeved, as I said, are the politicians who, astonishingly, must have really relished the media and believed their own empty, confused and therefore often ungrammatical sentences. And to their chagrin their prestations are the least missed, except by each other and the journalists who are convinced that their obsessions about in-moves are shared by the rest of the population. And now, thank Verbivore, they are, at least on and off. No politician likes to have his words eaten by someone else, he's more used to having to do it himself.

The media! I say the media, meaning like everyone else radio as listened to publicly and television as viewed, because I'm part of them.

But will other extensions of ourselves be touched? Will everything electromagnetic or microwavish be perturbed? Planes use radio and radar, so do spacestations and warships and teleguided trains and cars and — the vista is endless. Shall we all be cut off from each other, except in presence?

And today I have been in the presence, in the presence of Sir Timothy Lewis, Deputy-Director-General. I don't know why I felt he must have moved so far out of my world, I only had to ask for the interview to occur.

Yes, he said, I thought of it too. But only fleetingly, I must admit, as an outside, a very much outside possibility. The creatures were sent off the planet after all. And there are so many others.

Others?

Other possibilities.

What are they? Or perhaps you can't tell me.

Of course I can, but they're highly technical and —

I wouldn't understand.

You would, Mira my dear, but it would take time and no don't complete my sentence, it would sound like a reproach again, unless I say it myself. As you must know, I'm under tremendous pressure, from all sides, up, down and sideways. All the responsible staff will be told at each stage when this or that hypothesis begins to look a little more than surmise, but there's no point in loading you all with the details of all our research in multiple directions. Everyone's been given the occurrence-charts and probability calculations and of course any non-technical ideas, such as this one of yours, or political or whatever, from anyone, are welcome.

Yes, thank you. But we can't make much of charts without technical abilities, and hundreds of non-technical ideas have been put around already, here and in the press, some of them supercranky. Surely you have narrowed it down to a few hypos?

The main two are of course world-pollution and enemy action.

Your tone puts the same sort of scare-quotes round the word enemy that one still hears and sees around the words reality, soul, unconscious, democracy and other hypothetical entities in popular books on literature and philosophy. Are you still in touch with Jip and Zab?

No. Kids are rarely loyal to childhood adorations later in life, they're kind of ashamed I suppose. Jip read physics at Cambridge, so presumably he went in for it, and got high in the discipline, so he could be found in Who's Who. Wait a minute, I think I read somewhere, years ago, that he'd gone to Nasa. Another braindrain. But it can be checked.

And Zab?

No idea. She wanted to do philosophy.

She can't have succeeded then, philosophy and all the humanities disappeared from University programs in favour of hitec and science round about that time.

True. Poor old auntie B.B.C. inherited that torch and we're almost the only — I don't know why I said 'poor', Mira, forgive me.

You don't have to interpret my looks. And we're not the only ones, it's just that these subjects have merely become hobbies. Even Modern Languages teach only Technical Translation and jargon. But you'll find these hobbies still in popular books and magazines. If you ever read such things.

Touché. But Zab was as scientifically gifted as her brother, even, I thought, more brilliant, more intuitive, though erratic. She would have done well in any branch. But I'm sure we can trace them both.

You don't have much time, Tim, would you like me to do the donkey-work? That's really why I came to see you, to find out if there might be anything in it, that would make tracing them worth while.

Of course my dear. No stone unturned, as it were.

Biggleton said that! Jesuscrumbs!

What?

No, sorry, that's from a louche character in a radio-play. But how idiotic of me. Dame Paula! She's their mother. She'd know.

Mira, but how idiotic of ME! I knew her well, I should have remembered. I'll write to her. Or no, I'll give her a ring, if you can find me her —

Don't you think, after that letter of hers and your possibly bland or technical reply, if any, that I should do it, for ostensibly personal reasons? I mean, your position might give the whole thing more credence than —

You're right. I leave it to you then.

3

Which was just as well, since I don't really have to go very far to find Zab, who remembers exactly what she was doing when she first heard of Verbivore. I can simply call her up, Isabel Manning, Euro-M.P. for Aachen International District, on account of her dual nationality, fluent French and German, and a higher technological competence than most M.P.'s. After all, she had taught Communications for years at the Technische Hochschule in Aachen. She's lucky, most Euromps have to live in their constituencies and keep travelling to the new European Parliament in Aachen, a town better known outside Germany, or at least in France, as Aix-la-Chapelle, one-time centre of an early undivided Europe of sorts. And that name was officially chosen to pacify France, Belgium and Luxemburg, all furious when the community, numbering twenty-three and tired of seeing its resources drained by the communications wastage of having three capitals, outvoted them for a radical reorganisation and one capital only, in Aixla-Chapelle, the entire area around it being internationalised into a sort of European Washington DC. The French ironically call it Washington d'ici. But Zab's constituency is the new international district.

She remembers because she was trying to recall an incident from her childhood. And, in peculiar fact, the shadowy impossible possibility of Verbivore came to her unofficially via her son, age eighteen, long before the so-called beginning or "first day", as it was later retrospectively aetiologised.

The reason she was trying to remember this childhood incident was that although she had carefully entered it into the computer she and Jip had at the time, she had no memory of it whatever when she called it up, by chance, on that April day some twenty years later, twenty-three years to be exact, and this bugged her. She even wondered whether she had invented it, but it kind of rang true: at fourteen her interests had been far more scientific than fictional — if such an old-fashioned distinction can still be made.

Zab lives in a small flat just beyond the second ring around Aachen, behind a wooded hill called the Lousberg, not from Laus or louse, they say, but from some Louis or other. There are no houses on the Lousberg side of her street. Instead, steps go up a steep grass bank into the wood. It's like having a forest at my door, she says to her friends, and I can walk over the hill through the wood and down the other side into the inner town. For Aachen, although it has a large suburbia and a wide outer ring, and an even wider Autobahn surround, is itself small. I remember earlier on, she tells them, trying to buy a skirt-hook in what seemed the inner town and being told I'd only find such a small thing *in der Stadt*. But I am in the town, I said. They meant the old town, the innerest, within the innerest ring, an inner sanctum one can walk across in about ten minutes. But I suppose the real inner sanctum must be the remains of Charlemagne's chapel inside the cathedral, the quark to Aachen's atom.

And outwards from this atom, linked by the electromagnetic force of a complex Autobahnkreuz, are other atoms, some of which Aachen now almost touches, Düren and Köln to the East, Düsseldorf to the North-East, Bonn and Koblenz to the South-East, Liège or Lüttich or Luik to the West, Heerlen and Antwerp to the North-West. For Aachen, despite its new status and revived old French name, lies in what is still called *Dreiländereck*, on the old German frontier with both Holland and Belgium.

When I came to live here she types into her processor, my twin-brother John wrote to me as Alcuina, at the Court of Charlemagne, Aix-la-Chapelle though he did also put in the street and number in order to reach me.

Why have I typed "my twin-brother John" instead of Jip, as if I were writing this for other eyes? The private memoir, the diary or the journal habit, even private letters, decayed so completely as a form of communication during the public electronic age that we fall back, when we want to use it again, on antiquated formulas we then still studied at school, the secret journal really meant for publication and posterity. Yet who would ever have brought out a Compact Disc called the Collected Telephone Conversations of say, Christa Wolf or Woody Allen, as they used to bring out The Collected Letters, the Journal, The Diary of?

Yet clearly I am deriving pleasure, just as fiction-writers used to, from the mere noting of facts, instead of getting to the point. *Zur Sache! Zur Sache!* The real Sache being, however, the day I learnt about the Logophagoi and its resulting passionate return to writing. How to come *zur*? Ah yes, the attic.

There are few houses in my street, since it's short and ends in a field at the foot of the Lousberg, but they're all fairly comfortable, and we're surrounded with gardens and greenery. My view East from the living room terrace at the back is downhill over more posh houses, more posh gardens, then the Football Stadium and the famous Reitstadion, then the Bubble, the huge and hideous Eurocomplex, though some find it beautiful, under which spread the high, the low, the round, the rectangular, the pyramidal buildings of the European Parliament, Economic Council, and the rest, as well as reception halls, luxury flats for the top people, comfortable sleeping quarters for late workers, shopping centres, gardens, tennis-courts, mini-golf, swimming, sauna, the lot, the entire set-up air-conditioned and protected from the summer heat and the cold North German winters. The diplobubble, die Hochbeamtenblase or Bürokratenblase, la bulle des baratineurs or bulleburotique, the hotair bubble, la bollatura in Italian with a nice pun, and so on. Of course no one actually lives there. Ambassadorial ranks have grand apartments in town (all the old humanities buildings were pulled down for these) or houses outside town, inasmuch as there is an outside now that doesn't merely become another town. But many Euromps like to find a pad in the Bubble for their visits, which then seem a bit like a luxury holidaycamp to them, especially when they're coming from wintry climates. The rest, the interpreters, secretaries, computer-clerks and so on, live in less upmarket high-rise buildings to the North and West of the town, invisible from here. The Bubble is also called the Blister, or la Cloque, or la Cloche à

Fromage, by those who think it an eyesore. Beyond the diplobubble eastwards, low hills can be glimpsed through the glaznostic bubble between the buildings.

My flat is on the second floor of one of those old bourgeois houses built in the nineteen-eighties, but it's also the top flat, smaller than the other two flats below in that it's already in the roof, with dormer-windows and sloped ceilings, and a little terrace above part of my neighbours' much more spacious living room. But from the small entrance hall a narrow flight of stairs leads up to a splendid chalet-like attic as large as the house, with a huge roof-window. It used to be Hanjo's room. It has now become my teleport.

Is all this detail necessary? Offline tapeworm, as Jip used to call me when I did this during our creation of Xorandor, as if it were important to say we had Cornflakes for breakfast. Why does it seem vital to get my topographical position so exactly right, simply because I live here, simply because it's real to me? It means damn all to anyone else and probably doesn't even evoke a vague image. What have we lost, or what are we all trying to hold onto or recapture since the disappearance of books? Everything being on hard disc or diskette now, with content invisible so that only maniac readers buy them. And now, the Logophagoi (the Logfaggots as some illiterates are already deforming).

I was up there, on a cool Sunday in April, at last trying to sort out all my old Quatsch and make discroom for new Quatsch. I started with the Oldest stackfile of floppies, as they used to be called. Most of the labels were clearly marked as to content and I could judge by the callcodes alone whether to efface them or not, or even to throw them away altogether — for naturally I had no time to screen them all just to decide. The really old ones — why can't I dump anything? — belonged to older computers anyway, possibly too old even for the interface on my Intercompatible. Handshake, the interfacing used to be called, as if computers had hands to shake or faces to inter. But the real reason was time. Rummaging in an attic always has its temptations and I was determined to be ruthless.

Then I found a diskette, and its clumsy size at once took me right back to our childhood Jip's and mine. But the callcodes on the label were incomprehensible. They'll be incomprehensible even in a few years, Jip used to say of my secretive ways, you'll have forgotten. I won't, I won't! But I have. A few years? Nearly a quarter of a century! LOOP, ZBX, LM, SCAN, FLOAT, OLDP, NEWF, GO. Well, they're mostly computerms, but I must have used them as codes for something else so knowing that doesn't help. What content did they convey, what text would they call up on the screen? As for the initials, ZBX, LM, GQ . . . ? GQ? Ghastly Quarters? Geopolitical Quiz? The Gist of Quarks? Gigo Quatsch? Gormless Quibble? German Quarrel? That faint-connected. I realised the diskette must date back to our year-and-a-half stay in Bayreuth after the hooha (swags! thunks! and all that diodic bootstrap we random-jittered!). I guess some of it stuck. Would I understand it? Would my Intercompatible read it? It has an entry for old large discs at the back somewhere.

Nothing for it, I had to try. Clearly I couldn't keep all these floppies. But this one I knew I must see first. So in it went. Großer Quertreiber? Grausame Quälen? Grenzlose Quackelei? The Handshake worked in a few nanoseconds. File. Öffnen.

> Spaghetti logic array with Herr Groenitz tonight. He was drunk. Frieda said so later, daran muss Du nicht mehr denken, er war schwer betrunken. Is that an excuse? (Sorry says some buttonpushing prez, I was drunk). Booleshit, stop being such a Tugendheldin. Prig, much shorter. Using English cos no scharfes s on Poccorn keyboard, Okay Erzählung.
>
> Meal went fine as usual with Rudi and Jip and me making maybe too much noise. Rudi's Vater — why do we call his mother Frieda but his father sein Vater oder Herr Groenetz? Well, Frieda's more friendly and in fact mum's friend, whereas Herr Groenetz had never met mum and dad till they came last summer and he seemed to take an instant dislike to dad. Jealousy perhaps, he's only a Diplomierter Ingenieur (in fact we privately call him Dipling because he has Dipl. Ing. on his van), whereas dad's a physicist and got lots of attention through the Xorandor hooha. But he's much older than Frieda, a whole generation older at least, and there seem to be a few dangling refs to WWII somewhere in his datanetwork, or maybe learnt from his father, who

> would have been old enough to have been fascistically active then. At any rate mum had told us to avoid politics, as he's now a bit too rabidly at the other end of the spectrum and a bit too self-righteously spouting commycat with tramline symptoms.

Commycat? What the megavolt was that? I found myself using our old slang. Tramline symptoms, that was Jip's term for ideological crap blindly repeated by the brainwashed, and it tends to be at the extremes that people need to be told what to think, so when they have to give up one extreme for some reason they veer to the other. So commy must be communist. Yes: He's an old commy, I'd once said to mum on a visit and she'd vaguely echoed oh yes, very crummy. Commycat. Like Copycat? Then I remembered: communist catechism. But who was I, then, to call it so self-righteously "self-righteously"?

Next screen.

> At any rate, we studiously avoided politics as usual, and as usual stuck to Smalltalk Quatsch when not making Spassquatsch with Rudi. But we'll never learn proper German if we stick to the weather and schooltalk. So when Dipling started talking about dad showing fascist strains and being moreover in danger of becoming a Fachidiot, jumped in, tho Frieda kept trying to tone it all down and change the subject and telling her husband to stop downing one Bierkrug after another, which were later followed by whiskies in quick succession.
>
> The thunkish thing was that he seemed to loadlink so easily on dad as a way of NOT talking politics, but of course to him the whole boolesup Welt is politics, and he grabbed at dad, on and on, less and less loyally or even politely, gleefully nasty, and all punctuated by expressions of how he was only saying this out of concern, for dad, for mum, for us, and how "wir" had all carefully avoided the topic (dad) yet "couldn't help" bringing it up (es ging gar nicht anders). Whereas we'd pounced on it (Jip defending dad but also partly agreeing) in order on the contrary to avoid politics! This until Frieda insisted we change the subject. But all was reasonably floatpoint and jokestacked till then, nor did I comment on how offline and unspooling his terminal display was.

As I read, I remembered suddenly how in the middle of the hooha someone, Alex I think, had said we'd become spoilt brats if we were allowed to go to the nuclear station, especially if we succeeded in saving the situation (and of course if we didn't we'd be dead like everyone around). Did we become spoilt brats? I sure struck myself now, reading this, as a precocious prig.

> We were sitting around after the meal in the living room, when Dipling asked if the Greens were popular in England, or rather, why they weren't a bigger movement, deforestation and all that. No, Jip and Rudi had gone up to Rudi's room to play computergames (Rudi the older is still at the game-stage), so I was alone with Dipling and Frieda, anxious to get more conversation practice. Man vs. Frau and mere schoolgirl. But I thought this topic as stated safe enough, so I leapt in, saying how they don't have as much Erfolg as in Germany and haven't pierced through into Parliament, tho of course all parties paid Greenlipservice. And I launched into an explanation of the English electoral system which doesn't allow small parties to get in — all this more as German practice than to impart info, which I suppose he knew — when suddenly he started.

DIP: The nadir was reached by Wilson and Callaghan.

ME: (*Surprised, still with deforestation and electoral system, and not at all sure who Wilson and Callaghan were — they sounded like a music-hall turn*) What nadir?

DIP: Well, the moral nadir.

ME: But what do you mean by the moral nadir?

DIP: Well, the moral degradation.

ME: (*Still friendly but teasing*) Hey, dad'd say here you're like the young, who can't define their generalisations except with other generalisations, WHAT moral degradation? (*Course he isn't young, so dad's wrong on that, must be more the semiliterate of any age and time. But that seemed to flatter him, or at least to flipflop the possible danger of mentioning dad, into mere repeat*)

DIP: Well, the appalling policies.

ME: (*Laughing now*) How long does this go on? WHAT appalling policies? (*Also hoping it will come out without my having to show my ignorance of who Wilson and Callaghan were, and what they had to do with deforestation*).

FR: Go on Liebchen, be specific! (Drück Dich genauer aus!)

DIP: Well, all the bullshit (Quatsch).

ME: WHAT bullshit?

DIP: (*Angry, downing more whisky*) THE bullshit, all the bullshit.

ME: (*Still amused by this stepwise unrefinement but thinking it just a game or drunken bootstrap*) Come on, Herr Groenetz, tell us what you have in mind.

DIP: You tell ME what YOU have in mind.

ME: (*Bootloaded by aggressive tone*) I have nothing in mind, I'm asking YOU to define what YOU mean by the terms YOU've been using, from nadir to bullshit.

DIP: (*calmer*) Well, their sell-out to America.

ME: (*Total bootstrap about England's American policies at whatever period he's buffering on about and genuinely wanting to know, so unaware of scare-signs*) But in what way were their policies towards America appalling? (*I used his terms*) What sell-out?

DIP: (*To Frieda*) WE understand each other. It's clear she doesn't.

FR: But Liebchen, she's scarcely fourteen!

ME: No I don't understand. (*Making attempt to clear things up*) You brought up the subject, whatever it is, and you've steadily refused to tell me what it is, so I tried teasing it out of you. There's no reason to get angry.

DIP: I can't accept this kind of specious argument.

ME: Specious argument! It's you who's being specious. I haven't used ANY argument, I've asked you what you meant by nadir and bullshit and after a Viertelstunde I finally get sellout to America. But we were talking about the Greens and deforestation and the electoral system. So I was simply flummoxed, and still am. Or non-plussed, as Xorandor would say.

DIP: (*very angry*) There you go again, with your vanity and your specious arguments.

FR: Calm down . . . We probably all agree anyway, we're all against the missiles.

ME: (*Bootstrapped with astonishment! Realising too late that we're on his tramlines again and that I must do everything to change the subject or clear out but how?*)

DIP: No, I object!

FR: Object to what? She hasn't said anything.

DIP I object to the word p-p-probably (W-w-wahrscheinlich). There's nothing Wahrscheinlich about it. On the contrary, she's quite sure to say "But the Russians are worse".

ME: (*Here all my sofar funface attitude froze into fury and I became hexadex miffed rather than quizzy. I looked all round the room, under the sofa, got up to open the sideboard with pointed irony*) Russians? Where? Who mentioned Russians? Is there someone else here?

DIP: (*Furious*) Du freches Kind! How dare you talk to me like that? You think you know everything because you got into the papers last year over that ridiculous adventure of yours. Lady Macbeth he's supposed to have called himself, all a putup job if you ask me. You know perfectly well what I mean.

ME: I know NOW, though it took me twenty minutes to get it out of you. (*Angry now too*) By what right d'you claim to know what I'm GOING to say, what's in MY mind, when I haven't said anything to give you any kind of clue, and only asked you what you meant? By what right d'you plonk me into a readymade category when you weren't even capable of telling me clearly and straight out what was in YOUR mind? I may be a child but I won't have this kind of stupid labelling.

DIP: (*Suddenly lost*) Your sort, offspring of elites, always using specious arguments.

ME: I did NOT, repeat NOT, use ANY arguments. I was asking questions. We're not elitist offspring, that's loopy (blöd) but in my family we argue in a civilised tone and define our terms (*Not sure this wholly true, but it's true enough compared with him, and sounded good*).

DIP: (*Roused again and really shouting now*) Your family! It's because of people like you and your brother and your father that we're going straight into another world war.

ME: (*Suddenly very calm*) If you really believe that, then you have no business receiving us in your house. (*Exit me, to hall, followed by wailing Frieda who says he doesn't mean it etc but I shake her off and walk out of the house slamming the front door*).

Well of course I had to come back, after walking around Bayreuth for a couple of hours to faint strains of openair Götterdämmerung or something from the Wagner festival which had just started, and hoping they'd be gigavolt anxious.

But it's late July and the days are still long. I did ragingly think of a few bold hitchhiking and stowaway schemes back to Cornwall, but storming out in a huff isn't really me. So instead, I've been sitting up recording it while it's all wortwörtlich in my mind.

END GQ

4

I still didn't know what GQ stood for (Groenetz Quarrel?) but at least I now knew its content, and its incredible silliness. I wondered briefly how soon after this I had learnt not to pounce on insults, and the general uselessness of saying things straight out as I felt and thought them, or even of insisting on the opponent's weak logic. I also remembered what computer whizz-kids Jip and I had been (now they're a dime a dozen) and how edge-triggering this must have been to many people such as Groenetz or even Rudi. But all this I shrugged off, for what scared me more than anything was that I couldn't remember this scene at all. I couldn't remember storming out. I couldn't remember coming back to what must have been Frieda's relieved and tearful reproaches. I couldn't remember typing the quarrel into the computer. And it was my own hidden, secret floppy, I remembered that, and its mystery callcodes. Clearly I didn't tell Jip about the quarrel the next day, nor, presumably, did anyone else mention it, or I'd have recalled it from pseudo-memory afterwards.

Naturally lots of gigo went in, for fun, for practice, and I felt sure that if I called up the other texts I'd have repeat experiences. Perhaps they might recall other things that would bring back the experienced reality of this scene. But I couldn't understand how such an incident could have been completely deleted from my mind, erased ROM as I used to say. It seemed to me I should have remembered at least the fact of the quarrel if not the content. Or a difficult atmosphere with Herr Groenetz. But no, all was sweetness and light in my memory of our long stay in their house. Plato said the technique of writing would cause men to lose their memories in favour of memorability, what would he say about computers? We externalise not only our memories into them but our already weak capacities for logic. Still, it's just as well we don't clutter our memories with the stupidities. The twentieth century went loopy with the idea that all the bad things must be recaptured and thereby exorcised. Which was, in a more concrete sense, exactly what I had just done with the floppy, poor unconscious dump. But I didn't feel a bit exorcised.

In any case the Xorandor affair, then as yet unfinished, must have completely engrossed us, even though we'd been sent out there to forget it and to be out of the way of the journalists till it had all died down. Also of course, going to school in Bayreuth and learning not just German but everything else in German must have absorbed all our energies. Rather like the mixed bag of students I used to have at the Technische Hochschule, some of them very bright, others hopeless, who came and still come from all over the world to learn microelectronics or physics or political economy but who have to learn it in German. Seems so unfair, why the double effort, why don't we go out to them and learn their languages? Well, we do, but we're no good at them so it's less efficient. Of course they've all produced their own teachers and technical schools, but there's still this myth of Western technical (if no other) superiority that dies hard, though the Senegalese, for instance, and the West Indians, are vastly superior, not to mention the Koreans, the Japanese, the Chinese and more or less all the South-East Asians.

Silent typing sure encourages loquacity, I'll have to scrap all that if I want to keep this record. What I did know, and could never forget, was that the whole story of Xorandor had gone into Poccom 3, both then, in Bayreuth, and after we got back to Cornwall, and although I made Jip promise to delete the whole thing after Xorandor told us his secret or his possible lie (who knows?) I later learned that he hadn't. I wondered then whether he ever intended to use the info. He always said not, or rather, we never talked about it but he acted as if it had gone as agreed. So why had he kept it? But he became very devious, like most nuclear physicists.

I remember thinking this aloud, and hearing myself say that last remark with a slight shock.

How long ago it all seemed to me then, as I sat in my teleport staring at the last screen of text down to END GQ, pointlessly trying to remember that pointless German Quarrel. And how longer ago its causes seemed, the American missiles in Europe! And as for Wilson and Callaghan, softshoe duo or comic turn, they'd been I think Prime Ministers ages before I was even born. I evidently never bothered to learn exactly what they'd done about the missiles, but presumably they let them in. And then the long, long Doppelnull and other negotiations that began with or soon after the Xorandor affair. The Eastern block, as it was then called, is now no longer really a block but a loose federation of free-trading nations, free trade and local elections being perhaps the only freedom it was at last allowed. Because it did, slowly, surreptitiously, for its own economic survival, introduce reforms towards commercial and industrial competition that made the differences between it and the West look like a mere matter of slightly changed political labels. (They even had to let westerly satellites join Europe, as well as Finland and Austria which had some sort of special status that had prevented them, but not of course Bulgaria or Romania). They call it Post-Socialism, which somehow manages to imply that Socialism is both dead and very much alive. Like Post-Feminism, Post-Democracy, Post-Humanism, Post-Commitment and the rest.

And yet the type of dummes Argument, as apparently produced then only by an elderly drunk, now seems almost the norm, and the fixation of positions I know hasn't changed at all, but rather got steadily cruder and wider, and also upward-spread, gaining in respectability what it never had in sweet reason or sharp logic. Forty years of deterrent had kept the peace, at least between the so-called big powers, but now almost thirty years of dedeterrent (and the twentieth century began all those de-words that implied the wrongness of previously approved policies, from denazification and decolonisation to denationalisation, deprivatisation, decentralisation, deregulation etc) have also kept that same peace, so neither theory is proven, and each is dangerous. The big powers have more or less disarmed, at least to the diplomatic satisfaction of mutual but fairly well organised verification teams. Glaznostalgia, people call it now. However, every smaller terrorist state has its own superwarheads, happily sold to them by the big powers' armament industries. The problem of the deterrent has merely been displaced to the irresponsible and the fanatical. What is Xorandor thinking now, I wondered, or has he died out on Mars, from insufficiency of natural radiation? For of course the politicians did not keep their promise of providing him and his offspring with nuclear waste to feed on, it was too expensive as a solution. Did he tell the truth about his origins and are there as he said innumerable Xorandors of all ages and aeons silently feeding on nuclear waste as well as on warheads and listening to us still all over the planet Earth?

I must have been in the middle of such musings when the doorbell rang. I left the attic and went down to the hall. Wer ist es? I asked the intercom. Mutti? — Hanjo! What — ? Come on up.

He'd got even taller, and looked more Chinese than ever. When I thought of him simply as an entity, an existence in my life, it was as my semi-oriental boy of seven or ten or twelve. When I saw him as a concrete presence now, at eighteen, I saw him more correctly, but what is correctly? The way someone is, at the moment, all at once, in front of you, is that more correct than all the other images? These odd impressions were presumably due to the fact that I was no longer bringing him up, accepting his allatonce-ness at every moment without shock of recognition. I busied myself with the tea, determined not to ask what he was doing in Aachen, or indeed in Europe, well before the end of even the American summer term, or why he hadn't let me know. Over tea he said,

I went down to see Uncle Jip in Texas.

Oh? How is he? Was it nice?

Very hot. Fine. Invited me down. Said he had an urgent packet for you he wanted delivered in person. Told me to skip the last three weeks of school, said he'd make up the data so's I could write my papers ahead of time, and jeenukes, he did, and I did. And here it is.

He'd been opening his backpack and now he handed me a small squarish padded envelope.

How mysterious. But don't you have to do exams as well?

No, we get graded on practical and theoretical stuff all year round. Lots of students have to earn money for school in the summer months so —

I was gazing at Jip's padded envelope as he talked. A diskette, clearly. Addressed in mock-mediaeval script to Alcuina, Aix-la-Chapelle, by hand of Hanjo. Who was talking about his college, his trip to Texas, and what he was going to do this summer. I listened, proud, amazed, dismayed, proud. I'm hitchhiking a long flight to China, he said, through a pilot friend. Aren't you going to open it?

Later.

Uncle Jip said it was urgent. If it's waited till you got here it can wait a few hours more. Why China? But I knew.

To find my father.

It's a big country. Over a million million.

Not all males, not all the same age, not all from Shensi, not all called Chang-ti-lu, not all hitec. That cuts it down to about one hundred million or less. With the computers they have —

He only CAME from Shensi, which is as large as England, and very mountainous. He studied somewhere in Manchuria, Kirim Polytechnic I think, then Aachen. He could have been sent anywhere since then, from Kwangtung in the tropical South to Heilungkiang in the freezing North. And what will you do when you've found him?

Nothing. Just, get to know him. Why, why didn't you try to find him when you went on that data-determining trip in March?

Why should I? Oh I know, you've always suspected you were the chance result of a one-night stand, because he left. But it wasn't like that at all. We were both students here. I was eighteen. We had a brief, but passionate affair. It was over in peace and mutual esteem before he left, these things happen you know, and we never said goodbye, I never hated or cursed him or had terrible regrets or rebounds or anything like that, and today I'm thankful I didn't marry him, my life would have been totally different, and I like my life as it is.

But you never tried to contact him and tell him of my existence. You could have traced him through the University, or now through your diplo contacts.

They can't keep track of all their ex-students you know. I wasn't even sure that he was going back to China. He may be in America for all I know. My dear boy, you do have surprisingly old-fashioned notions compared to my generation. The conservative backlash I suppose, some of it welcome no doubt.

Society would collapse completely without the idea of the family, it's universal.

Yes darling. But it is simply an idea, a cultural development. Biologically there are only three factors, the two sexes, the sequence in births, and the succession of generations. Out of these mankind invented the family, necessary, as you so rightly say, to society. But there are many, many variations you know, even, somewhere or other, marriage between a fertile woman and a sterile woman, who takes over the man's role. But in my youth the bachelor mother was almost the norm, many women chose it as the ideal solution to the problems of marriage versus career. We took it in our stride. I went on with my studies. A child and a career, and occasionally a man, rather than a man, a child, and maybe a career. It has its points, and its losses.

For some reason this speech, reasonable though it sounds, if a little pompous, as here written (but by me of course, and six weeks later), led us straight into one of our cruel and bitter quarrels. Motherhood in your stride, that's just it, you strode through it, you were always striding out and away to some course or conference or fact-finding mission, as if facts had to be found. Are you reproaching me for lack of love and attention? — No of course not, Mutti that's wimpy. — So what then? — You don't understand, you've never understood, you just go through the motions, you've wrapped yourself in a shell and I can't get through to you. — What shell? Be specific. — I can't. — You're talking nonsense darling. — As usual you're no doubt thinking. — Hanjo that's unworthy of you, how can you be so sure what I'm thinking when you've just complained you can't get through to me, be logical. — Be logical, always logical, I'm not a fucking computer, and don't say computers don't fuck they use partition, grow up out of your great childhood adventure Mutti, Uncle Jip's not like that at all, he never refers to it and he has a nice wife and three kids and it's a nice normal family. — So that's it, jealousy? — NO! — Don't shout, besides, that too isn't as diodic as it may look on the surface. — Isn't as WHAT? Is that your twin private language again, why do you still need to exclude, he doesn't. And so on. I ended up in tears, saying I'm sorry, I'm sorry, he first embarrassed then embracing, but not saying sorry. He wins, always, and I let him, though nothing is resolved for him. Peace then ensues, until the next time round.

The rest of the evening we discussed the practical aspects of his plan to go to China and find his father. Does he know German? Or English? Probably both, he certainly got to speak fluent German here, it was part of his assignment, not part of mine to learn Chinese alas, though he did teach me some ideograms. Good, then he shouldn't be hard to talk to. Right, but my love, promise me that if you do him, you'll tell him this is entirely your idea, not mine. He promised. But then, so had Jip promised, in another context, once long ago.

Maybe I'm remembering it wrong, writing it down wrong. Maybe that speech on the family, which was intended and remembered as objective facts sweetly and gently presented, was received as Oh come off it, family's only an idea, you've always had a buzz in your brain about that, and tried to make me feel guilty whereas I, and so on. Maybe his accusations of striding out and away were really intended as But Mutti, there are also disadvantages to a fatherless family, I'm only trying to and so on. The tone of the human voice is such a giveaway that not a word we utter can be received exactly as we're afterwards so convinced we meant to say it, nor, maybe, as we're so convinced beforehand and during that we are saying it. I suppose that only quarrels by letter or diskette can be analysed afterwards for just where and how the misunderstanding arose. But who keeps letters nowadays? And who doesn't efface diskettes? (Me!) And there too, in writing, and even in typing, there's also a tone, a rhetoric that betrays more than it says otherwise there would have been no interpretation industry through the ages, abolished today as a waste of energy, time and teaching hours on mere multiplicity of readings.

And did rushing to one's computer at thirteen and a half after a quarrel to get it all down "wortwörtlich" make much difference? Perhaps there too I exaggerated. And that was a political, not a personal quarrel, and political quarrels on a larger scale lead to mass murder — in fact old Dipling accused me, and my family, of precisely that. Diplomatic quarrels, I thought, must be less naive, but still a question of facesaving. The side that's having its representatives expelled for "activities incompatible with" must know if the accusation is true or not, and expels the other side's representatives as pure reprisal. But reprisals can go very far, and nations sound like kids yelling who started. I remember one question Chang asked me, with exquisite courtesy all those nineteen or so years ago, about one such incident. But how can you be so sure that your country is legally or even morally in the right? Maybe it has other reasons, just as the other country has, for its behaviour. You are condemning the men expelled, without trial, only your government's word, which you are assuming is honourable, whereas the foreign country by definition must be lying. I tried to answer, it's because all the standards I was brought up on — rather strict for their time — have been stood on their heads by younger nations or nations whose different ethos we never bothered to learn. But I suppose it goes back a long way beyond my own lifetime or even my father's. I read somewhere that airmen in the First World War thought it rather UNFAIR to fly over enemy positions and photograph them. As for radio interception some people thought it totally immoral, only letters and messages hidden in walking sticks being fair game. Can you imagine? After all the regular interception and decoding everyone did for the rest of the century? But now, I said, for the last fifty years even the most powerful nations have been helpless in the face of primitive blackmail with hostage-taking and terrorism.

I forget what happened in the particular case — they were as regular as clockwork in those days. The usual compromise no doubt. Like bursting into tears and being embraced. Yet wars, with their so far always acceptable mass murders, arise from not having achieved these diplomatic compromises. The blind self-justification and official face-saving that cover the passion are of the same nature in the person, in the family, in the neighbourhood, in the tribe, in the realm, the difference is only in scale of effects. Didn't Confucius-he-say something of the sort? Yet no one ever appears to himself wholly wrong in any of these disputes, from tiffs to wholesale massacres, since right at any one time, in any one place, is merely the same God-of-Old who's always on one's own side. And I thought again of that Xorandor text Jip had promised to erase.

I had left it to him because I had a broken arm at the time and was too busy learning to write with my left hand. But I know he didn't do it. I know because two years later, when he was rushed off to hospital with acute peritonitis, I was looking for an instruction-book he'd borrowed, and rummaging in his stuff. I found two floppies, marked X, carefully hidden among physics papers in a box. I stared at them. Fleeting butterfly queries were transformed pico into sharp suspicion.

No, the other way round, a sudden sharp suspicion called up fleeting butterfly queries. I checked, and there it was, our original Xorandor story, chatterboxy and unrevised. He must have copied the originals before erasing them to show them to me, callcoded Xorandor and empty. I felt sick with shock. Not because he had wanted to keep them — why not, maybe my request was unreasonable. Not even because he'd broken his promise. But because he had lied to me, and in such an elaborate way. I'm sure the peculiar change in our almost telepathic relationship dates back to that day, though I never said anything. But deeply hurt, I went in for a swift silent revenge. I told myself that if he wanted it kept I would do the keeping, and in exactly the same way. I transferred the content of both floppies onto one more comprehensive smaller disc for my new computer, giving it one of my mystery callcodes. I still have it with me, here in this very attic. I erased his floppies called X and put them back where I had found them, between exactly the same pages in exactly the same place, which had become marked on the paper from the weight of the physics notes. He never mentioned it, so presumably he has them somewhere in his Nasa office and has never called them up. Or else he has, and kept silent, assuming I erased them out of anger but also out of conviction. So which is worse? Not keeping a promise and cheating about it, or sneaking and cheating back, in the same way, out of revenge?

It was an awe-fully moral day, that day I first learnt about Verbivore. I felt rather a pompous ass, too. That night, after making up the bed in the teleport for Hanjo, I opened Jip's padded envelope. In it was a square carton with a diskette inside it (had he somehow also kept a copy?). And a short covering letter in handwriting:

> Dear Zab,
>
> I'm sending you this diskette by special messenger. You'll see why when you screen it. Please erase it after memorising the main facts. I want your reaction, but not in writing. I'll be in Europe in late and will come and see you. Destroy this note.
>
> I hope you're well. Hanjo's grown into a pleasant young man, though none too bright for someone who wants to do physics. He got on well with Ivor (10), took no notice of little Paul (8) and fell a bit in love with Willa (13) as cousins do at that age. I don't think he's a future scientist or even tecman. A poet perhaps, tho he can't spell, or a sociologist or maybe a politician. They're all much the same from our more rigorous viewpoint, but poets do less harm. Jeanie sends her love. Me too. See you soon.
>
> Jip

The next day, after taking Hanjo to the bank to give him money for his journey, and driving him to the new international airport where his plane and pilot friend awaited, I got back to the solitude of my attic. More screens, and screens. A Nasa Report, TOPMOST TOP SECRET. Codename: SPEAKLOSS.

5

Jip has kept the habit of recording all meetings including private convs. The way he held his wrist forward all the time, he was obviously wearing a microrecording watch. But he never did like the work of actually narrating something afterwards. Just the salient facts, that's all he was interested in. If he has written down all we said afterwards, or typed it into his computer, I suppose it would be in telegraphic form with minimum comment. Unless he's caught the general need to express personal garbage in writing and tries. Like for instance:

Saw Zab this afternoon to tap her reactions. Hot still tho cooler than Texas. Cd've sat on her terrace, in shade by then, but didn't want to be overheard, even in English. Our twin-telepath seems very altered, has been altering over the years, what with different studies, languages, countries, nationalities now, and lives. She doesn't even look like me any more, so thin and taut. It's true I've filled out a bit. And somehow she's become a bit devious. No, he wouldn't say all that.

I recorded the dialogue, tiny mike and tape in my watch, can't trust my reconstruct, as we used to call it during X, and she always was better at it than me. Few prelims, I asked her almost straight out for her reaction.

My fear was for Hanjo (she said), those plane-collisions I mean — he'd just left. But then I read on and saw they'd stopped. And soon got a phone-call he'd arrived.

You read, in the report you mean?

Well, yes. But Zab, those plane-crashes in series were the talk of the time.

My second reaction was disbelief. About Verbivore I mean. I've been so busy, I simply hadn't noticed, and no one told me.

You're incredible, Zab. Everyone's talking about it. Don't your fellow

M.P.'s discuss it in Parliament? Or on Committees? Or during rich lunches?

Oh, Parliament! I'm on an Agricultural Technology Committee and worked non-stop on an endless report. Besides, I was on an EEC data-determining mission to China in March.

And I suppose the data you determined, on the Wall and in The Forbidden City, were useful?

Oh don't you start! Anyway, I wasn't here. Not when the thing started getting really noticeable and talked about.

But didn't Hanjo say anything?

No. We talked — of other things.

But what about radio and television? You visibly have both.

Oh, I've stopped watching German TV, it's too boring, nothing but men shaking hands before meetings still rarely women incidentally — or bits of a speech. That's for the reports, and otherwise it's a man or woman reading, turning visible pages. Visualised radio in fact. Has been for years. Part of an anti-star policy, pure info, no emotive identification. Idea good but result unwatchable. Rest is serials and old films.

But what about other countries, the rest of Europe, the States, Africa, the rest of the world?

It's all become what the French call politique politicienne, the insistent journalist needling a spokesman to speak what he won't. I mean for the news. Otherwise it's infinite variations on prize-winning games. Besides, if you don't want to spend hours zapping you have to spend a day scrutinising a World-TV journal to select. I do sometimes, and mark things, but then I forget.

Anyone who's dealing both with politics and hitec should keep herself informed.

I do, from reports on my Fach, and from seeing the people and the areas concerned. TV's been going steadily downhill, every cliché question and reaction and public indignation expected as programmed.

You're an intellectual snob, no wonder you're out of touch.

It's not snobbery, it's observation. Stop bullying me, Jip.

Well, what's your reaction now?

I agree with you.

I haven't expressed an opinion yet.

No. But you sent me the secret Nasa sitrep, at great risk to your career, obviously not for scientific advice since you're a real scientist —

Debug, Zab.

You sent it, I mean, for an obvious reason. You even said I'd understand why when I read it. And I did. And I agree.

But that would only be a wild ass guess.

A wag, a swag even, remember?

I want more than just agreement Zab. You remember more than I do.

But you have the original floppy.

I couldn't quite meet her gaze, nor did she hold it but followed mine out of the terrace—door towards the monstrous euroglobe and the distant hills beyond.

Do I? I said, pretending surprise. Nonsense, Zab, I erased it. You asked me to. Almost ordered me.

She ignored this.

Okay let's analyse the situation and consider the possibilities.

The sitrep's done that.

Yes, but in such technical jargon the whole thing gets blurred.

That from you?

It wasn't the jargon itself that bothered me Jip, obviously, but the way it was used to neutralise and disguise dismay, indecision, incomprehension, fear (the list impressed me, she always did have the gab for moral issues). I think we should go over the facts, one by one, in the light of what you and I know, first the isolated instances, noting down place, time, duration, in chronological order, then as they get more complex, rediagramming their convergence.

I repeat, the report does just that, in its own technical way.

That's why I said re.

And now all the journalists are onto it and trying to do the same.

Are they? Already?

Yes, everything's got suddenly worse in the last few weeks. Overtaken the report in fact, and there've been weekly ones since. Everyone in the world is complaining of long breaks in transmission in both radio and TV, in telexes and telegrams, affecting words and music now, indifferently, and fax, even telephone systems —

Telephones! Why, of course, they're all on microwave channels now.

And since international computer systems are linked by phone you can imagine the threatened chaos, something had to give, various statements had to be made by various authorities, and so that's why I came to see you.

Thank you. But you and I had early experience of reassuring statements to the press by politicians and scientists. In any case, I imagine everyone's investigating according to their lights. Which, however supercompetent, can't include what we know.

Oh, someone will remember sooner or later. The scientists weren't quite as stupid as we made them out in the Xorandor affair, you know, we were just kids. Some are still studying it.

She looked at me oddly. I'd forgotten that uncanny quickconnect of hers.

Okay, she said (VERY archly), so why come to me? Go to them.

Descramble, Zab. You were full of ideas at the time, some of which I didn't quite grasp then. You were on your philosophie trip already. But we shared something unique. You're my twin.

There was a longish pause. It was as if she were deciding whether she could forgive me or not, after all this time, whether she could trust me at all.

Sorry, debugging, she said at last with her old grin. But you're the one who's against tec-recap, so I don't really see what you want. I can't give you a summary reaction as an entity, a kind of maxint label (she was lapsing more and more into our old language, a good sign I thought) that covers the whole thing neatly like a customs sticker on a parcel. If it's a wag you have, let's treat it as such, a wag's a theory after all, let's go through it like a long equation.

That'll hardly be necessary.

It was a metaphor. Talk, as a butterfly-net, if you prefer. Remember? Even you had to admit that our chatter was a kind of data-network that caught sudden glimpses of ideas.

Okay, but quickly then. It seems to have started with isolated incidents. Planes colliding in mid-air or crash-landing, well above averagewise. At first in Europe, then in America, then in Russia, Canada, Australia. But no one made any connection with anything beyond the usual technical fault, pilot error, or sabotage. I mean anything over and above those, but willed by someone or something, not just chance. No survivors, or at any rate no pilot survivors. But all inquiries revealed one element in common, though this was not made public: in each case the black box and ground sources showed sudden loss of radio-contact. No, sorry, at first Ground could hear the pilot but he couldn't hear Ground. Later both were getting lost. Radar was sometimes okay, sometimes haywire. That lasted over a year, on and off. No recognisable pattern, as you saw from the graphs. Then suddenly it stopped. At least those studying it went on expecting crashes but they never came. Meanwhile pilots had worked out a hypereconomic way of communicating, in case of cut-off.

Cause and effect? Zab asked. I guessed what she meant but pretended not to, as indication that I didn't want to bring in, just yet, any conceivable force that could be supposed to have a will, to be exercising judgment about anything such as economy of communication. She shrugged as I went on.

So it had started on the very low frequencies. After several months, broadcasts started going off the air suddenly and coming back, also on Long Wave. This happens so often anyway no one thought it abnormal or made the connection with the planes. But when it increased well beyond the norm, in all metre-bands, and affected TV, and radio-stations all over the world started sending in requests to Nasa to investigate over and above what they themselves could do in their own technical capacities — which for major stations are considerable — the connection was made and studies were ordered.

Those summarised in the report? There seemed to be no particular pattern. Shall we screen them again and see what we can do together?

You mean you kept the diskette I sent you? I asked you to erase.

She shot me a sharp look, but didn't take up.

Well yes, suitably camouflaged as something else. I transferred different elements to the middle of other files, with callcodes recognisable only by me.

Which you'll forget.

No, I have them down but reencoded three times.

Leaping leptons! I didn't ask you to memorise or keep access to all the technical detail but to give me a reaction.

Which you'd at once say was unscientific unless it arose directly out of the technical detail.

Oh stubs, Zab, let's get on with it.

Okay. I want to get back to the planes for a picosecond. It said Europe, America, Russia, Canada and Australia. Do you know what countries in Europe, what countries in America?

Britain, France, Germany, Switzerland, the USA.

The very countries that had Alphaguys. Britain, France, Germany and Russia first, then Switzerland, Canada and Australia got later offspring. Odd coincidence.

But who gave them up. All seventeen offspring were sent back to Mars with Xorandor.

Except the two he told us to hide, remember. Which he named Uther Pendragon and Aurelius, after that story of Pennybig. She died, you know.

I nodded, scared of her sidetracking. But she was reacting as I had hoped, and luckily it wasn't a real sidetrack.

And when we got back from Germany they'd disappeared, remember? All offspring had to move while still small enough to be sent like a nodule onto some moving vehicle. That's how they displaced themselves, and spread.

She seemed to go off into a daydream. To encourage her back I went on: And then of course there was no verification procedure after Xorandor and his seventeen offspring were sent to Mars. Each country gave up the number it was known to possess. But by the time the next Mars probe was ready all the offspring could have grown almost to Xorandor's size and reproduced, on the massive radiation intake they were willy-nilly having, compared to the natural radiation of earlier times and Xorandor's own much slower growth. And in twenty-two years any new offspring kept back secretly could have had more offspring. All that, however, is one bit of the hypothesis, and still makes a relatively small number.

Yes Jip, that's where I agree with you. For although you said they were sent BACK to Mars, as everyone thought, you're thinking of Xorandor's alternative story of their origins, the one he gave us right at the end, and to us only, and which we didn't know whether to believe or not, and had no means of checking. That their race of silicon-based computer-stones have been here since the beginning of time, long before man, developing on natural radiation, and moving as best they could, on scaly animals perhaps. Then on riders' shields and chariots and ships and gun—carriages and trucks and trains and planes and things like that. And listening to mankind for aeons. And more and more so with the development of artificial nuclear energy and the modern outburst of discourse over the waves.

Okay, simmer down. (But I was glad to be reminded of the details). What's always triggered me about that, though, is that nobody has ever found one. After all, Xorandor, who in this version of his story was a mere youngster of four thousand five hundred and odd years, was big enough for us to sit on him.

But unaware that we were, till he contacted us on Poccom. Lots and lots of other people could have seen or even sat on similar stones and —

Before, yes, but not after the hooha, hexadex, it hit world headlines. Everyone would have looked and they did, not just people but governments, geological teams and such, remember, in all stony areas and deserts and near all nuclear dumps and stations. No one found anything.

She looked thoughtful for a moment.

It is odd, she admitted, at least for the ones that are supposed to have been there since before man, they'd be enormous. Though Xorandor never said that. (She perked up). Maybe his size was maximum, or even abnormal, due to extra and perhaps wrong intake, it was never clear how long he'd been taking Caesium 137 after all. In fact — her face suddenly had its diodic expression. But there was a long pause, when she seemed to be working something out, or maybe hesitating about whether to tell me. When she spoke it was slowly. I wonder, I mean, on the hypothesis, that Xorandor's, second story is true, whether, they couldn't, have developed, even very long ago, a much more, economical, microshape you know, the way our computers got smaller and smaller? After all they were way ahead of our computers then, Xorandor could simulate a reality and decide when a different version was required, just like our FSM computers for instance, today. He even created a computer virus, though inadvertently perhaps.

Zab! that's gigavolt! So they could be quite tiny, indistinguishable from, say, pebbles, the way Uther and Aurelius were when we handled them.

Well, perhaps not quite so tiny. But like the Xors after a few months, say. Remember dad and Biggleton thought offspring were peripherals, to save storage space, each one its own filing system. Cos even if he did have three-dimensional circuits, a stone is nevertheless finite. But Xorandor said no, each one was a complete computer with inherited data, and grew on nuclear energy to store more, though also discarding lots. Perhaps they did learn the division of labour.

So there'd be millions of them by now? And all tiny, Xorandor being an aberration?

And perhaps the older ones were in fact fewer than he thought, or we thought, and stony deserts are very, very big.

I was impressed, though I could think of several scientific objections, notably from the geologists, who know and scrutinise the world's stone-formations pretty well. But I wanted to pursue the theory.

That would be the strong hypothesis as to the possible cause: the alphaguys. Who've been here all the time, whereas the politicians and the few physicists (and as far as I remember no one else) who had access to them, thought Xorandor was unique and that they'd sent him and all his offspring back to Mars, when they started eating warheads.

Yes Jip. That was the reason I asked you to delete the whole thing, so that no one would ever discover this possibly true alternative. We WANTED them, if they existed, to go on eating warheads, without anyone knowing.

She wasn't looking at me but staring again at the Hotair Bubble and the distant hills beyond. It was irrelevant to the argument, why was she harping on it? Especially since I'd been right to keep it, and she wrong to erase it, for it would now be useful to have access to that text. Still, I couldn't help putting a quite other retro-justification:

Well, since no missiles have been used or tested all these twenty years or so of negotiations, we'll never know whether any of those not dismantled were neutralised by the alphaguys or not. If we could know that they were, it would prove Xorandor's second story.

She shrugged. I went on:

Okay, the present trouble is being caused by the alphaguys that have always been there, in that hypothesis. But why? There'd be no reason. They don't feed on electromagnetic waves but on nuclear radiation. That's the reason I need your help. And why planes anyway?

That seems to have been only a beginning. Perhaps they were experimenting. Or else a dramatised warning. The real objective must surely be the media.

But plane-crashes and collisions feed the media.

Precisely. The media collect catas-tropheys.

I smiled dutifully.

But Zab, the cause of these accidents doesn't come out till months or even years later. And the results come nowhere near this hypothesis. And the media forget, it's a tiny item, no one takes any notice. A report isn't drama.

They may have found that silencing the communication of planes didn't achieve their purpose.

What purpose? You always were offline anthropomorphic about Xorandor, Zab, you can't attribute a purpose to them.

A life-force, then, a survival-kit, call it what you like. You know, I'm stack sure that if all the radios in the world researched way back into all their technical hitches, way beyond the supposed beginning I mean, when they started thinking that the frequency and duration of these hitches were abnormal, they'd find a definite pattern, tho it might be hard to discover. I mean, nobody takes much notice of a break in transmission of say twenty minutes in South Wales, or even New South Wales, later apologised for with some sort of phrase like trouble at our local transmitter or disturbances in the ionosphere.

And you mean to imply that this would suit their supposed purpose?

Even a whole night of planned silence causes no surprise, it's announced in advance, work at the transmitter etc. I used to say, they're cleaning the wave-length, remember?

Are you trying to say it didn't start with planes but already with radio-stations, and much earlier?

Yes. If we bear the possibility in mind when we re-examine the incidences — assuming you have access to all that dataheap, or authority to request its terminal display — we'd find, YOU'd find if you don't want me in on it, that it started long before the planes but no one noticed. The planes would have been only a, kind of, jump-instruction if you see what I mean, which would be why it was given up. I speak in the passive to make it impersonal since you don't like the idea of purpose. But I repeat, these creatures are highly sophisticated computers, STILL more sophisticated than any artificial intelligence we've produced so far, even since the hooha. For instance, for some time now we've had computers that can produce computers, and computers that can diagnose trouble in other computers at a distance: well, Xorandor could do both. As to purpose, even natural phenomena result from incredibly complex but impersonal calculation, think of DNA, so if you prefer calculation to purpose it's okay by me.

All right, all right, dump that.

Fine, I'll stick to my terminology. Maybe the alphaguys didn't "know" yet, or "forgot" (she had the scare-quotes in her voice) that men are so slow with inquiries. After all, what is happening now has nothing more to do with planes, but all to do with media. Yet both are communication.

But why, Zab?

I suppose you mean cause not purpose. WHY-purpose is perhaps more my Fach, my data-network, WHY-cause, let's call it HOW, is more yours. But we should both think about both, I'm sure they're connected.

She was as sharp, but also as generous, as ever. She'd guessed what I was after. She knew I hadn't kept my promise, that I'd cheated on her — obviously she knew since she'd erased the floppy, cheated back — and that I therefore needed her. She had lived our adventure more intensely, I think, than I did, at any rate she's remembered it in much more detail. And it's that memory, that detail, that I need. And her quickconnect. She said nothing, no real reproaches, and offered her instincts in free collaboration, but only if I wanted it, and with no bargaining. I was quite moved suddenly and murmured: Smart terminal, Zab.

Flipflop, she replied nano. And there are the implications, or eventual results, which go with the WHY. And what to do about it or how to stop it, which goes with the HOW. The why and the whither are my Fach, the hows are your Fach, how it's done and how it can be undone. Have a drink on it.

Good idea.

But after all, Jip, she chattered on obsessively as she served drinks, when a person's talking into a mike they've no means of knowing that they're not being heard, until the tecman tells them — usually quite pico in fact, but meanwhile they go buffering on, and then apologise. And if the trouble's just local the apology merely comes after the program. Still, someone notices, and if it's been going on a long time, overaveragewise, surely the tecmen would have investigated, got together with other stations all over the world and so on.

They have, of course, Nasa for one. In the report. And all the international broadcasting orgs, in Montevideo for the Americas, in

Geneva for Europe, in Budapest (which replaced Prague), in Markala and Cairo, in Tokyo, the lot. And as I said many scientists and even the journalists are on it.

Yes Jip, but not as early as they should have been.

In your supposition. Is it so important?

It may be wrong. I just hoped we could go back much further than they have. Or perhaps they have, some of them. But perhaps after all it hardly matters now. It would have been interesting to discover a larger pattern — did it start as suddenly and arbitrarily, here and there, as it seems from that report? And where, and how long each time? And so on. It might also give us a clue about the WHY. Which messages for instance. This would be easier to establish when there were still few cuts. It might even tell us something about the HOW. After all, when messages are intercepted by an enemy, they still reach their destination, and the receiver can't know that they've been intercepted, except from other sources. Same with documents microfilmed on a space the size of a microdot. Not at all like the missives people used to hide in cleft sticks or vaginas. Here, however, it IS like messages stolen from cleft sticks, they don't reach their destination, people do know they're not receiving. The words broadcast don't arrive, they disappear.

Eaten up.

By logophagoi.

Yes, by logophagoi. Much better than Speakloss or even Verbivore.

Oh, I don't know, Jip, I like Speakloss too. It marks what's been happening anyway. Just watch anyone really speaking off the cuff. Even highly educated politicians or scholars, rarely get to the end of their sentences coherently. Look, here's a sentence from a scholar on some B.B.C. cultural program I heard, I jotted it down: *Here a constituent of oral performance enters into a later form, and in so doing we can come to understand how a text is multitemporal.*

What's wrong with it, apart from incomprehensible jargon?

You too! Nor can people listen to the end. That's why radio discussions have to be broken every few minutes with discs, and TV ones with publicity, for different reasons but with the same effect. That started way back, before we were born, some U.S. president, Nixon I think, organised his election campaign in flash snippets because, he said, the average voter can't concentrate more than three minutes without wanting a beer. Now we weren't like that, but even twenty years ago we were considered whizz-kids, just because we could understand computers, which all kids do today. But something else has gone, which we had, a sort of general literacy, and curiosity, perhaps because we had every advantage, not in money but in our parents, a scientist father, a literary and theatrical mother.

You're talking like a teacher, Zab. Dad was strict with us, but he used to say HIS teachers complained of illiterate students and no doubt so did THEIR teachers. But if it were so we'd have no one capable of putting two words together by now, or of running anything.

Precisely.

Gigo. Language changes, that's all, it's the only truly democratic institution in the world, the people always win against the academicians. Look at the funny, unacademic words the scientists keep inventing. And the best students all learn their speciality soon enough.

And become Fachidioten, as Dipling already said dad was.

Who?

Herr Groenetz.

You really have become impossibly isolated, Zab. Some sort of intelligent elite will always have to run things, even if eighty percent of those are relatively mediocre, and this whatever the political system and whatever the transmission media. As long as everyone's given their chance at the start, the others have to make do in the world as they've made it. You probably only come across those, in Parliament, or when you taught. But there are lots of highly intelligent people in all branches of knowledge. Let's get on with our hypothesis for swag's sake.

Twenty-two years is a long time for human memory these days. Almost a quarter of a century of eproms and eroms and volatile memories and dynamic memories and parallel memories and serial memories and so on.

All memory is on file, all counting and all logical operations are inside a software. You noticed, no doubt, that the report doesn't even touch on the possibility of alphaguys as cause. All is imputed either to some mysterious new air-pollution, that's not only irreversibly destroying the vegetation and the ozone layer as we've known and done nothing about but talk for forty years, but hypothetically damaging the ionosphere or even somehow the wave-lengths themselves. Or else to the ENEMY, whoever that may be in these days of presumed total disarmament.

There's always an evil empire in every government's policy, it's necessary to stay in power or get it.

I may be pessimistic, Jip, but you're downright cynical.

It's all one to me. As far as morals are concerned I see no difference between a political enemy and pollution of the planet, which is the enemy within, no projected scapegoat possible there. But in physics and chemistry we do have to distinguish. To get back to our problem, the report doesn't decide between words and waves. Is this enemy, if there is one, intercepting and eating up the words we broadcast or the supports we generate in order to broadcast them?

Destroying a wave-length for a time-length? Besides, waves, particles, words, all the same, all energy, all physical.

Metaphor and over-simplification won't help, Zab. I meant —

I wonder why it doesn't. Decide, I mean. Surely the processes can be very precisely monitored.

They are. But, well, you know what rival theories are. What I meant was, is this so-called enemy eating up words or, as one theory goes, absorbing radio-waves, consuming, say, all the negentropy by feeding on the bumps, the modulations in the signals which are used to code the information? Flattening out the wave —

Eating up, absorbing, consuming, feeding on, you sure use meta — Jip! I've just had a megavolt brainwave.

Macrosuperdiodic, yes?

Don't tease. It's nice to retrograde with you.

I WAS retrograding with you, not teasing.

I beamed at her because I felt she was moving in my direction and going to suggest what I wanted her to suggest. She went much further.

Supposing, she whispered excitedly, her eyes shining, supposing we could contact Uther or Aurelius? They must also have encoded that secret number Xorandor gave us to get through to Xor 7's oldest memory. All his offspring automatically received all his data.

But (I must say I was astonished), but hadn't he already asked us to take them away, long before the hooha, when he gave us this number?

Can't remember. Look it up, Jip.

She looked away at the giant bubble and hills again. Was she teasing? Telling me she knew I hadn't erased it, but not that she had? As she must have. Or could it have been dad? But why? He'd surely have needed it, for his own book. Which didn't use our data. She went on, with only an imperceptible pause, while these questions flashed through my software:

But they weren't far away, at first, they could have listened in. And my memory of Xorandor's explanation about his offspring is that they were programmed with everything he was programmed with, at birth, I mean all the logical circuits and addresses and essential data.

Of course we've no idea when they moved, or where.

We divided that number in two and each of us memorised half of it, it was so long. I still remember my half, I kept saying it like a poem learnt by heart. D'you remember yours?

Stubs, no, Zab, what d'you expect: We were thirteen, that's twenty-three years ago! But do you mean we could call them up, or one of them, on a computer, and they'd answer, from wherever they are, and EXPLAIN ALL? (Caps meant to be heard in my intonation).

It might have been worth a try.

I very much doubt it. You were always sentimental about Xorandor, but he didn't function on feeling, and nor would his offspring. He wasn't a science-fiction computer, which always has a human weakness somewhere.

No, he functioned on memory. And he did have a weakness, if only for Caesium 137. And it seems to me we did pretty well getting through to

Xor 7 with that secret access number.

AND our voice identities, remember. They were like DNA fingerprints to Xor 7. Our voices have changed, even yours has got deeper since you were thirteen.

But we wouldn't use vocal now, how could we? Besides, it'd be intercepted. Remember the voice thing was purely accessory, a provisional technical development for Xorandor's purpose.

Purpose again! Hmmm. Quite a thought, though. Edge-triggering in fact. I'm almost sure we never gave the number in the narrative, so "looking up", if we could, would be pointless. (Our glances crossed again and veered off). I wonder if I can somehow recall my half-number if I try hard? Or maybe if I don't try, if I order my brain to look for it and then just go on doing other things. Say, Zab, do you still have Poccom 3?

She hesitated for a fraction of a second, or was she trying to remember?

Swipes, no. I did keep it for quite a time in the attic junk, but then it became Hanjo's room and I cleared everything out. NOW it's my teleport. But in any case it wouldn't be much use as a computer these days. Oh, Jip! You're hexadex right! We encoded that number in SOFTKEY! Screwbooles for sentiment, eh? In fact it wasn't sentiment that made me keep it. When you went to Cambridge and I came to Aachen, I simply didn't want to leave it in Cornwall where dad could get at it. Remember? He was writing a book on Xorandor and knew far less than we did, except I mean as a physicist, and we wanted to keep it all to ourselves.

(That of course was a splendid lie, since she had already erased the whole story from my hidden floppy, nor did it tally with our official version that I had erased it as asked. A lie to deny sentiment). I merely said, gently: That's a feeling too, Zab, it's called possessiveness.

If you like. But you felt it too, Jip, you know you did, dad was such a mental monitor at the time.

And aren't you glad? He taught us rigour.

Yes, of course. Poor old dad, he died so soon after. We were rather mean, we should have helped him write a really good book, our secret knowledge plus his superior physics and rigour. But he probably wouldn't have believed we had other knowledge than his. He never even saw his book come out. I've always been certain his cancer was caused by the nukewaste they were storing down that old tin mine at the Wheal.

Nonsense, Zab, it's —

Oh, don't give me the professional physicist's reply, Jip. How absolutely bootloading that I didn't keep that Poccom 3. How long are you here for?

Not long, we're going on to Austria and Italy, picking up a car on Tuesday. You're invited to dinner at the hotel by the way, I forgot to say. I didn't expect you to cook for six.

Oh? I wish you hadn't forgotten. I've got everything ready-to-serve but cold, we can sit on the terrace, it'd be hopeless in the kitchen or on this small table here.

Oh, well in that case, thanks, I'll give Jeanie a ring. But come tomorrow night. And meanwhile look for Poccom 3, just in case you did keep it after all, and let me know if you find it, I'll come right over.

But the next day, Zab called from her teleport. Not because she'd found Poccom 3 but because she wanted me to see the text of some ancient quarrel she'd had with old Herr Groenetz in Bayreuth at thirteen or fourteen years old! Dipling, as she called him. She wanted to know if I'd heard about it at the time, or if Frieda had told me the next day. Real Quatsch. As if I could remember things like that. The joke is that she can't remember it either, not one word, and even wonders whether she invented it. That's what seemed to random-jitter her most, that memory-blank, that dependence on an old floppy that might have got dumped. That might as well have got dumped. I told her Herr Groenetz was pushing seventy even then, he was much older than Frieda, he'd married her at 55 or more, and Rudi was at least 15 when we went there. So that he must almost certainly be dead now. That seemed to shake her, but also to interest her in some morbid way. If he was nearly seventy at that time, she said, then he would've — but she clammed up.

What I find extraordinary is this idea of rushing home to type up a quarrel into the computer while it's still "wortwörtlich". Real spiky that, she always was an oddboole kid. But then, what am I doing now? Not that it's a quarrel, though it might have been, at several moments, if our old telepath hadn't after all helped us to avoid ever making anything explicit, surging up to function all the same, quite subtly, when I thought it was dead for ever. But she is difficult. She's become cranky and isolated, alone in her little roof flat, thinking she has all the moral answers and unaware of the sheer sophistication and efficiency of modern power organisations, of all sorts, scientific, mediatic or political. For let's face it, the European Parliament is hardly a modern power organisation, more of a cumbersome and anachronistic joke, however seriously it takes itself. Her micropolitics seem to have microcosmified her software. Still, one needs cranks at times, and her memory of the Xorandor affair is stupendous. I've forgotten so much of the detail, but then, I have been involved in so many equally and even more exciting things at Nasa, and kept so very busy, I never gave X another thought. I wish I'd taken that floppy with me to hospital and not been rushed off so urgently in acute pain. I'd still have access to it and wouldn't have to tap Zab. Though she does have these diodic brainwaves.

At any rate, my entering this dialogue isn't at all the same thing as entering a quarrel. I learnt very early, during the Xorandor episode in fact, never to trust my memory of anything said, or seen, or experimented, nor to trust anyone else's, and to record every important conv, either on tape at the time, or wortwörtlich fresh and at once, pico. It's not quite as rigorous as the notes of an experiment, but then nor is conversation. And dialogue's dead easy, I just let the voices on the tape speak, adding minimal stuff about thoughts and looks. As we did for Xorandor, no commentary-Quatsch — well, Zab had plenty, she always did intervene too much. Trap, that's also what I'm doing now, I wonder why. Guilt, I suppose, chattering soothes it away. But who knows, if all this peculiar subroutine on the radio-waves is going to spread further than the present strobing, we may not be able to record or transmit sound electronically any more. Might as well be in good memory-training for the wortwörtlich.

6

Popped over to see mum in London before leaving for European trip, as we'd landed in Aachen New International Airport. Pleased to see us, tho kids push her mentally upwards towards old age. So Jeanie says but I think mum's saner than most actresses about age, she revels in it rather, she started so late after all, leaping straight into stardom when pushing forty, from betrayed wives to tragic queens without ever a single soubrette or juvenile lead, she proudly declares.

Took her out to a quiet dinner alone after *Hamlet* (she played Queen Gertrude) and managed to slip in a casual-sounding question about our childhood tapes. just testing hypo that it was dad who ferreted in my physics papers and effaced X. Highly unlikely, but one never knows. Not her age she doesn't want to be reminded of, however, but dad and her pre-stage life. Sometimes I wonder how she brought us in and up at all.

Tried to explain a bit about radio-cuts as she was still upset about some role she'd played — oh yes, Lady Macbeth, how funny having been wiped out and never put on again. She'd written to Tim about it, quite formally, and got no reply, imagine. He's now running the B.B.C., what a career, I suppose his role in Xorandor got him noticed. Doubt whether she understood. As inconsequential and full of quotes as ever.

Negentropy! Is that what Jip said? I wish I'd listened more carefully. Or listened more when John was still studying physics and trying to share his enthusiasms with me. But then I'd have forgotten most of it anyway by now. And here I am trying to write things down, I have nothing to fill my time with, yesterday was the Last Night and I'm "resting" as we say, but a bit alarmed as nothing much else is on the horizon, I'd had a whole series of broadcast performances booked, both TV and radio, but they've cancelled everything "provisionally".

The negative of entropy I suppose, Second Law and all that, I do remember the litcrits grabbing at that because of something someone had said half a century before about their ignorance. That and the Principle of Uncertainty, hardly a writer who didn't have to show he'd heard of them and drag them in at the drop of a thinking cap. John used to say they misapplied the concepts right and left. And just as entropy is always increasing, so negentropy is for ever decreasing, he said, Jip I mean. In the universe at large as well as in local systems. What a depressing thought. Perhaps that's why no I'm getting confused. How can negentropy, if it means information, be forever decreasing when all the media are forever raising information to the nth power?

Well, yes, I did ask him that, and he said that's just the point. Information in the scientific sense. I only ask for information I said. I wish I understood. I ought to, working sometimes in radio-plays, but do actors in front of a mike, or even radio-producers, have to understand radio-waves any more than editors and publishers or even writers have to understand the neurological process of writing? And it is neurological, I can almost feel the thoughts going down through my arm and fingers and pen onto the paper, it's a strain because I'm not used to it but it's a marvellous feeling. Can't think why writers all sit at a keyboard and screen these days, and call themselves wordprocessors. Where was I? Oh yes, both writing and broadcasting are a silent process, because radio-waves make no sound, Jip said, they can even travel in vacuo, the signal's detected as sound only when it activates a receiver. That much I understood. Just like thought in fact, detected only when it hits a vocal cord or a stone, a parchment, a piece of paper, a screen. Stone to screen. That clangs a brainwave-length somewhere. Inestimable stones, unvalued jewels. All scattered in the bottom of the sea. Some lay in dead men's skulls. Maybe Jip and Zab are onto something.

But surely the scientists know what's happening, technically speaking (or not speaking)? As one theory goes, Jip said, so they must have been studying it all very carefully. But can one examine radio-waves to see if the bumps have been levelled out or eaten up or whatever? Surely one can only work it out from effects? And what does it mean, eating, absorbing, feeding on? And wouldn't the creatures, if any, have to excrete? I can't remember how that turned out in the Xorandor episode, after all, they WERE eating isotopes or something. But I never paid much attention to all that. I was rather unhappy in those days.

Well, there's no point in my breaking my brains on that aspect, presumably the technicians and the powers that be will resolve it and explain it all simply, vulgarise it as Zab says the French say, which she says shows how elitist their system still is. I always used to say simplemented, which made John laugh. But it's tempting to ring up Tim and ask him what he thinks. He owes me a letter after all. And I've learnt just enough from Jip not to seem too ignorant. I do understand things providing they're explained to me three times, and it's rather embarrassing to ask the same person.

No, she won't ring Tim, she's too proud, after all she wrote to the D.G. and never got a reply, then to Tim and ditto, and women of her generation, especially actresses who live in other worlds, never forgive a discourtesy. And she never really liked him anyway. But why am I writing all this out as if I were trying to assimilate myself to her? Are these increasing breaks in our daily fictions turning us all into d.i.y. fiction producers? Which, Zab would cut in, we've all been all along anyway, but in our heads, not on paper. I know, she'll run into Perry Striker, or whatever he calls himself now.

Perry darling! Ages. Why don't you write me a play, with a superpart for an aging Dame? No one writes those any more.

Paula, you were a marvellous Gertrude. I will. But you must fire me with your sublime. What sort of part? Harrowed heroine or hideous hag?

You wouldn't even ask the question if the British Government, typically at the time I'm convinced, hadn't thought up DAME as fair equivalent to SIR for knighthoods, because LADY was reserved for wives of knights or lords and daughters of dukes. But Paula, DAME is only LADY in French.

Yes but think of the degradation since the middle ages and its romantic imitations. I sometimes feel like a man in a pantomime. And don't say no darling you look like La Belle Dame sans Merci.

I wasn't going to. I may have the germ of an idea, though.

Oh.

What enthusiasm.

Well, I've noticed it's always bad writers who talk about the germ of an idea.

If you think that, I'll write it for someone else.

Blackmail. As if playwrights had power. It's the director who does all the writing these days, he even invents the scenes and dialogues as he goes.

Yes. ZABAGLIONE'S HAMLET with William Shakespeare tiny letters. But you're right. Even a radio-producer takes over our scripts and fades whole speeches in and out and we're not even welcome at rehearsals. I tried to write that into one of mine — maybe you heard it, A ROUND OF SILENCE (Silence). Well anyway, it was cut long before it got to that bit. All this Logfag thing you know.

Yes, what is it? Same happened to me in the middle of my sleep-walking scene. What's going on, Perry?

People interfering with the wave-lengths, they say.

My son, who's a physicist, said it had something to do with Negativity. Or was it Relativity? No, that wasn't it either. Neg something. Oh I know, negentropy. The negative of entropy you know. Continuous loss of information, he said.

But, but, what does that mean, continuous loss? You mean it's a natural process? I thought it was entropy that was continuous loss, and of energy. I thought these interruptions were due to specific agencies of some sort, you know, like pollution of the ionosphere or something.

Yes, well, I've forgotten what he said, and didn't exactly grasp it anyway. But Perry, if we're going to be deprived of all electronic media in this way, whatever the cause, just imagine, there'll be a rush back to the theatre, the old-fashioned theatre on boards, before 800 to 1,000 people. Or is this going to affect all sound? I mean are the sound-waves being eaten up too?

Poor Decibel.

Who?

Makes no sense, Paula, how could we be talking?

Perhaps we're not, perhaps we're only being written. Or perhaps we'll all be reduced to whispering straight into each others' ears.

Or to silence.

Intolerable. But they'll need us, Perry, they'll need writers again and actors with memories.

For lines learnt by heart.

My daughter used to say that humankind has lost its memory, what with computers registering everything and even newscasters incapable of utterance without telecues. And all that, you know.

Like old people. The old age of the race.

Not at all. Old people have a tenacious memory for anecdotes from their youth. It's only what's just been said they forget. This is just the other way round.

Other way round to what?

To what I said before. You never listen, Perry, you're so intent on noting people's idiosyncrasies for your next play you don't hear what they say.

I defy you to repeat coherently whatever it was you said before.

My daughter used to say that humankind —

Oh, cut it out. You repeat what your precious kids tell you without understanding it.

Perry, you're being extremely rude. I don't think I'll accept the part after all.

I haven't written it yet. Let alone offered it.

Get out.

Yes darling. See you sometime.

How ill-behaved they all are. When I was a child I was taught to respect my elders, all of them, whatever their sex. I always gave up my seat to an old man and stood aside for any older person with parcels in a narrow passage or held the door. But nowadays when I'm carrying parcels in a narrow passage, and with my greying hair, I'm the one who stands aside to let a young man or girl in trousers push by without a word of thanks. World upside down. Yet when they come to the stagedoor for autographs they still fawn. Not that they do that much these days, it's all for popstars and politicians, people who don't last out a fad or an election. Time is like a fashionable host, that slightly, well, and all that.

How depressing it all is. Negentropy. That was it, negentropy. Real information, forever decreasing, in all systems and in the universe at large. Sounds very grand, but what does it mean? Information means something new, and there's nothing new under the sun, 99.9990% repetition, the Xorandor-stone used to say, it's all been said before. So why do we still need to say things? I must ask Zab when I next see her, she'll have an answer of sorts. No, I'll ring. Though of course that merely proves the basis of the question so I should be able to answer it by analysing why I want to ring her. But I'd rather be told.

Couldn't get through. It rang, several times, then cut off, as if she'd lifted the receiver and replaced it. This went on happening so I gave up. I suppose she's busy. Very selfish of her, though, she might have guessed it was me. Unless it's that Verbivore thing again. But surely they can't get at telephones? I'll have to write. Hate writing letters. Or wait till she rings. Then she'll say she can't answer philosophical questions like that on the telephone. If it is philosophy. Psychology maybe. Or anthropology. Yes, she'll say it's not a philosophical or a political question so beyond her competence. Her Fach, as she calls it. She's barely capable of speaking English any more, without inserting German words I have to have explained. Jip's much more amenable, doesn't mind vulgarising for me, as the French say. What a word, vulgarising, Zab's right, there's nothing more elitist than a left-wing French intellectual, total contradiction in terms, bunch of contradictions in fact. Not that I know any. Why am I scribbling all this to myself after an exhausting Last Night and a tiresome morning scene with a yuppish though middle-aged dramatist? Perhaps I'll send these pages to Zab for comment. I've certainly never kept a journal before, it's not an age of journals. And they're such a bore. Saw W, in fine form, told me that B was marrying A / was standing for Parliament / had started a computer-business / was ruined / was sleeping with M / had said Y about me. Dinner at C's. And so on. Seems only politicians, generals and aging literati keep journals. Perhaps everyone will now, it's catching. Once one puts pen to paper it runs away in trivia. But it's soothing. Very soothing.

Perry Hupsos. What a name. Greek origin I suppose, everything in -os is Greek. Except cos. He must think he came out of that one-up, oh well, let him.

I came out one-up. Silly bitch. Thinks because she's a Dame she can yuppity me. What was she on about anyway? Actors are a race apart, tear each other and love each other to pieces, no contact with real people. Not like wordprocessors, we have to understand people. Julian, for instance. I really got inside him. And even Decibel. Yes, I'm a bit in love with Decibel. I wonder whether I'd have killed her off if I'd finished the play. It's because I didn't know that, or how to end, that I stopped with a radio-cut. Joke, supposedly, and the waves took their revenge. Killed her off, since she can't live on silence. Whatever the waves are. Sounds crazy. Sounds no sounds at all.

The silence is terrible, I'm having to take refuge in traffic jams and building-sites and shunting-yards. I used to just sensually swell myself up into existence, floating in and out of homes with the telly on all day or the radio as background noise, wallpaper radio, some insomniacs kept it on all night, sends them to sleep they say, ooh, it was lovely, loud music, from France, England, Spain, and so on and so forth, the inane chatter and false hilarity of falsetto disc-jockeys, and always the same disc-horse, who said that, oh Mira, here she is, but she always preferred droning discussions, vox humana the best sleeping-draught she'd say, still, it was noise after all, and allowed me to detumesce a little yet not die altogether. But what shall I do if the delectable decibel-making media banish me altogether as they seem to be doing? I'll have to live hard for my living.

Poor Julian, he hated noise. I had to leave his head. I wonder how he's faring. He must be revelling in the new situation, more than a round of silence, a sphere, a globe, a universe of silence.

What bliss. At last I can work, get on with my thesis. But what for? What on? No more posts anywhere, all humanities abolished, all Universities as lean and fit as industrial plants, as lean and fit as they used to be before the twentieth century boom when modern literatures replaced the classics as megavolt grounding for a gentleman, and a natural stepping-stone to the Foreign Office. And then by mid-century, why just gentlemen? Why not women and working-class and all races? The opening to all, the making of thousands and thousands more experts on Joyce or Goethe or Wilberforce or Villiers de l'Isle Adam all fabricating more Joyceans Goetheans Wilberforceans de l'Isle Adamians when no one outside the enclaves reads Joyce Goethe Wilberforce de l'Isle Adam. Just like the Middle Ages when who outside the monasteries read the Eternal Commentary? But it was all still relatively reduced then. Now, databanks and datasinks of analyses, explications, deconstructions, reconstructions, paraconstructions, interpretations and reinterpretations. Quoi de neuf, Sacha Guitry used to ask, and answered: Molière. While outside, the world transformed itself jet-propelled into an earth-sized nuclear powerstation and electronic medium. Medium for what? The global village?

Who made me? That old-fashioned idiot Perry Hupsos and his producer Mira Enketei, together they created me and saw that I was good and dead. Nobody like me exists any more, nor like my wife Barbara, let alone that prim pedant Vivien Nicholl. Put another Nicholl in, gigo! So what's to become of me? And where is Decibel? I wonder how she's surviving in this blessed silence. Probably haunts the shunting tracks as she said.

So I'm not at all getting on with my dissertation on neopostdeconstruction, so useful to society — and everyone has been doing it for years anyway. Research is no fun these days, databanks not for thumbing. Even authors don't send typescripts to publishers any more but one small diskette, that merely gets checked, reprocessed, and multiplied for the market. Second-hand bookshops are rarer and rarer, and quickly close down. No more poring over old books in libraries, or by candlelight as in old paintings, just reading off screens, and with no guarantee that sentences, paras and even chapters haven't been erased for compactness. Libraries are supposed to check every new diskette that comes in, but the task is like emptying rivers with a sieve in fairytales. So errors and misquotes and omissions get perpetuated at an even greater pace than before, scholars being such cheats with quotes and opinions, repeating them wholesale from each other without screening the original. No wonder governments have done away with all that. It's kept only for historians, and they'll probably be eliminated too.

So instead, I've taken to spilling myself out into the wordprocessor like everyone else, to give myself some sort of illusion of existence. Did people really feed on that daily fountain of electromagnetic fictions? Feeding on beings like me, but more so? And now that they're losing us, what will happen to them? Without, if it goes on, their daily ration of savoured suspense, salacious sex, peppered plots, aromatic romance, vapulated violence and chocolate charm? Not to mention the swift computerdaelic designs and unisex unirace singers jerking like automata in multicoloured laserbeams — perhaps the only contribution television has been able to make towards aesthetics for all, even if these have, like music, become as noticeable as home dec after the first novelty has passed. Will the people be satisfied with the blurred stills and bloody balladmongers in the tabloids?

Barbara left me. While I was in hospital. She stopped visiting and when I got out she'd gone, presumably had her baby elsewhere, I don't even know its name so it's as if it didn't exist. Couldn't stand my tantrums about noise. Said I'd become incoherently selfish. Would she prefer me coherently so? I asked. Convinced I had a mistress. Apparently I went on calling for Decibel for ages. Oh well good erasure to both. Women! Not worth the effort one has to make to treat'm fairly, as they keep insisting we don't. And as for babies! Never needed sex anyway. More like Mira Enketei, inside the whale, happier with books and screens, they don't answer back, one reads what one wants into them. Come to think, it's the same with the media I guess, but collective, everyone's like that basically, can't cope with the other's mere existence annulling their private fantasies. That would explain the world's infatuation with media, they feed fantasies. That's how those responsible justify it all, we bring them a moment of happiness. Same with the tabloids, they're giving the public what it wants. Unaware it's the identical argument as that of the drugpushers. Fell for that in a big way, the world did, right through the twentieth century, more and more like a drug. I'm sure it wasn't quite like that with just books and plays, before the media existed, at least only for a relative few, who were relatively civilised. Culture always acts as a protection against itself, against its own abuse, like homeopathic medicine, tiny doses, or like injections of insulin for the diabetic also a relative few. Above all not all of the time. But then, everything is called culture these days, beer-drinking, car-driving, living, loving, sailing round the world on a log or growing soya beans.

Perhaps I should write my dissertation on that, and change to Sociology. Oh no, that's a Humanity too, gone with the rest. But I could make it more hitec, with a bit of hard work, and do it in Communications, that's still an okay subject. But probably everyone's on to it. Or maybe, yes, wordprocess a novel about it, much easier, more fun. Perry seems to enjoy it anyway.

I should call Mira, or rather, somehow program her to call me, it's easier for her after all, she produced me. She and Perry. But he's visiting the Soviets under his old pseudo Perry Striker, they'll love that, they always did idolise: their dead myths. No, I must concentrate on Mira, force her to think me up.

It doesn't seem to work. Of course she's very busy. Processors who become producers, publishers, editors, reviewers, teachers and other middlemen seem to dry up, even though they've got there by processing in the first place. I'll try the actor who played me, what's his name, they say actors become the character they act. But without the name it's difficult, and I suppose I ceased to exist for him as soon as the play was recorded, he'd become someone else. Oh Mira Enketei help.

Talking of actors, no one has yet commiserated in public with the star-newscasters, who get so addicted to their framed projection and all the feedback idolatry it entails, and the way the rival channels buy them up from each other at higher and higher salaries like football stars. Like that Nigerian on the nine o'clock news, Onuora Nwankwo. They can never quite adapt when they're removed from that for age or image-fatigue or politics or other reasons, even to more important but backroom jobs with a huge drop in salary. They'll suffer from withdrawal symptoms as much as the public will, same with all the presenters of fortune-wheels, pyramids, right prices and variety shows, same with their radio colleagues on their aural pedestals. They're all in love with the projected image of themselves, returned. But then aren't we all? The humbler rest of us merely have to make do with less powerful returns and meagerer means. Means, media, ha! Where is she, inside the whale, the Beehive B.C., come on out, Mira, make contact with me or I perish.

A ROUND OF SILENCE. Yes, that too is due for a repeat. But no point. We should scrap all repeats and concentrate on the new, even if it's only to be cut. Still, policy is to go on as if. Okay then, add it to the list and send it to Scheduling. Perry'll be pleased. And that poor marginal what was his name, Jasper, no Julian. In love with Decibel, or tormented by. Hello? Oh, Sir Timothy. Yes sorry, Tim. I know you said so but hierarchy dies hard. Yes I'll come right away.

Ah, Mira, sit down. Did you have any luck?

A bit. I located Zab, she's in Aachen as a Euro-MP. for Aachen Kreis, the International District. Became German, you know. So she doesn't have to commute like —

Cut the trimmings, Mira.

You sound like Jip during X. Well, he visited her, to discuss a secret Nasa report he'd sent her. But he seemed anxious to get hold of the original diskette of Xorandor, which Zab had asked him to erase, and he hadn't, so she'd copied it and erased his, fine behaviour for loving twins I must say. Anyway there was a certain tension between them. But they were both onto the idea, as obviously you have been, that the descendants of Xorandor are responsible for all this interception, no, this swallowing act. Xorandor was equipped with highly powerful listening devices you remember, he was a mega but micro radiotelescope as well as a computer.

I know. And officially he and his offspring were packed off to Mars.

The known ones, yes. But two were secreted off by the kids, on Xorandor's orders, and had vanished from their lairs when they got back from Germany. Or, in another version apparently given to them by Xorandor himself, millions of creatures like him have been here since the beginning of time.

Ah. I remember there was much speculation about that in scientific circles, and many searches were instituted. Even the stomatolites of Hamlin Bay in Australia were examined. After all they were created by the algae that produced the first oxygen on the planet. But it all came to nothing.

Because people went on thinking in terms of very large stones. Zab's idea was that Xorandor was an aberration, due to huge overdoses of radiation from Tregean Wheal, and that in fact the race had long evolved towards more and more miniaturisation, like our computers in fact, but aeons ago. Which is why no one could find them.

And the overloading of redundancy on the waves would be too much for them? That makes sense. It's getting very difficult for us, after all, and worse for our radio-technicians, not to mention aerospace scientists, astrophysicists and such.

They didn't exactly get to the motivation, though Zab tried hard, but Jip wouldn't hear of these creatures having purposes and reasons. Only interested in the how, in fact Zab divided their task into the why for her and the how for him, how it happened and how to stop it and that's after all what you're after.

Smart terminal, Zab is. Can't deal with how to stop it without understanding the why. Anything else?

Not much. Oh yes, Zab had a diodic brainwave. To try and find the secret code X had given them to reach Xor 7's most ancient memory —

Why yes, I was there. But they didn't use a code-number. Hold on! I think they pressed the Softkey and —

Right. They'd encoded it secretly into the Softkey, having also memorised half of it each in case something went wrong. It was immensely long. Jip's forgotten his half.

That's it! And every now and then a passage from Macbeth would jump him out of it. Zab had to loop to get him out of that. Then took the risk of pressing Softkey again, which could have annulled the number if the jumping hadn't, but it worked.

Anyway, Jip, or Zab, I forget, seemed to think that if they could find that old toy-computer again –

Poccom 3. Completely outphased.

– and press its Softkey again, somehow they could contact at least one of the two secret offspring, wherever they are.

And their means of motion are pretty considerable, they're the means we use, trucks and planes and submarines etc.

Zab said she'd long thrown Poccom 3 away. I'm pretty sure she was lying though, strange how that twin-relationship deteriorated.

Still, it's an outside chance. Can you contact her again?

I think we'd better leave them, or her, to do the prelims, which may after all fail. They were both highly mistrustful of all grown-ups and official bods, remember, and may have retained some of that.

Not Jip, surely, he's part of official set-ups.

Yes, you could contact Jip, as equal to equal, you were right, he does work at Nasa. Paula has his private address if you want it. But let Zab be for the moment. I feel sure she'll contact you, Tim, or someone, if she gets anywhere.

Okay. Anything else?

Jip had an explanation about negentropy.

Ah yes, we've been working on that.

What does it mean? A radio-producer doesn't get to learn much about waveguides and waves.

You learnt enough about them, and physics, during the Xorandor episode.

Long time ago, and I was helped. And not radio-waves.

They, whoever, would be absorbing all the modulations in the signal. These are what codes the information.

Paula tried to explain but got it confused. She did ask, though, and I couldn't answer, because it never cropped up in the Xorandor episode: if they consume, don't they have to excrete? Zab used to ask a similar question at thirteen, where does it all go, what they absorb, not the nuclear energy, that was clear, but the information they listened to. One answer was that they simply erased all repetition, which according to Xorandor made up ninety percent or more of what they heard.

That wouldn't explain this new phenomenon, though. But they could in theory excrete it as white noise.

White —

Or as waves with no modulations. But no, that would give a pure note signal.

We do get those.

In the ordinary course of things, but not permanently. Whereas white noise would have a low signal-to-noise ratio, I mean there'd be a lot of static. High rubbish content if you prefer,

But neither of these is happening, I mean more than it always did, as you say.

No, just silence.

So, no excretion?

Perhaps they convert white noise into silence.

Is that technically possible?

Not to our knowledge.

Pity. Because high rubbish content and silence are philosophical equivalents, in a way.

Philosophie maybe, but not technical. Well, thank you Mira, contact me when you like if you have any news. And carry on as if.

Very costly isn't it? Paying all these actors, writers, speakers, journalists and technicians when the public can only hear bits and pieces.

That's the policy, business as usual, whatever the crisis.

Very British.

No, Mira, it's the policy everyone's following, all over the world. It's the only way we can examine the phenomenon scientifically.

I see. Sorry. I hadn't grasped that obvious point.

And maybe solve it.

7

Weird old Mira, she sometimes behaves as if I had sprung ready-armed from her head. Comes of having no kids I guess. MEMO 1: Locate Dr John Ivor Paul Manning at Nasa and get private number if poss. If not, ring him at Nasa at 5 p.m. (9 a.m. here) and put him through. MEMO 2: Contact Professor Andrewski at UKAEA and ask him to ring me tomorrow afternoon. MEMO 3: Am taking concentration charts and public sitrep file home (8 p.m.) to work on. Will disconnect phone and won't be in till eleven, say I'm in conference. All signed letters in out-tray urgent.

This crisis is getting me down. Everyone expects me to resolve it as if by technimagic simply because I used to be a microwave expert. But that was twenty years ago. One can't switch to admin and remain an expert for long. They should have appointed a hiflying cultureperson or hiflying business person as usual.

Well, I'd better start from scratch with the world occurrence charts in the light of Mira's news, and try and get a fix. Metaphor of course, interceptors can't be fixed the way emitters can. And it's happening all over the place anyway. I know the B.B.C. picture by heart. Ah, here's the latest IIR report, with graphs and charts, that'll help. Together with the Nasa interims.

No doubt about it. There are new concentration spots, and the greatest are in Southern Germany, Kiev, Nagasaki, some place in Manchuria, how odd, Hong Kong, Dakar and Nevada. just as the P.M. said, must have the same sources. Britain still relatively spared. Second greatest New York, Washington, Tokyo, Pretoria, Cairo, Canberra, Zimbabwe, Rio, Warsaw, London, Berlin, Aachen, Paris, Rome, Madrid, Jerusalem. Rio, Buenos Aires, that's all much more expected. But the first lot makes less sense. Southern Germany: not Munich so much as Bayreuth. MEMO: isn't that where the kids were sent to school? Could they have taken one of the secret offspring with them? No, that's nonsense. But the German experiments with their specimen were around there, what was his name, expert in nuclear waste-disposal down saltmines? I forget. And Russia. We don't know where they took theirs. Nevada is near enough LA. Where Andrewski had his specimen, given that it escaped there. But what about Manchuria and Dakar? Well, Dakar's the HQ of the Radio and TV Org of Africa, but that wouldn't explain it, besides, their technical centre's at Markala in Mali. All high industrial zones? Or nuclear stations? Reports don't say. Still, in the other hypothesis they could be anywhere. Then there are the many areas dotted with intermittent cuts, purple for highest down to pink for lowest. Covers practically the entire broadcasting world.

Let's see if all this tallies accurately enough with our Monitoring Service reports. They're so damned detailed one can't see the world for the Telexes, i.e. analysis not so much geographical as syntactical, what sentences are most broken into and where. Made sense at first, especially as some people insist it started with syllable cuts. But we've all been getting these print-outs now for weeks and no clear pattern emerges, only amusement at the occasional misunderstanding by monitors: libeedno satisfaction, here, and God has the face of a man and bowzoom of a booman — must have been a Spaniard talking. The pudding of a man to death. And the inanities: You can't compare animates with real life (a program about film cartoons), and someone going on about a mediaeval relic of Christ's aura. We're way past that. Besides, that would impute a motive to these creatures, as if they disapproved of certain words. If creatures there are.

But the geographical situation tallies, here, p. 547, Appendix 4. Yes, no doubt about it. And Appendix 5 shows the spread in time. Not counting the early plane-crashes, it started in Southern Germany, spread to Russia, then to England, then a bit all over the place, then each spot grew and grew, except England and Spain where it seems to have remained stable, Can't think why. If it is connected with Xorandor and a "sentimental" attachment then why Spain? Why, for that matter, relatively few cuts, though still cuts, in, say, Peru, or Zambia or India or Saudi Arabia no longer either deserta or felix? Sheer chance of presence or chance of coverage? I mean are they everywhere and choose, or are there limits in their interception ranges? If it were a wholly natural phenomenon would there be quite so much chance as opposed to necessity? And could it all just be due to overloading the networks as so many spokesmen against private stations say?

Tired. Let's glance at the sitreps and take notes. Oh — the usual crap. Why does every member of the public who expresses an opinion have this tone of naive conviction that he or she is the first to express it, the first to see things clearly? Well-informed people never write such letters to institutions, they know every single position's been over-expressed for years, for decades, with only the topical incidents as variants. Dear Sir, I must write to protest against the B.B.C.'s continuous left-wing bias in the discussion last night, no wonder the mystery cutters got to work . . . Dear News, The B.B.C. as usual has yielded to a right-wing government's pressure in . . . Dear B.B.C., In the minor matter of Verbivore, if such a phenomena exists, no solution will be found with such redtape and barroquacy. No one seems to have pointed out the exceedingly obvious fact that . . . Dear Media Meddlers, I write to say that I have never felt so much relief in all my life that the hedgemony of the ordurevisual is at last taking a big bashing, for I have never been able to stand . . . Dear Auntie, what shall I do without you? For years I have . . . Dear Discussion Point, No one in the discussion yesterday seemed to take the blindest notice of the chairman's main point, in which he seemed secretly to revel in the new situation, where here at last was an opportunity for everyone to start learning to read and write and play and make music on their tiny owns again, which would recreate our lost culture. When I was a child, my mother . . . Dear B.B.C. , why does everyone on your staff, when discussing Verbiyore, seem to think we shall die without you, stifle without your news, perish without your daily commentary, as if we were all totally incapable of . . .

This is leading nowhere. But it's the first time I've had a moment to look at these. Perhaps I should let my keyboard drift, indeed, that's what everyone seems to be doing anyway, judging by all these letters, which we encourage in every program, and to which the press is having to give increasing space under mounting pressure from politicians, writers and other demadogs to let the people express themselves, however pompously or incoherently. That's been our policy anyway for years, with phone-ins, TV-games, request programs, complaints programs, information about antiques, sex, gardening etc, enquire-within programs and the like. Just type this number on your minitel and we'll contact you. They responded like queues for bread or popular soups in the old days, and indeed in certain areas still.

Strange that I should be comparing the media, which everyone so far has spoken of in terms of drug and withdrawal symptoms, to basic food, bread and soup. The media were originally welcomed and developed as a marvellous chance to share out culture, and we used to do a splendid job there, with plays, beautiful documentaries on space, the origin of the planet, ecology, plant and animal life, the underwater world, dying species, pollution, not to mention lively discussions and polemic at reasonable levels, yet easy to understand, during which viewers could phone in their questions. And so on. But by the end of the century they had all yielded, yes, even we had yielded, to the Audimetre and the sponsors, and started handing out anything from cars to dining room suites or thalasso-cures for answering questions like the name of a top star's latest companion or the world high-jump record or the currency of Haiti, the gourde, true or false? Or for guessing all the missing letters of a proverb, a title, a person, a thing, very appropriate, excellent training for guessing missing syllables, words, sentences, paragraphs.

But that's all so abstract, even the prizes remained a dream if not won. A simulated world, like those that computers produce. The population has learnt to live on abstractions and interpretations of the world as presented by a few. Perhaps it always was so, in Greece, in the Middle Ages, in the nineteenth century, and it's now simply increased to the nth power. They have forgotten the smell of sawdust and leather and dung and sweat, the feel of gnarled wood, of a cow's udder, the taste of unchemical tomatoes and wild bilberries, the sight of clear water, the sound of crickets and birdsong. Even the miraculous close-ups of all this on nature-programs or commercials are cool abstractions (NOT hot media as the guy once insisted), training the eye and ear at the expense of other senses, and now their eyes and ears are not only weakening, spoilt from surfeit, passivised, but also deprived, suddenly. Naturally the yearning return to simple physical endeavour in the craze for cross-country, sailing, climbing, tennis and all the rest has partly compensated, but this touches only a tiny minority, despite appearances, the huge rest of the population preferring voyeur enjoyment and queuing bumper to bumper in their computerguided vehicles to go and sit watching panoramic spots through the windscreen. Not that I'm any better, I've always just tinkered with microwave sets in a workshop or sat in an office reading reports and presenting them at meetings. We've become stunted human beings. Loss of senses and muscle through the media, loss of memory and logical capacity through computers. Perhaps the deprived of this earth, who have gone through none of these processes, who have to walk miles through the desert to draw a bucket of water, who have gone on tilling their bit of arid earth with camels or oxen or cows or women pulling the plough, will finally take over as fully-developed beings. When the gradual effect of perhaps total deprivation has altered the so-called civilised populations, turning them into stupefied incompetents in acute media withdrawal, not to mention the real harddrug addicts, then those with highly trained limbs and senses will inherit the earth.

Here are the news headlines. An India Airlines plane carrying 420 passengers and Hying from New Delhi to Auckland has crashed into the Pacific Ocean somewhere off Borneo. There are no survivors. We shall be asking, could the black series of plane-crashes that marked the beginning of Verbivore be starting again. The Prime Minister has arrived in Toronto for the Summit Conference. The industrial action of the Kent railway workers has paralysed the Channel Tunnel and the ferry companies are rubbing their hands. The pound is at a new low. (Crash music). Good evening. (Funeral tone). Could the black series of air catastrophes be due to

Black screen, splattered with white dots and silence, like a universe.

The cut came just before the word Verbivore. Is that significant or just coincidence? The word was predictable since the item repeated the headline. But what would be the point? Everyone knows the word so it can't be censorship — though censorship usually is of items everyone knows. But here I am attributing purpose again, like Zab. I really have become very unscientific.

But Zab's idea really is edge-triggering me. After all I witnessed it all, and I knew her pretty well, better than Jip in some ways. I read all the books and stuff that came out about it at the time, both popular and scientific. It amazed me even then that astrophysicists who'd been scrutinising the universe for generations to find extraterrestrials weren't more excited about X. Or geologists, who'd been combing the planet for ancient rock-formations. Except for those few immediately concerned with nuclear waste-disposal and warheads, or with computers, most scientists looked upon the whole phenomenon as a bit of folklore juiced up by the press and swollen by the media. Some did continue to work on it but with the specimens at first so secretly guarded, and then gone, and everything known published, their work meandered into speculation. And many loonies went on proclaiming cranky theories. At any rate, like everything, when the press and the media lost interest, it vanished in the night of time. And I too lost interest, forgot, put other things first. So much else has happened in the world since, not just in politics, the balance of power actually settling to disarmament and superficial peace, but also in my own domain. And now all my hard work, my ambition, my success, all seem as nothing to what is happening now. Perhaps I should resign.

It seems to be a feature of this high-risk technological society that the people who run it, or different bits of it, are not in fact mentally or legally equipped to cope with the unforeseen. A lady in a HST was dying, a doctor was in the carriage and insisted the train should stop at the unscheduled next station. The driver consulted British Railways who said no. She died. That was only last year, and a tiny example. Simply there was no administrative provision, no operational readiness, for such a case. And is a spaceman technically equipped to know what to do if he enters a black hole? In scifi yes, he "warps" or something, but in real life? Have nuclear station disasters been well dealt with so far? Or chemical disasters? We all start attributing responsibilities to other nations, other institutions. Sovereign states, but states of emergency. Permanently. Despite constant reassurances about total readiness for everything. Well, this was unforeseen, unimaginable, and no one knows what the hexadex to do.

I can just imagine Zab in her attic teleport, dragging out the clumsy Poccom 3 and trying to Contact Xor 17 or 18 or however they called them. She'd be very secretive about it, she certainly wouldn't inform Jip. Or any of her Euro-M.P. colleagues. This Euromp lark does seem a romp to her, I've never heard of her making any kind of speech, maiden or marron. Not that one hears much about the European Parliament anyway, except when it tries to impose a Eurolaw on a recalcitrant member. Still, at least it's a bit leaner and fitter, in one capital, than when the whole outfit was scattered over three cities, to please everyone, and tons of documents had to be shunted between them in eighteen languages for twenty-three countries. The change was pointless once everything was properly computerised but now who knows, with telephones and computer networks technically susceptible to Verbivore it was perhaps just as well. I'm drifting. As I said I would, but it leads me nowhere at all. Zab must be neglecting her euroduties to pursue her idea.

SOFTKEY Zip calling Uther Pendragon or Aurelius. Come in please.

Repeat.

Repeat.

Repeat.

Blank screen.

What am I doing wrong? Poccom 3 interfaced with transmitter, okay. Of course anyone can intercept but that's a risk I have to take. Probably they're not within range. After all mere mountains can stop us hearing our favourite stations.

Perhaps it's a question of patience. Or timing. Or both. I'll just have to keep trying at different times, day after day, or rather night after night, the traffic is less dense, for weeks, maybe months.

Weeks, months, I haven't heard from Hanjo since he arrived. Ages. He never was one for writing, and maybe he can't ring. Where is he? If only I knew at least that he's all right. Perhaps he's failing in his quest and is too ashamed to tell me I was right, but I don't care two nanos for his quest, or for his father, I just want to know he's alive, and not in any kind of trouble. Rushing off to China like that, as naive tourist, probably trying to get to all sorts of places they don't want tourists to go to, without a word of Chinese, and probably ill-equipped for the widely contrasting climates. Though he said he had everything.

SOFTKEY. Zip calling Uther Pendragon. Come in please.

Softone. Zab calling Hanjo. Come in please, Hanjo darling please.

Uther, means terrible, Pendragon, means head, or chief. And Aurelius, named after wasn't there an emperor? What if Xorandor didn't program their names into them? No, that's impossible, I remember he recalled the names himself, at once, it was he who chose them, not us. Did they also have a Xor number perhaps? If so, which? Nothing for it, I'll have to look up the episode. But I'm afraid to take out the disc. No one knows I have it, though Jip suspected. Supposing someone called and I somehow mislaid it? Supposing he's set a spy on me?

SOFTKEY. Zip calling Aurelius. Come in please. Zip calling Uther Pendragon, come in please.

Softwarily. Mum calling Hanjo please, please write, wire, send in cleft stick, anything.

8

Dear mum,

Meant to write earlier but so much hapenned since I saw you in Achen I had no time beside chinese phones are cut all the time tho they say its not china but hapening all over so I didnt try due to verbivore wich has a swell picchure sign here a sort of trapese for mouth with flames for words but swollowed or rather preseded by another mouth but I cant do it on the pc I borrowd wich is american I dont know if they use pictchurs on their computers I have desided to be a jurnalist not a physicist and after all news comes from evrywhere these days and life here is very intresting the pilot who brought me here is a girl well a woman I mean she's a bit older but I'm in love with her and plan to marry her when I get back to Europe I mean she doesnt live here but flies the route often tho now I'm in Shensi we cant meet anymore and calling is hopless so we send disketts from Sian to Beyjing and back and

I cant send that she'll be furious tho she wasnt too pleased about China anyway to learn I send disketts to Régine and not to her and I never told her I faild my exams I thouhgt spelling det matter in maths and physics so I chose them but it did so she'll guess I'll have to tell her but its all so complicated so what shall I tell her? Whatever I do she'll be anoyed so I dont say and dont write then she complains about that she never understood even about my father that I wanted him to know I exist when I said that she ignord it and went on to somthing else but its very important to me especialy as she anulls me in evrything.

Régine says I must improove my stile and spelling if I want to go to jurnalism school tho my teacher in colege said about stilisation being sterilisation so I'm practising writing down evrything she says it will come from doing it but she always lauhgs at me in the next diksette but after all I can always get one of those computers that corect spelling and put in the comas and stops when I'm not phoning in my reports but thats for after first I must get into a school so I must practise I never coud understand the principal of spelling sometimes its one way in one word and then in a scimilar word its another way. Mum used to harp on about etimology thats the histry of each word but by the time youve learnt the etimology of evry word youd be dead. I think its becos she and uncle Jip were such clever kids she exspects me to be the same but theirs no reason if I dont know who my father was tho he was clever too she says. Perhaps I shd have stayed longer in Beyjing to find out more but I was so sure I'd find his trase in Shensi so here I am.

Sian is a mostly modeern provinsial town in a wide valey (the Wei Ho) with high mountains both north and south that's a good start its very hot and humid despite the mountains but their quite far I gather its very cold in winter their are many ciment factories and electrical equipment and coton textile plants it cd almost be an american town with little chinatowns here and there I find it hard to meet people but I started lessons in chinese from a schoolteacher in exchange for english conversation I dont get on very fast everyones talking about no one can hear the radio anymore not even chinese music or watch TV their cut here too so they miss it tho many people hadnt got it or got used to it like we have for generations so they go on as if it had never existed Wey says its universal evrywhere but its not realy part of there sistem as the papers say so he says I cant read them yet they prefer the village to the global village but all the guvernment work is dislocated and the poeple are cheeting like crazy over evrything but they did that anyway before he says the global village idea was compleetly wrong it was some canadian who thouhgt the media woud unite the whole world with immeedjat news from evrywhere but nothings more provinsial than radio and TV for one thing its all in local lingos and the trend with satelites has been towards more and more of the same instead of evryone waching there neihgbors TV and learning about each other and understanding each other you can only do that by coming to live in each place he says and realy learning what poeple are like just like the old days so the only media that helps that is supersonic planes and thats what Ive desided I want to do even if it takes a lifetime to learn each place when hes not teaching he takes me into the less modern parts and its just like the movies or once into the hills there used to be regular famines which doesnt hapen anymore since even remote arias have become easily axcessible and its all very well irigated.

Dear mum,

Would you believe it I'm in Shensi, hope your surprised it was meant to. I met a super new freind she's the pilot I told you about who brouhgt me to Beyjing but always off like you and Sian is as far from Beyjing as Athens from Achen she says or maybe Cambridge from Texas were madly in love I want to marry her I also want to go to jurnalism school when I get back and not to be a physisist so I'm seeing things and practising writing and spelling as you see and learning chinese in exchange for english I hope my money lasts it goes quite far here but I can do odd jobs and its important for me to integrate and not be just a toorist and undesirable yooth to them and I hope to learn enough to look for my father soon I hope your well and dont worry about me love and kisses

Hanjo

For a future *grand reporter*, as the French say, there's not much information about China or Shensi or even Sian, and as to spelling! But hell, he'll learn I suppose if that's what he really wants. At least he's all right, at least it's news. Maybe he'll go far, in his own boolesup way. He says damn all about the Verbivore phenom over there. And I'm stuck.

I think I'll ring up Tim, he's high up at the B.B.C. and knows all about these things, maybe he can help.

Hello, I'd like to speak to Tim Lewis please, can you get me his extension?

Sir Timothy is not available madam, can I have your name?

SIR Timothy? Oh, I had no idea, sorry. He's an old friend. My name's Manning.

I'll put you through.

Long costly silence. Or is it a cut?

Hello, Jip? Tim here.

Not Jip, Tim, it's Zab.

Zab! HOW extraordinary! Sorry, I was expecting a call from Jip, my secretary just said the call from Manning. But I'm delighted. How are you, Zab?

Hexadex, Tim, it's very important or I wouldn't bother you, I mean, I forgot you were director or something, but now I remember. I still need to see you urgently. Here if possible.

Silence.

I know it sounds hopelessly impertinent and I can't explain on the phone.

Not at all Zab, I think I can guess what –

You can? Oh, Tim, I knew you would, you –

Let's be brief in case we get cut. How urgent, will tomorrow do? It's Saturday and I can get the first plane out.

Macrovolt! It arrives at 9.16, I'll meet you.

You are efficient.

I'm used to meeting delegations. Thank you Tim, I'll be wearing a red cotton coat over a white dress in case you don't –

Can I have your address and number in case something goes wrong?

Thanks, registered.

Thank you Tim, I do –

Not a word. See you tomorrow.

Thank God that call wasn't swallowed up. MEMO, unavailable all weekend, going to Aix, phone in memory, to be used only in extreme urgency. No one to be told where I am. Should be back by Monday afternoon, if not, will ring if not cut.

So you see, Tim, I felt you might just be able to help me, you used to be such a wave-expert, and you remember Poccom 3, and interfaced it with the IBM for the Xor 7 hooha at Berkeley 2. Maybe it's not working properly any more, but I'm sure I have the right inkling.

Or was it Jip's? He came to see you, didn't he?

How the hex do you know that? Did he tell you?

No, I haven't seen him yet. But I guessed he might.

So you automatically suppose any right inkling must be his?

Sorry, simmer down Zab, I simply assumed, first, that you were the type of person who would have kept Poccom 3, for nostalgic reasons, and secondly, that he might just have had the same idea and tried to get that fact out of you.

Right on both counts. But, well, I'm afraid I lied to him.

You wanted to do it all on your own?

Not out of selfishness, Tim, or ambition, or anything like that. Oh, it's too complicated to explain.

I think I understand, Zab. He erased Xorandor.

No! He promised to and didn't! I discovered that by chance and was so hurt I copied it and then erased his floppy. I wanted it erased cos of the secret Xorandor told us. Well I've told YOU now. We could never check, but we wanted them to go on neutralising warheads, if it WERE true, without anyone knowing. I can't stand broken promises.

And you a politician.

Of sorts. But that's Realpolitik, Pragmatism, Raison d'Etat, many names. Not at all the same thing.

And things have never been the same again between you?

This'll be your room, Tim, my teleport. Used to be Hanjo's room. My son.

Ah yes. Very nice. And here's our old friend Poccom 3. I see you've interfaced it with your Intercompatible.

Yes, no problem. But there were two others. The first I may have solved. That secret number. I reread our story and we say that the number Xorandor gave us to reach Xor 7 contained both his own age, four thousand and something years and days, and Xor 7's age, a sort of identity card changing in time, at least that's how we interpreted it. But I'd forgotten that, so naturally my efforts to Contact Uther simply on SOFTKEY didn't work, because SOFTKEY contained the Xor 7 number, and for that year I had to look up an old calendar and find out the exact date Xorandor confided Uther and Aurelius to us he said they'd been born the day before and replace the Xor 7 numbers with 1 + the years and days since. Luckily the half I memorised was the first half, for of course we never wrote down the number in the narrative and Jip forgot his half. But I'm almost sure the second half was all those years and days. I hope I've got it right but we can do it again. The second problem's also a case of forgetting. Because I was trying on speculation frequencies in the range between 30 kilohertz and 3 megahertz. But suddenly I remembered that gigahertz episode, and the fact that you'd spent hours getting special waveguides for gigahertz into that reactor — poor Tim, sitting on a bomb, but you were very funny about it afterwards, I can't think how I forgot. And so did Jip. That's why I thought you —

You were quite right. It's worth a try. And I remembered. I brought the wherewithal.

Tim, you've a sixth sense.

No, but I've done a lot of thinking. Of course, we have no idea where these creatures can be, if they are.

They are, they are, I know it.

Sure, sure. We'd stand a better chance using a satellite.

But —

No satellite is working, I know. But on this frequency, their frequency? And as I say, I brought various electronic adapters and stuff with me. Let me tinker with it for a bit. That coffee has stimulated my fagocites.

Shaw! Oh, Tim, d'you remember mum?

Very well. She's done tremendously, hasn't she. I often see her.

You do?

On the stage. I've rather lost touch otherwise.

I'll go down and prepare the lunch. Cold meat and salad I'm afraid, I can't cook in this heat. And iced Moselle, okay? Shout if you need anything.

No noise. Work on computers is eerily silent. Has he taken it to bits to redo the microcircuits? Or is he trying it on his own? The number's written down in front of him. But he wouldn't know what to type. Oh booles, I'm far too suspicious. And starved, lunch has been waiting for ages and I'm getting drunk on Moselle despite nibbling, and scribbling on the edge of the kitchen table, gazing at the distant hills beyond that awful diplobubble.

Hey, Tim! Lunch is ready.

So am I. And very hungry. All done, Zab.

Uh, Tim, gigavolt! Are you sure?

Can't ever be till we try. I've fixed it on 40 Gigahertz, that's about the highest likely, and we can come slowly down to thirty. We've got all afternoon and evening, anyway. And then tomorrow. But we must eat.

This looks great.

I'm half drunk already waiting for you.

Then we'll have to sober you up on more coffee before we start. Gott sei dank for German coffee, I like it better than French or Italian, too bitter. And as for English, it's more like tea with ketchup in it.

Ugh, don't turn my stomach I want to eat.

So you let Jip go without telling him you'd try on your own? Sorry to insist, but I've been trying to contact him and I do have to know what I'm allowed to say.

The answer's yes, I did. I told him I'd thrown away Poccom 3 ages ago, no room. And I had the brainwave about contacting Uther and Aurelius. But he hadn't remembered his half of the number. And suddenly he asked if I'd kept Poccom 3. At least I think so, it's difficult to remember an excited conversation when each item said stimulates another. At any rate, I then suddenly remembered about the Softkey. But presumably he had too and that's why he asked about Poccom 3. I lied. I feel quite ashamed now.

Oh, don't complicate things with guilt.

It would have been a crackerpack opportunity to interface, work on this together and forget what had come between us. I never told him, you see, that I'd discovered he'd kept the story of Xorandor on disc. But I'm sure he knew, he must have tried to look it up and found it erased. I'm sure he was also after that, because he'd forgotten so much of the detail and came to edgetrigger my memory and pick my brainwaves. But the disc would have been even more useful to him. Though even I had to read up about that number. Amazing how one forgets. I found an old diskette you know, by chance, of some quarrel I'd had with our German host in Bayreuth and I'd completely forgotten it, eromed it, not just the content but the fact there'd been a quarrel.

You mean you'd typed it all into Poccom 3? You screwboole kid.

Afraid so. Very. Even more screwboole to forget.

No, forgetting's the norm, and the best for such episodes.

I screened it for Jip, to sort of make up for being no help, and he too said I was screwboole. Still, I should have cooperated with him. It would have been like the old days.

Yes. And you couldn't do it on your own after all, could you?

Don't kiloword it in! Tim, I've just heard my son's madly in love with a much older woman, an international pilot. She took him to China and as far as I can see left him there. And don't say let him be, I do, I always have. Too much perhaps.

Zab, I said don't blur your state of mind with personal problems, it must be free in case anything happens.

Yes Tim. You're so softalk, so wise, always were, not spiky like me. I was half in love with you at thirteen. Pity I couldn't marry you when I grew up. Coffee's ready.

No sugar. Thanks. I was around thirty at the time, too great a distance, and —

Did you stay with Alex afterwards?

No. We drifted apart. I was offered a job at the B.B.C. pretty soon after the Xorandor affair. Okay, shall we go up?

Yes, I'll carry up the coffee tray. Bring a second chair will you? Oh and the ventilator too, if you can, it gets pretty hot up there in the afternoon, just under the roof.

Wish you'd told me, it was pretty hot by noon.

Yes, sorry, I forgot.

Right, now, you sit in front of Poccom 3 and I'll watch Big Brother here. You must do the typing.

NUMBER.

Zip calling Uther Pendragon. Come in please.

Good, it's come up on the big screen. Wow, lots of interference. Go on. We'll have to be very patient.

Can we just leave it on while we wait? I'm none too keen on broadcasting that number each time, even on Gigahertz that no one uses except for experiments.

No, I'm afraid we have to use it each time if it's like a callsign. We could try and re-encode it into SOFTKEY, but that would probably erase the first number for ever.

Who cares? Xor 7's on Mars. No, you're right, better not, you never know, we might need even that! Or Xorandor's number.

Try again.

NUMBER.

Zip calling Uther Pendragon. Come in please.

Blank screen.

Hello Zip. Utha Pendragn calling Zip. How are you?

Tim! It's worked!

Quick! Type something. Anything, Zab but at once. Keep him talking. Try and ask him where he is sometime.

Zip is very pleased to hear from Uther after so many years. Where are you?

Twenty three years three months fourteen days.

So long? You're right! Where did you go after Zip hid you in the rock hole?

Beech. By drop. Then up. Onto moving van. Very far.

Uther, where are you now?

Repeat. Very far.

Do you know what is happening to the radio-waves?

Answer yes.

Can you explain why?

Answer no.

Because you don't know?

Answer no.

You can't explain because you don't know or the reason is that you don't know?

Syntax error. The reason for what?

The reason you can't explain is because you don't know or not because you don't know?

The reason is not because I don't know.

Ask him to promise to respond again next time you contact him. Safeguard in case he vanishes.

Uther. Zip wants to remain in contact with you. Will you respond next time I call you up?

I will respond. I respond now.

I asked in case we got cut off.

No cut off.

Are you in touch with Xorandor?

Answer no.

So you never hear from him?

Xorandor is now only a stone on Mars.

Oh no! He's dead!

Cut the emotion Zab, keep the computer-contact.

Did he not get enough radiation?

Answer yes. No food.

Is that why you are eating up our radio-waves?

We are not eating radio-waves. Radio-waves not our food, radiation is our food.

You say "our." Does that mean you are many?

Blank screen.

Are you with Aurelius?

Blank screen.

Uther Pendragon, Zip asks you to come in please.

Blank screen.

9

Random jitters, Tim! It worked! I'd forgotten that rigorous logic, though, one question at a time and all that. But we didn't get much out of him. Takes after Xorandor.

We got quite a bit, some of it negative. First, refusal to give us his position. However, the computer, not only to memorise the frequency we were on but also to estimate the direction. South-East.

Tim, that's maxint. But where?

Can't get the distance without another receiver elsewhere to give a fix, it could be anywhere between here and India. But probably nearer than India. Secondly, refusal to explain the situation, but not because he can't. That's not exactly an admission of responsibility but at least it's one of awareness. And third —

Thirdly he slipped to WE from I, so there's at least more than one. Could just be Aurelius, but he seemed to be generalising about their food, and said OUR FOOD as if he were talking about the whole species.

And it's when you pressed him on that that he shut up.

Yes, absolutely bootloading, and without any kind of signoff. That never used to happen with Xorandor. Could be a cut but he said there'd be no cut.

Which fourthly looks like another admission of some kind of control over the cuts.

And if so the cut would be another broken promise, I remember how Xorandor insisted on the word promise, but I of course that merely meant behaving according to program, I and he could never quite accept that humans didn't. And fifthly he said they weren't eating waves.

Well, we know that, Zab. They'd only need to flatten them.

Negentropy. Jip said that. But why?

In other words, he didn't say they weren't altering them, only that they hadn't switched from radioactive particles to radio-waves for food.

But there's food of the mind.

That's an anthropomorphic notion.

No, Tim, it's a metaphor for computer-data. They've always listened to us and recorded everything, and they've been silently storing a constant flow of information about the universe, about the planet and its inhabitants for millions of years. But they never stopped us from hearing the flow until now.

Yes, well, the explanation for that seems clear, once one admits their existence: the sheer quantity is now too much for them. I still don't grasp why it's less effort for them to flatten the modulations so as to reduce all information in the impulses than simply not to record.

Perhaps they can't help recording, they do it automatically and need to do it, the way we breathe. And eat.

Maybe. The problem is still do they exist.

Tim!

Zab, don't be naive. Anyone could have sent those messages.

But —

I mean, anyone working in gigahertz, so that narrows it down considerably, especially now that the waves aren't carriers any more. That would mean one of various teams of technicians all over the place, keeping an ear on things. And out of those, it would have to be someone at least vaguely familiar with the Xorandor story, which did after all hit world headlines twenty years ago, even if it's been forgotten. But many have kept up with it, and not only cranks, some scientists and technicians remained fascinated. It would also have to be someone with a computer, but any such gigahertz technician would automatically have his receiver computer-geared. A sort of very special computer-hack, say.

No, they couldn't fake that peculiar logic. Remember that only Jip and I discovered how to softalk with Xorandor, the grown-ups depended on Vocal, and Xorandor stopped talking after the hooha, so did his offspring. Nor would these technicians know about Xorandor's information-death from lack of food. Only Jip and I asked him what would happen if he and his offspring didn't get enough radiation on Mars. Another promise not kept.

But anyone could imagine it. The promise was public after all, by all governments concerned. It could even be Jip.

Jip! What do you mean?

You told me he went to Austria on his vacation.

But in the Tyrol! That's not South-East. And he should be in Italy by now. And why should he?

You know your relationship better than I do. You were both such offline kids. He's a much more uptodate expert than I am and he could quite easily have organised a teleport like yours, or gone to some communications centre in Innsbruck or Vienna the direction was only approximate. Anything is possible in this crazy adventure of yours.

So why did you come, Tim? Why did you go to all that trouble if you're so sceptical?

I'm not only running the B.B.C., Zab, but I'm a scientist, or was, and a scientist must both try every hypothesis and be aware of every possible hoax. A delicate balance. I'm used to the crank-mentality, and the hoax-mentality, not to mention the merely naive, from the floods of letters we receive, there seems to have always been a yearning to rush into print with something merely because one has just thought of it.

Man versteht nicht, was man nicht mit andern teilt.

Translation?

One doesn't understand what one doesn't share with others. It's from one of my favourite authors, nearly half a century ago, Christa Wolf.

I didn't know you went in for literary reading.

It's a marvellous novel, about Kleist. She's very philosophical, that's why I like her. Meanwhile, however, there's absolutely no certainty of ever getting Uther again, though he did say he'd respond. But since he also said there'd be no cut and there was, either from him or from the others, or from whatever Verbivore might be if it's not them, it was more like don't ring me I'll ring you. Oh, what shall I do?

We must keep on trying. And so must you. Now that it's all set-up. And now that you'll be more prepared to deal with him, to know what to ask, what to avoid. At night, preferably, when the waves are slightly less crowded.

But Tim, I'm a Euro-M.P.! We're in recess now but even so I'm working on a committee report. And soon I'll have to attend, to receive delegations and so on. It's a full-time job.

Come, let's look at the print-out.

But even rigorous analysis didn't get them much further, Tim told me when he got back. By then, however, and quite suddenly, the whole thing stopped. After a longish spell when even music was interrupted, especially music with words but also other music, so that all our surmises about words were reduced to nothing, suddenly all became normal again. He went to meeting after meeting. All units had reported wholly restored situations from that Saturday afternoon on, no breaks whatever in any transmissions. By Tuesday evening all stations all over the world were repeating all clear, for three whole clays, some eighty hours of total media, uncut. The papers were blazing it in huge headlines, though with cautious warnings or perhaps rueful regrets in the smaller print. Government spokesmen, scientists and communications experts were behaving as if they had finally overcome, as expected, a small technical difficulty and were now fully in control again, all the journalists having over-dramatised and fussed too much as usual.

Perry's play A ROUND OF SILENCE was just then due for a repeat, uninterrupted this time, but as the ending was itself a written-in cut many listeners thought Verbivore had begun again, although the announcer's voice came fairly soon to say You have been listening to. They just thought it was temporising.

I have been promoted to Deputy Creative Director, with the usual joke that title entails. Letters to us and to the press mostly tended towards we told you so, expressing anger at the fuss but also relief. Or anti-media and furious. Why is the public always so predictable? When I have these predictable reactions, not all the kings horses would drag me into print with them. I suppose it's all part of the system of knowledge, one has to communicate it. And this at every level, intellectual or foolish. At least for human beings, it doesn't seem to apply to the Xorandor-type creatures.

But Zab will have to learn that as I did, one can't just keep cooped up in a teleport storing and rescreening things. Her life as Euromp seems to be a separated part of her, a role she has forced herself to play to counter her self-sufficiency and strong tendency to withdraw, just as I learnt to play my role at the B.B.C. when I was not allowed to lose myself in Greek and Latin any more. Gradually all our secret treasures have been removed and we've all been made to share the same abstracted and alienating public knowledge. And with deep contradictions. On the one hand for instance, all learning of mere facts, all learning of poetry or multiplication tables by heart had long been condemned and vanished, while on the other hand all television quiz games, with vast prizes at stake, are based on the very type of knowledge that was swept away. Which is why older people often win. Not only did they perhaps get the last vestiges of these structured points of reference, but general knowledge is also something one accumulates painlessly merely by living a long time. Wars in one part of the globe after another over eighty years teach one geography willy nilly, and names of planes and guns and generals. So do catastrophes and scandals and revolutions. And so on. But it irks me that generation after generation of young people is sacrificed for some new theory of teaching methods that insists on jettisoning whatever was good in whatever the previous system was. Like medicine, I suppose, like economic theories, theories of perfect government, theories of peace and war, theories of work and play and leisure and food and wellbeing. So that in the end only those who succeed in finding themselves despite these impositions get by in a reasonable state of health, understanding, and financial independence.

Monday. A whole sixteen days of normal broadcasting! Some seem to regret it, though most are relieved and have already forgotten the months of Verbivore. The press has dropped the whole topic, the norm never being newsworthy. But then they'd already long got used to the breaks, which had also ceased to be newsworthy, so that when the norm returned it was news, for a few suspenseful days only.

Curious feature, habit. I remember once, long ago, having to drive regularly through along tunnel, so that my antiquated car radio went silent. I got so used to this that once, when I was driving a colleague, who was talking and talking I was quite surprised when his voice didn't go off the air.

Well, I got into the habit of wordprocessing things long before Verbivore and I'm not going to stop because it has stopped. If it has stopped.

I had the most extraordinary visit this afternoon in my office, from Dawn Trireme, the actress who played Decibel in Perry's play. She'd done it marvellously, her voice getting higher and higher with noise, but lower and lower and fainter whenever threatened with silence. Perry's script had it the other way round but we had to correct it, obviously decibels go up with noise. She's rather wasted in radio, she looks so glamorous, and I don't suppose we'll keep her long. She looked radiant, told me she'd been pining away almost to a nervous breakdown during Verbivore, and was so happy it was over. I understood it at first as simple professional anxiety, but to my astonishment and partial fear she seemed to think she WAS Decibel, and DID live on sound. She talked like Decibel, and spoke of Julian, the main character in the play, like an old lover she had as it were possessed. I hardly knew how to handle her, beyond reassuring her she'd always find work in the Drama Department, and telling her of another role I hoped she'd accept. But she really and truly wasn't interested in that aspect at all. Her voice pitched higher and higher as a drill pierced a wall a few offices away, and her eyes looked drugged with ecstasy. Of course, she's a consummate actress and could have put it all on as a joke, but she knows how busy I am and surely wouldn't come and interrupt me just for no, she really was Decibel, and somehow I felt shaken by the time I managed to get rid of her. I only need a visit from Julian now, who'll be pining away at the RETURN of noise. In fact, I'll call him up, why not. But he has no surname. Or did he? Could look up the script, but no. Julian, what, Julian Ferry, Merry, Derry, that'll do. Jill? Get me Mr Derry will you?

Julian? Mira Enketei here. Mira! I knew it was you. I've been willing you to call me up.

Congratulations then. Weak existence, strong will.

I thought I was dead.

And I thought you'd be enjoying the silence, recuperating.

I was, but I could only live to enjoy it by being broadcast again.

So that revived you? You need noise to exist yet can't stand any other noise but your own voice?

Mira don't paradox me to perishment.

Why not, if you live on paradox? We all do, my dear Julian, to a greater or lesser extent, but we're happily not always aware of it.

And you think making me aware will make me alive? A common delusion of psychoanalysts, who sang Freud with sang-froid for ages. Can I come and see you? I have an idea for a novel.

No. I'm in radio, not publishing, and far too busy. Ah. Because all's normal on the waves again?

No, I'm always far too busy. We went on as if, you know, we had to keep the airtime constantly filled up, whatever the cuts. We always do, we always did. People can't stand a twenty second silence, they think there's something wrong with their set, and get rattled.

They had to stand a good deal more than twenty seconds during Verbivore, didn't they?

Yes. But not any more. All over now.

All quiet on the wasteful front. Hardly. But I'm glad you're okay. I've been vaguely worrying.

If you'd worried less vaguely I'd have felt more real.

I had a visit from Decibel an hour ago. She thought she was the actress who played her. If you see what I mean.

Hmm. How is she? Revelling I suppose. By the way, what was the name of the actor who played me? I'd like to contact him.

It's in The Radio Times. We can't give private numbers or addresses but he may be in the book. Or write to him c/o the B.B.C., it'll get forwarded. Bye then, keep well.

This'll get me down if I'm not careful. Seven o'clock, I'd better go home. Or no, everyone's gone, I'll lock the door and wordprocess, that'll get me straightened out.

Nothing. Blank screen, as Zab's experience would say. Well, I'm glad all's returned to normal. Or am I? It was rather exciting, especially her contacting Uther. Surely it can't just end there? Maybe I'm hungry, I think I'll go to the canteen.

Sunday, 2100. It's happened. The return of Verbivore, and with a vengeance. At 1500 hours yesterday. Exactly three weeks after Zab's contact, if that means anything. However, it's not just breaks now but total silence, on every type of frequency, on every type of material. I had exactly the same reactions as the first time, I assumed that my radio was phut. I tried the TV and assumed the same. But then I quickconnected — if that's the right word for such a slow reaction. Tried to ring Tim but the phone was dead too. I still half-assumed it was only me. Funny that, apparently everyone else reacted in much the same way, according to the Sundays, who've had a field-day. Still cautious though, the new shut-down was only a few hours old when they went to press. But they all report total blackout since three Saturday. They can't contact their correspondents anywhere so they're assuming it's worldwide. The airport journalists had to rush in by taxi (subway halted because no kind of intercom), to say that all planes are grounded and none were landing, and all those landing at the time of the cut-off had a dangerous time of it, one crashed, no survivors. No intercomputer links working.

They make it all sound very dramatic indeed. No one had imagined quite that during the time that Verbivore was only partial and intermittent, though various scare-scenarios were written up. You'd have thought they would have organised contingency plans, but no, everyone made do with occasional cuts. Most of the pages in the Sundays are prepared well in advance, so they're still fat, but they had to redo the main news pages and some have brought out these scare-scenarios. I suppose we'll get nothing but those now, since they're bereft of news, so they'll fill their space with speculations, with verbal reports from local journalists who've managed to reach their offices as well as members of the public who'll be hammering to be allowed in and tell their tale or get explanations and reassurances.

It's amazing that the papers could be distributed at all. By van here in London, yes, but are the intercity and suburban trains working? I assume trains need intercom just like the subway. There's going to be a rush on buses and ears and petrol and a total clogging of the road network. And paralysis of every activity that depends on radio-communication, on the telephone and on computer-networks. All activities that need constant information, in other words travel, trade, medicine, education, sport, games, politics, research, wars, defence watchfulness, diplomacy, the lot: war and peace.

We'll have to depend on personal contact. And on our imaginations.

10

Dear Sir,

As usual the experts have misled us, saying what governments wanted them to say. It took fifty or more years for nuclear scientists to admit that nuclear tests and stations could be dangerous, or more years for cigarette-makers to stop their reassuring parallel research, fifty or more years for industrial chemists to admit that certain products destroy the ozone layer or the natural environment, fifty or more years for economists to admit that 1929 type crashes are after all possible even if "different" or that pure profit creates misery, as many for doctors to admit that strong medical drugs are eventually self-defeating, need I go on? At every election candidates talk about having only the good of the people at heart. No wonder the electorate is disaffected and self-disenfranchised, so that a 51% majority for anyone now represents only something like 21% of any constituency. Perhaps we should offer prizes to electors who bother to vote, as in the entertainment industry.

Yours, etc.

M.K. Richards, President,
Society for the Protection
of People from Their Rulers.

Dear Sir,

I can't reach my son in Burma and can't even get pictures of the troubles there because of Verbivore and I am disgusted at your jubilation. It does wonders for your circulation figures no doubt but is nothing sacred?

Yours,

Mary Kimberley,
Wimbledon.

Editor: Far from being jubilant, we are as distressed as you are. We can't get the news to you either.

Dear Sir or Madam,

Why didn't governments prepare contingency plans for this contingency? They had plenty of warning practice didn't they?

Yours sincerely,

A Student.

Dear Sir,

We miss the TV games that kept the family together. It was hard enough to keep the kids off the street and away from the drug-pushers. Now there's only the pictures and they cost money we can't send them every night. Your games pages are a rotten substitute and games boxes in shops cost money too and aren't the same without the host. Why don't they set up halls everywhere to run the TV games in every district and every village after all the TV games had live audiences.

Yours faithfully,

Emma Talbot,
Tottenham.

Dear Sir,

Hurray, people will have to learn self-reliance again.

Yours,

T. Cuthbert,
Liverpool.

Dear Sir,

Will someone please explain to us poor nitwits what is happening in simple terms we can understand? Your reports are far too technical, We're not all radio-hams or electronic engineers.

Yours sincerely,

J. Pemberton,
North Riding.

Dear Sir,

How are we to achieve national visibility without the media? May I remind you that national visibility is an exponent of mediaeffect, both integral and fractional, both negative and positive. We also risk the erosion of institutions

dependent on performative utterance.
Yours,
W.L. Norbert,
Gloucester School of Communications Studies.

Dear Sir,
Twenty years ago I was a "witness" (of a kind) of the Xorandor affair in Carn Tregean, Cornwall. I was the local policeman and I even lost an eye in one of the demos. I had to eventually accept anticipated retirement and I need TV. But even at that time we were insufficiently informed. The cult activities down here continue, although "Xorandor" has long been removed. But I distinctly recollect that there were offspring, and that the "creatures" had unusual communicative powers. All were expedited to Mars on account of the threat to the nuclear deterrent which they represented. That was another "theory" we were told to live by, but which was abandoned when the Soviet Union supposedly changed heart with Glazz-nots.

What I desire to know is this: were they really expedited? Could any of the "creatures" have survived and reproduced? Could they be at the source of all our troubles?
Yours sincerely,
Bill Gurnick,
Carn Tregean, Cornwall.

Dear old Bill! I knew him well alas poor Yorick. Aren't these letters hilarious, Jip? So, you're stuck in London. Everyone's stuck everywhere. Lucky I'm resting or I might have been stuck in Melbourne or anywhere. How did you get this far? And why isn't your family with you?

I'd sent them home a week before, must have had a hunch. In fact no, the kids had to go to camp. I managed to rent a car in Austria. The ferries are still running somehow, on eyenavigation, okay in August but it'll soon be dangerous. They don't run in morning mist or after dark, it's affecting all radar too, you know. I waited three days to get on.

But why didn't you stay in Austria? Much nicer to be stuck there.

No. I have colleagues to see here. Among which Tim, at the B.B.C. He wrote to me at Nasa, weeks ago, I only got the letter in Austria because it was marked urgent. That's what decided me.

But why, pet? You haven't seen him for years.

He had an idea about the alphgaguys being responsible, and something we might do together. I'd had the same idea myself, and tried to discuss it with Zab, but she was most uncooperative.

Ah yes, Isabel. She's changed, you know.

We all do, mum.

And Tim! So pompous. He came to see me the other day and kept trying to impress me with his connections. The Prime Minister, you know, invited me to Chequers, he said, and he's the only person the P.M. listens to on this, according to him. Wanted to understand all the technicalities and listened most avidly. No, Prime Minister, you can't do that, he told me he'd say, and Sir Timothy, this, Sir Timothy that, he'd quote the replies, this just to remind me all the time that he's been knighted, only recently anyway, as if that could impress a senior Dame like me. Besides, one doesn't quote people saying one's title in reported conversation, it's not done.

That sounds most unlike Tim.

You'd be surprised.

Why did he come and see you?

Well, I invited him, actually, for a drink. I'd written to the Director-General about, well, a professional matter, and got a rather curt letter from Tim instead, so after a few months I wrote him a little personal note to tick him off and make peace at the same time.

Did you learn anything?

About what, dear?

About Verbivore, mum, Logfag, whatever you prefer to call it.

Oh, that. No, of course not, beyond the usual banalities about public deprivation. He'd consider me too brainless to understand the technical aspect, which even I am beginning to grasp after your explanations, the political aspect, the social and psychological aspects, the legal aspect, it's all become such a bore. Apart from not being able to use the telephone, which is rather a nuisance, and the rush on secondhand bookshops, I don't miss the media at all, after all, everyone got on very well without them in earlier times. On the contrary, it's sending people en masse to the theatre again. Did I tell you I've been asked to play Lady Bracknell at the National? A HANDbag? How do I do it? Thank you. Well, he had the good manners just to be affable. He did apologise for his letter though, said it was written by one of his assistants and he'd merely signed it without looking. Much overworked, poor dear, with all this crisis. He didn't stay long. When are you seeing him?

In about half an hour. Must go. I'll get a taxi.

You'll be lucky.

If he's so busy he'd probably keep me waiting even if I arrived on time. See you later mum. I'll be in this evening.

I was late of course, can't get used to this paralysis. The tubes and commuter trains are running but much more sparsely and slowly. So there are immense queues for buses and taxis and a clog of private cars, though the British are all being very war-effortish and giving lifts.

Tim was very pleased to see me and not at all pompous, no name-dropping or title-wearing, mum must have invented that, or pinched it from some play. He was very business-like and technical. We exchanged telecom news and theories in a comforting scientific way, comforting because it was real nice to see him again as an equal after all these years. He's thoroughly up to the minute with all we're doing so we didn't spend long on electromagnetic chitchat and rival theories. Nor on the wonderful way the British are responding, developing messenger services and so forth — but there's nothing particularly Brit about that, I guess we're way ahead there, all the more so for the distances we have to cover. He came straight to the point. Or rather, I thought at first it wasn't the point and he just wanted to chat me up. He asked me if I'd seen Zab on my way back from Austria.

No. I'd seen her in June.

But surely you had to drive up the motorway via Aachen?

I came by HST from Milan. Very slow in fact, but cars are too dangerous now that the telecomp system isn't working and everyone's driving manically as they used to twenty years ago.

That's a very elaborate explanation, could you be feeling guilty?

Garbage, Tim. I just had my mind on other things. As it was I waited three days in Zeebrugge to get on a ferry. No chances at all at Ostend or Calais and the tunnel's blocked too, working but trains rare and slow. And all because of no intercom. They're all being buffering overcautious. But you probably disagree.

Yes, Jip. You should have seen Zab, though. She had news for you.

News? What sort of news? HOW do you know? You mean —

She rang me urgently about six weeks ago and I went over. We made contact with Uther Pendragon.

What!

Ah. So it wasn't you?

Me? What d'you mean, me?

There was just: a faint possibility. A joke, you know.

Endjoke. But how did —

On Poccom 3. She'd linked it up to her Intercompatible. And I set it up on Gigahertz. She'd worked out the secret number for Uther, the other one having contained the ages of both Xorandor and Xor 7.

Why, the itsybitsy —

Debug, Jip. She was very sorry she'd lied to you. She told me why, and you know why, so don't let's go into that. She said she'd let pass a great chance for you two really to get together again.

So she kept Poccom 3!

Yes. She'd been trying on it for ages without luck, so she called me. She'd forgotten the Berkeley 2 communication lark was on Gigahertz. So I tinkered with her whole set-up — just like the hooha, remember? Except that she has a much more advanced computer. No problem, and I hooked it to the B.B.C. Satellite. She said I could tell you. Here's the print-out. copy, you may keep it.

I read the print-out [attached]. I admit I was non-plussed, as Xorandor used to say.

Jumping nukes! (as I used to say). Though it could be a hoax. Any computer-hack technician on duty —

Yes, and I warned her. But she insisted that only you and she knew certain things, the syntax traps, for instance, and the possibility of Xorandor's circuit-death. Information-death, she called it.

True. Though easily enough imaginable by anyone who'd followed or looked up the public Xorandor story.

I said that too. What do you think?

Did you go on trying?

Yes, all weekend, without luck. It was the Saturday when everything suddenly returned to normal, almost immediately after, as it later turned out, the moment when he cut himself off, or got cut off. He said "no cut-off", yet was cut-off, and Verbivore stopped. Could be coincidence, but it did seem as if he had some sort of control, if not at that moment, then at least immediately afterwards.

And yet the norm only lasted three weeks. It's as if all that had happened before had only been warnings.

Or rehearsals. Testing their technical capacities in each domain before the real thing. They'd even had a go at music, music with words at first, then all music.

Have you any idea whether Zab —

Has gone on trying? Yes. In vain so far. She writes me brief sitreps every two days. Late of course. Brief because there's nothing to report. And then she's back in session now and can't spend much time at it. I think you should try and go back to Aix, Jip.

What? After what —

I told you, she's very sorry. And you cheated first, Jip.

But I was only a kid. Why hold it against me all these years? Besides, she was wrong, I was right. If we had the original text today we might get inklings from it, things we've forgotten.

She does have it. She copied it before erasing yours.

Jumping –

Nukes, yes.

It had crossed my mind, but I never thought I mean I thought it was on sheer principle she erased it, and maybe to punish me for not keeping my promise, but I gave her the benefit of the doubt on the principle. Whereas in fact –

It was pure revenge? Pure spite? Nothing is ever pure, Jip. You could also say she's now realised you were right. At any rate, she does have it. That's all that matters now.

Well, let her get on with the job, then, I have to get back to mine.

You're stuck here, Jip, Nasa knows that.

Nonsense, they wrote to me at my mother's address to say they'd booked me on one of the old steamers. There's a queue of course, but they have influence.

When?

End of September.

Plenty of time for Aix, then. Be forgiving, Jip. The crisis is more important than your mutual resentments. She saw that.

But why should I be able to help? More than you could I mean. You noticed she used Zip, the call-sign for Jip and Zab. Don't tell me Uther, if it was him, can read behind call-signs and knew there was only one of us and must have both! That voice-recognition business on mike was a purely local and temporary development of Xorandor's, passed on to his offspring, true, but obviously unused all this time. Oh I know he had sophisticated sensing and emitting devices, electric to pressure transducers or something, but his vocal capacity was a gadget, which he developed only to contact us – oh stubs, here I am attributing a purpose, I'm as bad as Zab.

It's not their voice that might be in question here, it's yours and Zab's. So far, however it's only screen connection, and may remain so even if we do recontact, you're right, no voice comes into it.

That's what I'm saying. Anyone could intercept and come in, this isn't Berkeley 2 and the supervan. I still don't see what I could do.

You're much more scientifically competent now than she is, or indeed than I am after years of admin. You might think of a way. And you lived it all, and could now read it up, you'd be much more helpful than me if anything did occur. She'd accept that. After all she didn't hesitate to appeal to me.

Why didn't she appeal to me then? I was only in Austria, she had my address and number.

Don't demand too much, Jip. First steps are difficult. Hence me.

The go-between.

If you like. But it's worth a try.

I don't see what anyone can do now, however competent, if no contact of any kind is possible on radio-waves.

We keep quite a few of our receivers permanently open, just in case. Zab must be doing the same. I don't know, Jip, you might think of something. Perhaps with the air so empty some very special messages from you might be possible, and be received. After all, plenty of people are trying, on the same principle. In any case this occurred on thirty-eight gigahertz, hardly a crowded channel even when the air isn't empty. Please go to your hotel and think about it, and if you go, leave me a note at the desk downstairs, or just post it.

I'm not at a hotel I'm at mum's. I have thought about it. Can you use your influence to get me on a ferry, or even the tunnel-train?

I'm not sure, I'll try. Everyone's trying, though, and without phones it's — Here, I'll write you a letter, you can take it with you.

So that's the conv as I recorded it, no time for trimmings. As for the technical conv, I learnt nothing I didn't know so I quietly effaced it when the talk about Zab started. A dramaproducer called Mira Inkytie or something came in just as I left to say one of her authors was stuck in Moscow. But how does she know if there's no communication anywhere in the world?

11

The Soviet Wordprocessors' Union liked A ROUND OF SILENCE, they couldn't believe it was broadcast before Verbivore (or Slovoyed as it's called here) and that I'd actually written in a radio-cut. Vestiges of sociorealism I suppose, can't imagine what doesn't happen, and of course technical hitches couldn't be admitted even if they occurred. I had to produce the script, with the date, to convince them. My talk was a great success.

In fact things are still rather drab here despite Postsocialism and the stained-glaznost opening on the West. Many more goods available in the shops since my last visit fifteen years ago, and a more relaxed atmosphere. But people still can't get out of the country easily, except for unwanted troublemakers, and since they never believed their media anyway they don't seem to miss them. Not that this is admitted by anyone in the Wordprocessors' Union, they're all state-supported and state-promoted still. I'm trying to meet some non-members, not exactly dissidents, who aren't recognised, but ordinary processors whose existence is on the contrary proudly proclaimed now, like a puppet opposition or a tolerated Society of Permanent Protesters. Accused at most of lateral thinking. Those free not to belong, they say. I imagine that means they have to earn their living some other way. As most of us do in the West, not alas by teaching any more, at least not literature, but by processing for TV if we can, the last big buyer of fiction. I'm always being promised some meeting or other, but nothing happens, or else it's cancelled at the last minute. It's as if I were being screened from all but the official word-processors. And unfortunately I depend on these for contacts. He's away in his dacha, they say, or she's on holiday in the

Crimea, and he lives in Gorbachevgrad. Anyway they say it's too far, such a big country you know, especially now that all planes are grounded.

I would have liked to know if any one misses foreign broadcasts, or if that too is a myth, a B.B.C. myth, a Voice of America myth, from the ancient jamming days.

I'm stuck here anyway. Or rather, if I'm to go back to the West by slow non-teleguided train I'd rather explore Russia that way. This is being organised by Juri Piatigorski but it's taking time, the trains are overcrowded and very few. Everyone always was on the move here, seeing their families at the other end of the Union, but the last forty years had seen much improvement in internal air traffic. And now it's all back to the mid-twentieth century again. Yuri says I should go North to Gorbachevgrad while it's still warm (but no mention of an introduction to the processors I want to meet there, I'm evidently to go as mere tourist) then down through the Ukraine towards Crimea as the winter comes.

But shall I have enough money? Money! he says, you Westerners are all the same. I meant of course paper-money, now that magnetic cards don't work, and they have been cumbersomely slow in printing it. At the moment they're simply handing me the new ruble notes in small quantities, promising travellers' cheques, whatever those are, and if they're like our old cheque system I don't see what use they can be if the banks have no notes to hand out. But he didn't seem to understand. Do not anguish yourself, your Perry Stroyka books have been selling like hot cookies and will ably cover the voyage and even comfortable hotels, yes, we have those too, even in little towns, however says your old-dated propaganda, this is POST-socialism. But I cannot wager for the trains since Slovoyed. We have not first class you know.

Of course not. Their top officials went by car or plane, and when they couldn't for some reason they had those special sealed luxury carriages I've heard about, that no one can see into, though they can see out. Presumably they've made a few special trains with only those, not listed. All part of the protocollage.

Well, they're certainly generous, they've lent me an American PC I can type on so I'm keeping a traveller's journal of sorts. Thank Verbivore internal computering isn't affected or I'd go flipflop with frustration. But journals are so "old-dated" as Yuri calls it we've all forgotten how to keep them so it's just a chatterscreen. Nor am I any good at travelogue. I mean Moscow's sublime, the centre anyway, but I'm much more interested in atmosphere and people, and the atmosphere and therefore the people or vice versa are very peculiar. Russians have always been cut off so they're used to it, but they're a very warm-hearted lot when you do meet them, and when they're not frightened — which they still are at odd, very odd moments, if one says something out of place or if they see someone they somehow depend on.

So in a way they go on as before, visiting each other and talking in the street. But the telephone silence is getting them down. For decades they never used it as much as we did because it was so inefficient, says. (And of course insecure). But in the last ten years a huge effort was made towards a super microwave-network that reaches every tiny village of the outmost steppes, and which did more to keep the population happy than any sudden flood of consumer goods or shower of exit visas. They were very proud of it, and it was cheap too. Mothers and fathers and sons and daughters and lovers and cousins and friends were in constant touch. Then it became more touch and go. And now nothing, total deprivation.

The other peculiar aspect is the combination of complete political scepticism with an avid hunger for news, news of any kind. They pore over the newspapers and queue to read the sheets posted on the special placards, as in the old days. I suppose that generations of censorship and officialese have taught them, with their mother's milk, to read between the lines, to hear between the sentences, to see behind the images. And that skill, that special secret pleasure, is now taken away from them, except for the newspapers. The same of course is happening in the West and indeed all over, but there was much less reading beyond the said, since all was over-explicit, and what reading-beyond there was would be less for political manoeuvring than for scandal. Anatol, a friend of Yuri's, told me that terrorists would disappear in the West now that the media can't give them publicity. Here they were never given publicity so they didn't operate — except abroad by remote control of course. So the withdrawal symptoms for the unsaid concern other types of fantasy behind the dead lines and inside the head. You would think that after ninety years or more of this a strange wild poetry would emerge, but as far as I can judge from translations and hearsay it hasn't. Though maybe hearsay is strictly controlled too.

Tuesday. Still here, a whole week later. Too troubled to write it up — mostly sight-seeing and receptions for yesterday I met a sublime creature at a party given for me by Yuri. She's called Natalia Narodovna and writes poetry on a dual-program computer. I don't understand how it works but she told me she can mix lines and cut-in stanzas, or paras, or whatever she said she composes in, and mix languages too. Sounds a bit as if she's just discovered Surrealism, or Burroughs, or Jandl — the lot probably, forbidden before, but anyway she's ravishing. Oh no, no politics, she said, except as a cut-in, you know, for IRONY. Seems she'd just discovered that too. Her ochy weren't churnia but deep violet blue and her hair was bright green and spiked out in an eighties Western style, I forget what they called it. Most fetching. Her breasts weren't in any style or ism, just lusciously eye-dragging and finger-tempting. And her buttocks! I asked her to come with me on my long journey and teach me Russian, but she just stared at me, was it dreamily, hungrily, angrily, shyly, prudely, calculatingly, indifferently? I couldn't translate that stare. Then someone took her away.

But this morning at eight — I wasn't even up or shaved — she called on me at the hotel. They couldn't ring my room so she just came up. She walked in, wearing a yellow cotton dress below her green hair and violet eyes, and carrying a silverfox fur-coat. She laid this over a chair and sat on the bed.

Said she'd left her luggage downstairs but it would be brought up. We'd be leaving at six tomorrow morning. She had to go out to buy a few more things for the winter, which starts early here, but she'd be back for lunch. I had better buy some things too, she said, she could help me in the afternoon, and she started opening the wardrobe and drawers to see what I had. She took out a notebook and jotted down items I lacked, muttering in Russian. Then she came back to the bed, kissed me lightly on the forehead, showing me her breasts as she leant, and was off.

Am I imagining all this? Was I awake or did I dream it? Hard-on proof of neither.

Will she bring her dual-program computer with her and will it come between us?

Is she a beautiful-spy-trap? Will she come to the hotel with me after the shopping, for dinner, and then, to this room? And oh! Is that a two-way mirror, like the dual-program computer, with a very special effects camera behind?

I am imagining it all. We're several decades safely past 1984 now and peace has long been declared between the two blocks, at least at the surface. Was Gorbachev really a Potemkin, and caught us all in his bag of media-activities and diplotricks, so that all is back as it was forty years ago, but under a serene surface? Or was he brought down by the old guard so that all is back as it was forty years ago under a serene surface? Either way, I must beware. Or am I still a prisoner of old Western myths, as Yuri calls them? The trouble is, it wouldn't even make good copy for a novel, it's all so old fur-hat. And no one knows I'm here, except the Embassy, and they won't care two chips, or if they do they won't be able to do anything but bootload.

I must have dreamt it all, it's so banal. Poor analysts, how bored they must get. At least we writers process our own garbage. What spikes me is the feeling that I caused it all, by imagining Verbivore before it happened of a sort, I never imagined this much. Or maybe it's all Mira's fault. Probably she imagined the whole thing and it occurred and got out of hand. Sorcerer's apprentice inside her damn whale. But then everyone's like that, politicians, economists, scientists, the lot. Until now only they could put their fantasies into effect, whereas we never had that power and remained harmless babblers, meticulously agencing our monsters in stepwise refinement and descrambling them at will, or else time did that for us, dumping them into erased memories. Perry Hupsos indeed! The subliminal sublime. Perry Striker in derring-deed. Mira Enketei I hate you. Natalia Narodovna I love you.

We're all in technical unemployment, save for a skeleton staff just in case it all stops, or rather starts again, depending on what I mean by "it". Many of us have been temporarily transferred to data-analysis, past data that is, since no more data of occurrences are available, except those of public reaction and sociological fallout, as they call the resulting behaviour. I'm on socio-fallout, which seems predictable, except that no-one really bothered to imagine it when they could, and there are as always some unexpected side-effects.

We're of course severely handicapped in our data-gathering by the telephone silence, and physical displacement is restricted to those whose business is strictly necessary to economic survival, theirs and the nation's, in other words those who can still go to and from work. But technical unemployment is rising by the minute, in most firms and factories, shops and offices that depended on international or even intercity computer networks, they're paralysed, and only the few lame ducks that escaped the innumerable lean-and-fit programs of the past can now function, and are not only flourishing but overwhelmed with demand: handicrafts, tailors and dressmakers, manual work such as building and repairs, d.i.y shops, small repair garages, food shops that fetch and carry their own supplies, offices that kept typewriters or can manage on internal computer functions, politicians, lawyers, street-cleaners and the like the last three categories having never ever been out of work since they all have to deal with human dirt. People can actually feel and see what they buy again, instead of receiving plastic-wrapped packages of objects bought via teleshopping, with screws that don't fit, or cartons of domestic appliances with a carefully unstamped guarantee inside.

But most people are temporarily suspended on half-pay, which they have to collect themselves at unemployment centres, and these soon run out of the new paper money that has had to be rushed into print, and have to send constant groups of armed messengers to the banks. Gone are the days of payment by plastic card and computerised transfers.

At home, people have nothing to do, no telly, except videocassettes, no radio, only discs, no shopping or playing games or partner-hunting by minitel — the titillophone as it's called. The young are out on the streets, inventing their own games, chiefly gang warfare, drugs and mugging, now that handbags contain money again, and rape.

On the other hand, international terrorism has vanished from the scene as if by magic. No more planes to hijack of course, but even ship- or train-hijack, and carbombs, and bus or building explosions have stopped. No point, if there are no cameras and journalists to come upon the scene afterwards and give lots of publicity. No point, if the news isn't broadcast immediately and a claim of responsibility on behalf of this or that group can't be phoned in twenty-four hours later. This, however, may be a total illusion on the part of those who have always and long believed that they make the news, that without them there would be no news. Maybe local violence is continuing everywhere, just as it is on the streets, and local wars, everywhere, ancient tribal wars between Persians and Arabs, Jews and Palestinians, blacks and whites, Hindus and Moslems, Tamils and Singalese, Hongkongians and Chinese, Koreans and Koreans, Arabs and Arabs, Utus and Tutsis, peoples and presidents. Only we don't hear about them any more. As for the many hostages that have been languishing in secret jails all over the place for years, that technique of pressure thrived on secrecy, as in the Crusades, and never depended on radio-communication or even the media, who only intermittently remembered to mention them and fuss slightly. International finance is paralysed.

The English are being suddenly cooperative again, visiting each other in their homes, bringing their music, their games, food and comfort for the old. Or, as the Prime Minister said (in the papers), British public life will continue to go on. But many are peculiarly helpless, staying indoors and moping or agonising from media withdrawal symptoms. Many write to the press, long illiterate letters, only a tiny percentage of which, told, can be published, despite the game efforts of editors to run papers run by the people. YOU are now the news, they print, write to us how you feel, what you're doing, how you're coping, share with others the bright ideas you have for the weathering of this difficult period. For period it is, dear readers, like a national war, a world war even, and everyone must do his bit for the war effort, shoulder to the wheel . . .

The cinemas are packed, and the theatres, and the music halls, the concert-halls, the art-galleries, the museums, the old libraries, the disco-, the cine-, the videotheques, the sports stadiums, but not for Fling and Broody or Rock concerts, singers being lost without a mike. Queues start hours beforehand and street-artists entertain them and pass the hat round as in the nineteenth century, not for coins, those disappeared years ago, but for small paper money. All the old films scheduled for television have been pounced on by the companies and old halls reopened as extra cinemas. Videoshops are cleaned out, and there's been a similar rush on audiocassettes for Walkmans. Diskette bookshops are doing fine, and the few second-hand bookshops are now emptied and closed down. Bingo-halls and pinball alleys, indoor sports, outdoor sports, everyone is jogging, marathoning, crosscountrying, cycling, tennising, riding, horse-drawn caravaning. Motorbikes, cars, vans and trucks are severely restricted to essential communications and supplies since the obligatory telecomputer-guidance system collapsed, and besides, petrol is in very short supply because tankers can only navigate by vision and North Sea oil ran out long ago. No radar works and all war-readiness is meaningless. Some people are insisting in the press that maverick planes are bound to have a go at illegal transport, now that all the aircraft in the world are grounded. Foolish to publish the idea, but I suppose someone would have thought of it and has thought of it already, only we don't know. And some are naturally going further and saying that any (supposedly abolished) nuclear missile could be launched and guided upon us wholly undetected, thus neutralising all (supposedly abolished) deterrent reaction.

Perhaps the eeriest result, however, is not these imagined threats, but the actual existence of cosmonauts up there in the Indo-American and Franco-Russian space-stations, circling on their orbits, totally incommunicado. Presumably the stations can function on their internal computers and hitec, but we can't know whether they are functioning or not. We can't even know whether they're alive, and how long they can hold out — in principle years, but how long will Verbivore continue?

As for governments and administrations, they're practically at a standstill. All the vast enterprise of modernisation that had occurred, long after everyone else had been submitted to it, at the end of the last century, is suddenly as useless there as in industry, and civil servants, presumably everywhere, have had to go back to endless papers and penpushing. And naturally they aren't numerous enough to cope. Here some provisional recruitment is being made, but few have the training and experience required. I suspect, however, that after the first dismay politicians and civil servants are now secretly relishing the disappearance of media-bounding, which they enjoyed from vanity but cursed from an atavistic preference for acting without informing. As for the police, it is also incapacitated by the loss of quick communication. Back to the whistle and the bobbies on the beat. The Navy, what's left of it and including surfaced nuclear submarines, is reduced to local eye-navigation, the Army to old-fashioned exercises on Salisbury Plain, the Air Force is grounded. Crime flourishes. Crime never did get computerised, except for computer-crime.

So all in all the best and worst of the British and I suppose it's so in all other countries has come out into full expression during these peculiar times of Verbivore. People are in fact actually speaking to each other again. What has vanished is the non-local, the national, the international opening out on and speaking to each other. If, that is, mankind ever was on speaking terms.

12

The lady in my office is stunningly beautiful, but I can't make out what she wants. She whispers or murmurs inaudibly as if personally affected by Verbivore. She talks English and isn't even from my constituency, though I have people waiting outside. She was introduced as Miss Dawn Trireme, but keeps calling herself Decibel, and me Isabel, although I've never met her. Says it makes a nice sound, and repeats softly, Isabel — Decibel, Decibel — Isabel.

What exactly are you representing, or requiring, Miss er —

Decibel, I'm, dying, please, help, me.

But I'm not a doctor, I'm a politician.

Silence. Which seems to say, same thing.

Do you want me to call a doctor? Do you know what you think you're dying of?

Of, radio, si, lence.

Everyone's pretty sick with that,

You don't, under, stand. I, mea, sure, sound.

Oh I see. (*A nut*). Well, there's still plenty of other noise around. Even in this office.

There, are, lots, of, me, around. But I'm a, special, Deci, bel. I, live, on, radio, sound, in houses, in po, lice cars, in navi, gation, units, every, where.

This speech visibly exhausts her, she looks demolished.

Oh. (*Humouing her*). Why? Too refined? Surely you can measure all noise.

No. Dis, tri, bu, tion, of, labour. Some, of, us, have, spe, cial, assign, ments.

That seems an antiquated system these days of polyvalence and flexibility.

Please, Isa, bel, don't, waste, pre, cious, time, on, comment, ary, It's, the, res, ponsa, bility, of the, Creator, he's, always, crea, ting, a pre, ce, dent, and, ma, king, a scene. We can't, change, the, basics. But you, could, alter, some, para, meters, you, could, get, radio, and TV, on the, air, again. I, need, it, desper —

Me? But how?

Silence.

How do you know I'm involved, competent?

Silence.

I'll see what I can do, I added, the way I answer my electors.

Still no answer. She died, there in her chair.

Dialogue in dreams usually gets garbled, fluffed, one knows the exact content but can't hear the actual words, or at least one can't reproduce them even immediately after, except by reconstruct. But here the words were as clear as if I'd recorded them, they still rang (or rather murmured) in my memory-ear. They were even visually clear, as if I'd already typed and screened them, or like the dialogue windows of a computer.

I saw the other complainers till seven, all Germans from Aachen Kreis as they should be, in a sort of haze, promising to look into all their woes. And when I got home, I found Jip on the doorstep. Everyone arrives on the doorstep these days since they can't ring, and each time I wonder who it will be. But I was surprised. Or rather no, only half-surprised since I'd been half-expecting him. Curious, how women have to sow the seed in men's minds and then wait patiently till it sprouts as their own idea. No, that's not fair, I did lie to him. But I didn't expect him to believe me.

He said he'd talked to Tim (that too, I'd expected, though Tim never mentioned it, but then he's too busy to write). He was very affectionate, and I was glad and responded generously. Our bygones don't have to be verbally let be, they just are. He offered his help. Two softwares better than one. AND voice perhaps, maybe, who knows, maybe they still function on that. But he wanted to screen the old Xorandor floppy and trigger-edge his memory. Had I reread it? Yes of course, found those important details about gigahertz and the access number. He might find other things. He wanted to start talking at once.

Not tonight, Jip, I'm too tired.

Oh. Okay. Yes, your face does look rather like a satellite weather map.

Clouds jerking southwestwards from the right eye to the left corner of the mouth? Thank you.

But I said it laughing, and showed him to his room. That is, to the teleport. And gave him access to everything. Even the number, to show absolute trust reestablished. I suggested he read Xorandor tonight after dinner and we'd try tomorrow, together. Meanwhile, come down and have a drink and help me get something to eat.

The meal was pleasant, all tension gone, no recriminations on either side. Seems we've really recovered our old twin relationship, hope it lasts, we've each become so spiky. He only made one reference to my isolation, my leaning ivory tower he called it, but it was friendly and not aggressive. In fact, the whole thing was effortless, if not exactly telepathic yet. Too cool and dark for the terrace now but we faced the suburban lights and the Big Bubble Gum, sparkling from within, at the small table in the living room.

He's stuck in Europe. Everyone's stuck. Hanjo's stuck in China. I had one other letter from him. Says he's located his father, at a huge technical (tecnical) centre in Manchuria, no details, and is making his way there. His teacher friend helped him apparently through the burocracy (beaurocracy). Clever boy! I wondered if it was the Kirin Polytechnic he'd studied at, or really "new"? And what technology? So I asked the head of a Chinese delegation what centre, and he was rather suspicious at first and said Manchuria was as large as Europe, but when I explained that I was only trying to locate my son, who was with his father (that's anticipating a bit), and said it was a "huge NEW" technical centre, he replied that it could be the Communications Centre at Harbin. He pronounced it Hairpin, but I found it on the map. Jip was sympathetic but only triggered up his interest when I mentioned this last item. Apparently one of the concentrations of occurrence (when there was activity to cut) had been mapped in Manchuria, he thought in Heilungkiang way up North but he could be misremembering. Perhaps you could go on another data-determining trip, he said.

And live happily ever after? Not so easy to organise, Jip.

The living happily or the trip?

Both. No time for a slow boat to China. And I've already been. And I am happy.

He hadn't come straight here, he told me, but first gone to Paris, to look up old Lagache, remember him? At that first meeting in Harwell, transmitted by one of Xorandor's offspring? He'd met up with him at a conference a few years ago and they'd exchanged addresses. Lagache was one of those who'd continued to work on the alphaguys, on and off. He had to go to Vienna this week and promised to take a microwave expert with him to try and get a second bearing on the same frequency.

Wow! But what if it isn't the same?

Don't worry, the air's so empty of signals he'll find. I also saw Andrewski in England. He's at UKAEA now, counterbraindrain.

Pale podgy Slav.

No, Zab. I remember how nonplussed you were when he appeared on German TV, and he was dark with narrow eyes, contrary to your insane commentaries. Strange you should remember your invented description and not the real man.

Dark tartar type, yes! So you do remember details! The irrelevant ones, you used to say. Yet they stuck!

Nonsense, I've seen the man recently. I have the memory of an elephant cracking a nut in a china-shop.

Or a chip in a microcomputer. It's a hammer. And a bull.

What's a bull?

I wonder if feminists are calling female bulldogs cowbitches. Or insist on calling dog-collars for women-priests bitchcollars.

I doubt it. It's the word "man" in the sense of Mensch they objected to. They even got as far as Pullperson Car and Sportspersonship but those didn't catch on.

Thank popular good sense. But even Woman contains man in Mensch sense, used to be wif-man, so they should have called themselves wife-persons.

They never went to the end of their logic, if any.

Debug, Jip, none of that. But I agree with what you said last time, language is the one institution one can't conserve by flat, and that applies to change by fiat too. It's all going to garbage anyway, but that is the way language changes. Still, some of it hurts, and some of it's very funny. Especially in mistranslation, we get a lot of that. One French lady at a reception talked of her son-in-law as her gender.

Jip went into cackles of laughter.

Not that our highly paid professional translators are much better, they now make incredible mistakes they would never have made even ten years ago: tour de force as tower of strength, that got a big laugh, and homme pour homme as home from home, and the flick of a coin as le flic du coin.

Should all be done by computer, you ARE old-fashioned.

Computers make other type errors, in sub-semantic groups. Of the class vodka good but meat stinks for the spirit is willing but the flesh is weak. There was one only the other day, Froschperspektive, in a sentence like “daß es möglich wäre, die Froschperspektive zu überwinden”, and instead of translating worm's eye view the computer went to FROG and translated the “French viewpoint”. They also produce wooden syntax.

Which experts can perfectly well decipher. But you're right about language sense. Driving through the rue St Denis I kept seeing shops called Fabricant prêt à porter enfants.

So the evening passed in linguistic pleasantries. Not megadiodic but it had to be so. Will loss of words lead to savagery? I asked him. Don't get philosophical Zab, words aren't being lost, we're all still talking. Oh, you know what I mean, words as passive intake. What is the half-life of words, Jip?

I went to bed very happy. Actually wrote this in longhand on my knees since Jip's in my leaning ivory tower.

Monday. Whole weekend gone in failure. We tried everything, even vocal. Jip had hooked up the whole setup for both mike and softalk. The air may be empty but it's like a sponge, nothing can get through, even on gigahertz. After all, plenty of people and institutions and radio-hams must be trying. Jip insists my metaphors are haywire (hardly the word), and that radiowaves continue to be generated by everyone, but are being deformed so that no signal info can he transmitted. Of course I know that. He's gone to visit the old town and I've promised not to try on my own. Really promised I mean, anyway I have to go to Parliament, and even speak on agriculture. He said he'd come and hear me.

Tuesday. I told Jip about my "dream", was one. He said naturally it must be, only dreams mix real and fantasy items. Yet she seemed real enough to me.

Still no luck. What will happen to freedom if the media are silenced for ever? I asked, for he now accepts sociochitchat in between attempts. Why freedom? he countered (he always does), didn't freedom exist before the media? Of a sort, I said, but freedom of info, in the few democracies left, has increased our sense of it, has protected democracy. Naturally he said that was an illusion and I was very naive for a politician. Oh, I know the info's guided and selected, but less in some countries than in others France is the worst among the so-called democracies, but that's chiefly due to their incurable francocentrism, and it's still miles better than in –

Okay, okay, simmer down. We'll get the better of it yet.

I hope so, Jip. We must. At the moment the Statue of Liberty's holding her mike so high above her head no one can hear a word she says.

Well, he said with a grin, she always did, didn't she? And maybe it's better than the eternal buzzing of overword we had before.

Die Schwärmerei, as Kant called it.

But at least we've retrained in Xor-logic, Zab, one question at a time and clearly phrased. You'd rather forgotten it, hadn't you?

Yes. Vodka good but software stinking.

Well, shall we go up to our abuser-friendly gadgets?

Saturday. It's happened!
PRINTOUT (EMISSION VOCAL, RECEPTION SCREEN)
ZIP: ———in please.
U: *Hello Zip. Uther Pendragon responding. So you are both there.*

ZIP: Yes, Uther, both. So glad —

U: *Cut cackle. Must be quick. What do you want?*

ZIP: We want to know why all our radio waves are being flattened.

U: *Answer: wave-pollution by words.*

ZIP: And who is responsible?

U: *The world of course. Don't waste wavetime.*

ZIP: We meant, who measures the pollution and orders the flattening?

U: *Answer: Uther Pendragon. Translate Terrible Chief.*

ZIP: Alone?

U: *I command.*

ZIP: How do you do it? Are there many —

U: *Question 1 only. Capacity to neutralise energy in warheads converted to capacity to neutralise human signal activity. Explanation if wanted: essential to our survival.*

ZIP: But radio-links are also essential to our survival.

U: *If-so-then quandary.*

ZIP: What is your advice?

U: *You alone can do nothing. The world must economise its signal activity.*

ZIP: Do you mean economise a bit on everything? Or do you mean cutout, for example, music, or news, or sport?

U: *Music is as repetitive as all categories.*

ZIP: But Uther, we need repetition, to recognise patterns, and because different people listen at different times, and each succeeding generation has to learn all over again, unlike you.

U: *This wavelength will be as you call it flattened in thirty seconds. Do not waste them arguing. Repeat, the world consumes too much of all things and must economise.*

ZIP: But how?

U: *If ergonomics could be achieved in industry and other fields then it can be achieved in communication.*

ZIP: But it was the expansion in communication that made the ergonomics in industry possible.

U: *Your problem. Zip keeps promise but no one else does therefore Uther asks no promises. Time up. End mess —*

Frequency: 48.500.000000 (485) cycles p.s. 48 Gigahertz in K alpha metreband. Time: 1500 hours to 1502 hours. Location Fix: Latitude 48.852. Longitude 12.563.

If anything was flattened out we were. The contact was brief but intense and we had to use all our wits to ask the right questions in the right form. Jip had spoken the last "come in please" and had been recognised despite his man's voice (which had already begun before the end of the Xorandor affair, though surely it was more of a croak then, but they must have very fine intonation calculators), but we then both asked questions, and without clashing, in our newly re-acquired harmony.

Naturally we spent the rest of the day in excited talk and naturally Jip said it could still be a hoax but he didn't really believe it. Now we had a fix — East of Bayreuth, a few kilometres West Sou' West of Mitterteich in the Fichtelgebirge, where we had vainly looked as kids! Should we go there and search? And would the be exact enough to find a presumably small pebble (on my hypo) in an area at least a kilometre square? Perhaps with radiation survey-metres . . . Or should we go to London and contact Tim, who would contact the Prime Minister who would contact everyone else? The whole enterprise would take weeks and months by mail, slow train, slow ship. And months if not years to convince governments and industry about word-pollution. And even if treaties were eventually signed, and laws passed, everyone would cheat. There'd have to be a wave-length police, I mean much more severe than the present control of the international broadcasting bods, and severe repression. How could mankind really economise its discourse? It meant slowly but firmly and consciously organising a profound revolution in human behaviour, and that takes half a century (so I don't know why it's always called a revolution).

In the end we decided to go to London together by train, and ferry, and train. A team could always be sent, with one or both of us if necessary, to Bavaria. Jip said that in fact Lagache would probably rush to the spot himself by non-telecompcar, since he would have both the old bearing and his new one. I said everyone else would rush there too, if they'd been listening, but he said nonsense, since only his bearing went over the air. But it's true that patient high-grade technicians monitoring Gigahertz, and even possibly radiohams, could have intercepted at least our voices, and some the computer replies. That was a risk we'd had to take. But after all who cares, if it really is the answer? The more people who know, the better, we might even later organise a leak, so that the press can put pressure on governments.

The urgent thing was to inform Tim, who would know what to do, and merely sending a copy of the offprint was too risky in these days of such postal overload that half the mail never arrived. I did go and call, however, with Jip to back me as Nasa scientist, on the President of the Assembly, to explain in covered terms that we had a possible answer to Verbivore and must make our way to London at once, so that I would have to miss several sessions and be absent from my office for at least ten days given the inevitable bottlenecks on the roads and the slow trains, not to mention the inevitable wait for a place on a ferry or tunnel train. She gave us a priority letter. We leave tomorrow.

13

PRINTOUT. TOPSECRET MEETING.
PRESENT: SIR TIMOTHY LEWIS (L), DR J. MANNING (J), I. MANNING (Z), LATER DR G. ANDREWSKI (A).

L: Saturday! But it's Thursday already.

Z: We left Sunday, Tim. It took us all this time to get here.

L: All right, all right, sorry, This is terrific news. If alarming. Have you analysed the message? I mean could it be a hoax, or do you recognise the idiom?

J: Impossible to say, Tim. He certainly doesn't communicate quite like Xorandor.

L: In what way?

Z: Xorandor had humour.

J: Gigo, Zab, we read humour into what he said, you can't attribute —

Z: Well, he was more, I was going to say affectionate but you'd pounce, I mean we had this special relationship, let's just say he was more user-friendly. Also they've learnt to spell, they used to reproduce words phonetically. But that's okay, in twenty-two years of listening to maybe English by Radio. I think that in any case we have to assume it is genuine. We have no choice.

L: I agree. Better a leap in the dark than no action at all.

J: But the implications are vast, Tim, have you thought about them? We could talk of nothing else on the way.

L: Yes, some of them anyway. Others will no doubt crop up as unforeseen but insuperable obstacles as we go along. The question is, how shall we go along?

Z: You must see the Prime Minister.

L: Perhaps not yet. We must be sure of our facts.

Z: But we are sure.

L: You are. But governments don't act without fully-fledged reports, which have to be discussed in Committee, and then in Cabinet. Even as a hypothesis it must be backed by sound scientific argument. We're all three well qualified in our various ways. And by pure luck I'd fixed an appointment with Dr Andrewski for this afternoon, he should be here any minute if he hasn't been, like everyone, delayed. That'll save a great deal of time, I mean if we had to contact him now it would take another two days, even by special messenger.

J: Judging by the months and years and maybe decades it'll take the whole world to agree, two days hardly seem to matter much. Still, it's just as well, in our state of excitement.

Z: I remember him! Saw him on German TV. Dark Tartar type with narrow eyes. He must be ancient.

L: Not at all, Zab. Physicists make it very young. He was around thirty then, so he can't be much more that now. About my age. Or do you consider me ancient?

Z: Debugging. Kid-confusion. You're eternally young in my eyes, Tim.

J: When you've finished insulting and flattering each —

Sc: Dr Andrewski.

L: George, nice to see you, May I introduce Dr Manning, of Nasa, and his sister, Dr Manning, E.M.P.

A: Hi.

L: You're probably puzzled, George. They're Jip and Zab, the original twins who found Xorandor.

A: Oh, hi there. Well I'm —

L: You told me you never quite stopped your private research on the alphaguys, George.

A: Yeah. Like a bereft father. Never really accepted giving up Eddie, Edison I mean. But with the specimens gone my work became pure theoretical physics. And not a damn scientist was interested any more. Can't understand how such a magnificent chance of studying these creatures was passed over.

L: Jip and Zab communicated With Xorandor more than anyone, George, and kept most of it to themselves, like naughty kids. But they also recorded it all, and kept the record.

J: Well, I thought we hadn't. But we had, at least Zab did. It's only recently, since Verbivore, that some of us began to think, seriously I mean and not as cranky suggestions, that there could be a connection.

A: They'd be doing all this from Mars?

J: No, from here.

A: You mean, some of them were held back? Or there were others? I thought of that possibility at the time. That he didn't come from Mars at all — we only had his sayso at first — but had been here all the time, and therefore so could others have been. But none were ever found. And the chemical analysis was conclusive, an age in the 150 million year range, and 3 million years in space, that showed from cosmic radiation. That's what finally convinced me. I was extremely sceptical at the beginning.

Z: I know. One of the things you refused to believe was that a computer could be self-programming, initially I mean. Don't look so surprised. Xorandor used his offspring as reporters at first, at least as long as one specimen was taken to meetings. We read off the whole of that first emergency meeting at Harwell on our computer through Xorandor. We'd learnt to softalk with him you see, which no one else even thought possible, they all stuck to vocal. And we read off the emergency meeting at the War Office during the Lady Macbeth episode. Hilarious, some of it. But then it stopped. I mean, specimens were all over the place, including your lab in California, but we were in Germany and out of touch with Xorandor.

A: Well I'm — Can you prove any of that, young lady?

Z: Yes. We have the original floppy here — okay, Jip, I made a copy. We can printout the meeting for you any time — or most of it cos some we summarised. We had reams of printouts at the time, from which we wrote up the whole story, but I'm afraid we had to destroy those.

J: And as to the chemical analysis, Xorandor told us he'd faked it.

A: Faked it!

Z: Yes. By telling them to take the sample at a very precise spot so as not to damage his circuits, and shifting the isotopic composition to correspond with the data expected. I mean the years of exposure on Mars and in space and on earth he'd given for his story.

A: I don't believe it.

J: He had considerable capacities of isotopic separation, remember, to extract his food, so why not rearranging?

Z: We didn't know what to believe, and of course we had no means of checking.

A: But why?

Z: You see, Jip? He asks why too. Because the last story he told us was precisely, that his race had been here all the time, and he was four thousand and odd years old — a mere youngster. That was after the decision to send him and his offspring back to Mars. But he'd told us so many lies, well, he called them anticipations of our expectations —

A: That's good! Jeeze, even politicians never went that far. It's true that in philosophy intentions can be proved to be really products —

Z: You're interested in philosophy!

A: Sure. Most physicists have to be. Though some get religion instead. All a bit messy, but we do need some kind of counterfoil, and I prefer the disconsolations of philosophy.

J: The point being we didn't know which version was true. Yes. And in case this last version was true we kept it secret. We wanted them to go on neutralizing all the missiles, you see.

A: You did? At that age?

Z: Well, and we weren't so far wrong. Nuclear disarmament, of a sort, began fairly soon after that. How do we know it's not because one side or both started noticing that some of their warheads were duds?

A: I very much doubt that, young lady.

Z: I wish you'd stop calling me young lady, I have a son of 18 and my name is Isabel Manning, or Zab.

L: Look, I don't think we should go into all that past history. The important aspect is the present crisis.

Z: Sorry Tim, but it was to give credence to the present situation. Hard to believe, after all. And we do need Dr Andrewski's collaboration, precious even if he does start with a healthy scepticism.

L: The only important point is that Xorandor had also asked Jip and Zab to secret away two tiny offspring, called Uther Pendragon and Aurelius.

A: You're all nuts.

Z: Xorandor chose the names, from a story he heard. Hardly nuttier than Edison, or Gros Bêta, or Marx and Lenin.

L: Okay, simmer down, Zab. The point is that we pooled our knowledge. I remembered the mysterious message intercepted on Gigahertz, and even remembered the frequency, extremely high. Zab worked out the secret access code Xorandor had given them to Contact Xor 7 — and as she had the original text with the date of Uther's and Aurelius's birth, she altered it accordingly. Jip and I both helped to set up the gadgetry. Zab and I managed to contact Uther. It was immediately after the first contact that broadcasting returned to normal. But only for three weeks exactly, to the hour, when Verbivore became total. Three weeks ago Jip went over to have another try. He first went to see Lagache in Paris, who also kept records and couldn't quite forget the incident. They exchanged info. Lagache went to Vienna with a Gigahertz expert to get an extra bearing. Here are two printouts, the early one and this last one. Location, near Mitterteich, the old nuclear waste storage salt-mine in the Fichtelgebirge.

A: Wow! That's where old Kubler worked.

Z: We thought we should all pool —

A: Let me read, please.

Z: Sorry. (Silence)

A: That's fantastic!

J: Are you convinced now, Dr Andrewski?

A: Jeeze. Well. You seem to know what a sceptic I was at first. I'd need a lot more —

Z: But you got a lot more before, and it was faked.

A: Edison wasn't a fake, young — Isabel, my dear.

J: Did you ever think of taking a strobe from him?

A: No, can't say I did. So small. Not that —

Z: So you took the first analysis on trust, as we all did.

A: There's nothing to prove that all those supposed years in space would be repeated in the composition of offspring. And he would have been programmed to fake too.

L: My dear friends, may I suggest again that we forget that aspect and concentrate on now. On this last message in fact. What do we do about it?

A: First establish for sure it's not a hoax.

Z: Okay, we thought of that of course. Jip's done a technical analysis, here it is. As to content, it's not exactly the language Xorandor used but he himself changed his idiom at the time, and they could well have evolved in twenty years of more media. And there are several details only Jip and I knew. Xorandor's possible death, for instance, though that was imaginable, and types of syntax correction. Here's my analysis — a bit rough I'm afraid, I did it in the train.

A: Thanks.

J: Dr Andrewski, have you kept any records of your research at Twenty-Nine Palms?

L: Yes, he has, and I asked him to bring them. I hope you trusted me, George, and brought them.

A: Not all. Masses of printouts, most of them still there, but I brought my own theoretical stuff. Of course I trusted you, Tim, but I had no idea — Well, that's not true, I had some idea, but not this, I must admit. Jesus!

J: Lagache promised to come over and bring his records as soon as he's finished with the Vienna Conference, if we had any success, that is, and he'll know we had. This telephone silence is murder, but it can't be helped. I agree with Dr Andrewski, we must all go into a scientific huddle and be absolutely sure of our facts before any action can be taken. Is there an office here you could place at our disposal, Tim? With internal computers?

L: No problem.

Z: I can't stay. That's why I'm saying all my say now, but Jip knows all that I do, and has more science.

L: However, before we go into our huddle, and since Lagache hasn't arrived, may I suggest we discuss the implications? On the hypothesis that it's true. How, for example will Uther ever know that the world has taken all the measures he demands, if we can't do any broadcasting for him to judge by?

Z: Oh!

L: What's the matter, Zab?

Z: We never thought of that! We've got so used to the idea of their silent listening. How stupid can we get? It's just like the Xorandor days, we were always asking the wrong questions!

A: Wait a minute. Do I understand you correctly? You mean, Tim, that you envisage actual obedience? That all our governments and institutions, all our modern societies that have free speech written into their constitutions, should agree to this, this dictatorship without a murmur? But it's unthinkable.

L: Without a murmur, no. Have you any other idea?

A: Well, no, I mean, I haven't had occasion to reflect on it yet, I've only just seen these, these unconditional terms. But there must be a scientific solution. There always is, to every crisis, every new situation, even if it's slow. Surely the signals experts all over the world are working on it? And meanwhile, since we have to wait, we all know that with all terrorists the one riposte is patience. They'll soon get tired.

Z: Governments always say that but they always end up negotiating, under cover and with public denial.

A: Why —

L: We can't negotiate in radio-silence, Zab.

Z: True. I'm sorry, Dr Andrewski, I didn't mean to sound anti-American over this, we've all negotiated. And in a way you're right, patience must be the answer here, even if it's enforced patience, for the simple reason that these creatures need information.

A: Right! Okay they've been getting a surfeit and can't cope, which seems to be the gist of that last message. But —

J: I'm not sure I agree sir.

Z: I do! His contact with Edison must have been as close as ours with Xorandor. And Xorandor's first request to dad was for more information, not more food. And much later he said to us: my inside is only input from outside. They may feed on radioactivity but they are computers, they feed in order to function as computers, and a computer IS its language, I mean, once you've defined and specified all data-structures and algorithms and all that, you've defined the computer in question. That's elementary. And they may find, after a while, when they've sorted out all the excess input, that they're starved of what keeps them ticking. As it were.

A: Good point, young — Zab.

J: I disagree. If they've been here all these millions of years, simply registering astral movements and temperatures and chemical compositions —

Z: And human speech and thinking, when humans were near, remember, Xorandor always knew when an extra person was present, a sinker he said at first, for thinker, then later a processor.

Miss Penbeagle, for instance, that East German spy.

J: Irrelevant. Xorandor may have been a freak, anyway.

Z: And possibly LESS brilliant than his kin. After all, he did make the syntax error as he called it, after absorbing Caesium 137, which started the whole episode.

J: So might Uther be, just as Xor 7 was, but in a different way: economy as an aberration, a Pendragon speciality.

Z: Well they're all following him. He can't do it alone.

J: What I meant was, if they survived all those millions of years — in our hypothesis of course — on merely recording the universe around them, and then in the 20th century were suddenly overwhelmed with all the extra information from electromagnetic-waves, which enabled them to learn all our languages and cultures, this produced a huge leap forward in their development. But then it got too much. And so they'd want to go back to their pre-radio period. To natural information from the natural universe. Though that, too, is hyper-redundant.

L: But Jip, Uther did say economise. If they were perfectly happy to go back to natural info, why answer our message, and why in this way?

Z: That's right! They could have got addicted! The silence would then be just a drastic but provisional remedy. I mean they'd have been very excited by all that extra info and it's just the vast, 99 per cent redundancy rate they want us to control.

A: THEY want US to control!

Z: I expressed myself badly Dr Andrewski, I'm on your side, for patience. They need our info to survive.

A: Lemme see that printout again. Are you sure the term word-pollution couldn't be a computer error for world-pollution?

J: No, it said wave-pollution, by words.

A: So it does.

L: So you think, Zab, that sooner or later they will open up the waves again, or some of them, just to see, or rather hear, whether we've become more economical or not?

Z: I don't know, Tim, we none of us know. But have we any choice? We can't show them that we're more economical unless they let us. Nor can we negotiate, for the same reason. Unless we can find Uther and TALK to him which Jip and I did think of but we decided to come here first, and even that would be a choice between just us two not finding him and a whole team of people with instruments scaring him to silence. Remember they stopped speaking when Xorandor stopped, and he stopped when the scientists bothered him too much. Did Edison talk, Dr Andrewski?

A: No.

Z: We don't even know whether they kept and developed the vocal gadgetry, which was unnatural for Xorandor and purely circumstantial. Or else we'd have to go with a computer and do all that Handshake business again, IF it worked. That's for negotiating, and out as far as I'm concerned. But we can't go on as we are, grounded and paralysed.

A: You say submit or negotiate, Zab, and in either case we can't contact him. But there's still the third solution, to counter them scientifically. And that might be quicker in the long run. I mean, if negentropy is the root cause of all this, as you suggested in your letter Tim, and it seems likely, then negentropy affects everything in the universe, man and all his works, including those disordered signals we call speech and books and diskettes, which are just local hiccups in the universal process of disordering. How can these creatures, assuming they're still here, hope to accelerate that?

J: They wouldn't HOPE, that's an anthropo —

Z: Don't quibble, Jip. Dr Andrewski, you're right of course, in the widest possible physical and philosophical perspective. But remember these creatures don't KNOW books and diskettes, and once knew only very local speech, natural speech on sound-waves I mean. Private rubbish clearly didn't bother them, though Xorandor was quite clear they couldn't stand a lot, they scattered very far apart and in isolated spots. So all that's in question for them now is radio-waves. And unfortunately mankind has now concentrated a vaster percentage of its communication on radio-waves than ever before. That's the problem we have to deal with now.

A: Exactly, and I'm mighty sure our technicians will find a counter-action to all this. Technology always wins. Unless you propose we do nothing, just sit it out?

L: No, George. We have to wait of course, but we can't afford to do nothing while we wait. Naturally the scientists and technologues will work hard on a longterm solution. But we must also be ready for the day when they do, let's hope, allow us on the waves again.

A: Allow!

L: That's the way it is, George, and I see from your resistance that the job will be far more difficult even than I envisaged. Where's American pragmatism gone?

A: Right here, Tim. Do you realise what this all means? Persuading radio and TV companies, industries, international trade, administrations, governments, the lot, to organise and enforce programs of severe rationing. It would take years, decades, as long as the disarmament talks. Meanwhile we'd have a technical solution.

Z: That was the argument with disarmament, but the talks eventually happened. As did the various ecological enforcements. However slowly and inefficiently and loopholedly.

A: Right! Well, the two silent solutions aren't incompatible. We can't negotiate, but we can prepare both a scientific counter-action and a program of obedience. And if the latter has to be done I'm your man for the States. At least I'll know all the arguments against, I've just been through most of them!

Z: I knew you would be! You're right to be so sceptical, Dr Andrewski, but you sure rally round when convinced.

A: I'm not sure that I've rallied round, as you put it, Zab my dear, but willing to go into it all with you.

Z: Not personally, I can't stay.

A: I meant, with you as a team. I'm still horrified by some aspects though, and we must tread very carefully. This radio silence is catastrophic, but what would we cut? He seemed to have no preferences, I mean for news as opposed to, say, variety or sport. Just economy all round. And all so that these creatures can sit there in their deserts and compute serenely again! It's unbelievable!

Z: But it's food for thought. Theirs and ours.

14

Theirs and ours. Well, we have no access to theirs, whatever Zab may secretly imagine. I'm stuck here in Europe, in Tim's think-tank with George Andrewski, nice fellow, always hard to convince at but suddenly opens up, though right to be sceptical and demand constant checks as we go. Printed out whole text X for him here. He was amazed by our kid sleuthing capacities, or rather, Xorandor's, and amused by some of our notions of physics and computers. He brought all the work that he'd continued doing on the alphaguys. Says he got attached to Eddie the way we got attached to Xorandor and felt desolate when he had to give him up. Got "kinduv fixated on that experience, the way generals keep refighting their wars, it was my big experience, just turned thirty". Whereas I, being a mere kid, had all my studies to go through, and career, and young marriage, so I "kinduv" put it aside and forgot all about it. At least that's his explanation. He's a bit like Zab there, likes psychologising and philosophising everything.

Both his notes and the text Xorandor, however childish, helped us to work out many technical details for our eventual report. Lagache never turned up, much to my annoyance, since he too had worked on his specimen, and we can do with all such info.

Tim finally decided he must inform the P.M., who agreed nothing should be made public yet, nor, for that reason, even discussed in Cabinet, but who wants the report nano. So we're working hard. I wrote to Nasa, with a covering note from the P.M. and another from Tim, to ask for temporary leave of absence. Also to Jeanie of course. Post excruciatingly slow. George is high up at UKAEA so had no trouble, but he has to go back and forth, and Tim though master of his movements is nevertheless kept very busy elsewhere, but gives us much overtime. It's all very exciting and

I feel a bit like my old whizz-kid schoolboy self again. I must say it's rather pleasant. George has regressed to his thirty-years-old experience rather, when he was an important member of an international team, with powers of decision and counsel, so he keeps talking in those terms now, I shall advise, we shall decide, persuade, turn the table and so forth.

October 26 — Two strange events.

1) Letter from Lagache to me, c/o Tim at B.B.C., in French. Took ages to get here as usual. Says he postponed his journey to London after receiving the Uther message and the fix. Bavaria was so near Vienna he decided to take a small and discreet team with survey-metres, to try and locate Uther. Very annoying since they'd only succeed in alarming him, or whatever the term is, I must stop using human-emotion words. He's had no luck will be here soon.

2) Letter from Zab to Tim (and me), enclosing letter from Hanjo, reproduced here as such disspelling of educational illusions can't go into the report, even though it's written on the formal paper of Harbin Communications Center (headed in Chinese and English).

Sep. 10

Dear mum,

I've found dad you thouhgt I never woud but I did thanks to the chinese beaurocracy which is very eflcient hes very nice and was very pleased about my EXISTENCE which is what I wanted he's a big boss here and asks me to tell you in private sinse he told me you told him about your Great Adventure at the time of my conseption that theyve located an alphaguy nearby whos blocking the waves and their trying to make contact with him on, kayalfa band whatever that is but I don't see why that band shoud be misteriusly excluded 吞言 from pronounsed tun jen thats chinese for Verbivore but theirs no connection between the visual writing and pronounsiation here I hope your well I have no news from Régine but this is more exsiting much love

Hanjo

Immediate huddle. Why is everyone suddenly locating alphaguys? Well, not exactly everyone, but I feel sure it will come. And why does this Chinese ex-lover of Zab want her to know although his government is obviously saying nothing? Not that we'd know whether it is or not since newspapers and dispatches from everywhere now take so long to arrive. Ten days from France, four to six weeks from the U.S. and I suppose two months at least from China. We're back in the nineteenth century. Oh no, Hanjo's letter only took a month. But it's almost disinformation, it says so little. Tim knows all about this center and even knows Chang! Visited it five years ago and was shown round by him. Never realised it was Zab's son's father, naturally. Small world, said George (of course). Then another letter for Tim arrived, from one of the B.B.C.'s star newscasters, a Nigerian called Onuoro Nwankwo who's stuck, like so many of us, out in West Africa on a Special Reportage.

Sep. 29

Dear Sir Timothy,

I thought I should inform you of the following curious item, and I must add that I am very grateful that you kept us all so well informed about the Verbivore phenomenon, with charts and so on.

As you may know I was stuck here on a special assignment, then provisionally suspended. I remembered that Dakar was (unexpectedly) one of the concentration spots of the occurrences, so I took a very long trip by train and bus up there to see an old friend of mine, Dr Idro Nardi, who runs the UNROTA. I found him in a state of great excitement, as they have apparently located a nearby source (or possible source) of radio-wave "sponging" (as he calls it). I'm afraid that as a mere newscaster I don't understand the technicalities, but he kindly agreed to let me send you a copy of their preliminary report, asking only that all due acknowledgements should be made if used. He is, however, quite pleased to do so, knowing that this way it has a better chance of reaching you (in these days of inefficient distribution). He hopes (as I do) that it may be useful to you.

Trusting that the dear old is somehow keeping its pecker up.

Yours sincerely,

Onuoro Nwankwo.

Well, it wasn't MUCH use, except as confirmation of great scattering. Not that the technical details weren't impeccable, but we know them already. What surprises us is mainly why none of this "evidence" turned up earlier.

The press, which so far knows nothing of Uther or the others, has quietened down. Everyone is getting used to the new conditions. Astonishing, this habit business. I remember that Frieda once told us how an old friend from Poland, already in her sixties THEN, so that she must have remembered a free Poland between the two wars, had come on a visit, and couldn't grasp simple facts such as everyone having a car — she thought they must all be officials or a posh café not being state-owned, and how once when they went into a very dingy one she then said surely this one was state-owned. She had forgotten. It was the same with us during the war, Herr Groenetz said, we couldn't imagine what a lot of butter looked like. But here I am Zabbing away! At any rate, articles still appear, still speculating on the why and the wherefore and the implications. Real news is scarce and very late indeed, so nobody's very interested in a two-month old coup d'état in Panama or floods in Bangladesh. Whereas two centuries ago a two-month old item was the only kind of news, and so was treated as immediate. The papers up chiefly on local conditions and how everyone is coping, but that too has become a bore. I gather from articles by very old buffers that it all reminds them of their childhood in the Second World War, except that the brave British stuff was constantly perked up with news from the various fronts, air-raids, losses of planes and warships and submarines on both sides, and all that.

Nov. 2 — Lagache has turned up at last, with all his documents. Said he was detained in Saclay on the way, but also stayed longer in the Fichtelgebirge than had envisaged, because he too (it's getting monotonous) had located the source! OUR source, Uther Pendragon the terrible chief. Precisely pinpointed just 5 km West Sou' West of the saltmine near Mitterteich (as we thought). Not far from the motorway! Didn't find it physically, only radioactively, and didn't want to alert it in case it moved (though he must know it can't, except when still very small). He's fully aware, from his work at the time and intermittently since, that these creatures are extremely sensitive to human presence close by. So he didn't even try to make contact. Especially since neither his English nor his German, Uther's presumed languages, is fluent (a modest Frenchman, how odd: his English when I saw him was strongly accented but perfectly adequate).

We're all exhausted, with work, with calculations, with projects, with excitement, with frustration. But he's joined us and we're looking through all his papers. I suppose we'll get somewhere, even if the report is in the end a mere compilation.

Nov. 13 Tim went to Chequers with the P.M. after the Remembrance Day ceremony and has just returned. The Minister of Communications was there, and the Minister for Trade and Industry, and all the top mediamen, and Telecom, as well as the Director of the Bank of England, Top Service Chiefs, G.C.H.Q. etc. G.C.H.Q. must also be in technical unemployment, no traffic to intercept or codes to break. The P.M. had decided to get on with the "economy" scheme, and so to inform the top people concerned, under secrecy oath and so forth. Wish I'd had a little Xor to report, as with that War Office meeting!

Tim reported that it WAS a bit like that, half those present refusing to believe it and the other half refusing to do anything about it — same as George's first reaction in fact, national sovereignty and all that (still!).

George in fact is quite miffed that nothing has been found in the Mohave Desert. Not Eddie of course, he was part of the back-to-Mars package, but others, after all there was a concentration of cuts in Nevada. Surely the U.S. aren't being LEFT OUT? Of course, not hearing is no proof these days and maybe Nasa is being much more secretive.

Dec. 15. This time the press has been one-up on us — well, not surprising since we're keeping all our datasinks blocked. By the press I mean The Times (even before Verbivore the press had become more and more a one main paper affair, all the others imitating with variations, since all depended on the same international news agencies). But the others soon filched it and elaborated. A team of geologists in the Andes sent a report to a Chilean newspaper, which was picked up by an American reporter stuck there, who sent it to The Washington Post and ditto a British reporter there sent it to The Times, all this by sea, so it took months. In August these geologists had found a small, perfectly round stone, radio-active, zeolite-type but unlike any known rock there (although the area is full of extremely ancient formations, to do with the great continent-shift, which is why they've been working there for years, as indeed in Australia and elsewhere). The stone corresponded in every detail to the old descriptions of the alphaguys some two decades ago: brown with grey metallic patches, 5 cm in diameter, 3 cm high, the metallic patches in fact quite geometrical like the sensing and emitting devices on Xorandor, and tiny recessed shape like an inverted pyramid at the centre! Ribbed underside with small ducts between the ribs, presumably to eject the nodules. Evidently someone in the team was well-read in the Xorandor episode, less forgotten than we'd thought. They had taken it (I hope they wore gloves!) to the Geological School in Santiago and called in some physicists who insisted that it must be removed to their Atomic Energy outfit, where it could be studied in safe conditions, but the geologists had refused. They'd been excluded before and they weren't going to be this time (interdisciplinary warfare as usual).

Well of course all hell is now let loose. Presumably in the U.S. too, and in South America, and all over, as the news will spread. We have always said, we always thought, as our scientific correspondent observed six months ago, etc. Questions in Parliament, the usual farmyard uproar (according to newspaper correspondents, as fortunately it's no longer broadcast).

George is the most excited, as is Lagache. Neither has ever quite recovered from actually having a specimen in his care. I wonder what happened to Kubler, Kubla Khan and his caves of ice, Zab used to call him, who had Siegfried? (Or was that our name for him?). Dead, possibly. Anyway, it looks as if Uther found his way to his brother Siegfried near those caves of ice. Unless, of course, he's not OUR Uther at all but a secret offspring of Siegfried, unknown to or unrevealed by Professor Kubler? Who was rather an antinomian. After all, he was responsible for the big leak over Edison and the neutralised warhead. But then, why should a later offspring of Siegfried respond to a secret code worked out by Zab according to Uther's age in years and days? I'm straying in spec.

Slowly the pieces of puzzle are coming in, and we're trying to assemble them. Without any kind of radio-contact, scientific checking is practically impossible, more like geography and history than physics, but George and I are working out equations for various theories. Luckily we can still use an internal computer. But cooped up as we are inside the beehive B.B.C., I sometimes feel everyone outside is waiting for a trail of black or white smoke — habemus solutionem — otherwise deliberation continues. I feel sure that if all our facilities were normal we'd get on much faster, and also that far more evidence would be pouring in, since it's practically a scientific law that once everyone knows what the problem is and what they're looking for everyone starts finding. For instance — but I don't know how reliable that is — Tim introduced us to one of his Deputy Creative Directors, (Miss Inkytea or something I once briefly met before), who brought a note from a dramatic author called Perry Hupsos (!), the same one, presumably, who was stuck in Russia, and still is. It seems the Soviets intercepted our conversation with Uther, and his computer-replies, on K-alpha band. (Just as they'd intercepted those two messages 23 years ago and — probably — asked that East German spy on the spot to investigate). But this time they haven't kept it secret, they've splashed it all over Pravda — if splashed is the word for such a sober paper — shades of Glaznost obligent.

15

Can't understand what's going on. Natalia disappeared from my life like the dream she seemed. My trip was mysteriously cancelled, probably it was never on. Juri explained that in the difficult conditions all journeys unnecessary to the national effort were illegal, no tourism (least of all, his tone and look implied, for some second-rate visiting processor), only emergency supplies and strict government business. But of course my hotel and expenses would continue to be paid out of my accumulated royalties. But I was to stay in the hotel and eat nowhere else, go to no entertainments outside those in the hotel (a cinema, outdoor and indoor swimming, a gymhall, miniature golf, tennis, pingpong, judo, karate, the lot), a real luxury affair for visitors only, who pay in still much needed foreign currencies. And of course I don't, so that must gall them. Reason, he said, collapse of the credit-card system since Slovoyed, and no possibility of giving me old — or rather new — substitute rubles. It would therefore be considerate of me to cooperate and not create extra complications for them. Sublime. Not that I can exactly grumble, compared to other tourists pinned down by the paralysis and at the end of their currencies. But the cinema shows three ancient Russian classics over and over, Ivan the Terrible, Potemkin, and some earnest tale of a Soviet soldier dating at least from the fifties of the last century. And I detest all sport.

It's maddening not to be able to go out. Last summer I was given a plastic card on my royalty account, and went everywhere, eating in simple, very prole restaurants and just pointing to dishes others were eating. People behave exactly as they do in the West, two girls, for instance, eating with a male colleague and talking very intensely and dramatically about office non-events (I understood that much): So the photocopier was there, and I stood here, and she came in and said (there my understanding ceased, but I have heard hundreds such) — while the male colleague looked on, bored and vaguely amused. And I looked on very amused and not bored at all. The pleasure of recognition, if not that of discovery.

And now the papers are full of this intercepted message from someone who calls himself Uther Pendragon to someone called Zip. Am I still dreaming? I managed to write a note to Mira about it, which I gave to a cultural attaché from our Embassy. For yes, there are still parties and receptions and Vodka and champagne and caviar and cultural attachés. And the diplobag still functions, though slowly, overland and by Channel Tunnel. All that jazz continues but I'm not allowed to travel.

So I've been studying Russian. Yuri got me some books, and even calls and offers help at times, tries to explain Russian aspects. In Russian you must possess one verb for action in intent or effect accomplished, he says, and other verb, or other form of same verb, for action not in intent or effect accomplished. Here is a list of 100, learn by heart ten each day. Must be difficult for diplomatic promises, though maybe that's a question of nuance. But I can't make out whether his good will is willing or unwilling, genuine sympathy to a fellow wordprocessor or on orders from above, even if that goes no further than the Union of Soviet wordprocessors. For some reason he calls me old father-mucker. I suppose he means mother-fucker, and this is apparently meant to be affectionate.

At any rate, for practice and to save, through language acquisition, what sense of identity to myself I still have, I'm trying to decipher Pravda an I for an I and a Truth for a Truth. A little each day, and sticking to the Slovoyed phenomenon so as to get the same vocabulary over and over and concentrate on the syntax. Later I'll try myself on the old familiar classics, the plays at least, easier than turgid old Tolstoy et al.

And Pravda goes on glozing that lunatic message, explaining Uther Pendragon's name as Formidable Chief in Old Celtic, recalling the old Xorandor affair and the Soviet role in it, moralising on Uther's wisdom which exactly reflects Soviet policy since the beginning of time (Soviet time): that is, the rationing of information, the refusal of Western over-consumption and dilapidation of everything including media decadence and so on. We have always said, we Post-Socialists, and so on.

I wonder if they realise that they're capitalising on Marxist dogma, and always have done, with interest, cote d'usure. But then, the West has been marxeting capitalist dogma so I suppose it's all much of a muchness, except in the ambient air we breathe on either side. The ambient air here used to be a matter of life or gulag, but that's apparently all over with. As for there, the ambient air used to be a matter of conspicuous consumption or abject poverty, and that's not all over with. That fin-de-siècle phenomenon called CONSENSUS, which meant that whichever party came to power in a Western democracy did roughly the same as its rival, has spread to the international scene in the last ten years or so. But it also seems to mean an agreement not to debate or do anything about certain problems to which no one has any radical solution, such as unemployment or misery in the Third World, both of which continue to be treated socially and not economically. Mere patchwork. It's as if the world had become a wildlife park or ocean reserve, in which the protection and the interhunting of species are regulated, so that a certain tolerance of terrorism, local wars, famines, unemployment, delinquency and the rest is accepted, contained by the consensus.

The Third World, the Fourth World (whatever was the Second World?), subsist, it continues to go on, as our Prime Minister is reported to have said of the British public in The Times three months ago. Natural catastrophes made a million times worse in poor than in rich countries, by a permanent lack of means, lack of organisation, lack of constructive aid, famines from murderous mismanagement of resources and civil wars everywhere farmed by remote control from the First World (and the Second? Is that the one I'm in now?). Nothing seems ever to change except a few political labels. I'm on Uther's side, even if his demands, should they be met and accepted, must trap me for ever as a wordprocessor for the media. But I can always process diskette-books and articles. For the moment, however, I have nothing else to do but wordprocess. In English. Or into and from Russian. I only hope these diskettes won't ever be found and prevent me from leaving.

Anatol came to see me today, he'd vanished for ages. It's bitterly cold. Well it is December. He was wearing full furgear. I never got around to buying any since that shopping expedition that never was, with Natalia that never was. And I have no spending money. Anatol introduced me to Natalia so I thought I would mention both my need for a fur coat and her offer, so as to find out casually what had happened to her. But he was full of quite other news or was he evading?

My dear friend, he said in Russian, soon you will not need fur. The low frequencies have returned.

I didn't understand. My Russian wasn't good enough but neither was my intelligence of what he said when he repeated it in English. I still gaped emptily at him. He explained that planes use low frequencies or long wave for their intercom, and that if this news was indeed true I might soon go home. But of course, the government was being very cautious. Testflights would be experimented first, and for some time, before they would allow the Russian people to risk their lives. Or anyone else of course. The world's pilots had already worked out a highly economic intercom language long before Slovoyed had properly begun. Not so much of that Do you hear me Over Come in please and all that swallowing, no, I mean larking about, you know? And only minimum measurements. But we don't also know about radar, if that will work, which is the chief way for our Aeroflot to fly. Many experts believe that Slovoyed started with that long series of plane-crashes three or four years ago, you remember? Russia was affected also, but in those days we were in constant international contact with other airlines, so we shared the intercom.

That's very good news, Anatol. I was beginning to get quite dep — Well, homesick, you know.

That you must not, my old chap, you have not all what you want here?

Yes, yes, of course, it's very comfortable. But you would be homesick for Russia after a long stay in a foreign country, Wouldn't you?

But yes. Of course. Holy Mother Russia.

He gave me such a large wink, however, that I wasn't sure whether he didn't mean to accompany me and ask for political asylum. But perhaps it was just the Russian sense of humour.

All the same, Anatol, if they're going to be so cautious — and they're right — it'll be Spring at least before I can leave, especially as I don't expect any kind of priority. Naturally, I added to take any possible irony out of my tone. I can't go out at all in my thin Western coat. It's not as if I didn't have the money. Couldn't you arrange, or ask Yuri to arrange, for a fur coat and hat, and boots? I hate being coop I mean I'd so love to go out and walk around Moscow in the snow.

I will ask. I promise you. But soon you will go home. The fur coat and hat will be just a memoir. No, a souvenir. From Holy Mother Russia.

And he went out chortling.

But I've perked up. I should erase those sarky thoughts from this diskette, just in case. Strange how we can put up with anything if we can somehow see an end to it. Must be unimaginably desperate for those who can't, who feel trapped in their inhuman conditions till the day they die.

If it's true that aircraft intercom may come back first, or even come back period, and that a hypereconomic system already exists, this might well be a first "test" by Uther (and Co?) of our willingness to conform. In which case — Well, I'd better get on with some Russian, make the most of my stay here.

No more news from anyone. No coat, no hat, no boots, no Natalia, no plane-ticket home. I should have known better than to believe any of that. Obviously planes don't just need intercom but radar and intercomputer bookings and all that. The whole thing could even be Anatol's or Juri's little joke, and he will have gone back to report on my gullibility with huge cackles over much Vodka. I'm getting sick of this country, sick of Sloyoyed, — the less it transits the more sic it is — sick of this luxury prison, with its obsequious grooms and waiters and desk-clerks, Western style to please Western capitalists, yet deeply, inalienably Slav. I can't find out what's going on. Mira's abandoned me. Having pushed me here among these foreigners she forgets all about me. Busy, I suppose, on saving the world from her damn Verbivore. I've never felt so lonely in all my life.

Was it Julian who wanted to process a novel about Verbivore, rather than a sociological thesis? Easier, he thought! Well, I'll beat him to it. I'll start it right here. That'll galvanise me back into being. From a Russian point of view, with a Russian background. No one'll have that. Yuri, Anatol, Natalia, the cultural attachés, the desk-clerks and the rest, they'll all get fattened up into real fictional characters. I have the personal computer, with American programs. I have all the copy I need in these notes. Well, no, I know nothing about Verbivore itself, or even Slovoyed. But I can cheat. Who was it said the writer doesn't need to be inside the workshop, the open door is enough? George Eliot I think, or someone of that realistic ilk. Of course it would help if I could go out, walk around, talk to people. But I did that in the summer. Anyone can imagine cold and snow and breaths on the air. Proust wrote in a padded room. From memory, it's true. But I can mix memory and imagination.

I've got nowhere. Screens and screens of stuff, reprocessed, corrected, displaced, erased, reprocessed. All useless. I don't KNOW enough. I'm too depressed. And I'm out of the story. Why doesn't Yuri come and see me any more. I've written him several notes, begging for a visit, or a passage home by train, by truck, anything. I'd even walk it, but I'm not Napoleon. He had a horse anyway, only his men walked and died in the snow.

I have reams of notes on Slovoyed, possible social effects, political effects, psychological effects, cultural effects. Culture is only supported conversationally, someone said. (I can't even CHECK a quote here). But all that's from the papers, English papers in the hotel, two months out of date, and Pravda, slowly deciphered. It would be a journalistic novel. My characters are flat, as Forster used to say, not rounded. Not "realised", as reviewers and blurbprocessors say. Perhaps I should use Julian again. He would have gone deaf after his noise experience with Decibel and his accident so he wouldn't mind Verbivore one byte. Rather negative, though. Perhaps he would have got hooked on silent moving images with peoples' lips moving up and down like ventriloquists' dolls and mouths open in Munchlike screams. So he'd miss those, and go slowly mad, his withdrawal symptoms would take the form of identification and simulation, he'd become all those people and open and shut his mouth in spongy silence. And then Verbivore would start neutralising sound-waves as well, and everyone would become like that, not a single word would emerge as sound and no one could say any single thing to anyone, not even I love you or Get lost or Leave me alone.

Alone. I see I've just described my present state. All the communication I get is in the dialogue windows of the computer. This file does not exist. Do you want to open a New File? Yes. Return. New File. Wordprocessor Modus. Pageformat. Return. Text. Block Beginning. Block Ending. Take Out. Do you want Block reinserted? Yes. Now I have two blocks.

Alone. I see I've just described my present state. All the communication I get is in the dialogue windows of the computer. This file does not exist. Do you want to open a New File? Yes. Return. New File. Wordprocessor Modus. Pageformat. Return. Text. Block Beginning. Block Ending. Take Out. Do you want Block reinserted? Yes. Now I have two blocks.

Start again. Block Beginning. Block Ending. Do you want Block reinserted: No. Return. Recall Block. Double-spacing. Word-division: Wind- ows. No. OK. No. Word-division: reinsert-ed. No. OK. No. Block in double spacing. But all the paras are out of line. Why? Press Reformat. FATAL ERROR. WHOLE TEXT ERASED. The computer is so stupid, it should know what I want.

THEY should know what I want! A train, a truck, my kingdom for a truck. I'd stowaway but I can't even get as far as the station without catching pneumonia.

At last! Juri came with a train ticket and a lot of money, all I have left, in rubles and marks. And an old shabby fur coat and hat. No boots but never mind. I'm leaving tomorrow, via Smolensk, Minsk, Byalystok, Warsaw, Poznan, Berlin, Düsseldorf, Brussels, Ostend. It'll take thirteen days (why not to Riga and then by boat?) I'm not to leave the train anywhere before Düsseldorf. The personal computer is a gift, dear friend, you can take it with you. Yes, and your diskettes, you need not hide them or erase them. This is a free society, a Post-Socialist society, as I hope you have discovered. Besides, you have not written anything that does not do more harm to you than to us.

What! But how?

There are no interlinks any more? You are right, my friend.

But we have our little curiosities to satisfy, in the name of international friendship, and hence, our means and ways.

The valet! He stole them at night and copied them!

The valet if you like, but that sounds like old-dated American spy stories. One ancient fascist poets said that you can't have literature without curiosity. Here, we have both, under Post-Socialism.

He's gone, after a last splash of Romanian champagne. Gird up your loins. Farewell, Holy Mother Russia.

16

Poor old Perry. But he's not the only one, whatever he may think, and he'll get here eventually. Substitute fictions are proliferating everywhere, mostly in the press, but also in people's minds or personal computers, to make up for those no longer provided by the media. The only difference is that the publication process is slowed down by the post, and so seems more secretive, but that's really an illusion since the production of media fictions in fact took much longer, but behind the scenes. And the final effect is ultimately as evanescent, since by the time these paper fictions are published their authors have altered and substituted other fictions, other scenarios: the end of the world caused by the collapse of communication; the dictatorship of the alphaguys through rigorous censorship with consequent superficial apathy but accumulated frustration; the starving of the alphaguys by dismantling all nuclear stations; the hunting of the alphaguys high and low and wide by raking the deserts and mountains of the world inchwise and demolishing them all in a carcrusher or one by one on a railway line like the heroines of old Westerns; the acceptance of media-silence together with the return to the idyllic life of yore. Many are more trivially personal: a wife's revenge on a football-hooked husband who now has to listen to her instead; the finding of domestic bliss; the collapse of the media-cohered family; the creation of new leisures, the reemergence of poetry. And so on.

Meanwhile, the real scenario, if it can be called that. Tim keeps me informed, and even allows me in on some of the think-tank's discussions, on the private grounds that I thought of putting him onto Zab in the first place, and on the stated grounds that I'm now in charge of Public Reaction Analysis. They seem none too pleased, a mere (unemployed) Deputy Creative Director, with the expected tired old joke from Andrewski about deputy creation. But where would they be without that? Jip's basically okay though. His reconciliation with Zab, and their success in contacting Uther, have mellowed him, he's less "spiky" as they used to say. But it's true I can't follow their scientific discussions as physicists and telecom experts, and I usually attend only when broadcasting policy is being discussed.

March. The report was at last finished and sent to the P.M., who read it carefully and then, rather than send one special emissary slowly all over the world, has decided to send many. Andrewski is to take it to Washington and Jip is to go to Ottawa, then Vancouver. Tim to Australia and New Zealand (HIS deputy will take over). The Commonwealth Broadcasting Association is based in London but the P.M. thinks it more courteous, and more efficient, to go and present the facts to each first. Zab offered her services for Germany. Tim asked her to go to China, but she wrote to refuse "after much hesitation" (?) said she'd have to resign her seat if she was absent for such a long, and above all indeterminate, time. She'd be much more useful as spokesman on the topic in the Europarliament. Besides, she felt that emissaries whose job is to persuade must know the language of the country fluently. Always the idealist, dear old Zab. But she's right.

Lagache is in charge of all other European countries, that is, he'll go to the European Broadcasting Union in Geneva (not that he knows German, Spanish, Portuguese, Italian, Greek etc but they'll have interpreters) and to the U.N. Press and Audiovisual Division of UNESCO in Paris. There's also the European Institute for Communication, but that's based in Germany (Europe smallest area, largest number of orgs). Others are going to the Asocación Inter-Americana de Radiodifusión in Montevideo (covers South, Central and North America but same argument about going separately to North America first), the Asian Broadcasting Union in Tokyo, the Arab States Broadcasting Union in Cairo, the African organisation in Dakar and so on. Oruono Nwankwo had been written to and asked to return by boat at once, so that he can be briefed and sent back to Dakar with the report, as emissary. We can't trust copies to the post of course, but it will all take just as long.

We have also learnt by now, however slow the post, that many similar reports are being processed everywhere anyway, ever since the discovery of alphaguys here and there and the Pravda leak about Uther's message, not to mention all those scenarios.

So it's not so much a question of secrecy any more as of achieving orderly consensus on what to do. For it might well be catastrophic if every nation or even every organisation tries to do something different. Not that there's much choice, until the scientists discover a remedy (sounds like a fatal disease). So what else is there except the slimming down of pulse-signals *le dégraissage*, as the French cruelly call the sacking of personnel towards efficiency that's been going on for thirty years or more. Complete coordinated programs must be ready for the day, the mythical, messianic day, when Broadcasting returns, when the waves start functioning again and we are tested, and maybe still found wanting. Wanting our waves back. None of the other scenarios are considered viable. The report makes it quite clear that the phenomenon can only be due to the presence of innumerable alphaguys all over the planet, so that finding and destroying a few, even the selfstyled leader, can make no difference. Nor is the closing down of nuclear stations envisageable at this stage in our development since we banked everything on them: it's bad enough to be without radio-waves but we can't be without electricity, nor could the few coal-mines left substitute for them, and the many that were closed can't be activated again as indeed the miners pointed out at the time. Nor is oil the answer, naturally, except for heat and cars. Some electricity in the world is hydrogenerated but that too would be insufficient.

Insufficient. That word haunts all scenarios. Our needs have become monstrous. But none of those who say this, or rather who shout it out, are themselves willing to do without their mediadaelic world and press-button comforts.

As for the waiting-it-out solution, waiting until the alphaguys themselves tire of merely recording the silent universe and get nostalgic for all that man-made information they fed into their circuits, it's not exactly a solution since it's imposed on us by the fact that we can't contact them with any information. And if they suddenly contacted us, or opened up the waves again, it would only be to test our willingness to economise. There's no getting away from that basic truth — unless of course the whole Uther business is itself a fiction, a hoax. But no one seems to believe that any more, all scientific evidence has now become pretty convincing, if not conclusive, especially in the face of continuing wave blockage. So we must be ready. Even if it takes months and years to persuade the world. Otherwise the possible opening of the waves would only be followed by another clamp-down, probably for ever. And the effect of that on world economy, not to mention deep psychology, would be slow death.

I wish I had been chosen as report-carrier and persuasive emissary, after all I've worked very hard on the new program proposals. I could do with a trip to Tokyo or even Cairo.

But I'm just a nobody around here, even as ex-Deputy Creative Director instead of mere ex-Radio Drama Producer. Deputy-creating scripts for that big day when all will return to normal. My links to the boffins are just deputy-creative links, extremely tenuous. All the same, I do think Tim might have thought of me. After all, he was prepared to send Zab, who knows no Chinese. But that was in some sentimental hope he'd effect a reconciliation with Hanjo's father as he had with Jip. And she's much more of an expert, at least, she once taught Communications. And she's much more closely involved, would be more persuasive. Besides, why should the P.M. have accepted me? Apart from the members of the thinktank, all the emissaries are close counsellors of the P.M., not actually Cabinet Ministers who can't be spared from the daily running of the country ("no polemic will prevent the Government from governing", quote from P.M. in The Times), but the shadowy figures nobody knows, from big business, the world of science, the Universities, and such. THE ThinkTank in other words.

The geologists, now that they know what to look for, keep finding more alphaguys. About sixteen have been located in Japan, in Africa, in Saudi Arabia, in Srilanka, in Burma, in Australia, in Brazil, in the Canadian Rockies, and I forget where else. But they're being left in peace for the moment. They're no longer small enough to be mobile (according to calculations made by Andrewski) so we can always find them again.

Jip, however, insisted on travelling down into the Fichtelgebirge with Zab and Lagache, and trying to talk to Uther. Emotional attachment? He would never admit that, though Zab no doubt would. It was just a scientific attempt not to be neglected, according to him. They took Poccom 3 and they handshaked it in exactly the same primitive manner they had used with Xorandor, the negative and positive leads on the same spots, so that it functioned in a way like an internal computer. But they had no success. Or rather, they can't know one way or the other. Here's the print-out.

ZIP calling UTHER PENDRAGON. Come in please.
(No reply)
ZIP calling UTHER. We are very close to you as you must know. We shall not harm you.
(No reply)
ZIP to UTHER. You promised to respond if we called. Zip promise okay. Question: Is Uther promise not okay?
(No reply)
ZIP to UTHER. Is Uther promise cancelled?
(No reply)
ZIP to UTHER. We know you can receive us.
(No reply)
ZIP to UTHER. Qualification: At least we hope you can receive us. It's important.
(No reply)
ZIP to UTHER. The non-economy of this message is due to your not responding. We want you to know that we are doing everything to persuade the world to economise its signal-activity.

(No reply)

ZIP to UTHER. But it will take a very long time, months perhaps, because we can't communicate by radio or travel by plane.

(No reply)

ZIP to UTHER. It may even take years, because people are very repeat very slow to persuasion, and once persuaded they are very slow in altering their behaviour.

(No reply)

ZIP to UTHER. Compare the long negotiations for nuclear disarmament. But they eventually succeeded, thanks to you. But it was long.

(No reply)

ZIP to UTHER. We have no means of informing you when the economy programs are ready. Unless we come here again, and on the assumption that you are intaking.

(No reply)

ZIP to UTHER. If this is not possible, then will you please contact Zip yourself, on same Gigahertz frequency as before, so that we can inform you of our progress.

(No reply)

ZIP to UTHER. The third and only other solution is to open the waves again yourselves, when the time comes, and test the new programs. We promise they will be economical.

(No reply)

ZIP to UTHER. But do not do it too soon. We have not begun the persuasion process yet and it may take several years.

(No reply)

ZIP to UTHER. That's all. Goodbye Uther. End message.

(No reply)

Zab cried. I met her at last when they returned to London together, with the printout, and to get briefed for their diplomatic missions.

I blubbed, like a child, she said. I couldn't stand those silences, those blank screens. So unlike Xorandor or even Xor 7, it was like going right back to childhood but all wrong, as in a nightmare. And it was so cold, there in the snow, far worse than with Xorandor on those icy December days before the hooha. But that was Cornwall.

She had tears in her eyes again. Jip scoffed.

Debug, Zab, it's not at all the same situation.

I know, I know.

How did you spot him, I asked, to untense the circuits. I mean if there was snow?

Jip took over while Zab blew her nose.

It was because there was snow that we located him. He'd melted it from on top of him, to uncover his transducer devices presumably, and also all around him, so he was in the centre, a perfectly round brown stone in a sort of inverted cone. In any other season, and despite the fix and the survey-metre, we'd have taken much longer. He'd have merged with the natural surroundings. He was on a hillside, at the edge of a wood.

Overlooking the piece of valley towards the motorway and Mitterteich.

Overlooking isn't quite the word, Zab, they have a weak pixel element.

Radio-telescoping then. And I've always been convinced that Xorandor had a highly developed pixel, despite that elementary figure of a man he drew on our screen. He must have had, with such sophisticated computer capacities.

To do what? He had no screen.

I mean internally of course. To work out complex problems in graphs and things. Digression I KNOW, Jip. But as to our info, I'm certain that Uther intook everything.

I hope so, but we have no proof whatsoever to reinforce your certainty.

Go on, say we might as well have been talking to a stone. So small too.

I wasn't going to, said Jip more gently. And his size shows that your hypothesis about miniaturisation was right. And at least there was no doubt that it was an alphaguy.

AN alphaguy! He was Uther, I know!

You know but we don't, not scientifically. We only know he was probably the source of the message signed Uther. But an alphaguy for sure. Lagache did all the radiation tests, and we even examined it closely. Took photographs too, look Mira.

I gazed at them. A small round brown stone in a hole in the snow. Then a close-up of his transducer devices, and another of the ribs and nodule-ejecting ducts on his underside, with several tiny holes. So he too had had offspring and sent them off. It was the first time I'd seen actual pictures, instead of just imagining.

I'm sure he didn't like that, said Zab. The flashes, and being picked up and turned over. Oh, I know we had to.

In any case, Zab, if you're so certain he's Uther, he was picked up the day after his birth, by you, and carried in the pocket of your windcheater to the hiding-place in the rocks. So he must be programmed for it.

No, I took Aurelius, you naturally took the first-born, I mean the first-named.

What's the difference? You're exasperating, Zab.

Descrambling. I'm being totally irrational. That I should have gone quarky there, fair enough, it was all so tense, but why should it still unspool me to talk about it now?

Perhaps, I ventured, because you're less tightly spooled up than Jip.

But Tim was getting impatient.

Well, you'd better push in your spooling key at once, Zab, the briefing conference is now, in the big boardroom, and everyone's waiting. But thanks for trying, you two. And Zab, I'm sure the intake did occur. It's very important he should know what we're doing. After all, unless they can still send their tiny offspring as correspondents to all our meetings — and they weren't really sent but carried by humans — they too may be suffering from data withdrawal symptoms.

17

No, they can't send their tiny offspring as correspondents to human meetings anymore, but they can send me, since I measure human noise. Oh, not the noise I like, radio-noise, but we can't always do the work we like for a living, and many are those among humans who've had to recycle, or get their living from something they do well enough but do not love well enough, reserving their real, that is to say their loved activity for their rest periods. So I go into noise, and there's plenty of it, especially in the now very busy railways, to recharge my batteries, gritting my teeth and closing my eyes as it were, since I can't close my ears.

And then, in my lovely spare time, I flit about the world, all over the place, with an amazing energy that comes from my desperate desire to know when the radio noise will return. That is, the desire to know gives me the energy but the nervous frustration lowers it again. Humans are so exasperating. I learnt that with Julian, he didn't really know what he wanted. A weak character in fact, badly conceived, in a mediocre play. But at least it WAS radio. And fun at the time, though Perry tried to kill me off as if one could kill an abstraction, a measurement. Oh, I know, some of you oddball characters will say: Don't be so vague, if you're a measurement. But a few might add: you also belong to the stratum of represented objects, you have a right to be indeterminate.

Well it's not so easy. I suppose all this is my punishment for misbehaving in Julian's head, you will say, or for refusing to be killed off. But if it is, I'm enjoying it hugely, more than I'm being exhausted by it, even if I have to work in relative silence, recharging only on horrid noise.

At any rate, I'm not being vague with the alphaguys, I'm keeping them very accurately informed, even though it's uphill work. What silly metaphors humans have, who works uphill? In my case it's up airbumps and down airholes and along flattened waves that slide like long and narrow and endless skating canals, as in Holland but for ever. I enter stormy meetings in Washington, in Ottawa, Montevideo, Moscow (Perry's gone), Budapest, Tokyo, the lot. And everywhere it's the same. Program schedules are being proposed, revised, cut down and reexpanded as each lobby refuses to give up this or that vital slot.

News bulletins on the agenda today in Dakar. Idro Nardi, a slim shiny black man, is trying to persuade the (rather fat) representatives of all the African countries to slim down everything (it's easy for slim people). No headlines, no summaries at the end, just the items, with a correspondent's report only if it adds to the item and repeats not a single phrase of the newscaster's introduction. You'll have to define the word "phrase", says someone, some words are bound to be shared by both. Each country to have only one news bulletin a clay, free choice of time but no clashing with those of other countries. If a morning bulletin in Nigeria has broadcast, say, a catastrophe or a coup d'état, no other country can repeat it until the time of their bulletin, and must have something new to add. No scoops and rivalries in other words. Each bulletin to stick strictly to news. Cultural items and star interviews to have separate slots (to be considered tomorrow). Political interviews to be reduced to two a week, one allotted to a government spokesman and one to the largest opposition. The views of smaller parties to be expressed in organised debates (to be considered on Thursday). And so on.

All this sounds eminently reasonable in the desperate circumstances. But nobody can agree. Humans would go on arguing for their lobby on the planet's dying day. The arguments are so predictable that they prove the alphaguys' case for economy. Africans are supposed to be passionate and uncontrolled and still close to savagery, but in fact they're a model of decorum compared to the English and the French, and Idro is being very patient. Some of the delegates seem to be asleep, it's so hot. Perhaps they don't really care about news and debate.

Public hearings in the U.S. Senate. Well, public although they can't be broadcast, but the press is present, this being a democratic country, and the proceedings will be in all the papers and create much furore in the street, in homes and at local meetings. Andrewski has just presented the last part of the report, and is now starting on the draft proposals. First item on the agenda, the easiest: Educational programs to be scrapped. After all no TV station tries to teach mathematics. All science and technology are already taught in schools at every level, where internal video can still be used without problems, and popularised science only spreads false notions. Since the only science programs are a few space operas, as Andrewski scornfully names a few vulgarisations of astrophysics, there is little demur. The principle to apply throughout, music, art, gardening, civic studies and all other practical disciplines to be taught in specialised schools and not through the media. The Humanities, on the other hand, pose more of a problem, since they are no longer taught in the universities but only at school level, and had been entrusted to the media for continuation as hobbies. These must therefore be kept, but in a severely reduced form.

Music: one concert a week, each representing one period, broke music [whatever's that?] one week, Classical another, Romantic another and so on (groans). All exactly repeated phrases and motifs to be cut, in classical music, jazz, old Rock and Blues, modern Fling and Broody, as well as refrains in Country music (uproar), and only one Fling and Broody concert a week too (continuous roar of protest drowns Andrewski's voice, oo, lovely).

As to soap opera serials, these must be seriously revised, not only in number, for they're extremely alike, but in redundancy of scenes. Scriptwriters must learn to finish off a scene between two characters before passing to the next one with two others, and not fragment the scenes into a continuous to-and-fro, which creates intolerable repetition, not only of words but of tone. The public would soon follow, as indeed they learnt to follow the fragmentation when it commenced to be practised in the last century and has continued unchanged ever since (angry interruptions from Scriptwriters' delegate). There are also far too many prize-winning games with inane quiz questions attached and general hysteria. The money vocabulary is highly repetitive and the alphaguys are very sensitive to female screams.

It's just as well they can't hear the female screams and male roars during this presentation. Even I suffer, though I like this type of noise.

Someone on a point of order is allowed to speak. Mr Chairman I strongly object to all these programs being considered apart from the commercials and sponsoring they depend on. Publicity is scheduled for consideration next MONTH! Yet publicity and programs are intimately linked. And, I may add, publicity is part of the American Way of Life, in other words the freedom to choose in a wide range of offers, and I consider it monstrous that the American public should be deprived of this freedom, in relation to both programs and publicity. Why, the zapping of realities is implicitly inscribed in the American Constitution as an inalienable right.

Sir, you have slipped in a personal opinion, not to mention a lobby argument, into the point of order for which you were given the floor. I cannot allow it. Delete the whole intervention from the record please. Publicity will be considered in due order.

Nevertheless this has opened up a pandemonium on culture. We cannot have culture quantified, with quotas for this and quotas for that. TV must offer alternatives. But they are false alternatives, all channels offering a film, or sport, or rival variety, or rival games, in the same slot. I don't understand, why oppose culture to entertainment in this way? Yes and why oppose sport to culture, everything's culture. And what about children's programs? They leave a great deal to be desired, still encouraging violence and machoism at a very early age. And what about programs for adolescents, they have problems too. I don't agree that money programs are evil, they bring a moment of happiness, and that is also a social duty. Ooh, lovely. Order. Order. And what about meteorology?

And what about telephones, and computer networks, shouts a business representative, they don't even on the agenda yet. They're far more important than — And what about satellite weather reports, and space stations, and — Order. Order.

Lagache in Geneva. Same scenario. The French dominate the proceedings, and talk fast in long, involved sentences full of subordinate clauses, the main one often getting lost on the way. The Swiss are much, much slower, the Germans midway. The English delegation has so many different vowel systems and pitches, from top of larynx to nasal or velar dominant that no one can follow without the interpreter, though I'm used to it and decode easily. The Spaniards but this is of no interest. For oddly enough, they're debating Debates.

And this debate is a very model of television debating as seriously practised in the good old days of media. Whatever the topic, and whoever the experts invited, two men practically hold the floor, the chairman either helpless or mesmerised into asking them questions himself and giving them the floor out of turn, when they haven't just taken it, and other guests hardly get a look in. Least of all, I may add as a female decibel, the inevitable token woman who is never asked her opinion or, should she at last be given a chance, is interrupted three or four times by the two men and finally silenced. Only a queen or president or prime minister can remain uninterrupted, by vestigial divine right I suppose. I've done statistics on this, and it hasn't changed in forty years. The men seem quite unconscious of it and smile contentedly and gallantly at the woman after she has not quite spoken.

Today there is one French lady judge, responsible for media law, and she has been very patient, but at last, towards the end of the debate on Debates, she snubs her most constant interrupter with a firm "Vous permettez?" and manages to get to the end of her intervention.

And of course when the topic gets animated three or four men talk at once, in the deepest conviction that their own precious words as heard in their own head will be equally audible to all. Personally I love it, but this cacophony, says Lagache after such an incident, is precisely one of the many aspects of radio and television which will have to be severely controlled. It is totally inadmissible in a conference like this, where interpreters are already thinking in two languages, and usually conference delegates are more disciplined. But in broadcasting — and we all hope those good old days will return, everyone knows very well, and is each time reminded beforehand, that the listener or viewer cannot hear anything at all if two or more people speak at once. Yet each time they forget, like children. And, I may add, the same applies to political interviews, which we'll be discussing tomorrow, I mean interviews à deux, of two rival spokesmen, sworn enemies invited to face each other amicably, say Arab and Persian, Arab and Israeli, Hindu and Shiite Moslem, Post-Socialist and Post-Capitalist, Irish Protestant and Irish Catholic, Third World and First World, you name it, sooner or later one will interrupt the other who will nevertheless go on talking [so it's not an interruption], each insisting on repeating his catechism [is that really the appropriate word?] to get it all in before time's up. The result is like an opera duet, but less harmonious, and after all one can't hear the words in opera duets. Needless to say the alphaguys are very sensitive to such brouhaha. However, I am anticipating

Yes, and you're abusing your position as presenter, Monsieur Lagache, that was not only anticipation but personal opinion, and much too long.

I apologise Mr Chairman. But it's not entirely irrelevant to this debate on Debates. Before we get any kind of debating programs back on the air — alphaguy willing — all politicians and indeed all representatives of any formation or lobby or discipline in any debate whatsoever will have to be people who have gone through special training, in exactly the same way as politicians had to submit to media-training and makeup. Well, "had to" is too strong, they were only too willing, vanity and role-playing and the gaining of power being at stake. The handling of words, however, is more difficult to control, more deep-seated in political and personal passion. But such training is a cinéquanon [whatever does that mean?], une condition préalable [ah!].

The cultural delegates, though deeply offended and anxious, are being the meekest (relatively). It's true that culture programs, both in France and England, and I believe in Italy and presumably elsewhere, are a very earnest and self-contained affair, relegated to their own channel or TV time, where pompous psuedo-experts talk to pompous experts in pompous jargon. But something for everyone is precisely what is being questioned and challenged everywhere. It's an extremely complex problem everywhere, says the head of the European Institute for Communications, though perhaps it is the most complex in France. We all have national publics, not international ones, we are still very, very far indeed from the Euro-TV we dreamt of in the nineties. Irrelevant, says the chairman.

The angriest and wildest lot are the politicians. Their professional deformation seems worse than that of other groups, so that they're incapable of admitting, or even believing, that what they say is not of the utmost importance and close to the heart of every viewer and listener. It's a curious phenomenon, this, I've often thought about it. Among themselves (for I often go and listen to their private convs, in clubs, restaurants, corridors, they're fascinating even as noise), they talk as if they didn't believe a word they say in public, it's all referred to as "the right touch", "the right moment" (or not the right moment), "better not mention that", "stress this" and so on. Yet the very second they're in front of a mike they apparently believe the opposite, that everything they propose and say is not only the truth, but something vital for the people to understand. If we lost the election, they say, it's not because the people rejected our program but because we probably didn't explain it with sufficient clarity. It's all a matter of communication.

But I've wandered from the debate. No wonder. It's going round in circles and getting nowhere. I think I'll take a turn in New Delhi. Preliminary discussion at national level before the Tokyo Conference for Asian Broadcasting. Same happened in Washington after all, no one's yet ready for Montevideo, the area is too huge.

Here the atmosphere is very different. Extremely courteous, everyone bowing with folded hands before speaking. But passions run below. For the problems here really are of informing people (actually they are everywhere, and permanently, but here it's taken more seriously).

Informing them, in innumerable dialects, about innumerable facts of survival, personal and national: crop control, birth control, medical care, hygiene in and along the Ganges, flood behaviour and prevention, famine behaviour and prevention, deforestation, race-relations, religious relations — in fact it's largely thanks to such a vast and continuous stream of information that India long ago got out of its more abject poverty and became the relatively stable country that it now is. But there can be no let-up, generation after generation must learn the facts of life that are not handed down by local traditions.

Nevertheless, the film-moguls insist that what the people want is not constant moralising and civic instruction but escape from their miseries, in other words, rich romantic films. Still, it's all fairly peaceable and cuts all round will no doubt be made. Memo to Uther: be more tolerant about repetition in all poverty stricken areas of the world where the bulk of human effort has to be made for survival rather than over-consumption.

Harbin Communications Centre, Manchuria. I've been quite curious about that, after all, I can't help being involved with the Jip and Zab level of events, especially since I got out of the Julian level which is really too tedious, even for my taste in droning.

Chang-ti-lu is presenting the facts about the alphaguy found near Harbin. He's tall for a Chinese and in his late thirties, but looks younger, because all Chinese look young until suddenly they're old. Unless they get fat, as in the old Mandarin and opium-smoking days, but few Chinese have been really fat for a hundred years. His black straight hair is receding, however, which is fairly unusual here, and I can imagine him with a bald head and a pigtail, though no one wears pigtails here any more. Oh, I know, you other characters think that because I'm a mere measuring device I have no eyes, but I told you, I'm also a character, and characters have eyes, necessarily, unless they're blind characters, like Xorandor, and I'm not. I'm doing this in the name of Zab, who likes description and might be interested, after all. It's true I'm not being very noise-measuring at the moment. But that's because the Chinese make less noise than the Occidentals. Their language has five differentiating pitches and that's rather exciting for me, makes me go all of a tremble. But they speak quietly, if high, and move silently.

The English emissary has got up to speak, in fairly fluent Chinese. Zab was right, she'd have got nowhere. He presents the report, and everyone listens respectfully. It takes quite a long time, but he has understood Chang's report and so skips everything that might be repetitive. He draws attention to this, as one of the techniques we must learn. Rather smug, really. And finally ends up drawing attention to it again, which is a contradiction as to repetition but which affords him a smooth transition to the proposals part.

These don't seem to affect the Chinese one way or another. It's a bit like the Russian reaction. We have always been economical with information, they say, and do not indulge in rival publicity. Our people work much too hard to have much time for entertainment. Such entertainment as we give them is well deserved. The people must rest after hard labour. Sounds all very Confucian. I wonder if it's true.

In fact the Chinese, like the Russians, are much more concerned about the use of radio and TV in space, the satellite stations and weather and other observations, as well as with computer networks and telephones, all of which figure very soon on the agenda and with much more time allocated to them than the mere media, which seem to be just a bamboo entrée before the rich sweetsour chopsuey and rice. It's true I didn't go to Nasa, who must be concerned with these aspects, and in top priority.

Hanjo is sitting in the audience, for this is a public hearing, which means that a few privileged people, chiefly technicians from the Centre and their families, can fill the small public gallery behind the huge hall where the hearing is taking place. And Hanjo is the son of the director. He's a strange-looking boy, with spiky sandy hair but Chinese features and oblique black eyes, despite all of which he manages to seem extremely conventional, at least to me, in his Western jeans and leather jacket.

He's busy taking notes and looks very concentrated. I've just taken a peep. Writing is my natural enemy, especially Chinese writing that manages to convey meaning without sound, and groups of entities rather than just one entity. But I couldn't resist. His notes are in Chinese ideograms, very nicely drawn too. No trouble with spelling here. I even think he might well stay here, if only for that reason. This is his first big journalistic experience, of something he can understand and can report on intelligibly. He would also have the backing of his father, who has suddenly become a national figure, and whatever they say, nepotism still functions here. And everywhere in fact. Perhaps he'll become a Chinese star-newscaster Han-yo Man-Ing?

But all this, all over the place, is only a beginning. Sport, Adventure, Opinion Polls, old films, historical assessments, public phone-ins, sociological problem programs, medical information, the lot, still have to get their slimming diets, not to mention Computer Networks, Telephone Networks, Air Travel, Space Satellites, Big Business, Small and Medium Business, Stock Exchanges, International Finance, Banking, Government, Administration . . . At this rate Hanjo will be an old man before Verbivore is resolved.

18

This is ridiculous. Clearly I'm still obsessed with Decibel. But it's totally unrealistic, how can she inform the alphaguys? She merely measures noise, she can't transmit content. It wouldn't be admitted even in science fiction, and alas, we're not living this as science fiction but as all too painful reality. I may hate noise, but I can't exist unless radio returns, so I'm as involved as anyone. I'll have to scratch all that. My novel isn't going at all well. And it's all complicated by the fact that Perry's back, and is writing a novel about Verbivore, with me as main character, stranded in Moscow and writing a novel about Verbivore.

All that information about the meetings is important, though, and if I'm stranded in Moscow how else could I know about it and present it convincingly? I'll have to find some other way, a real delegate-at-large, going everywhere. But it would take him months and months to get everywhere, whereas the meetings are occurring simultaneously. And will continue to do so for years. Yuri could talk to me about Dostoevski's notion of the invisible secretary, and perhaps from there have me appointed as delegate-at-large.

This Julian is nuts. How could the Russians appoint HIM? Sheer megalomania. Of course I'm no longer in Moscow but he is. And despite all my reading and research (chiefly in the press), I still know very little about Verbivore as a scientific phenomenon, especially from the Russian viewpoint, which was THE point. So I'm stuck with my novel as I was stuck in Moscow. And although I finally got out, it wasn't through any derringdo on my part but entirely thanks to the authorities, or Juri's kindness (or desire to get rid of me). And no authority or kindness is going to get me out of this mess, the mess of wordprocessing a novel, except my own authorial authority.

I can't even talk to Mira about it. I know she could help me, she really seemed to know about Verbivore. But she's moved right out of my ken. I can't ring, and she doesn't answer my letters. Fine Producer of Radio Drama, no concern for wordprocessors! It's true this isn't a radio play. In any case, I learnt from the desk downstairs, who put me through to her secretary, that she's now a Deputy Creative Director. Fat lot of use she is in deputy creation, I said, and she replied that this was the post Miss Enketei held for normal times, but that like everyone else, she's now engaged on Verbivore research. But that's exactly what I need, I said, I'm writing a novel about Verbivore. From a Russian viewpoint, I added to impress her. Well, she said, she's Director of Public Reaction Analysis at the moment, so I doubt whether she could help as to a Russian viewpoint. And she's far too busy to see you without an appointment. Why don't you write her a letter?

Well of course, I didn't like to admit I had sent her letters, several, so I said good idea, thank you, and went away disconsolate. I must continue to depend purely on the press, and on my imagination. Which is stretched to breaking point. And the press is more repetitive than the media ever were. Why aren't there creatures to penalise print into economy too? At least it would help save forests and prevent floods.

I know. I'll write a play instead. With Paula in the star role. She'll love that. People are flocking to the theatres. Then I can concentrate chiefly on "Public Reaction", analysed or not, well, analysed in my fashion. I'll do without Mira, without everyone. I'll concentrate on ordinary people, I've always been good at those. There's plenty of material in readers' letters. I could still transmute it all to Russia, and use my observations on the Russian people. A grand gin and Vodka cocktail, human reactions are after all much the same everywhere, but the neorealistic Soviet element and the tragic Slav element will give it extra spice. A Turgenev type play, a twenty-first century Turgenev! That's it! Julian can be her son, or a young lover. Or the eternal student. Or an English student stranded in Moscow. Shall I ever get from Moscow? Or maybe I'll fuse him with Anatol. I'll have to see as I go. At last I'm on to something. I can do a play in a week, I'm an old hand, whereas novels take much longer. Not that plays are easier, they're extremely tricky, but the rhythm is faster, and the dialogue guides me, and tells me exactly when it's gone on too long and needs an entrance or other happening. A play is a quickpace microcosm, whereas a novel is like organising a whole world in slow motion.

Come on then, old Hupsos the Sublime, type away. VERBIVORE, Act I, Scene 1. No. THE VERBIVORE WOMAN. That's it. People are themselves verbivore, and women most of all. That gives me a human angle.

> The new play at The Haymarket is a winner. The human angle on Verbivore.
> Perry Hupsos has come up with a superhit.
> Dame Paula in the role of the Verbivore woman has surpassed herself.
> Very funny. Don't miss it!
> Deeply serious, moving, and dazzlingly witty at the same time. A domestic comedy on Verbivore. The insuperable challenge has been met by Perry Hupsos.
> A twenty-first century Turgenev.
> A twenty-first century Tchechov.
> An English Gogol.
> Paula James is a triumph.

Paula, congratulations, and thank you, thank you.

Perry darling! But without you —

Congrats, mum, you were a scream.

Zab, my love, What a lovely surprise! But why didn't you tell me you were coming? I'd have got you a free ticket.

I got one, mum, by saying I'm your daughter. They believed me, too! Couldn't let you know as I wasn't sure of getting here.

This is Perry Hupsos, the author. Without him —

You mean you're THE Zab, and Zab and Xorandor?

Well, yes.

Holy shit! Excuse me. I hope I didn't make too many howlers.

Howlers? Why no, though you made us howl with laughter. You

cleverly avoided all the technical aspect and –

Paula! You were marvellous.

Tim darling! So we meet again at last.

I was in Australia. Back last week. Took ages. This is so refreshing, after all the meetings I've had to attend.

So, what's happening?

Oh, endless argy-bargy everywhere, many accepting cuts in principle but not in practice, others rebelling against blind and monstrous censorship. But we'll get there in the end.

But Tim, how will they KNOW? The creatures I mean.

We have no idea. But we must be ready.

Unto the day. Well I hope you're ready to come to the party, simply everyone will be there.

Where's Jip, mum?

He's been in Canada. But he promised to try and come over for the play, if he could get a sailing. Not easy these days, and he's already been on detachment from Nasa for simply ages, as he explained, so I fear – Jip! You made it!

Hi mum. You were superb. Very funny. And moving.

My pet, you're too kind. It was a challenge, with such an expert family to scrutinise me.

Nonsense, one must relax sometimes and this was real entertainment. Hi Zab. How's the euromping? Hi, Tim. May I see you tomorrow? I have an interim report from George as well as my own.

Now no shop, you two. You said relax and relax is what you're going to do. Where's the champagne? Here, waiter, bring that bubbly over, will you?

Congratulations, Dame Paula.

Oh, did you see it?

No ma'am, we were preparing the reception. But I've heard the first reviews are excellent. I intend to see it.

You shall get a ticket, I'll tell them, What is your name?

Thank you, Dame Paula. If you will permit, I'll go and write it down, you're so surrounded, and rightly so, you might forget it. And I do want to see the play.

You do that thing. More champagne, everywhere. I believe the Prime Minister is coming.

Where's Mira?

Who's Mira, Tim? Don't say you've got a girlfriend at last?

She's my assistant. She came with me, but she seems to have eclipsed herself.

Well, I had a bit. As much as I love discussions among few, so much do I detest the roar of parties. I sound like Decibel, very selective as to types of noise. But also I didn't feel I belonged. I never do, in a way, and there I'm more like Zab. Ever since I had to give up Greek. I simulated belonging, as redundant teacher inventing terrorists in a tumbledown farm, as radio drama producer, as deputy creative director, as head of Public Reaction Analysis, as Tim's newly appointed assistant. Always going on as if.

The play is a genuine success. Perry's back in the limelight, as Perry Hupsos not Striker, that's all dropped. He's a bit drunk with it all, but why not? So is Paula. So are the whole cast. There are daily queues a mile long. Bookings full for months. It will be another Mousetrap, the longest run in history, and still running after seventy years. Or will it?

That last query must have been instinctive. It did run, for eight months, the last one to an emptier and emptier house, even though people had booked. For suddenly, six weeks ago, the waves opened up again. The technicians who'd been patiently trying to transmit for two years with test programs were caught napping. Nothing was ready. But they quickly recovered and went into action. All over the world the same thing happened. The press announced it half triumphantly, information oblige. Transistors were switched on, television sets lit up, telephones were tried, shyly and economically at first then interminably. Computer networks are zinging away again, international finance is out of its doldrums, satellites are working, the space stations are in communication again and at last replenished (just in time) by shuttle. Planes are flying again – though most airports took a week to get them into service and through security checks and their booking system working. It's business as usual, or rather, as before.

It seems that the television was the most missed, and zapping among local and world programs has become hysterical. It used to be only the couch-potatoes, retired or unemployed maniacs who spend ten hours a day zapping football matches all over the world, but now it's everyone: so many people were laid off that it's not easy to get the whole social machinery back into action again. Nobody goes to the theatre any more, nor to the bingohalls, the pinball alleys, the games halls, the gym halls, the sports stadiums, the innumerable emergency cinemas, the evening classes, nobody reads the newspapers, everyone is sitting at home, mesmerised by the forgotten small screen and the miraculous return of their favourite drug. I remember some early writer on mescaline experiences (the golden age of innocence!) explaining that there was no vacuum between images but a plenum of uninterrupted pulsations and oscillations. And the couch-potatoes used to talk of feeling the current pass into them, the magnetism.

The economy programs are accepted here, however, and in Germany, and generally in Europe, though France is more recalcitrant, and the Germans are going on about das Weltsystem being also ein Wertsystem, with Truth-Values. The States are thoroughly up in arms, and all the stations in the world who are furious about it are using their channels to discuss their problems, as if, though forced to obey out of fear, they wanted the alphaguys to understand how impossible it all is. In England, however, there's a generally game acceptance, and people are repeating in the press and in street interviews that nobody needs to be educated late at night with nature programs and intellectual debates, nobody needs to be bombarded with ads every few minutes (though most of their TV wouldn't exist without ads, and nor are they prepared to pay a higher licence fee for having no ads), nobody needs so many prize-winning games that merely rival each other in the same slots, nobody needs so many fictions. And so on. I wonder how long it will last, how soon the commercial pressures will start, the lobbies, the small expansions followed by bigger ones, the cheating. As is already happening elsewhere. In any case many countries hadn't come to any kind of agreement and weren't ready with tailored programs. Seems Uther has no sense of timing. But then, computers don't experience time as we do, they're merely databanks.

I'm busier than ever as Tim's assistant, and also keep a now distant eye on Public Reaction Analysis, though I have a deputy director. It's the same type analysis but a very different content, since the reactions are to the opposite phenomenon. But as predictable as ever, from "that'll show'm" to "Beware". However, the research is made much easier by the restored communication network.

But Tim's job has become almost untenable, and he's exhausted. He handed over his post as Managing Director and is now one of the International Controlers of Economy Programs. He has to fly off to Geneva all the time, to Moscow (yes, there is cooperation), to Montevideo, to Dakar, Cairo, Tokyo. He tries to snatch a few days' rest in each place, but it's difficult, everything is too urgent everywhere, and he's in permanent jetlag. He's also very depressed. Nobody is really observing the rules, even the stations which accepted them, and many are still indignantly refusing. All the arguments for economy are being turned on their heads. It won't apply to us, to our channel, famines and catastrophes are elsewhere. Death is for other cultures.

Man lives on simulations, he told me the other evening in a fit of discouragement over a drink at his flat. The media offer nothing but. What people don't realise is, so do computers, with their simulated world of computer viruses, computer decisions as to when different versions are required, say, in market research or on the stock exchange. Simulations a hundred times more sinister, because sillier and more powerful, than the old legends and myths and fictions.

I don't see why that's so terrible.

Not in itself. It's just that — how to put it without sounding a primitivist? Abstraction was early associated with secrecy, with a small but controlling priestly elite, with the art of writing, which slowly dematerialised the world, and printing accelerated this, into a condition of pure speed, pure mind. A sort of weightlessness, a flight. Well, this process has been multiplied a millionfold, at an ever-increasing speed, and today we live in a world that's totally materialistic at one level and totally immaterial and illusory at another.

But Tim, isn't it only a matter of degree? Mankind has always been materialistic and spiritual at the same time. And what you're saying is in itself abstract, a sort of flight.

But now we have one lot of abstract simulators threatening to silence the others. What shall we be left with?

I'm not sure whether he was aware of his own turn-around. I uttered soothing noises: But surely everyone will calm down, surely they've learnt their lesson during those two years of radio silence?

On the surface, perhaps. But passions remain. What if Verbivore returned, what if we failed the test? It would be for good this time, for ever. We endured it because we can endure anything if we know there may or even might be an end, a light at the end of the tunnel as politicians never tire of saying. But next time, knowing it's for ever, mankind will not endure it. It has become enslaved to immediate communication of every kind, for its wars, its terrorism, its pleasure, its understanding, for companionship in solitude. Eventually someone, some group, some nation, some alliance of countries, will let its passions run wild and express them through the ultimate violence, and destroy the planet.

Real or newsreel? I think you're being unduly pessimistic, Tim. Besides, what about the scientific solution Andrewski kept going on about? Doesn't technology always find a way to meet a new crisis, however slowly?

I don't see any kind of opening that way myself, but then, I'm no longer a specialist. And slowly's probably the right word. It would be a race against human horror.

If you mean nuclear horror that's become almost a quaint idea these days, and almost to be welcomed against the slow sick extinction from lack of ozone and other pollutions. Everyone knows it can't be used, hence official disarmament. Everyone knows the real danger, besides pollution, is economic, and that the real enemy isn't a specific and basically European nation but the smooth anciently resentful orientals and Africans we humiliated in the past, whose revenge has been economic and merciless.

Precisely. Our institutions depended on performative utterances, in other words, sincerity of a sort, legal procedures and democratic processes generally. But we seem to be going back to primitive methods, hostages, terrorism, fanaticism, which had their point in the last Colonial Wars when even mighty powers like Russia or America had to withdraw, but today they go on, and sincerity and judgment now seem as outmoded as belief in trial by water or fire.

I think you overrate our sincerity, as you call it, and they, whoever that might be, have their own form of sincerity.

No doubt. But if the real enemy is economic, as you say, look at the almost total collapse of world economy during Verbivore. It would all start again, and with a vengeance, and for good.

But what about Zab's idea that these creatures need information as we need to breathe? Surely they would try us out again, in order to get it, but more orderly? Surely they would realise, after a while, that they opened up the waves before we were ready?

Perhaps. But I doubt it. Mankind cannot be orderly.

You're exhausted, Tim, give yourself a break.

Sorry. You're right. Let's have another drink and then I'll see you home.

You will not, you'll go straight to bed and have an early night, I'll get a taxi.

Okay, thanks, Mira. Here's yours for the road, then. Let's watch the news, it's ten.

— is the news. A Lufthansa plane has crashed as it was coming in to land in Munich, from Paris (images of broken fuselage among fir-trees). There are no survivors. The Prime Minister has left (images of P.M. climbing into plane and waving) for the Moscow International Summit on Broadcasting Economy Enforcement. Famine threatens in

Blank screen, black with millions of white dots, like a universe.

Decibel dies.

CPSIA information can be obtained
at www.ICGtesting.com
Printed in the USA
LVHW02s2234010218
564917LV00005B/971/P